LIVE BY THE WEST,
DIE BY THE WEST

LIVE BY THE WEST, DIE BY THE WEST

THE SMOKE JENSEN SAGA

Journey of the Mountain Man
Triumph of the Mountain Man

William W. Johnstone

PINNACLE BOOKS
Kensington Publishing Corp.
www.kensingtonbooks.com

PINNACLE BOOKS are published by

Kensington Publishing Corp.
119 West 40th Street
New York, NY 10018

All Kensington titles, imprints, and distributed lines are available at
special quantity discounts for bulk purchases for sales promotions,
premiums, fund-raising, educational, or institutional use. Special book
excerpts or customized printings can also be created to fit specific needs.
For details, write or phone the office of the Kensington sales manager:
Kensington Publishing Corp., 119 West 40th Street, New York, NY 10018,
attn: Sales Department; phone 1-800-221-2647.

PINNACLE BOOKS, the Pinnacle logo, and the WWJ steer head logo
are Reg. U.S. Pat. & TM Off.

ISBN-13: 978-0-7860-4322-4
ISBN-10: 0-7860-4322-9

First printing of *Journey of the Mountain Man:* March 1989
First printing of *Triumph of the Mountain Man:* January 1997
First printing of omnibus edition: March 2019

10 9 8 7 6 5 4 3 2 1

Printed in the United States of America

Electronic edition available:

ISBN-13: 978-0-7860-4462-7 (e-book)
ISBN-10: 0-7860-4462-4 (e-book)

JOURNEY OF THE MOUNTAIN MAN

Dedicated to James Albert Martin

It is only the dead who do not return.
—Bertrand De Vieuzac

ONE

"I didn't think you had any living relatives, except for your sister."

"I didn't either. But then I forgot about Pa's brother. He was supposed to have gotten killed at Chancellorsville, back in '63. I guess this letter came from his kids. It would have to be; it's signed Fae Jensen."

"I wonder how they knew where to write?" Sally asked. "Big Rock is not exactly the hub of commerce, culture, and industry."

The man laughed at that. The schoolteacher in his wife kept coming out in the way she could put words together.

It was 1882, in the high-up country of Colorado. The cabin had recently been remodeled: two new rooms added for Louis Arthur and Denise Nicole Jensen. The twins were approaching their first birthday.

And the man called Smoke was torn between going to the aid of a family member he had never seen and staying at home for the birthday party.

"You have to go, Smoke," Sally spoke the words softly.

"Gibson, in the Montana Territory." The tall, wide-shouldered and lean-hipped man shook his head. "A long way from home. On what might be a wild goose hunt. Probably is. I don't even know where Gibson is."

Sally once more opened the letter and read it aloud. The handwriting was definitely that of a woman, and a woman who had earned high marks in penmanship.

> *Dear Cousin Kirby,*
>   *I read about you in the local paper last year, after that dreadful fight at Dead River. I wanted to write you then, but thought my brother and I could handle the situation ourselves. Time has proven me incorrect. We are in the middle of a war here, and our small ranch lies directly between the warring factions. I did not believe when this range war was started that either Mr. Dooley Hanks or Mr. Cord McCorkle would deliberately harm us, but conditions have worsened to the point where I fear for our lives. Any help you could give us would be greatly appreciated.*
>
>   *Respectfully, your cousin*
>   *Fae Jensen*

"Have you ever heard of either of those men, Smoke?"

"McCorkle. He came into that country twenty years or more ago. Started the Circle Double C. He's a hard man, but I never heard of him riding roughshod over a woman."

"How about this Dooley Hanks?"

Smoke shook his head. "The name sort of rings a bell. But it isn't ringin' very loud."

"When will you be leaving, honey?"

He turned his brown eyes on her, eyes that were usually cold and emotionless. Except when he looked at her. "I haven't said I was going."

"I'll be fine, Smoke. We've got some good hands and some good neighbors. You don't have to worry about me or the babies." She held up the letter. "They're blood kin, honey."

He slowly nodded his head. "I'll get things squared away around the Sugarloaf, and probably pull out in about three days." He smiled. "If you just insist that I go."

She poked him in the ribs and ran laughing out of the room.

"That's him," the little boy said to his friend, visiting from the East. "That's the one ever'body writes about in them penny dreadfuls. That's Smoke Jensen."

Smoke tied his horse to the hitchrail in front of the Big Rock *Guardian* and went inside to speak with Haywood Arden, owner and editor.

"He sure is mean-lookin'," the boy from back East said. "And he really does wear them guns all whopper-jawed, don't he?"

The first thing Haywood noticed was Smoke wearing two guns, the left-hand .44 worn butt forward for a cross draw, the right-hand .44 low and tied down.

"Expecting trouble, Smoke?"

"Not around here. Just getting used to wearing them again. I've got to take a trip, Haywood. I don't know how long I'll be gone. Probably most of the spring and part of the summer. I know Sheriff Carson is out of town, so I'd be beholden if you'd ask him to check in with Sally from time to time. I'm not expecting any trouble out there; Preacher Morrow and Bountiful are right over the ridge and my hands would fight a grizzly with a stick. I'd just feel better if Monte would drop by now and then."

"I'll sure do it, Smoke." He had a dozen questions he'd like to ask, but in the West, a man's business was his own.

Smoke stuck out his hand. "See you in a few months, Haywood. Give Dana my best."

Haywood watched the tall, broad-shouldered, ruggedly handsome man stroll up the boardwalk toward the general store. Smoke Jensen, the last mountain man. The hero of dozens of dime novels. The fastest gun in the West. A man who never wanted the title of gunfighter, but who at sixteen years of age was taken under the tutelage of an old he-coon named Preacher. The old mountain man had taught the boy well, and the boy had grown into one of the most feared and respected men in the West.

No one really knew how many outlaws and murderers and gunslingers and highwaymen had fallen under Smoke's thundering .44's. Some said fifty, others said two hundred. Smoke himself didn't really know for sure.

But Haywood knew one thing for a fact: if Smoke Jensen had strapped on his guns, and was going on a journey, it would darn sure be interesting when he reached his destination.

Interesting and deadly.

The next morning Smoke saddled a tough mountain-bred horse named Dagger—the outline of a knife was on the animal's left rump—checked his canvased and tied-down supplies on the pack horse, and went back into the cabin.

The twins were still sleeping as their father slipped into their rooms and softly kissed each child's cheek. He stepped back out into the main room of the cabin—the den, as Sally called it. "Sally, I don't know what I'm riding into this time. Or how long I'll be gone."

She smiled at him. "Then I'll see you when you get back."

They embraced, kissed, and Smoke stepped out the door, walking to the barn. With the pack horse rope in his left hand, Smoke lifted his right hand in farewell, picked up the reins, and pointed Dagger's nose toward the north.

Sally watched him until he was out of sight, then with a sigh, turned and walked into the cabin, quietly closing the door behind her.

Smoke had dressed warmly, for it was still early spring in the high lonesome, and the early mornings and nights were cold. But as the sun touched the land with its warming rays, he would shed his heavy lined jacket and travel wearing a buckskin jacket, made for him by the squaws of Indian friends.

He traveled following a route that kept the Rocky Mountains to his left and the Medicine Bow Mountains to his right. He crossed the Continental Divide and angled slightly west. He knew this country, and loved it. Preacher had first shown this country to him, back in the late sixties, and Smoke had fallen in love with it. The columbine was in early bloom, splashing the countryside in blue and lavender and white and purple.

Smoke's father, Emmett Jensen, was buried at Brown's Hole, up near the Utah line, in the northwest corner of Colorado. Buried lying atop thousands and thousands of dollars in gold. No one except Smoke and Preacher knew that, and neither one of them had any intention of spreading it about.

Old Preacher was in his early eighties, at least, but it had filled Smoke with joy and love to learn that he was still alive.

Cantankerous old billy-goat!

On his third night out, Smoke made camp halfway between Rabbit Ears Pass and Buffalo Pass, in the high-up country of the Rockies. He had caught some trout just before dusk dropped night on the land and was frying them in a dollop of lard when he saw Dagger's ears come up.

Smoke set the frying pan away from the flames, on a part of the circle of stones around the flames, and slipped back a few feet from the fire and put a hand on his Winchester .44.

"Hallo, the fire!" the voice came out of the darkness. "I'm friendly as a little wolf cub but as hongry as a just woke-up bar."

Smoke smiled. But his hand did not leave his Winchester. "Then come on in. I'll turn no hungry man away from a warm fire and a meal."

The stranger came out of the brush, keeping one hand

in view, the other hand tugging at the lead rope which was attached to a reluctant donkey. "I'm aheadin' for the tradin' post on the Illinois," he said, stripping the gear from the donkey's back and hobbling the animal so it could graze and stay close. "Ran slap out of food yesterday and ain't seen no game atall."

"I have plenty of fish and fried potatoes and bread," Smoke told him. "Spread your blanket and sit." Smoke poured him a tin cup of coffee.

"Kind of you, stranger. Kind. I'm called Big Foot." He grinned and held up a booted foot. "Size fourteen. Been up in Montana lookin' for some color. Got snowed in. Coldest damn place I ever been in my life." He hooked a piece of bread and went to gnawing.

"I run a ranch south of here. The Sugarloaf. Name's Jensen."

Big Foot choked on his bread. When he finally got it swallowed, he took a drink of coffee. "Smoke Jensen?" he managed to gasp.

"Yes."

"Aunt Fanny's drawers!"

Smoke smiled and slid the skillet back over the flames, dumping in some sliced potatoes and a few bits of some early wild onions for flavor. "Where'bouts in Montana?"

"All around the Little Belt Mountains. East of the Smith River."

"Is that anywhere close to Gibson?"

"Durn shore is. And that's a good place to fight shy of, Smoke. Big range war goin' on. Gonna bust wide open any minute."

"Seems to me I heard about that. McCorkle and Hanks, right?"

"Right on the money. Dooley Hanks has done hired Lanny Ball, and McCorkle put Jason Bright on the payroll. I reckon you've heard of them two?"

"Killers. Two-bit punks who hire their guns."

Big Foot shook his head. "You can get away with sayin' that, but not me. Them two is poison fast, Smoke. They's talk about that Mex gunhawk, Diego, comin' in. He's 'pposed to be bringing in half a dozen with him. Bad ones."

"Probably Pablo Gomez is with him. They usually double-team a victim."

"Say! You're right. I heard that. They gonna be workin' for Hanks."

Smoke served up the fish and potatoes and bread and both men fell to it.

When the edges had been taken off their hunger, Smoke asked, "Town had to be named for somebody . . . who's Gibson?"

"Well, it really ain't much of a town. Three, four stores, two saloons, a barber shop, and a smithy. I don't know who Gibson is, or was, whatever.

"No school?"

"Well, sort of. Got a real prissy feller teachin' there. Say! His name's Jensen, too. Parnell Jensen. But he ain't no kin to you, Smoke. Y'all don't favor atall. Parnell don't look like nothin'!"

Parnell was his uncle's middle name.

"But Parnell's sister, now, brother, that is another story."

Smoke dropped in more lard and more fish and potatoes. He sopped up the grease in his tin plate with a hunk of bread and waited for Big Foot to continue.

"Miss Fae would tackle a puma with a short switch. She ain't no real comely lass, but that ain't what's keepin' the beaux away. It's that damn temper of her'n. Got her a tongue you could use for a skinnin' knife. I seen and heared her lash out at that poor brother of her'n one time that was plumb pitiful. Made my old donkey draw all up. He teaches school and she runs the little ranch they got. Durnest mixed-up mess I ever did see. That woman rides astraddle! Plumb embarrassin'!"

Big Foot ate up everything in sight, then picked up the skillet and sopped it out with a hunk of bread. He poured another cup of coffee and with a sigh of contentment, leaned back and rolled a smoke. "Mighty fine eats, Smoke. Feel human agin."

"Where you heading, Big Foot?"

"Kansas. I'm givin' 'er up. I been prowlin' this country-side for twenty-five years, chasin' color. Never found the motherlode. Barely findin' enough color to keep body and soul alive. My brother's been pesterin' me for years to come hep work his hog farm. So that's where I'm headin'. Me and Lucy over yonder. Bes' burro I ever had. I'm gonna retire her; just let 'er eat and get fat. You?"

"Heading up to Montana to check out some land. I don't plan on staying long."

"You fight shy of Gibson, now, Smoke. They's something wrong with that town."

"How do you mean that?"

"Cain't hardly put it in words. It's a feel in the air. And the people is crabby. Oh, most go to church and all that. But it's . . . well, they don't like each other. Always bickerin' about this and that and the other thing. The lid's gonna blow off that whole county one of these days. It's gonna be unpleasant when it do."

"How about the sheriff?"

"He's nearabouts a hundred miles away. I never put eyes on him or any of his deputies. Ain't no town marshal. Just a whole bunch of gunslicks lookin' hard at one another. When they start grabbin' iron, it's gonna be a sight to see."

Big Foot drank his coffee and lay back with a grunt. "And I'll tell you something else: that Fae Jensen woman, her spread is smack in the middle of it all. She's got the water and the graze, and both sides wants it. Sharp tongue and men's britches an' all . . . I feel sorry for her."

"She have hands?"

"Had a half a dozen. Down to two now. Both of them old men. Hanks and McCorkle keep runnin' off anyone she hires. Either that or just outright killin' them. Drug one young puncher, Hanks's men did. Killed him. But McCorkle is not a really mean person. He just don't like Hanks. Nothin' to like. Hanks is evil, Smoke. Just plain evil."

TWO

Come the dawning, Smoke gave Big Foot enough food to take him to the trading post. They said their goodbyes and each went their own way: one north, one east.

Smoke pondered the situation as he rode, trying to work out a plan of action. Since he knew only a smattering of what was going on, he decided to go in unknown and check it out. He took off his pistols and tucked them away in his supplies. He began growing a mustache.

Just inside Wyoming, Smoke came up on the camp of half a dozen riders. It took him but one glance to know what they were: gunhawks.

"Light and set," one offered, his eyes appraising Smoke and deciding he was no danger. He waved toward the fire. "We got beef and beans."

"Jist don't ask where the meat come from," a young man said with a mean grin.

"You talk too much, Royce," another told him. "Shut up and eat." He looked at Smoke. "Help yourself, stranger."

"Thanks." Smoke filled a plate and squatted down. "Lookin' for work. Any of you boys know where they're hirin'?"

"Depends on what kind of work you're lookin' for," a man with a long scar on the side of his face said.

"Punchin' cows," Smoke told him. "Breakin' horses. Ridin' fence. Whatever it takes to make a dollar."

Smoke had packed away his buckskin jacket and for a dollar had bought a nearly worn-out light jacket from a farmer, frayed at the cuffs and collar. He had deliberately scuffed his boots and dirtied his jeans.

"Can't help you there," the scar-faced man said.

Smoke knew the man, but doubted the man knew him. He had seen him twice before. His name was Lodi, from down Texas way, and the man was rattlesnake quick with a gun.

"How come you don't pack no gun?" Royce asked.

Smoke had met the type many times. A punk who thought he was bad and liked to push. Royce wore two guns, both tied down low. Fancy guns: engraved .45 caliber Peacemakers.

"I got my rifle," Smoke told him. "She'll bang seventeen times."

"I mean a short gun," Royce said irritably.

"One in the saddlebags if I need it. I don't hunt trouble, so I ain't never needed it."

One of the other gunhands laughed. "You got your answer, Royce. Now let the man eat." He cut his eyes to Smoke. "What be your name?"

"Kirby." He knew his last name would not be asked. It was not a polite question in the West.

"You look familiar to me."

"I been workin' down on the Blue for three years. Got the urge to drift."

"I do know the feelin'." He rose to his boots and started packing his gear.

These men, with the possible exception of Royce, were range-wise and had been on the owlhoot trail many times, Smoke concluded. They would eat in one place, then move on several miles before settling in and making camp for the night. Smoke quickly finished his beef and beans and cleaned his plate.

They packed up, taking everything but the fire. Lodi lifted his head. "See you, puncher."

Smoke nodded and watched them ride away. To the north. He stayed by the fire, watching it burn down, then swung back into the saddle and headed out, following their trail for a couple of miles before cutting east. He crossed the North Platte and made camp on the east side of the river.

He followed the Platte up to Fort Fred Steele, an army post built in 1868 to protect workers involved in the building of the Union Pacific railroad. There, he had a hot bath in a wooden tub behind a barber shop and resupplied. He stepped into a café and enjoyed a meal that he didn't have to cook, and ate quietly, listening to the gossip going on around him.

There had been no Indian trouble for some time; the Shoshone and the Arapahoe were, for the most part, now settled in at the Wind River Reservation, although every now and then some whiskeyed-up bucks would go on the prowl. They usually ended up either shot or hanged.

Smoke loafed around the fort for a couple of days, giving the gunhands he'd talked with ample time to get gone farther north.

And even this far south of the Little Belt Mountains, folks knew about the impending range war, although Smoke did not hear any talk about anyone here taking sides.

He pulled out and headed for Fort Caspar, about halfway between Fort Fetterman and Hell's Half Acre. The town of Casper would become reality in a few more years.

At Fort Caspar, Smoke stayed clear of a group of gunslicks who were resupplying at the general store. He knew several in this bunch: Eddie Hart, Pooch Matthews, Golden. None of them were known for their gentle, loving dispositions.

It was at Fort Caspar that he met a young, down-at-the-heels puncher with the unlikely handle of Beans.

"Bainbridge is the name my folks hung on me," Beans explained with a grin. "I was about to come to the conclusion that I'd just shoot myself and get it over with knowin' I had to go through the rest of my life with everybody callin' me Bainbridge. A camp cook over in the Dakotas started callin' me Beans. He didn't have no teeth, and evertime he called my name, it come out soundin' like Beans-Beans. So Beans it is."

Beans was one of those types who seemed not to have a care in the world. He had him a good horse, a good pistol, and a good rifle. He was young and full of fire and vinegar . . . so what was there to worry about?

Smoke told him he was drifting on up into Montana. Beans allowed as how that was as good a direction as any to go, so they pulled out before dawn the next day.

With his beat-up clothes and his lip concealed behind a mustache and his hair now badly in need of a trim, Smoke felt that unless he met someone who really knew him, he would not be recognized by any who had only bumped into him casually.

"You any good with that short gun?" Smoke asked.

"Man over in Utah didn't think so. I rattled my hocks shortly before the funeral."

Now, there was two ways to take that. "Your funeral or his?"

"He was a tad quicker, but he missed."

'Nuff said.

On the third night out, Beans finally said what he'd been mullin' about all day. "Kirby . . . there's something about you that just don't add up."

"Oh?"

"Yeah. Now, to someone who just happened to glance over at you and ride on, you'd appear to be a drifter. Spend some time on the trail with you, and a body gets to thinkin'."

Smoke stirred the beans and laid the bacon in the pan. He poured them both coffee and waited.

"You got coins in your pocket and greenbacks in your poke. That saddle don't belong to no bum. That Winchester in your boot didn't come cheap. And both them horses are wearin a brand like I ain't never seen. Is that a circle double snake or what?"

"Circle Double-S." As his spread had grown, Smoke had changed his brand. S for Smoke, S for Sally. It was registered with the brand commission.

"There ain't no 'S' in Kirby." Beans noted.

"Maybe my last name is Smith."

"Ain't but one 'S' there."

"You do have a point." Beans was only pointing out things that Smoke was already aware of. "How far into Montana are you planning on going?"

"Well," Beans grinned, "I don't know. Taggin' along with you I found that the grub's pretty good."

"You're aware of the impending range war in Montana?"

"There's another thing that don't ring true, Kirby. Sometimes you talk like a schoolteacher. Now I know that don't necessarily mean nothin' out here, but it do get folks to thinkin'. You know what I mean?"

Smoke nodded and turned the bacon.

"And them jeans of yours is wore slick on the right side, down low on the leg. You best get you some other britches or strap that hogleg back on."

"You don't miss much, do you, Beans?"

"My folks died with the fever when I was eight. I been on my own ever since. Goin' on nineteen years. Startin' out alone, that young, a body best get savvy quick."

"My real name is Kirby, Beans."

"All right."

"You didn't answer my question about whether you knew about the range war?"

"I heard of it, yeah. But I don't hire my gun. Way I had it figured, with most of the hands fightin', them rich ranchers is gonna need somebody just to look after the cattle." He grinned. "That's me!"

"I'd hate to see you get tied up in a range war, Beans, 'cause sooner or later, you're gonna have to take a stand and grab iron."

"Yeah, I know. But I don't never worry about bridges until I come to them. Ain't that food about fitten to eat?"

They were lazy days, and the two men rode easy; no reason to push. Smoke was only a few years older than Beans—chronologically speaking; several lifetimes in experience—and the men became friends as they rode.

Spring had hit the high country, and the hills and valleys were blazing in God's colors. The men entered Johnson County in the Wyoming Territory, rode into Buffalo, and decided to hunt up a hot bath; both were just a bit on the gamey side.

After a bath and a change of clothes, Smoke offered to buy the drinks. Beans, with a grin, pointed out the sign on the barroom wall: "Don't forget to write your mother, boys. Whether you are worth it or not, she is thinking of you. Paper and inveelopes free. So is the picklled eggs. The whiskey ain't."

"You got a ma, Kirby?"

"Beans, *everybody* has a mother!" Smoke grinned at the man.

"I mean . . . is she still alive?" He flushed red.

"No. She died when I was just a kid, back in Missouri."

"I thought I smelled a Missouri puke in here." The voice came from behind them.

Smoke had not yet tasted his whiskey. He placed the shot glass back on the bar as the sounds of chairs being pushed back reached him. He turned slowly.

A bear of a man sat at a table. Even sitting down he was huge. Little piggy eyes. Mean eyes. Bully was invisibly stamped all over him. His face looked remarkably like a hog.

"You talking to me, Pig-Face?" Smoke asked.

Big Pig stood up and held open his coat. He was not wearing a gun. Smoke opened his jacket to show that he was not armed.

Beans stepped to one side.

"I think I'll tear your head off," Big Pig snorted.

Smoke leaned against the bar. "Why?"

The question seemed to confuse the bully. Which came as no surprise to Smoke. Most bullies could not be classified as being anywhere close to mental giants.

"For fun!" Big Pig said.

Then he charged Smoke, both big hands balled into fists that looked like hams. Smoke stepped to one side just at the last possible split second and Big Pig crashed into the bar. His bulk and momentum tore the rickety bar in half and sent Big Pig hurling against the counter. Whiskey bottles and beer mugs and shot glasses were splintered from the impact. The stench of raw whiskey and strong beer filled the smoky barroom.

Hollering obscenities and roaring like a grizzly with a sore paw, Big Pig lumbered and stumbled to his feet and swung a big fist that would've busted Smoke's head wide open had it landed.

Smoke ducked under the punch and sidestepped. The force of Big Pig's forward motion sent him staggering and slipping across the floor. Smoke picked up a chair and just as Big Pig turned around, Smoke splintered the wooden chair across his teeth.

Big Pig's boots flew out from under him and he went crashing to the floor, blood spurting from smashed lips and cuts on his face. But Smoke saw that Pig was a hard man to keep down. Getting to his feet a second time, Pig came at a rush, wide open. Smoke had already figured out that the man was no skilled slugger, relying on his enormous strength and his ability to take punches that would have felled a normal man.

Smoke hit him flush on the beak with a straight-from-the-shoulder right. The nose busted and the blood flew. Big Pig snorted away the pain and blood and backhanded Smoke, knocking him against a wall. Smoke's mouth filled with the copper taste of blood.

Yelling, falsely sensing that victory was his, Pig charged again. Smoke dropped to his knees and drove his right fist straight up into the V of Big Pig's legs.

Pig howled in agony and dropped to the floor, both hands cupping his injured parts. Still on his knees, Smoke hit the man on the side of the jaw with everything he could put into the punch. This time, Big Pig toppled over, down, but still a hell of a long way from being out.

Spitting out blood, Smoke got to his feet and backed up, catching his breath, readying himself for the next round that he knew was coming.

Big Pig crawled to his feet, glaring at Smoke. But his eyes were filled with doubt. This had never happened to him. He had never lost a fight; not in his entire life.

Smoke suddenly jumped at the man, hitting him with both fists, further pulping the man's lips and flattening his snout.

Pig swung and Smoke grabbed the thick wrist with both hands and turned and slung the man, spinning Big Pig across the room. Pig crashed into the wall and went right through it, sailing across the warped boardwalk and landing in a horse trough.

Smoke stepped through the splintered hole in the wall and walked to the trough. He grabbed Big Pig's head and forced it down into the water, holding him there. Just as it appeared the man would drown, Smoke pulled the head out, pounded it with his fists, then grabbed the man by his hair and once more forced the head under water.

Finally, Big Pig's struggling ceased. Smoke wearily hauled

him out of the water and left him draped half in, half out of the trough. Big Pig was breathing, but that was about all.

Smoke sat down on the edge of the boardwalk and tried to catch his breath.

The boardwalk gradually filled with people, all of them staring in awe at Smoke. One man said, "Mister, I don't know who you are, but I'd have bet my spread that you wouldn't have lasted a minute against old Ring, let alone whip him."

Smoke rubbed his aching leg. "I'd hate to have to do it again."

Beans squatted down beside Smoke. When he spoke his voice was low. "Kirby, I don't know who you really are, but I shore don't never want to make you mad."

Smoke looked at him. "Hell, I'm not angry!" He pointed to the man called Ring. "He's the one who wanted to fight, not me.

"Lord, have mercy!" Beans said. "All this and you wasn't even mad."

Ring groaned and heaved himself out of the horse trough.

Smoke picked up a broken two-by-four and walked over to where Ring lay on the soaked ground. "Mister Ring, I want your attention for a moment. If you have any thoughts at all about getting up off that ground and having a go at me, I'm going to bust your head wide open with this two-by-four. You understand all that?"

Ring rolled over onto his back and grinned up at Smoke. One eye was swollen shut and his nose and lips were a mess. He held up a hand. "Hows 'bout you and me bein' friends. I shore don't want you for an enemy!"

THREE

The three of them pulled out the next morning, Ring riding the biggest mule Smoke had ever seen.

"Satan's his name," Ring explained. "Man was going to kill him till I come along. I swapped him a good horse and a gun for him. One thing, boys: don't never get behind him if you've got a hostile thought. He'll sense it and kick you clear into Canada."

There was no turning Ring back. He had found someone to look up to in Smoke. And Smoke had found a friend for life.

"I just can't handle whiskey," Ring said. "I can drink beer all day long and get mellow. One drink of whiskey and I'll turn mean as a snake."

"I figured you were just another bully," Beans said.

"Oh, no! I love everybody till I get to drinkin' whiskey. Then I don't even like myself."

"No more whiskey for you, Ring," Smoke told him.

"Yes, sir, Mister Kirby. Whatever you say is fine with me."

They were getting too far east, so when they left Buffalo, they cut west and crossed the Bighorn Mountains, skirting north of Cloud Peak, the thirteen-thousand-foot mountain rearing up majestically, snowcapped year-round. Cutting south at Granite Pass, the men turned north, pointing their horses' noses toward Montana Territory.

"Mister Kirby?" Ring asked.

"Just Kirby, Ring. Please. Just Kirby."

"OK . . . Kirby. Why is it we're going to Montana?"

"Seeing the sights, Ring."

"OK. Whatever you say. I ain't got nothin' but time."

"We might find us a job punchin' cows," Beans said.

"I don't know nothin' about cows," Ring admitted. "But I can make a nine-pound hammer sing all day long. I can work the mines or dig a ditch. There ain't a team of horses or mules that I can't handle. But I don't know nothin' about cows."

"You ever done any smithing?" Smoke asked.

"Oh, sure. I'm good with animals. I like animals. I love puppy dogs and kitty cats. I don't like to see people mistreat animals. Makes me mad. And when I get mad, I hurt people. I seen a man beatin' a poor little dog one time back in Kansas when I was passin' through drivin' freight. That man killed that little dog. And for no good reason."

"What'd you do?" Smoke asked him.

"Got down off that wagon and broke his back. Left him there and drove on. After I buried the little dog."

Beans shuddered.

"Dogs and cats and the like can't help bein' what they are. God made them that way. If God had wanted them different, He'd have made 'em different. Men can think. I don't know about women, but men can think. Man shouldn't be cruel to animals. It ain't right and I don't like it."

"I have never been mean to a dog in my life," Beans quickly pointed out.

"Good. Then you're a nice person. You show me a man who is mean to animals, and I'll show you a low-down person at heart."

Smoke agreed with that. "You born out here, Ring?"

"No. Born in Pennsylvania. I killed a man there and done

time. He was a no-good man. Mean-hearted man. He cheated my mother out of her farm through some legal shenanigans. Put her on the road with nothin' but the clothes on her back. I come home from the mines to visit and found my mother in the poor farm, dying. After the funeral, I looked that man up and beat him to death. The judge gimme life in prison."

"You get pardoned?" Beans asked.

"No. I got tired of it and jerked the bars out of the bricks, tied the guard up, climbed over the walls and walked away one night."

"Your secret is safe with us," Smoke assured him.

"I figured it would be."

They forded the Yellowstone and were in Montana Territory, but still had a mighty long way to go before they reached Gibson.

Smoke and Beans had both figured out that Ring was no great shakes when it came to thinking, but he was an incredibly gentle man—as long as you kept him away from the whiskey. Birds would come to him when he held out his arms. Squirrels would scamper up and take food from his fingers. And he almost cried one day when he shot a deer for food. He left the entrails for the wolves and the coyotes and spent the rest of the journey working on the hide, making them all moccasins and gloves.

Ring was truly one of a kind.

He stood six feet six inches and weighed three hundred pounds, very little of it fat. He could read and write only a little, but he said it didn't matter. He didn't have anyone to write to noways, and nobody ever wrote to him.

At a small village on the Boulder, Smoke resupplied and they all had a hot bath. Ring was so big he made the wooden tub look like a bucket.

But Smoke had a bad feeling about the village; not about the village itself, but at what might be coming at them if they stayed. Smoke had played on his hunches before; they had kept him alive more than once. And this one kept nagging at him.

After carefully shaving, leaving his mustache intact, he went to his packhorse and took out his .44s, belting them around his lean hips, tying down the right-hand gun. He carefully checked them, wiping them clean with a cloth and checking the loads. He usually kept the chamber under the hammer empty; this time he loaded them both up full. He stepped out from behind the wooden partition by the wooden tubs and walked into the rear of the store, conscious of the eyes of Beans and Ring on him; they had never seen him wear a short gun, much less two of them, one butt-forward for a cross draw.

"Five boxes of .44s," Smoke told the clerk.

"You plannin' on startin' a war?" the clerk said, sticking his mouth into something that didn't concern him.

Smoke's only reply was to fix his cold brown eyes on the man and stare at him. The clerk got the message and turned away, a flush on his face.

He placed the ammunition on the counter and asked no more questions. Smoke bought three cans of peaches and paid for his purchases. He walked out onto the shaded porch, Ring and Beans right behind him. The three of them sat down and opened the peaches with their knives, enjoying a mid-morning sweet-syruped snack.

"Don't see too many people wearin' twin guns thataway," Beans observed, looking at Smoke's rig.

"Not too many," Smoke agreed, and ate a peach.

"Riders coming," Ring said quietly. "From the south."

The men sat on the porch, eating peaches and watching the riders come closer.

"You recognize any of them?" Smoke tossed the question out.

Beans took it. "Nope. You?"

"That one on the right is Park. Gunfighter from over in

the Dakotas. Man next to him is Tabor. Gunhawk from Oklahoma. I don't know the others."

"They know you?" Ring asked.

"They know of me." Smoke's words were softly spoken.

"By the name of Kirby?"

"No."

The five dusty gunhands reined up and dismounted. A ferret-faced young man ducked under the hitchrail and paused by the porch, staring at Smoke. His eyes drifted to Smoke's twin guns.

The other gunhawks were older, wiser, and could read sign. They were not being paid to cause trouble in this tiny village, therefore they would avoid trouble if at all possible.

The kid with the acne-pocked face and the big Colts slung around his hips was not nearly so wise. He deliberately stepped on Smoke's boot as he walked past.

Smoke said nothing. The four older men stood to one side, watching, keeping their hands away from the butts of their guns.

Ferret-face laughed and looked at his friends, jerking a thumb toward Smoke. "There ain't much to him."

"I wouldn't bet my life on it," Park said softly. To Smoke, "Don't I know you?"

Smoke stood up. At the approach of the men, he had slipped the leather hammer-thongs from his guns. "We've crossed rails a time or two. If this punk kid's a friend of yours, you might better put a stopper on his mouth before I'm forced to change his diapers."

The kid flushed at the insult. He backed up a few yards, his hands hovering over the butts of his fancy guns. "They call me Larado. Maybe you've heard of me?"

"Can't say as I have," Smoke spoke easily. "But I'm glad to know you have a name. That's something that everybody should have."

"You're makin' fun of me!"

"Am I? Maybe so."

"I think I'll just carve another notch on my guns," Larado hissed.

"Yeah? I had you pegged right then. A tinhorn."

"Draw, damn you!"

But Smoke just stood, smiling at the young man.

Two little boys took that time to walk by the store; perhaps they were planning on spending a penny for some candy. One of them looked at Smoke, jerked a dime novel out of the back of his overalls, and stared at the cover. He mentally shaved off Smoke's mustache. His mouth dropped open.

"It's really him! That's Smoke Jensen!"

All the steam went out of Larado. His sigh was audible. He lifted his hands and carefully folded them across his chest, keeping his hands on the outside of his arms.

Beans and Ring sat in their chairs and stared at their friend.

"You some distance from Colorado, Smoke," Tabor said.

"And you're a long way from Oklahoma," Smoke countered.

"For a fact. You headin' north or south?"

"North."

"I never knowed you to hire your guns out."

"I never have. It isn't for sale this trip, either."

"But you do have a reputation for buttin' in where you ain't wanted," Park added his opinion.

"I got a personal invitation to this party, Park. But if you feel like payin' the fiddler, you can write your name on my dance card right now."

"I ain't got nothin' agin you, Smoke. Not until I find out which side you buckin' leastways. McCorkle or Hanks?"

"Neither one."

The gunslicks exchanged glances. "That don't make no sense," one of the men that Smoke didn't know said.

"You got a name?"

"Dunlap."

"Yeah, I heard of you. You killed a couple of Mexican sheepherders and shot one drunk in the back down in Arizona. But I'm not a sheepherder and I'm not drunk."

Dunlap didn't like that. But he had enough sense not to pull iron with Smoke Jensen.

"You was plannin' on riding in with nobody knowin' who you were, wasn't you?" Tabor asked.

"Yes."

"Next question is why?"

"I guess that's my business."

"You right. I reckon we'll find out when west to Gibson."

"Perhaps." He turned to Beans and Ring. "Let's ride."

After the three men had ridden away, toward the north, one of the two gunhands who had not spoken broke his silence.

"I'm fixin' to have me a drink and then I'm ridin' over to Idaho. It's right purty this time of year."

Larado, now that Smoke was a good mile away, had reclaimed his nerve. "You act like you're yeller!" he sneered.

But the man just chuckled. "Boy, I was over at what they's now callin' Telluride some years back, when a young man name of Smoke Jensen come ridin' in. He braced fifteen of the saltiest ol' boys there was at that time. Les' see, that was back in, oh, '72, I reckon." He looked directly at Larado. "And you bear in mind, young feller, that he kilt about ten or so gettin' to that silver camp. He kilt all fifteen of them so-called fancy gunhandlers. Yeah, kid, he's that Smoke Jensen. The last mountain man. Since he kilt his first Injun when he was about fifteen years old, over in Kansas, he's probably kilt a hundred or more white men—and that's probably figurin' low. There ain't nobody ever been as fast as he is, there ain't never gonna be nobody as fast as he is.

"And I know you couldn't hep notice that bear of a man

with him? That there is Ring. Ring ain't never followed no man in his life afore today. And that tells me this: Smoke has done whipped him fair and square with his fists. And if I ain't mistaken, that young feller with Smoke and Ring is the one from over in Utah, round Moab. Goes by a half a dozen different names, but one he favors is Beans.

"Now, boys, I'm a fixin' to have me a drink and light a shuck. 'Cause wherever Smoke goes, they's soon a half a dozen or more of the randiest ol' boys this side of hell. Smoke draws 'em like a magnet does steel shavin's. I had my say. We partin' company. Like as of right now!"

Down in Cheyenne, two old friends came face-to-face in a dingy side-street barroom. The men whoopped and hollered and insulted each other for about five minutes before settling down to have a drink and talk about old times.

Across the room, a young man stood up, irritation on his face. He said to his companion, "I think I'll go over there and tell them old men to shut up. I'm tared of hearin' them hoot and holler."

"Sit down and close your mouth," his friend told him. "That's Charlie Starr and Pistol Le Roux."

The young man sat down very quickly. A chill touched him, as if death had brushed his skin.

"I thought them old men was dead!" he managed to croak after slugging back his drink.

"Well, they ain't. But I got some news that I bet would interest them. I might even get to shake their hands. My daddy just come back from haulin' freight down in Colorado. You wanna go with me?"

"No, sir!"

The young man walked over to where the two aging gunfighters were sitting and talking over their beers. "Sirs?"

Charlie and Pistol looked up. "What can I do for you?" Le Roux said.

The young man swallowed hard. This was real flesh-and-blood legend he was looking at. These men helped tame the West. "You gentlemen are friends with a man called Smoke Jensen, aren't you?"

"You bet your boots!" Charlie smiled at him.

"My daddy just come home from haulin' freight down to a place called Big Rock. He spoke with the sheriff, a man called Monte Carson. Smoke's in trouble. He's gone up to some town in Montana Territory called Gibson to help his cousin. A woman. He's gonna be facin' forty or fifty gun-hands; right in the middle of a range war."

Pistol and Charlie stood up as of one mind. The young man stared in astonishment. God, but they were both big and gray and gnarled and old!

But the guns they wore under their old jackets were clean and shiny.

"I wish we could pay you," Charlie said. "But we're gonna have to scratch deep to get up yonder."

The young man stuck out his hand and the men shook it. Their hands were thickly calloused. "There's a poke of food tied to my saddle horn. Take it. It's all I can do."

"Nice of you," Pistol said. "Thankee kindly."

The men turned, spurs jingling, and were gone.

The silver-haired man pulled off his boot and looked at the hole in the sole. He stuck some more paper down into the boot. "Hardrock, today is my birthday. I just remembered."

"How old are you, about a hundred?"

"I think I'm sixty-seven. And I know you two year older than me."

"Happy birthday."

"Thankee."

"I ain't got no present. Sorry."

Silver Jim laughed. "Hardrock, between the two of us we might be able to come up with five dollars. Tell you what. Let's drift up to Montana Territory. I got a friend up in the Little Belt Mountains. Got him a cabin and runs a few head of cattle. Least we can eat."

"Silver Jim . . . he died about three years ago."

"Ummm . . . that's right. He did, didn't he. Well, the cabin's still there, don't you reckon?"

"Might be. I thought of Smoke this mornin'. Wonder how that youngster is?"

"Did you now? That's odd. I did, too."

"I thought about Montana, too."

The two old gunfighters exchanged glances, Silver Jim saying, "I just remembered I had a couple of double eagles I was savin' for hard times."

"Is that right? Well . . . me, too."

"We could ride back to that little town we come through this morning and send a message through the wires to Big Rock."

The old gunslingers waited around the wire office for several hours until they received a reply from Monte Carson in Big Rock.

"Let's get the hell to Montanee!" Silver Jim said.

FOUR

"I thought you would be a much older man," Ring remarked after they had made camp for the evening.

It was the first time Smoke's real identity had been brought up since leaving the little village.

Smoke smiled and dumped the coffee into the boiling water. "I started young."

"When was you gonna tell us?" Beans asked.

"The same time you told me that you was the Moab Gunfighter."

Beans chuckled. "I wasn't gonna get involved in this fight. But you headin' that way . . . well, it sorta piqued my interest."

"My cousin is in the middle of it. She wrote me at my ranch. You can't turn your back on kin."

"Y'all must be close."

"I have never laid eyes on her in my life. I didn't even know she existed until the letter came." He told them about his conversations with Big Foot.

"This brother of hers sounds like a sissy to me," Beans said.

"He does for a fact," Smoke agreed. "But I've found out this much about sissies: they'll take and take and take, until you push them to their limits, and then they'll kill you."

* * *

The three of them made camp about ten miles outside of Gibson, on the fringes of the Little Belt Mountains.

"There is no point in any of us trying to hide who we are," Smoke told the others. "As soon as Park and the others get in town, it would be known. We'll just ride in and look the place over first thing in the morning. I'm not going to take a stand in this matter unless the big ranchers involved try to run over Fae . . . or unless I'm pushed to it."

The three topped the hill and looked down at the town of Gibson. One long street, with vacant lots separating a few of the stores. A saloon, one general store, and the smithy were on one side of the street, the remainder of the businesses on the other side. Including a doctor's office. The church stood at the far end of town.

"We'd better be careful which saloon—if any—we go into," Beans warned. "For a fact, Hanks's boys will gather in one and McCorkle's boys in the other."

"I don't think I'll go into either of them," Ring said. "This is the longest I've been without a drink in some time. I like the feeling."

"Looks like school is in session." Smoke lifted the reins. "You boys hang around the smithy's place while I go talk to Cousin Parnell. Let's go."

They entered the town at a slow walk, Ring and Beans flanking Smoke as they moved up the wide street. Although it was early in the day, both saloons were full, judging by the number of horses tied at the hitchrails. A half a dozen or more gunslicks were sitting under the awnings of both saloons. The men could feel the hard eyes on them as they rode slowly up the street. Appraising eyes. Violent eyes; eyes of death.

"Ring," they heard one man say.

"That's the Moab Kid," another said. "But who is that in the middle?"

"I don't know him."

"I do," the voice was accented. Smoke cut his eyes, shaded by the wide brim of his hat. Diego. "That, *amigos,* is Smoke Jensen."

Several chair legs hit the boardwalk, the sound sharp in the still morning air.

The trio kept riding.

"Circle C on the west side of the street," Beans observed.

"Yeah." Smoke cut his eyes again. "That's Jason Bright standing by the trough."

"He is supposed to be very, very fast," Ring said.

"He's a punk," Smoke replied.

"Lanny Ball over at the Hangout," Beans pointed out.

"The Pussycat and the Hangout," Ring said with a smile. "Where do they get the names?"

They reined up at the smith's place; a huge stable and corral and blacksmithing complex. Beans and Ring swung down. Smoke hesitated, then stepped down.

"Changed my mind," he told them. "No point in disturbing school while it's in session. We'll loaf around some; stretch our legs."

"I'm for some breakfast," Ring said. "Let's try the Café Eats."

Smoke told the stable boy to rub their horses down, and to give each a good bait of corn. They'd be back.

They walked across the wide street, spurs jingling, boots kicking up dust in the dry street, and stepped up onto the boardwalk, entering the café.

It was a big place for such a tiny town, but clean and bright, and the smells from the kitchen awakened the taste buds in them all.

They sat down at a table covered with a red-and-white checkered cloth and waited. A man stepped out of the kitchen. He wore an apron and carried a sawed-off double-barreled ten-gauge express gun. "You are velcome to eat here at anytime ve are open," he announced, his German accent thick. "My name is Hans, and I own dis establishment. I vill tell you what I have told all the rest: there vill be no trouble in here. None! I operate a nice quiet family restaurant. People come in from twenty, terty miles avay to eat here. Start trouble, und I vill kill you! Understood?"

"We understand, Hans," Smoke said. "But we are not taking sides with either McCorkle or Hanks. I do not hire my guns and neither does Beans here." He jerked his thumb toward the Moab Kid. "And Ring doesn't even carry a short gun.

"Uummph!" the German grunted. "Den dat vill be a velcome change. You vant breakfast?"

"Please."

"Good! I vill start you gentlemen vith hot oatmeal vith lots of fresh cream and sugar. Den ham and eggs and fried potatoes and lots of coffee. Olga! Tree oatmeals and tree breakfasts, *liebling*."

"What'd he call her?" Beans whispered.

"Darling," Ring told him.

Smoke looked up. "You speak German, Ring?"

"My parents were German. Born in the old country. My last name is Kruger."

The oatmeal was placed before them, huge bowls of steaming oatmeal covered with cream and sugar. Ring looked up. *"Danke."*

The two men then proceeded to converse in rapid-fire German. To Beans it sounded like a couple of bullfrogs with laryngitis.

Then, to the total amazement of Smoke and Beans, the two big men proceeded to slap each other across the face several times, grinning all the time.

Hans laughed and returned to the kitchen. "Y'all fixin' to fight, Ring?" Beans asked.

Ring laughed at the expression on their faces. "Oh, no.

That is a form of greeting in certain parts of the old country. It means we like each other."

"That is certainly a good thing to know," Smoke remarked drily. "In case I ever take a notion to travel to Germany."

The men fell to eating the delicious oatmeal. When they pushed the empty bowls away, Hans was there with huge platters of food and the contest was on.

"*Guten appetit,* gentlemans."

"What'd he say?" Beans asked Ring.

"Eat!" He smiled. "More or less."

Olga stepped out of the kitchen to stand watching the men eat, a smile on her face. She was just as ample as Hans. Between the two of them they'd weigh a good five hundred pounds. Another lady stepped out of the kitchen. Make that seven hundred and fifty pounds.

When they had finished, as full as ticks, Ring looked up and said, *"Prima! Grobartig!"* He lifted his coffee mug and toasted their good health. *"Auf Ihre Gesundheit!"*

Olga and the other lady giggled.

"I didn't hear nobody sneeze." Beans looked around.

Ring stayed in the restaurant, talking with Hans and Olga and Hilda and drinking coffee. Beans sat down in a wooden chair in front of the place, staring across the street at the gunhawks who were staring at him. Smoke walked up to the church that doubled as a schoolhouse. The kids were playing out front so he figured it was recess time.

The children looked at him, a passing glance, and resumed their playing. Smoke walked up the steps.

Smoke stood in the open doorway, the outside light making him almost impossible to view clearly from the inside. He felt a pang of . . . some kind of emotion. He wasn't sure. But there was no doubt: he was looking at family.

The schoolteacher looked up from his grading papers. "Yes?"

"Parnell Jensen?"

"Yes. Whom do I have the pleasure of addressing?"

Smoke had to chew on that for a few seconds. "I reckon I'm your cousin, Parnell. I'm Smoke Jensen."

Parnell gave Smoke directions to the ranch and said he would be out at three-thirty. And he would be prompt about it. "I am a very punctilious person," Parnell added.

And a prissy sort too, Smoke thought. "Uh-huh. Right." He'd have to remember to ask somebody what punch-till-eous meant.

He was walking up the boardwalk just as the thunder of hooves coming hard reached him. The hooves drummed across the bridge at the west end of town and didn't slow up. A dozen hard-ridden horses can kick up a lot of dust.

Smoke had found out from Parnell that McCorkle's spread was west and north of town, Hanks's spread was east and north of town. Fae's spread, and it was no little spread, ran on both sides of the Smith River; for about fifteen miles on either side of it. McCorkle hated Hanks, Hanks hated McCorkle, and both men had threatened to dam up the Smith and dry Fae out if she didn't sell out to one of them.

"And then what are they going to do?" Smoke asked.

"Fight each other for control of the entire area between the Big Belt and the Little Belt Mountains. They've been fighting for twenty years. They came here together in '62. Hated each other at first sight." Parnell flapped his hand in disgust. "It's just a dreadful situation. I wish we had never come to this barbaric land."

"Why did you?"

"My sister wanted to farm and ranch. She's always been a tomboy. The man who owned the ranch before us hired me—

I was teaching at a lovely private institution in Illinois, close to Chicago—and told Fae that he had no children and would give us the ranch upon his death. I think more to spite McCorkle and Hanks than out of any kindness of heart."

Smoke leaned against a storefront and watched as King Cord McCorkle—as Parnell called him—and his crew came to a halt in a cloud of dust in front of the Pussycat. When the dust had settled, Jason Bright stepped off the boardwalk and walked to Cord's side, speaking softly to him.

Parnell's words returned: "I have always had to look after my sister. She is so *flighty*. I wish she would marry and then I could return to civilization. It's so primitive out here!" He sighed. "But I fear that the man who gets my sister will have to beat her three times a day."

Cord turned his big head and broad face toward Smoke and stared at him. Smoke pegged the man to be in his early forties; a bull of a man. Just about Smoke's height, maybe twenty pounds heavier.

Cord blinked first, turning his head away with a curse that just reached Smoke. Smoke cut his eyes to the Hangout. Diego and Pablo Gomez and another man stood there. Smoke finally recognized the third man. Lujan, the Chihuahua gunfighter. Probably the fastest gun—that as yet had built a reputation—in all of Mexico. But not a cold-blooded killer like Diego and Pablo.

Lujan tipped his hat at Smoke and Smoke lifted a hand in acknowledgment and smiled. Lujan returned the smile, then turned and walked into the saloon.

Smoke again felt eyes on him. Cord was once more staring at him.

"You there! The man supposed to be Smoke Jensen. Git down here. I wanna talk to you."

"You got two legs and a horse, mister!" Smoke called over the distance. "So you can either walk or ride up here."

Pablo and Diego laughed at that.

"Damned greasers!" Cord spat the words.

The Mexicans stiffened, hands dropping to the butts of their guns.

A dozen gunhands in front of the Pussycat stood up.

A little boy, about four or five years old, accompanied by his dog, froze in the middle of the street, right in the line of fire.

Lujan opened the batwings and stepped out. "We—all of us—have no right to bring bloodshed to the innocent people of this town." His voice carried across the street. He stepped into the street and walked to the boy's side. "You and your dog go home, *muchacho*. Quickly, now."

Lujan stood alone in the street. "A man who would deliberately injure a child is not fit to live. So, McCorkle, it is a good day to die, is it not?"

Smoke walked out into the street to stand by Lujan's side. A smile creased the Mexican's lips. "You are taking a side, Smoke?"

"No. I just don't like McCorkle, and I probably won't like Hanks either."

"So, McCorkle," Lujan called. "You see before you two men who have not taken a side, but who are more than willing to open the *baile*. Are you ready?"

"Make that three people," Beans's voice rang out.

"Who the hell are you?" McCorkle shouted.

"Some people call me the Moab Kid."

"Make that four people," Ring said. He held his Winchester in his big hands.

"Funf!" Hans shouted, stepping out into the street. He held the sawed-off in his hands.

The window above the café opened and Olga leaned out, a pistol with a barrel about a foot and a half long in her hand. She jacked back the hammer to show them all she knew how to use it. And would.

"All right, all right!" Cord shouted. "Hell's bells! Nobody was going to hurt the kid. Come on, boys, I'll buy the drinks." He turned and bulled his way through his men.

At the far end of the street, Parnell stepped back from the open doorway and fanned himself vigorously. *"Heavens!"* he said.

FIVE

"Almost come a showdown in town this morning, Boss," Dooley Hanks's foreman said.

Hanks eyeballed the man. "Between who?"

Gage told his boss what a hand had relayed to him only moments earlier.

Hanks slumped back in his chair. "Smoke Jensen," he whispered the word. "I never even thought about Fae and Parnell bein' related to him. And the Moab Kid and Lujan sided with him?"

"Or vicey-versy."

"This ain't good. That damn Lujan is poison enough. But add Smoke Jensen to the pot . . . might as well be lookin' the devil in the eyeballs. I don't know nothin' about Ring, except he's unbeatable in a fight. And the Moab Gunfighter has made a name for hisself in half a dozen states. All right, Gage. We got to get us a backshooter in here. Send a rider to Helena. Wire Danny Rouge; he's over in Missoula. Tell him to come a-foggin'."

"Yes, sir."

"Where's them damn boys of mine?"

"Pushin' cattle up to new pasture."

"You mean they actually doin' some work?"

Gage grinned. "Yes, sir."

Hanks shook his head in disbelief. "Thank you, Gage."

Gage left, hollering for a rider to saddle up. Hanks walked to a window in his office. He had swore he would be kingpin of this area, and he intended to be just that. Even if he bankrupted himself doing it. Even if he had to kill half the people in the area attaining it.

Cord McCorkle had ridden out of town shortly after his facedown with Smoke and Lujan and the others. He did not feel that he had backed down. It was simply a matter of survival. Nobody but a fool willingly steps into his own coffin.

His hands would have killed Smoke and Lujan and the others, for a fact. But it was also hard fact that Cord would have gone down in the first volley . . . and what the hell would that have proved?

Nothing. Except to get dead.

Cord knew that men like Smoke and Lujan could soak up lead and still stay on their feet, pulling the trigger. He had personally witnessed a gunfighter get hit nine times with .45 slugs and before he died still kill several of the men he was facing.

Cord sat on the front porch of his ranch house and looked around him. He wanted for nothing. He had everything a man could want. It had sickened him when Dooley had OK'd the dragging of that young Box T puncher. Scattering someone's cattle was one thing. Murder was another. He was glad that Jensen had come along. But he didn't believe anyone could ever talk sense into Hanks.

Smoke, Ring, and Beans sat their horses on the knoll overlooking the ranch house of Fae and Parnell Jensen. Fae might well be a bad-mouthed woman with a double-edged tongue, but she kept a neat place. Flowers surrounded the house, the lawn was freshly cut, and the place itself was attractive.

Even at this distance, a good mile off, Smoke could see two men, with what he guessed were rifles in their hands, take up positions around the bunkhouse and barn. A woman—he guessed it was a woman, she was dressed in britches—came out onto the porch. She also carried a rifle. Smoke waved at her and waited for her to give them some signal to ride on in.

Finally the woman stepped off the porch and motioned for them to come on.

The men walked their horses down to the house, stopping at the hitchrail but not dismounting. The woman looked at Smoke. Finally she smiled.

"I saw a tintype of your daddy once. You look like him. You'd be Kirby Jensen."

"And you'd be Cousin Fae. I got your letter. I picked up these galoots along the way." He introduced Beans and Ring.

"Put your horses in the barn, boys, and come on into the house. It's about dinnertime. I got fresh doughnuts; 'bear-sign' as you call them out here."

Fae Jensen was more than a comely lass; she was really quite pretty and shapely. But unlike most women of the time, her face and arms were tanned from hours in the sun, doing a man's work. And her hands were calloused.

Smoke had met Fae's two remaining ranch hands, Spring and Pat. Both men in their early sixties, he guessed. But still leather-tough. They both gave him a good eyeballing, passed him through inspection, and returned to their jobs.

Over dinner—Sally called it lunch—Smoke began asking his questions while Beans skipped the regular food and began attacking a platter of bear-sign, washed down with hot strong western coffee.

How many head of cattle?

Started out with a thousand. Probably down to less than five hundred now, due to Hanks and McCorkle's boys running them off.

Would she have any objections to Smoke getting her cattle back?

She looked hard at him. Finally shook her head. No objections at all.

"Ring will stay here at the ranch and start doing some much needed repair work," Smoke told her. "Beans and me will start working the cattle, moving them closer in. Then we'll get your other beeves back. Tell me the boundaries of this spread."

She produced a map and pointed out her spread, and it was not a little one. It had good graze and excellent water. The brand was the Box T; she had not changed it since taking over several years back.

"If you'll pack us some food," Smoke said, "me and Beans will head out right now; get the lay of the land. We'll stay out a couple of days—maybe longer. This situation is shaping up to be a bad one. The lid could blow off at any moment. Beans, shake out your rope and pick us out a couple of fresh horses. Let's give ours a few days' rest. They've earned it."

"I'll start putting together some food," Fae said. She looked at Smoke. "I appreciate this. More than you know."

"Sorry family that don't stick together."

They rode out an hour later, Smoke on a buckskin a good seventeen hands high that looked as though it could go all day and all night and still want to travel.

The old man who had given the spread to Fae had known his business—Smoke still wondered about how she'd gotten it. He decided to pursue that further when he had the time.

About ten miles from the ranch, they crossed the Smith and rode up to several men working Box T cattle toward the northwest.

They wheeled around at Smoke's approach.

"Right nice of you boys to take such an interest in our cattle," Smoke told a hard-eyed puncher. "But you're pushing them the wrong way. Now move them back across the river."

"Who the hell do you think you are?" the man challenged him.

"Jensen."

The man spat on the ground. "I like the direction we're movin' them better." He grabbed iron.

Smoke drew, cocked, and fired in one blindingly fast move. The .44 slug took the man in the center of his chest and knocked him out of the saddle. He tried to rise up but did not have the strength. With a groan, he fell back on the ground, dead. Beans held a pistol on the other McCorkle riders; they were all looking a little white around the mouth.

"Jack Waters," Smoke said. "He's wanted for murder in two states. I've seen the flyers in Monte's office."

"Yeah," Beans said glumly. "And he's got three brothers just as bad as he is. Waco, Hatley, and Collis."

"You won't last a week on this range, Jensen," a mouthy McCorkle rider said.

Smoke moved closer to him and backhanded the rider out of his saddle. He hit the ground and opened his mouth to cuss. Then he closed his mouth as the truth came home. Jensen. Smoke Jensen.

"All of you shuck outta them gun belts," Beans ordered. "When you've done that, start movin' them cattle back across the river."

"Then we're going to take a ride," Smoke added. "To see Cord."

While the Circle Double C boys pushed the cattle back across the river, Smoke lashed the body of Jack Waters across his saddle and Beans picked up the guns, stuffing guns, belts, and all into a gunny sack and tying it on his saddle horn. The riders returned, a sullen lot, and Smoke told them to head out for the ranch.

A hand hollered for Cord to come out long before Smoke and Beans entered the front yard. "Stay in the house," Cord told his wife and daughter. "I don't want you to see any of this."

Beans stayed in the saddle, a Winchester .44 across his saddle horn. Smoke untied the ropes and slung Jack Waters over his shoulder, and Jack was not a small man. He walked across the lawn and dumped the body on the ground, by Cord's feet.

Cord was livid, his face flushed and the veins in his neck standing out like ropes. He was breathing like an enraged bull.

"We caught Jack and these other hands on Box T range, rustling cattle. Now you know the law out here, Cord: we were within our rights to hang every one of them. But I gave them a chance to ride on. Waters decided to drag iron."

Cord nodded his head, not trusting his voice to speak.

"Now, Cord," Smoke told him, "I don't care if you and Hanks fight until you kill each other. I don't think either of you remember what it is you're fighting about. But the war against the Box T is over. Fae and Parnell Jensen have no interest in your war, and nothing to do with it. *Leave . . . them . . . alone!*"

Smoke's last three words cracked like whips; several hard-nosed punchers winced at the sound.

"You all through flappin' your mouth, Jensen?" Cord asked.

"No. I want all the cattle belonging to Fae and Parnell Jensen rounded up and returned. I'm not saying that your hands ran them all off. I'm sure Hanks and his boys had a hand in it, too. And I'll be paying him a visit shortly. Get them rounded up and back on Box T range."

"And if I don't—not saying I have them, mind you?"

Smoke's smile was not pretty. "You ever heard of Louis Longmont, McCorkle?"

"Of course, I have! What's he have to do with any of this?"

"He's an old friend of mine, Cord. We stood shoulder to shoulder several years back and cleaned up Fontana. Then last year, he rode with me to New Hampshire . . . you probably read about that."

Cord nodded his head curtly.

"He's one of the wealthiest men west of the Mississippi, Cord. And he loves a good fight. He wouldn't blink an eye to spend a couple of hundred thousand putting together an army to come in here and wipe your nose on a porcupine's backside."

From in the house, Smoke heard a young woman's laughter and an older woman telling her to shush!

The truth was, Louis was in Europe on an extended vacation and Smoke knew it. But sometimes a good bluff wins the pot.

Cord had money, but nothing to compare with Louis Longmont . . . and he also knew that Smoke had married into a great deal of money and was wealthy in his own right. He sighed heavily.

"I can't speak for Hanks, Jensen. You'll have to face him yourself. But as for me and mine . . . OK, we'll leave the Box T alone. I don't have their cattle. I'm not a rustler. My boys just scattered them. But I'm damned if I'll help you round them up. You can come on my range and look; any wearing the Box T brand, take them."

Smoke nodded and stuck out his hand. Cord looked startled for a few seconds, then a very grudging smile cut his face. He took the hand and gripped it briefly.

Smoke turned and mounted up. "See you."

Beans and Smoke swung around and rode slowly away from the ranch house.

"My back is itchy," Beans said.

"So is mine. But I think he's a man of his word. I don't think he'll go back on his word. Least I'm a poor judge of character if he does."

They rode on. Beans said, "My goodness me. I plumb forgot to give them boys their guns back."

"Well, shame on you, Beans. I hate to see them go to waste. We'll just take them back to Fae and she can keep them in reserve. Never know when she might need them. You can swap them for some bear-sign."

"What about hands?"

"We got to hire some, that's for sure. Fae's got to sell off some cattle for working capital. She told me so. So we've got to hire some boys."

"Durned if I know where. And there's still the matter of Dooley Hanks."

Fae would hire some hands, sooner than Smoke thought. But they would be about fifty years from boyhood.

SIX

They made camp early that day, after rounding up about fifty head of Box T cattle they found on Cord's place. They put them in a coulee and blocked the entrance with brush. They would push them closer to home in the morning.

They suppered on the food Fae had fixed for them and were rolled up in their blankets just after dark.

Smoke was the first one up, several hours before dawn. He coaxed life back into the coals by adding dry grass and twigs, and Beans sat up when the smell of coffee got too much for him to take. Beans threw off his blankets, put on his hat, pulled on his boots, and buckled on his gun belt. He squatted by the fire beside Smoke, warming his hands and waiting for the cowboy coffee to boil.

"Town life's done spoiled me," Beans griped. "Man gets used to shavin' and bathin' every day, and puttin' on clean clothes every mornin'. It ain't natural."

Smoke grinned and handed him a small sack.

"What's in here?"

"Bear-sign I hid from you yesterday."

Beans quit his grousing and went to eating while Smoke

sliced the bacon and cut up some potatoes, adding a bit of wild onion for flavor.

"The problem of hands has got me worried," Beans admitted, slurping on a cup of coffee. "Ain't no cowboy in his right mind gonna go to work for the Box T with all this trouble starin' him in the face."

"I know." Smoke ladled out the food onto tin plates. "But I think I know one who just might do it, for thirty and found, just for the pure hell of it. I'll talk to him this afternoon if I can. First we have to see Hanks."

"You got a lot of damn nerve, Jensen," the foreman of the D-H spread told him. "Mister Hanks don't wanna see you."

"You tell him I'm here and I'll wait just as long as it takes."

Gage stared into the cold eyes of the most respected and feared gunfighter in all the West. He sighed, shook his head, and finally said, "All right, mister. I'll tell him you insist on seein' him. But I ain't givin' no guarantees."

Hanks and McCorkle could pass for brothers, Smoke thought, as he squatted under the shade of a tree and watched as Dooley left the house and walked toward him. Both of them square-built men. Solid. Both of them in their early to mid forties.

Dooley did not offer to shake hands. "Speak your piece, Jensen."

Smoke repeated what he'd told Cord, almost word for word, including the bit about Louis Longmont. Grim-faced, Hanks stood and took it. He didn't like it, but he took it.

"Maybe I'll just wait you out, Jensen."

"Maybe. But I doubt it. You're paying fighting wages, Dooley. To a lot of people. You're like most cattlemen, Dooley: you're worth a lot of money, but most of it is standing on four hooves. Ready scratch is hard to come up with."

Dooley grunted. Man knew what he was talking about, all right. "You won't get between me and McCorkle?"

"I don't care what you two do to each other. The area would probably be better off if you'd kill each other."

"Plainspoken man, ain't you?"

"I see no reason to dance around it, Dooley. What'd you say?"

Something evil moved behind Dooley Hanks's eyes. And Smoke didn't miss it. He did not trust this man; there was no honor to be found in Dooley Hanks.

"I didn't rustle no Box T cattle, Jensen. We just scattered them all to hell and gone. You're free to work my range. You find any Box T cattle, take them. You won't be bothered, and neither will Miss Fae or any punchers she hires." He grinned, and it was not a pleasant curving of the lips. He also had bad breath. "*If* she can find anyone stupid enough to work for her. Now get out of my face. I'm sick of lookin at you."

"The feeling is quite mutual, Hanks." Smoke mounted up and rode away.

"I don't trust that hombre," Beans said. "He's got more twists and turns than a snake."

"I got the same feeling. See if you can find some of Fae's beef and start pushing them toward Box T graze. I'm going into Gibson."

"You're serious?"

"Oh, yes," Smoke told him. "Thirty and found, and you'll work just like any other cowboy."

The man threw back his head and laughed; his teeth were very white against his deeply tanned face. He tossed his hat onto the table in Hans's café.

"All right," he said suddenly. "All right, Smoke, you have a deal. I was a vaquero before I turned to the gun. I will ride for the Box T."

Smoke and Lujan shook hands. Smoke had always heard how unpredictable the man was, but once he gave his word, he would die keeping it.

Lujan packed up his gear and pulled out moments later, riding for the Box T. Smoke chatted with Hans and Olga and Hilda for a few moments—Hilda, as it turned out, was quite taken with Ring—and then he decided he'd like a beer. Smoke was not much of a drinker, but did enjoy a beer or a drink of whiskey every now and then.

Which saloon to enter? He stood in front of the café and pondered that for a moment. Both of the saloons were filled up with gunhands. "Foolish of me," he muttered. But a cool beer sounded good. He slipped the leather thongs from the hammers of his guns and walked over to the Pussycat and pushed open the batwings, stepping into the semi-gloom of the beery-smelling saloon.

All conversation stopped.

Smoke walked to the bar and ordered a beer. The barkeep suddenly got very nervous. Smoke sipped his beer and it was good, hitting the spot.

"Jack Waters was a friend of mine," a man spoke, the voice coming from the gloom of the far end of the saloon.

Smoke turned, his beer mug in his left hand.

His right thumb was hooked behind his big silver belt buckle, his fingers only a few inches from his cross-draw .44.

He stood saying nothing, sipping at his beer. He paid for the brew, damned if he wasn't going to try to finish as much of it as possible before he had to deal with this loudmouth.

"Ever'body talks about how bad you are, Jensen," the bigmouth cranked his tongue up again. "But I ain't never seen none of your graveyards."

"I have," the voice came quietly from Smoke's left. He did not know the voice and did not turn his head to put a face to it.

"Far as I'm concerned," the bigmouth stuck it in gear

again, "I think Smoke Jensen is about as bad as a dried-up cow pile."

"You know my name," Smoke's words were softly offered. "What's your name?"

"What's it to you?"

"Wouldn't be right to put a man in the ground without his name on his grave marker."

The loudmouth cursed Smoke.

Smoke took a swallow of beer and waited. He watched as the man pushed his chair back and stood up. Men on both sides of him stood up and backed away, getting out of the line of fire.

"My name's John Cheave, Jensen. I been lookin' for you for nearabouts two years."

"Why?" Smoke was almost to the bottom of his beer mug.

"My brother was killed at Fontana. By you."

"Too bad. He should have picked better company to run with. But I don't recall any Cheave. What was he, some two-bit thief who had to change his name?"

John Cheave again cursed Smoke.

Smoke finished his beer and set the mug down on the edge of the bar. He slipped his thumb from behind his belt buckle and let his right hand dangle by the butt of his .44.

John Cheave called Smoke a son of a bitch.

Smoke's eyes narrowed. "You could have cussed me all day and not said that. Make your grab, Cheave."

Cheave's hands dipped and touched the butts of his guns. Two shots thundered, the reports so close together they sounded as one. Smoke had drawn both guns and fired, rolling his left-hand .44. It was a move that many tried, but few ever perfected; and more than a few ended up shooting themselves in the belly trying.

John Cheave had not cleared leather. He sat down in the chair he had just stood up out of and leaned his head back, his wide, staring eyes looking up at the ceiling of the saloon.

There were two bloody holes in the center of his chest. Cheave opened his mouth a couple of times, but no words came out.

His boots drummed on the floor for a few seconds and then he died, his eyes wide open, staring at and meeting death.

"I seen it, but I don't believe it," a man said, standing up. He tossed a couple of dollars on the table. "Cheave come out of California. Some say he was as fast as John Wesley Hardin. Count me out of this game, boys. I'm ridin'."

He walked out of the saloon, being very careful to avoid getting too close to Smoke.

The sounds of his horse's hooves faded before anyone else spoke.

"The barber doubles as the undertaker," Pooch Matthews said.

Smoke nodded his head. "Fine."

The bartender yelled for his swamper to fetch the undertaker.

"Impressive," a gunhawk named Hazzard said. "I have to say it: you're about the best I've ever seen. Except for one."

"Oh?"

Hazzard smiled. "Yeah. Me."

Smoke returned the smile and turned his back to the man, knowing the move would infuriate the gunhawk.

"Another beer, Mister Smoke?" the barkeep asked.

"No."

The barkeep did not push the issue.

Smoke studied the bottom of the empty beer mug, wondering how many more would fall under his guns. Although he knew this showdown would have come, sooner or later, one part of him said that he should not have come into the saloon, while another part of him said that he had a right to go wherever he damned well pleased. As long as it was a public place.

It was an old struggle within the man.

The barber came in and he and the swamper dragged the body out to the barber's wagon and chunked him in. The thud of the body falling against the bed of the wagon could be heard inside the saloon.

"I believe I will have that beer," Smoke said. While the barkeep filled his mug, Smoke rolled one of his rare cigarettes and lit up.

The saloon remained very quiet.

The barkeep's hand trembled just slightly as he set the foamy mug in front of Smoke.

Several horses pulled up outside the place. McCorkle and Jason Bright and several of Cord's hands came in. They walked to a table and sat down, ordering beer.

"What happened?" Smoke heard Cord ask.

"Cheave started it with Jensen. He didn't even clear leather."

"I thought you was going to stay out of this game, Jensen?" McCorkle directed the question to Smoke's back.

Smoke slowly turned, holding the beer mug in his left hand. "Cheave pushed me, Cord. I only came in here for a beer."

"Man's got a right to have a drink," Cord grudgingly conceded. "I seen some Box T cattle coming in, Jensen. They was grazin' on range 'bout five, six miles out of town. On the west side of the Smith."

"Thanks." And with a straight face, he added, "I'll have Lujan and a couple of others push them back to Box T range."

"Lujan!" Jason Bright almost hollered the word.

"Yes. He went to work for the Box T a couple of hours ago."

A gunslick that Smoke knew from the old days, when he and Preacher were roaming the land, got up and walked toward the table where Cord was sitting. "I figure I got half a month's wages comin' to me, Mister McCorkle. If you've a mind to pay me now, I'd appreciate it."

With a look of wry amusement on his face, Cord reached into his pocket and counted out fifty dollars, handing it to the man. "You ridin', Jim?"

"Yes, sir. I figure I can catch up with Red. He hauled his ashes a few minutes ago."

Cord counted out another fifty. "Give this to Red. He earned it."

"Yes, sir. Much obliged." He looked around the saloon. "See you boys on another trail. This one's gettin' crowded." He walked through the batwings.

"Yellow," Hazzard said disgustedly, his eyes on the swinging and squeaking batwings. "Just plain yellow is all he is."

Cord cut his eyes. "Jim Kay is anything but yellow, Hazzard. I've known him for ten years. There is a hell of a lot of difference between being yellow and bettin' your life on a busted flush." He looked at Smoke. "There bad blood between you and Jim Kay?"

Smoke shook his head. "Not that I'm aware of. I've known him since I was just a kid. He's a friend of Preacher."

Cord smiled. "Preacher pulled my bacon out of the fire long years back. Only time I ever met him. I owe him. I often wonder what happened to him."

"He's alive. But getting on in years."

Cord nodded his head, then his eyes swept the room. "I'll say it now, boys; we leave the Box T alone. Our fight is with Dooley Hanks. Box T riders can cross our range and be safe doin' it. They'll be comin' through lookin' for the cattle we scattered. You don't have to help them, just leave them alone."

A few of the gunslicks exchanged furtive glances. Cord missed the eye movement. Smoke did not. The gunfighters that Smoke would have trusted had left the area, such as Jim

Kay and Red and a few others. What was left was the dregs, and there was not an ounce of honor in the lot.

Smoke finished his beer. "See you, Cord."

The rancher nodded his head and Smoke walked out the door. Riding toward the Box T, Smoke thought: You better be careful, McCorkle, 'cause you've surrounded yourself with a bunch of rattlesnakes, and I don't think you know just how dangerous they are.

SEVEN

The days drifted on, filled with hard honest work and the deep dreamless sleep of the exhausted. Smoke had hired two more hands, boys really, in their late teens. Bobby and Hatfield. They had left the drudgery of a hardscrabble farm in Wisconsin and drifted west, with dreams of the romantic West and being cowboys. And they both had lost all illusions about the romantic life of a cowboy very quickly. It was brutally hard work, but at least much of it could be done from the back of a horse.

True to his word, Lujan not only did his share, but took up some slack as well. He was a skilled cowboy, working with no wasted motion, and he was one of the finest horsemen Smoke had ever seen.

One hot afternoon, Smoke looked up to see young Hatfield come a-foggin' toward him, lathering his horse.

"Mister Smoke! Mister Smoke!" he yelled. "I ain't believing this. You got to come quick to the house."

He reined up in a cloud of dust and Smoke had to wait until the dust settled before he could even see the young man to talk to him.

"Whoa, boy! Who put a burr under your blanket?"

"Mister Smoke, my *daddy* read stories about them men up

to Miss Fae's house when he was a boy. I thought they was all dead and buried in the grave!"

"Slow down, boy. What men?"

"Them old gunfighters up yonder. Come on." He wheeled his horse around and was gone at a gallop.

Lujan pulled up. "What's going on, *amigo*?"

"I don't know. Come on, let's find out."

Fae was entertaining them on the front porch when Smoke and Lujan rode up. Smoke laughed when he saw them.

Lujan looked first at the aging men on the porch, and then looked at Smoke, When he spoke, there was disapproval in his voice. "It is not nice to laugh at the old, my friend."

"Lujan, I'm not laughing at them. These men are friends of mine. As well known as we are, we're pikers compared to those old gunslingers. Lujan, you're looking at Silver Jim, Pistol Le Roux, Hardrock, and Charlie Starr."

"Dios mio!" the Mexican breathed. "Those men invented the fast draw."

"And don't sell them short even today, Lujan. They can still get into action mighty quick."

"I wouldn't doubt it for a minute," Lujan said, dismounting.

"If I'd known you old coots were going to show up, I'd have called the old folks' home and had them send over some wheelchairs," Smoke called out.

"Would you just listen to the pup flap his mouth," Hardrock said. "I ought to get up and spank him."

"Way your knees pop and crack he'd probably think you was shootin' at him," Pistol laughed.

The men shook hands and Smoke introduced them to Lujan.

Charlie Starr sized the Mexican up. "Yeah, I seen you down along the border some years back. When them Sabler brothers called you out. Too bad you didn't kill all five of them."

"Wasn't two down enough?" Lujan asked softly, clearly in awe of these old gunslingers.

"Nope," Silver Jim said. "We stopped off down in

Wyoming for supplies. Store clerk said the Sabler boys had come through the day before, heading up thisaway. Ben, Carl, and Delmar."

Lujan sighed. "Many, many times I have wished I had never drawn my pistol in anger that first time down in Cuauhtemoc." He smiled. "Of course, the shooting was over a lovely lady. And of course, she would have nothing to do with me after that."

"What was her name?" Hatfield asked.

Lujan laughed. "I do not even remember."

The old gunfighters were all well up in years—Charlie Starr being the youngest—but they were all leather-tough and could still work many men half their age into the ground.

And the news that the Box T had hired the famed gun-slingers was soon all over the area. Some of Cord McCorkle's hired guns thought it was funny, and it would be even fun-nier to tree one of the old gunnies and see just what he'd do. The gunfighter they happened to pick that morning was the Louisiana Creole, Pistol Le Roux.

Ol' Pistol and Bobby were working some strays back toward the east side of the Smith when the three gunhawks spotted Pistol and headed his way. Just to be on the safe side, Pistol wheeled his horse to face the men and slipped the hammer thong off his right-hand Colt and waited.

That one of the men held a coiled rope in his right hand did not escape the old gunfighter. He had him a hunch that these pups were gonna try to rope and drag him. A hard smile touched his face. That had been tried before. Several times. Ain't been done yet.

"Well, well," the hired gun said, riding up. "What you reckon we done come across here, boys?"

"Damned if I know," another said with a nasty grin. "But it shore looks to me like it needs buryin'."

"Yeah," the third gunny said, sniffing the air. "It's done died and gone to stinkin'."

"That's probably your dirty drawers you smellin', punk," Pistol told him. "Since your mammy ain't around to change them for you."

The man flushed, deep anger touching his face. Tell the truth, he hadn't changed his union suit in a while.

"I think we'll just check the brands on them beeves," they told Pistol.

"You'll visit the outhouse if you eat regular, too," Pistol popped back. "And you probably should, and soon, 'cause you sure full of it."

"Why, you godda—" He grabbed for his pistol. The last part of the obscenity was cut off as Pistol's Colt roared, the slug taking the would-be gunslick in the lower part of his face and driving through the base of his throat.

Pistol had drawn and fired so fast the other two had not had time to clear leather. Now they found themselves looking down the long barrel of Pistol's Peacemaker. The dying gunny moaned and tried to talk; the words were unintelligible, due in no small measure to the lower part of his jaw being missing.

"Shuck out of them gun belts," Pistol told them, just as Bobby came galloping up to see what the shooting was all about. "Usin' your left hands," Pistol added.

Gun belts hit the ground.

"Dismount," Pistol told them. "Bobby, git that rope."

"Hey!" one of the gunnies said. "We was just a-funnin' with you, that's all."

"I don't consider bein' dragged no fun. And that's what you was gonna do, right?"

"Aw, no!"

Pistol's Colt barked and the bootheel was torn loose from the gunny's left boot. "Wasn't it, boy?" Pistol yelled.

On the ground, holding his numbed foot, the gunny nodded his head. "Yeah. We all make mistakes."

"Git out of them clothes," Pistol ordered. "Bare-butted nekkid. Do it!"

Red-faced, the men stood before Pistol, Bobby, and God in their birthday suits.

"Tie 'em together, Bobby. But give them room to walk. They got a long way to hoof it."

The gunny on the ground jerked and died.

The bare-butted men tied, their hands behind their backs, Pistol looped the rope around his saddle horn and gave the orders. "Move out. Head for your bunkhouse, boys. Git goin'."

"What about Pete?" one hollered.

"He'll keep without gettin' too gamy. Now *move*!"

It was a good hour's walk back to the Circle Double C ranch house, and the gunnies hoofed it all the way. They complained and moaned and hollered and finally begged for relief from their hurting, bleeding feet. They shut up when Pistol threatened to drag them.

"Pitiful," Pistol told him. "Twice the Indians caught me and made me run for it, bare-butt nekkid. Miles and miles and miles. With them just a-whoopin' and a-hollerin' right behind me. You two are a disgrace."

Cord stood by the front gate and had to smile at the sight as the painful parade came to a halt. He had ordered his wife and daughter not to look outside. But of course they both did.

The naked men collapsed to the ground.

"Mister McCorkle, my name is Le Roux. They call me Pistol. Now, sir, I was minding my own business, herdin' cattle like I'm paid to do, when three of your hands come up and was gonna put a loop around me and drag me. One of them went for his gun. He was a tad slow. You'll find him dead by that big stand of cottonwoods on the Smith. He ain't real purty to look at. Course, he wasn't all that beautiful when he was livin'. I brung these wayward children back home. You want to spank them, that's your business. Good day, sir."

Pistol and Bobby swung their horses and headed back to Box T range.

Cord looked at the naked men and their bloody feet and briar-scratched ankles and legs. "Get their feet taken care of, pay them off, and get them out of here," he instructed his foreman. He looked at the gunslicks on his payroll. "Pete was one of your own. Go get him and bury him. And stay the hell away from Box T riders." He pointed to the naked and weary and footsore men on the ground. "One man did that. One . . . old . . . man. But that man, and those other old gunfighters over at the Box T came out here in the thirties and forties as mountain men. Tough? You bet your life they're tough. When they do go down for the last time, they'll go out of this world like cornered wolves, snarling and ripping at anything or anyone that confronts them. Leave them alone, boys. If you feel you can't obey my orders, ride out of here."

The gunfighters stared at Cord. All stayed. As Cord turned his back to them and walked toward his house, he had a very bad feeling about the outcome of this matter, and he could not shake it.

"It's stupid!" Sandi McCorkle said to her friend. "They don't even know why they hate each other."

Rita Hanks nodded her head in agreement. "I'm going to tell you something, Sandi. And it's just between you and me. I don't trust my father, or my brothers."

Sandi waited for her friend to continue.

"I think Daddy's gone crazy." She grimaced. "I think my brothers have always been crazy. They've never been . . . well, just right; as far as I'm concerned. They're cruel and vicious."

"What do you think your dad is going to do?"

"I don't know. But he's up to something. He sent a hand out

last week to Helena. Then yesterday this ratty-faced-looking guy shows up at the ranch. Danny Rouge. Has a real fancy rifle. Carries it in a special-made case. I think he's a back-shooter, Sandi."

The two young women, both in their late teens, had been forbidden by their fathers to see each other, years back. Of course, neither of them paid absolutely any attention to those orders. But their meetings had become a bit more secretive.

"Do you want me to tell Daddy about this, Rita?"

"No. He'd know it came from me and then you'd get in trouble. I think we'd better tell Smoke Jensen."

Sandi giggled. "I'd like to tell him a thing or two—in private. He's about the best-looking man I've ever seen."

"He's also married with children," Rita reminded her friend. "But he sure is cute. He's even better looking than the covers of those books make him out to be. Have you seen the Moab Kid?"

"Yes! He's *darling*!"

The two young women talked about men and marriage for a few minutes. It was time for them to be married; pretty soon they'd be pegged as old maids. They both had plenty of suitors, but none lasted very long. The young women were both waiting for that "perfect man" to come riding into their lives.

"How in the world are we going to tell Smoke Jensen about this back-shooter?"

"I don't know. But I think it's our bounden duty to tell him. People listen to him."

"That Bobby's been gettin' all red-eared everytime he gets around me," Sandi said. "I think maybe he could get a message to Smoke and he'd meet us."

"Worth a try. We'll take us a ride tomorrow over to the Smith and have a picnic and wait. Maybe he'll show up."

"Let's do it. I'll see you at the pool about noon."

The young women walked to their buggies. Both buggies were equipped with rifle boots and the boots were full. A pistol lay on the seat of each buggy. Both Sandi and Rita could, would, and had used the weapons. With few exceptions, ranch-born-and-raised western women were no shrinking violets. They lived in a violent time and had to be prepared to fight. Although most western men would not bother a woman, there were always a few who would, even though they knew the punishment was usually a rope.

Very little Indian trouble now occurred in this part of Montana; but there was always the chance of a few bucks breaking from the reservations to steal a few horses or take a few scalps.

With a wave, the young women went their way, Sandi back to the Circle Double C, Rita back to D-H. Neither noticed the two men sitting their horses in the timber. The men wore masks and long dusters.

"You ready?" one asked, his voice muffled by the bandanna tied round his face.

"I been ready for some of that Rita. Let's go."

EIGHT

Silver Jim found the overturned buggy while out hunting strays. The horse was nowhere in sight. He noticed that the Winchester .44 carbine was a good twenty feet from the over-turned buggy. He surmised that whoever had been in this rig had pulled the carbine from its boot and was makin' ready to use it. Then he found the pistol. He squatted down and sniffed at the barrel. Recently fired.

He stood up and emptied his Colt into the air; six widely spaced shots. It took only a few minutes for Smoke and Lujan to reach him.

"That is Señorita Hanks's buggy," Lujan said. "I have seen her in it several times."

"Stay with it, boys," Smoke said. "Look around. I'll ride to the D-H."

He did not spare his horse getting to the ranch, reining up to the main house in a cloud of dust and jumping off. "Switch my saddle," he told a startled hand. He ran up the steps to face a hard-eyed Dooley Hanks. "Silver Jim found Miss Hanks's buggy just north of our range. By that creek. Over-turned. No sign of Miss Hanks. But Silver Jim said her pistol had been fired. I left them looking for her and trying to cut some trail."

The color went out of Dooley's face. Like most men, his daughter was the apple of his eye. "I'm obliged. Let's ride, boys!" he yelled.

Already, one of his regular hands was noosing a rope.

Within five minutes, twenty-five strong, Dooley led his hands and his hired guns out at a gallop. The wrangler had switched Smoke's saddle to a mean-eyed mustang and was running for his own horse.

Smoke showed the mustang who was boss and then cut across country, taking the timber and making his own trail, going where no large group of riders could. He reached the overturned buggy just a couple of minutes before Dooley and his men.

"Silver Jim cut some sign," Bobby told him. "Him and Lujan took off thataway. Told me to stay here."

Dooley and his party reined up and Dooley jumped off his horse. Smoke pointed to the pistol, still where Silver Jim had found it.

"That's hers," the father said, a horrified look in his eyes. "I give it to her and taught her how to use it."

"Look!" Bobby pointed.

Heads turned. Silver Jim was holding a girl in his arms, Lujan leading the horse, some of its harness dragging the ground.

The cook from the D-H came rattling up in a wagon, Mrs. Hanks on the seat beside him. "I filled it with hay, Boss," he told Dooley. "Just in case."

Dooley nodded.

Smoke took the girl from Silver Jim and carried her to the wagon and to her mother. She had been badly beaten and her clothing ripped from her. One of her eyes was closed and discolored and blood leaked from a corner of her mouth. Silver Jim had wrapped her in a blanket.

"How did you . . . I mean," Dooley shook his head. "Had she been . . . ?"

"I reckon," Silver Jim said solemnly. "Her clothes and . . . underthings was strewn over about a half a mile. Looks like they was rippin' and tearin' as they rode. Two men took her, a third joined them over yonder on that first ridge." He pointed. "He'd been waitin' for some time. Half a dozen cigarette butts on the ground."

"She say who done this?" Dooley's voice was harsh and terrible sounding.

"No, señor," Lujan said. "She was unconscious when we found her."

"Shorty!" Dooley barked. "Go fetch that old rummy we call a doctor. If he ain't sober, dunk him in a horse trough until he is. Ride, man!"

Smoke had walked to the wagon bed and was looking at the young woman, her head cradled in her mother's lap. He noticed a crimson area on the side of her head. "Bobby, bring me my canteen, hurry!"

He wet a cloth and asked Mrs. Hanks to clean up the bloody spot.

"Awful bump on her head," the mother said, her voice calm but the words tight.

"For sure she's got a concussion," Smoke said. "Maybe a fractured skull. Cushion her head and drive real slow, Cookie. She can't take many bumps and jars."

Smoke and his people stood and watched the procession start out for the ranch. Dooley had sent several of his men to follow the trail left by the rapists. "Bring them back alive," he told them. "I want to stake them out." He turned his mean and slightly maddened eyes toward Smoke. "Ain't that what you done years back, Jensen?"

"That's what I did."

The man's gone over the edge, Smoke thought. This was all it took to push him into that shadowy, eerie world of madness.

"They're going to find out what we didn't tell them,

Smoke," Lujan said. "The trail leads straight to Circle Double C range."

"And one of them horses has a chip out of a shoe. It'll be easy to identify." Silver Jim said.

Smoke thought about that. "Almost too easy, wouldn't you think?"

"That thought did cross my mind," the old gunfighter acknowledged, rolling a cigarette.

"I better get over there." Smoke swung into the saddle and turned the mustang's head.

He looped the reins around the hitchrail and walked up to the porch, conscious of a lot of hard eyes on him as he knocked on the door.

A very lovely young woman opened the door and smiled at him. "Why, Mister Jensen. How nice. Please come in."

Smoke removed his hat and stepped inside the nicely furnished home just as Cord stepped into the foyer. "Trouble, Cord. Bad trouble." He looked at Sandi.

"Go sit with your mother, girl," the father said.

Sandi smiled sweetly and leaned up against the wall, folding her arms under her breasts.

Cord lifted and spread his big hands in a helpless gesture. "Boys are bad enough, Smoke, but girls are impossible."

Smoke told them both, leaving very little out. He did not mention anything about the chipped shoe; not in front of Sandi. Nor did he say anything about the trail leading straight to Circle C range.

"I've got to get over there," Sandi said, turning to fetch her shawl.

"No." Smoke's hard-spoken word stopped her, turning her around. "There is nothing you can do over there. Rita is unconscious and will probably remain so for many hours. Dooley is killing mad and likely to go further off the deep end. And those who . . . abused Rita are still out there. Your going over there would accomplish nothing and only put you in danger."

She locked rebellious eyes with Smoke. Then she slowly nodded her head. "You're right, of course. Thank you for pointing those things out. I'll go tell Mother."

Smoke motioned Cord out onto the porch where they could talk freely, in private. He leveled with Cord.

"Damn!" the man cursed, balling his fists. "If the men who done it are here, we'll find them and hold them for the law . . . or hang them," he added the hard words. "No matter what I feel about Hanks himself, Rita and my Sandi have been friends for years. Rita and her momma is the two reasons I haven't gone over there and burned the damn place down. I've known for years that Dooley was crazy; and his boys is twice as bad. They're cruel mean."

"I've heard that from other people."

"It's true. And good with short guns, too. Very good. As good and probably better than most of the hired hands on the payroll." He met Smoke's eyes. "There's something you ought to know. Dooley has hired a back-shooter name of Danny Rouge."

"I know of him. Looks like a big rat. But he's pure poison with a rifle."

Cord looked toward the bunkhouse, where half a dozen gunhands were loafing. "Worthless scum. I was gonna let them go. Now I don't know what to do."

Smoke could offer no advice. He knew that Cord knew that if Dooley even thought his daughter's attackers came from the Circle Double C, he would need all the guns he could muster. They were all sitting on a powder keg, and it could go up at any moment.

A cowboy walked past the big house. "Find Del for me," Cord ordered. "Tell him to come up here."

"Yes, sir."

"You want me to stick around and help you?" Smoke asked.

Cord shook his head. "No. But thanks. This is my snake. I'll kill it."

"I'll be riding, then. If you need help, don't hesitate to send word. I'll come."

Smoke was riding out as the foreman was walking up.

Smoke rode back to the site of the attack. His people had already righted the buggy and hitched up the now calmed horse.

"I'll take it over to the D-H," Smoke offered. "I've got to get my horse anyway."

"I'll ride with you," Lujan said.

"What are we supposed to do?" Silver Jim asked. "Sit here and grow cobwebs? We'll all ride over."

Bobby had returned to chasing strays and pushing them toward new pasture.

The foreman of the D-H, Gage, met them halfway, leading Smoke's horse. "You boys is all right," he said. "So I'll give it to you straight. Don't come on D-H range no more. I mean, as far as I'm concerned, me and the regular hands, you could ride over anytime; but Dooley has done let his bread burn. He's gone slap nuts. Sent a rider off to wire for more gunhands; they waitin' over at Butte. Lanny Ball found where them tracks led to McCorkle range and that's when Dooley went crazy. His wife talked him out of riding over and killing Cord today. But he's gonna declare war on the Circle Double C and anybody who befriends them. So I guess all bets is off, boys. But I'll tell you this: me and the regular boys is gonna punch cows, and that's it . . . unless someone tries to attack the house. I'm just damn sorry all this had to happen. I'll be ridin' now. You boys keep a good eye on your backtrail. See you."

"Guess that tears it," Smoke said, after Gage had driven off in the buggy, his horse and the horse Smoke had borrowed tied to the back. "Let's get back to the ranch. Fae and Parnell need to be informed about this day."

* * *

Rita regained consciousness the following day. She told her father that she never saw her attackers' faces. They kept masks and hoods on the entire time she was being assaulted.

Cord McCorkle sent word that Dooley was welcome to come help search his spread from top to bottom to find the attackers.

Dooley sent word that Cord could go to hell. That he believed Cord knew who raped and beat his daughter and was hiding them, protecting them.

"I tried," Cord said to Smoke. "I don't know what else I can do."

The men were in town, having coffee in Hans's café.

Parnell had wanted to pack up and go back east immediately. Fae had told him, in quite blunt language, that anytime he wanted to haul his ashes, to go right ahead. She was staying.

Beans and Charlie Starr had stood openmouthed, listening to Fae vent her spleen. They had never heard such language from the mouth of a woman.

Parnell had packed his bags and left the ranch in a huff, vowing never to return until his sister apologized for such unseemly behavior and such vile language.

That set Fae off again. She stood by the hitchrail and cussed her brother until his buggy was out of sight.

Lujan and Spring walked up.

"They do this about once a month," Spring said. "He'll be back in a couple of days. I tell you boys what, workin' for that woman has done give me an education I could do without. Someone needs to sit on her and wash her mouth out with soap."

"Don't look at me!" Lujan said, rolling his dark eyes. "I'd rather crawl up in a nest of rattlesnakes."

"Get back to work!" Fae squalled from the porch, sending the men scrambling for their horses.

"There they are," Smoke said quietly, his eyes on three men riding abreast up the street.

"Who?" Cord asked.

"The Sabler brothers. Ben, Carl, and Delmar. They'll be gunning for Lujan. He killed two of their brothers some years back."

"Be interesting to see which saloon they go in."

"You takin' bets?"

"Not me. I damn sure didn't send for them."

The Sabler boys reined up in front of the Hangout.

"It's like they was told not to come to the Pussycat," Cord reflected.

"They probably were. No chipped shoes on any of your horses, huh?"

"No. But several were reshod that day; started before you came over with the news. It's odd, Smoke. Del is as square as they come; hates the gunfighters. But he says he can account for every one of them the morning Rita was raped. He says he'll swear in a court of law that none of them left the bunkhouse–main house area. I believe him."

"It could have been some drifters."

"You believe that?"

"No. I don't know what to believe, really."

"I better tell you: talk among the D-H bunch—the gunslicks—is that it was Silver Jim and Lujan and the Hatfield boy."

Smoke lifted his eyes to meet Cord's gaze. Cord had to struggle to keep from recoiling back. The eyes were ice-house cold and rattler deadly. "Silver Jim is one of the most honorable men I have ever met. Lujan was with me all that morning. Both Hatfield and Bobby are of the age where neither one of them can even talk when they get around women; besides he was within a mile of me and Lujan all morning. Whoever started that rumor is about to walk into a load of grief. If you know who it is, Cord, I'd appreciate you telling me."

"It was that new bunch that came in on the stage the day after it happened. They come up from Butte at Hanks's wire."

"Names?"

"All I know is they call one of them Rose."

Lujan came galloping up, off his horse before the animal even stopped. He ran into the café. "Smoke! Hardrock found young Hatfield about an hour ago. He'd been tortured with a running iron and then dragged. He ain't got long."

NINE

Doc Adair, now sober for several days, looked up as Smoke and Cord entered the bedroom of the main ranch house. He shook his head. "Driftin' in and out of consciousness. I've got him full of laudanum to ease the pain. They burned him all over his body with a hot iron, then they dragged him. He isn't going to make it. He wouldn't be a whole man even if he did."

No one needed to ask what he meant by that. Those who did this to the boy had been more cruel than mean.

Bobby was fighting back tears. "Me and him growed up together. We was neighbors. More like brothers than friends."

Fae put her arm around the young man and held him, then, at a signal from Smoke, led him out of the bedroom. Smoke knelt down beside the bed.

"Can you hear me, Hatfield?"

The boy groaned and opened his one good eye. "Yes, sir, Mister Smoke." His voice was barely a whisper, and filled with pain.

"Who did this to you?"

"One of them was called . . . Rose. They called another one Cliff. I ain't gonna make it, am I, Mister Smoke?"

Smoke sighed.

"Tell me . . . the truth."

"The doc says no. But doctors have been wrong before."

"When they burned my privates . . . I screamed and passed out. I come to and they . . . was draggin' me."

His words were becoming hard to understand and his breathing was very ragged. Smoke could see one empty eye socket. "Send any money due me to . . . my ma. Tell her to buy something pretty . . . with it. Watch out for Bobby. He's . . . He don't look it, but he's . . . cat quick with a short gun. Been . . . practicin' since we was about . . . six years old. Gettin' dark. See you, boys."

The young man closed his good eye and spoke no more. Doc Adair pushed his way through to the bed. After a few seconds, he said, "He's still alive, but just. A few more minutes and he'll be out of his pain."

Smoke glanced at Lujan. "Lujan, go sit on Bobby. Hog-tie him if you have to. We'll avenge Hatfield, but it'll be after the boy's been given a proper burial."

Grim-faced, and feeling a great deal more emotion than showed on his face, the Mexican gunfighter nodded and left the room.

Hatfield groaned in his unconsciousness. He sighed and his chest moved up and down, as if struggling for breath. Then he lay still. Doc Adair held a small pocket mirror up to the boy's mouth. No breath clouded the mirror. The doctor pulled the sheet over Hatfield's face.

"I'll start putting a box together," Spring spoke from the doorway. "Damn, but I liked that boy!"

The funeral was at ten o'clock the following morning. Mr. and Mrs. Cord McCorkle came, accompanied by Sandi and a few of their hands. Doc Adair was there, as were Hans and Hilda and Olga. Olga went straight to Ring's side and stood there during the services.

No one had seen Bobby that morning. He showed up at the last moment, wearing a black suit—Fae had pressed it for him—with a white shirt and black string tie. He wore a Remington Frontier .44, low and tied down. He did not strut and swagger. He wore it like he had been born with it. He walked up to Smoke and Lujan and the others, standing in a group.

"Bobby just died with Hatfield," he told them. "My last name is Johnson. Turkey Creek Jack Johnson is my uncle. My name is Bob Johnson. And I'll be goin' into town when my friend is in the ground proper and the words said over him. '

"We'll all go in, Bob," Smoke told him.

The preacher spoke his piece and the dirt was shoveled over Hatfield's fresh-made coffin.

"Cord, I'd appreciate it if you and yours would stay here with Fae and Parnell until we get back."

"We'll sure do it, Smoke. Take your time. And shoot straight," he added.

The men headed out. Four aging gunfighters with a string of kills behind them so long history has still not counted them. One gunfighter from south of the border. Smoke Jensen, from north of the border. The Moab Kid and a boy/man who rode with destiny on his shoulders.

They slowed their horses as they approached Gibson, the men splitting up into pairs, some circling the town to come in at different points.

But the town was nearly deserted. Hans's café had been closed for the funeral. The big general store—run by Walt and Leah Hillery, a sour-faced man and his wife—was open, but doing no business. The barber shop was empty. There were no horses standing at the hitchrails of either saloon. Smoke walked his horse around the corral and then looked inside the stable. Only a few horses in stalls, and none of them appeared to be wet from recent riding.

The men gathered at the edge of town, talked it over, and

then dismounted, splitting up into two groups, one group on each side of the street.

Smoke pushed open the batwings of the Hangout and stepped inside. The place was empty except for the barkeep and the swamper. The bartender, knowing that Smoke had on his warpaint, was nervously polishing shot glasses and beer mugs.

"Ain't had a customer all morning, Mister Smoke," he announced. "I think the boys is stayin' close to the bunkhouse."

Smoke nodded at the man and stepped back out onto the boardwalk, continuing on his walking inspection.

He met with Beans. "Nothing," the Moab Kid said. "Town is deserted."

"They are not yet ready to meet us," Lujan said, walking up.

"We're wasting time here. We've still got cattle to brand and more to move to higher pasture. There'll be another day. Let's get back to work."

The days passed uneventfully, the normal day-to-day routine of the ranch devouring the men's time. Parnell, just as Old Spring had called it, moved back to the ranch and he and Fae continued their bickering. Rita improved, physically, but was not allowed off the ranch. And to make sure that she not try any meetings with Sandi, her father assigned two to watch her at all times.

Bob Johnson was a drastically changed young man. Bobby was gone. The boy seldom smiled now, and he was always armed. Smoke and Charlie Starr had watched him practice late one afternoon, when the day's work on the range was over.

"He's better than good," Charlie remarked. "He's cursed with being a natural."

He did not have to explain that. Smoke knew only too well what the gunfighter meant. With Bob, it was almost as if gun was a physical extension of his right arm. His draw was oil-smooth and his aim was deadly accurate. And he was fast, very fast.

Old Pat rode out to the branding site in the early morning the sixth day after Hatfield's burying.

"Hans just sent word, Smoke. Them Waters brothers come into town late yesterday and they brought a half dozen hard-cases with them."

"Hans know who they are?"

"He knowed two of 'em. No-Count George Victor and Three-Fingers Kerman. Other four looked meaner than snakes, Hans said. 'Bout an hour later, four more guns come in on the stage. Wore them big California spurs."

"Of course they went straight to the Hangout?" Charlie asked.

"Waters's bunch did. Them California gunslicks went on over to the Pussycat. McCorkle's hirin' agin."

Smoke cursed, but he really could not blame Cord. Every peace effort he had made to Hanks had been turned down with a violent outburst of profanity from Dooley. And Hanks' sons were pushing and prodding each time they came into town. Sonny, Bud, and Conrad Hanks had made their brags that they were going to kill Cord's boys, Max, Rock, and Troy. They were all about the same age and, according to Cord, all possessing about the same ability with a short gun. Cord's boys were more level-headed and better educated—his wife had seen to that. Hanks's boys were borderline stupid. Hanks had seen to that. And they were cruel and vicious.

"We're gonna be pulled into this thing," Hardrock remarked. "Just sure as the sun comes up. There ain't no way we can miss it. Sooner or later, we're gonna run up on them no-goods that done in Young Hatfield. And whether we do it together, or Young Bob does the deed, we'll have chosen a side."

"I'm curious as to when that back-shootin' Danny Rouge

is gonna uncork," Pistol said. "I been prowlin' some; I ain't picked up no sign of his ever comin' onto Box T range."

"Hanks hasn't turned him loose yet." Smoke fished out the makings and rolled him a cigarette, passing the sack and the papers around. He was thoughtful for a moment. "I'll tell you all what's very odd to me: these gunhawks are drawing fighting wages, but they have made no move toward each other. I think there's something rotten in the potato barrel, boys. And I think it's time I rode over and talked it out with Cord."

"You would have to bring that to my attention," Cord said, a glum look on his face. "I hadn't thought of that. But by George, you may be right. I hope you're not," he quickly added, "but there's always a chance. Have you heard anything more about Rita's condition?"

"Getting better, physically. Hanks keeps her under guard at the ranch."

"Same thing I heard. Sandi asked to see her and Dooley said he wouldn't guarantee her safety if she set foot on D-H range. He didn't out and out threaten her—he knows better than that—but he came damn close. His sons and my sons are shapin' up for a shootin', though. And I can't stop them. I want to, but I don't know how, short of hogtyin' my boys and chainin' them to a post."

"How many regular hands do you have, Cord?"

"Eight, counting Del. I always hire part-timers come brandin' time and drives."

"So that's twelve people you can count on, including yourself and your sons."

"Right. Cookie is old, but he can still handle a six-gun and a rifle. You think the lid is going to fly off the pot, don't you, Smoke?"

"Yes. But I don't know when. Do you think your wife and Sandi would go on a visit somewhere until this thing is over?"

"*Hell,* no! If I asked Alice to leave she'd hit me with a skillet. God only knows what Sandi would do, or say," he added drily. "Her mouth doesn't compare to Fae's, but stir her up and you' got a cornered puma on your hands."

"How about those California gunhands that just came in?

"I don't trust them any more than I do the others. But I felt had to beef up my gunnies."

"I don't blame you a bit. And I may be all wrong in my suspicions."

"Sad thing is, Smoke, I think you're probably right."

Smoke left McCorkle's ranch and headed back to the Box T. Halfway there, he changed his mind and pointed his horse's nose toward Gibson. Some of the crew was running out of chewing tobacco. He was almost to town when he heard the pounding of hooves. He pulled over to the side of the road and twisted in the saddle. Four riders that he had not seen before. He pulled his Winchester from the boot, levered in a round, and eared the hammer back, laying the rifle across his saddle horn. He was riding Dagger, and knew the horse would stand still in the middle of a cyclone; he wouldn't even look up from grazing at a few gunshots.

The riders reined in, kicking up a lot of unnecessary dust. Smoke pegged them immediately. Arrogant punks, would-be gunslicks. Not a one of them over twenty-one. But they wore two guns tied down.

"You there, puncher!" one hollered. "How far to Gibson?"

"I'm not standing in the next county, sonny, and I'm not deaf, either."

"You 'bout half smart, though, ain't you?" He grinned at Smoke. "You know who you're talkin' to?"

"Just another loudmouthed punk, I reckon."

The young man flushed, looked at his friends, and then laughed. "You're lucky, cowboy. I feel good today, so I won' call you down for that remark. I've killed people for less. I'm Twain."

"Does that rhyme with rain or are you a half-wit?"

"Damn you!" Twain yelled. "Who do you think you are, anyways?"

"Smoke Jensen."

Twain's horse chose that moment to dump a pile of road apples in the dirt. From the look on Twain's face, he felt like doing the same thing in his saddle. He opened and closed his mouth about a half dozen times.

His friends relaxed in their saddles, making very sure both hands were clearly visible and kept well away from their guns.

"You keep on this road," Smoke told them. "Gibson's about four miles."

"Ah . . . uh . . . yes, sir!" Twain finally got the words out. "I . . . uh . . . we are sure obliged."

"You got any sense, boy, you won't stop. You'll just keep on ridin' until you come to Wyoming. But I figure that any-body who cuts kill-notches in the butt of their gun don't have much sense. Who you aimin' to ride for, boy?"

"Ah . . . the D-H spread."

Smoke sat his saddle and stared at the quartet. He stared at them so long they all four began to sweat.

"Is . . . ah . . . something the matter, Mister Smoke?" Twain asked.

"The rest of your buddies got names, Twain?"

"Ah . . . this here is Hector. That's Rod, and that's Murray."

"Be sure and tell that to the barber when you get to town."

"The . . . barber?" Hector asked.

"Yeah. He doubles as the undertaker." Smoke turned his back on the young gunhands and rode on toward town.

TEN

Among the many horses tied to the hitchrails, on both sides of the street, the first to catch Smoke's eyes was Bob's paint, tied up in front of Hans's café. Smoke looped his reins and went in for some coffee and pie. He wondered why so much activity and then remembered it was Saturday. Parnell sat with Bob at a table. They were in such heated discussion neither noticed as Smoke walked up to their table. They lifted their eyes as he pulled back a chair and sat down.

"Perhaps you can talk some sense into this young man's head, Mister Jensen," Parnell pleaded. "He is going to call out these Rose and Cliff individuals."

Smoke ordered apple pie and coffee and then said, "His right, Parnell. I'd do the same was I standing in his boots."

Parnell was aghast. His mouth dropped open and he shook his head. "But he's just a boy! I cannot for the life of me understand why you didn't call the authorities after the murder!"

"Because the law is a hundred miles away, Parnell. And out here, a man handles his own problems without runnin' whining to the law."

"I find it positively barbaric!"

Smoke ate some apple pie and sipped his coffee. Then he surprised the schoolteacher by saying, "Yes, it is barbaric,

Parnell. But it's quick. Don't worry, there'll be plenty of lawyers out here before you know it, and they'll be messin' things up and writin' contracts so's that only another lawyer can read them. That'll be good for people like you . . . not so good for the rest of us. You haven't learned in the time you've been here that out here, a man's word is his bond. If he tells you he's sellin' you five hundred head of cattle, there will be five hundred head of cattle, or he'll make good any missing. Call a man a liar out here, Parnell, and it's a shootin' offense. Honorable men live by their word. If they're not honorable, they don't last. They either leave, or get buried. Lawyers, Parnell, will only succeed in screwing that all up." He looked at Bob. "You nervous, Bob?"

"Yes, sir. Some. But I figure I'll calm down soon as I face him."

"As soon as *we* face *them,* Bob," Smoke corrected. "Yes, you'll calm down. Ever killed a man, Bob?"

"No, sir."

Smoke finished his pie, wiped his mouth with the napkin, and waved for Olga to refill his cup. He sugared and stirred and sipped. "A man gets real calm inside, Bob. It's the strangest thing. You can hear a fly buzz a hundred yards off. And you can see everything so clearly. And the quiet is so much so it's scary. Dogs can be barking, cats fighting, but you won't hear anything except the boots of the man you're facing walking toward you."

"How old was you when you killed your first man, Smoke?" Bob asked.

"Fifteen, I think. Maybe fourteen. I don't remember."

"That must have been a terribly traumatic time for you," Parnell said.

"Nope. I just reloaded 'er up and went on. Me and Preacher. I killed some Indians before that . . . in Kansas I think it was. Pa was still alive then. They attacked us," he added. "I always got along with the Indians for the most part.

Lived with them for a while. Me and Preacher. That was after Pa died. Drink your coffee, Bob. It's about time."

Smoke noticed the young man's hands were calm as he lifted the cup to his mouth, sipped, and replaced the cup in the saucer.

Parnell looked at the men, his eyes drifting back and forth. He had heard from his sister and from the old gunfighters at the ranch that Smoke was a devoted family man: totally faithful to his wife and a loving father. A marvelous friend. Yet for all of those attributes, the man was sitting here talking about killing with less emotion than he exhibited when ordering a piece of pie.

Parnell watched with a curious mixture of fascination and revulsion as Smoke took his guns from leather, one at a time, and carefully checked the action, using the napkin to wipe them free of any dust that might have accumulated during his ride to town. He loaded up the usually empty chamber under the hammer.

Bob checked his Remington .44 and then pulled a short-barreled revolver out of his waistband and checked that, loading both guns full. He cut his eyes to Smoke. "Insurance," he said.

"Never hurts." Smoke pushed back his chair and stood up. "You know these people, Bob?"

"They been pointed out to me." He stood up.

"Their buddies are sure to join them. We're probably not going to have much time for plan-making. At the first twitch, we start shooting. Take the ones to your left. I'll take care of the rest."

"Yes, sir."

"Let's go."

Both men had noticed, out of the corners of their eyes, the horses lining both sides of the wide dusty street being cleared from the line of fire.

They stepped out of the café and stood for a moment on the boardwalk, hats pulled down low, letting their eyes adjust to the bright sunlight.

"Your play," Smoke said. "You call it."

"Rose!" Bob yelled. "Cliff! And any others who tortured and dragged Hatfield. Let's see if you got the backbone to face someone gun to gun."

Rose looked out the window of the Hangout. "Hell, it's that damn kid."

"And Smoke Jensen," he was reminded.

"Let's shoot 'em from here," Cliff suggested.

"No!" Lanny Ball stepped in. "They're callin' you out fair and square. If you ain't got the stomach for it, use the back door and cut and run . . . and don't never show your faces around here agin. I've killed a lot of men, and I've rode the owlhoot trail with a posse at my back. But I ain't never tortured nobody while they was trussed up like a hog. I may not be much, but I ain't no coward."

Only a few of the other gunhawks in the large saloon murmured their agreement, but those few were the best-known and most feared of their kind. It was enough to bring the sweat out on the faces of Cliff and Rose and the two others who had taken part in the dragging and torture of Hatfield.

When open warfare was finally called by Hanks, Lanny and few others who still possessed a modicum of honor would back-shoot and snipe at any known enemy . . . that was the way of war. But when a man called you out to face him, you faced him, eyeball to eyeball.

With a low curse, Rose checked his guns and stepped out through the batwings, Cliff and the others behind him. It was straight-up noon, the sun a hot bubbling ball overhead. There were no shadows of advantage for either side.

Smoke and Bob had drifted down the boardwalk and now stood in the middle of the street, about ten feet apart, waiting.

Rose and Cliff and their two partners in torture stepped off the boardwalk and walked to the center of the street.

"Rose to my left," Bob said. "Cliff is to your right."

"Who are those other two?"

"I don't know their names."

"You two in the middle!" Smoke called, his voice carrying the two hundred odd feet between them. "You got names?"

"I'm Stanford and this here is Thomas!"

"You take Stanford, Bob. Thomas is mine." Smoke's voice was low.

"You ready?" Bob asked.

"I been ready."

Smoke and Bob started walking, their spurs softly jingling and their boots kicking up small pockets of dust with each step toward showdown.

"You boys watch this," Lanny told the others. "I doubt they's many of you ever seen Jensen in action. Don't make no mistakes about him. He's the fastest I ever seen. Some of you may want to change your minds about stayin' once you seen him."

"I do not have to watch him," Diego boasted. "I am better." He knocked back a shot of whiskey.

Several of the others in the saloon agreed.

Lanny smiled at their arrogance. Lanny might be many things, but he was not arrogant when it came to facing Smoke Jensen. He did not feel he was better than Smoke, but he did feel he was as good. When the time came for them to meet, as he knew it would, it would all come down to that first well-placed shot. Lanny knew that he would probably take lead when he faced Smoke, therefore he would delay facing him as long as possible.

"You shoulda heard that punk squall when we laid that hot runnin' iron agin him!" Thomas yelled over the closing distance. "He jerked and hollered like a baby. Squalled and bawled like a calf."

Neither Smoke nor Bob offered any comment in reply.

The loud silence and the artificial inner brightness consumed them both.

There was less than fifty feet between them when Rose made his move. He never even cleared leather. None of the four managed to get clear of leather before they began dancing and jerking under the impact of .44 slugs. Thomas took two .44 slugs in the heart and died on his feet. He sat down in the dirt, on his knees, his empty hands dangling in the bloody dirt.

Bob was nearly as fast as Smoke. His .44 Remington barked again and Stanford was turned halfway around, hit in the stomach and side just as Cliff experienced twin hammerblows to his chest from Smoke's Colt and his world began to dim. He fell to the dirt in a slack heap, seemingly powerless to do anything except cry out for his mother. He was still hollering for her when he died, the word frozen in time and space.

"Jesus Christ!" a gunslick spoke from the saloon window. He picked up his hat from the table and walked out the back door. He had a brother over in the Dakotas and concluded that this was just a dandy time to go see how his brother and his family was getting along. Hell would be better than this place.

Smoke and Bob turned and walked to the Pussycat, reloading as they walked. Inside the coolness of the saloon, they ordered beer and sat down at a table, with a clear view of the street.

Neither of them spoke for several minutes. When the barkeep had brought their pitcher of beer and two mugs and returned to his post behind the long bar, Bob picked up his mug and held it out. "For Hatfield," he said.

"I'll drink to that," Smoke said, lifting his mug.

Parnell entered the saloon, walking gingerly, sniffing disdainfully at the beery odor. Smoke waved him over and kicked out a chair for him.

"You want something to drink?" the barkeep called.

"A glass of your best wine would be nice." Parnell sat down.

"Ain't got no wine. Beer and whiskey and sodee pop."

Parnell shook his head and the bartender went back to polishing glasses, muttering under his breath about fancy-pants easterners.

Outside, in the bloody street, the barber and his helper were scurrying about, loading up the bodies. Business certainly had taken a nice turn for the better.

Smoke noticed that Parnell seemed calm enough. "Not your first time to see men die violently, Parnell?"

"No. I've seen several shootings out here. All of them as unnecessary as the one I just witnessed."

"Justice was served," Smoke told him, after taking a sip of beer.

Parnell ignored that. "Innocent bystanders could have been killed by a stray bullet."

"That is true," Smoke acknowledged. "I didn't say it was the best way to handle matters, only that justice had been served."

"And now you've taken a definite side."

"If that is the way people wish to view it, yes."

"I have a good notion to notify the army about this matter."

"And you think they'd do what, Parnell? Send a company in to keep watch? Forget it. The army's strung out too thin as it is in the West. And they'd tell you that this is a civilian matter."

"What you're saying is that this . . . ugly boil on the face of civilization must erupt before it begins the healing process?"

"That's one way of putting it, yes. Dooley Hanks has gone around the bend, Parnell. I suspect he was always borderline nuts. The beating and rape of his daughter tipped him the rest of the way. He's insane. And he's making a mistake in trusting those gunslicks he's hired. That bunch can turn on a man faster than a lightning bolt."

"And McCorkle?"

"Same with that bunch he's got. Only difference is, Cord knows it. He's tried to make peace with Hanks . . . over the past few weeks. Hanks isn't having any of it. Cord had no choice but to hire more gunnies."

"And now . . . ?"

"We wait."

"You are aware, of course, about the rumor that it was really some of your people who beat and sexually assaulted Rita Hanks?"

"Some of that crap is being toted off the street now," Smoke reminded the schoolteacher. "When Silver Jim and Lujan hear of it—I have not mentioned it to them—the rest of it will be planted six feet under. But I think that rumor got squashed a few minutes ago."

"And if it didn't, there will be more violence."

"Yes."

"Why are we so different, Cousin? What I'm asking is that we spring from the same bloodlines, yet we are as different as the sun and the moon."

"Maybe, Parnell, it's because you're a dreamer. You think of the world as a place filled with good, decent, honorable men. I see the world as it really is. Maybe that's it."

Parnell pushed back his chair and stood up. He looked down at Smoke for a few seconds. "If that is the case, I would still rather have my dreams than live with blood on my hands."

"I'd rather have that blood on my hands than have it leaking out of me," Smoke countered. "Knowing that I could have possibly prevented it simply by standing my ground with a gun at the ready."

"A point well put. I shall take my leave now, gentlemen. I must see to the closing of the school for the summer."

"See you at the ranch, Parnell."

Both Smoke and Bob had lost their taste for beer. They left the nearly full pitcher of beer on the table and walked out onto the boardwalk. Most of the gunnies had left the Hangout, heading back to the D-H spread. Lanny Ball stood on the boardwalk in front of the saloon, looking across the street at Smoke.

"He's a punk," Smoke said to Bob. "But a very fast punk. I'd say he's one of the best gunslicks to be found anywhere."

"Better than you?" Bob asked, doubt in the question.

"Just as good, I'd say. And so is Jason Bright."

Lanny turned his back to them and entered the saloon.

"Another day," Smoke muttered. "But it's coming."

ELEVEN

Smoke was riding the ridges early one morning, looking for any strays they might have missed. He had arranged for a buyer from the Army to come in, in order to give Fae some badly needed working capital, and planned to sell off five hundred head of cattle. He saw the flash of sunlight off a barrel just a split second before the rifle fired. Smoke threw himself out of the saddle, grabbing his Winchester as he went. The slug hit nothing but air. Grabbing the reins, Smoke crawled around a rise and picketed the horse, talking to the animal, calming it.

He wasn't sure if he was on Box T range or D-H range. It would be mighty close either way. If the gunman had waited just a few more minutes, Smoke might well be dead on the ground, for he had planned to ride in a blind canyon to flush out any strays.

Working his way around the rise of earth, Smoke began to realize just how bad his situation was. He was smack in the middle of a clearing, hunkering down behind the only rise big enough to conceal a human or horse to be found within several hundred yards.

And he found out just how good the sniper was when a hard spray of dirt slapped him in the face, followed closely by the boom of the rifle. Smoke could not tell the caliber of the rifle, but it sounded like a .44-40, probably with one of those fancy telescopes on it. He'd read about the telescopes on rifles, but had never looked through one mounted on a rifle, only seen pictures of them. They looked awkward to Smoke.

He knew one thing for an iron-clad fact: he was in trouble.

Whatever the gunman was using, he was one hell of a fine rifleman.

Hanks had cut loose his rabid dog: that rat-faced Danny Rouge.

What to do? Smoke judged his chances of getting to the timber facing him and rejected a frontal run for it. He worked his way to his horse and removed his boots, slipping into a pair of moccasins he always carried. The fancy moccasins Ring had made were back at the house.

Smoke eased back to his skimpy cover and chanced a look, cursing as the rifle slammed again, showering him with dirt.

No question about it, he had to move, and soon. If he stayed here, and tried to wait Danny out—if it was Danny, and Smoke was certain it was—sooner or later the sniper would get the clean shot he was waiting for and Smoke would take lead. He'd been shot before and didn't like it at all. It was a very disagreeable feeling. Hurt, too.

Smoke looked around him. There was a drop-off about fifty yards behind him; a natural ditch that ran in a huge half circle, the southeast angle of the ditch running close to the timber. He studied every option available to him, and there weren't that many.

His horse would be safe, protected by the rise. If something happened to Smoke—like death—the horse would eventually pull its picket pin and return to the ranch.

Smoke checked his gun belt. All the loops were full. Returning to the horse, he stuffed a handful of cartridges into his jeans' pocket and slung his canteen after first filling his hat with water and giving the horse a good drink. Squatting down, he munched on a salt pork and biscuit sandwich, then took a long satisfying pull at the canteen. He patted the horse's neck.

"You stay put, fellow. I'll be back." I hope, he silently added.

Smoke took several deep breaths and took off running down the slope.

Smoke knew that shooting either uphill or downhill was tricky; bad enough with open sights. But with a telescope, trying to line up a running, twisting target would be nearly impossible.

He hoped.

The gunman started dusting Smoke's running feet, but he was hurrying his shots, and missing. But coming close enough to show Smoke how good he was with a rifle.

Smoke hurled himself in the ditch, managed to stay on his feet, then dive for the cover of the ravine's wall. Now, Danny would have to worry about which side Smoke would pop up out of. Catching his breath, Smoke began working his way around, staying close to the earthen wall. He knew the distance was still too great for his .44, and besides that, he didn't want to give away his position.

Smoke took his time, smiling as the ravine curved closer to the timber and began narrowing as the timber loomed up on both sides. When he came to a brushy spot, Smoke carefully eased out of the ravine and slipped into the timber. His jeans were a tan color, his shirt a dark brown; he would blend in well with his surroundings.

He began closing the distance. Smoke had been taught well the ways of a woodsman; Preacher had been his teacher, and there was no finer woodsman to be found than the old mountain man.

He moved carefully while still covering a lot of ground, stopping often to check the terrain all around him. Danny not only looked like a big rat, the killer could move as furtively as a rodent.

Before making his run for it, Smoke had inspected the

area on the ridges as carefully as possible—considering that he was being shot at—and kept Danny's position highlighted in his mind.

But Smoke was certain the sniper would have changed positions as soon as he made his run for it. Where to was the question.

He moved closer to where he had last seen the puff of smoke. When he was about a hundred yards from where he thought Danny had been firing from, Smoke made himself comfortable behind a tree and waited, every sense working overtime. He felt he could play the waiting game just as good as, or better than, Danny.

He waited for a good twenty minutes, as motionless as a snake waiting for a passing rat. Then the rat he was waiting for moved.

It was only a very slight move, perhaps to brush away a pesky fly. But it was all Smoke needed. Very carefully, he raised his rifle and sighted in—he had been waiting with the hammer eared back—and pulled the trigger. The rifle slammed his shoulder and Smoke knew he had a clean miss on his target.

The gunman rolled away and came up shooting, shooting way fast. Maybe he had two rifles, one a short-barreled carbine, or maybe he was shooting one of those Winchester .44-40's with the extra rear sight for greater accuracy. If that was the case, the man was still one hell of a marksman.

Smoke caught a glimpse of color that didn't seem right in the timber and triggered off two fast rounds. This time he heard a squall of pain. He fired again and something heavy fell in the woods. A trick on the man's part? Maybe. Smoke settled back and waited.

He listened to the man cough, hard, racking coughs of pain. Then the man cursed him.

"Sorry, partner," Smoke called. "You opened this dance, now you pay the fiddler."

"You Injun bastard!" the man said with a groan. "I never even heard you come up on me."

Smoke offered no reply.

"I'm hit hard, man. I got the makins but my matches is all bloody. Least you can do is give me a light."

"You're gonna have lots of fire where you're goin', partner. Just give it a few minutes."

That got Smoke another round of cussing.

But Smoke was up and moving, working his way up the ridge to a vantage point which would enable him to look down on the wounded man. If he was as hard hit as he claimed.

The man was down, all right, Smoke could see that. And the front of his shirt was badly stained with blood. But it wasn't Danny Rouge.

It was a man he'd seen riding with Cord's hired guns.

What the hell was going on?

The man had stopped his moaning and was lying flat on his back, both hands in plain sight. He was not moving.

Smoke inched his way down the ridge to just above the gunman. He was dead. He had taken a round in his guts and one in his chest. Smoke had been right: it was a .44-40, and a brand spanking new one from the looks of it.

It took him a few minutes to find the man's horse and get him roped belly-down across the saddle. He shoved the dead man's Winchester in the boot and led the animal down the ridge to his own horse. His horse shied away from the smell of blood and death, pulling his picket pin, and Smoke had to catch him and calm him down.

Now what to do with the McCorkle rider?

If the gunnies on Cord's payroll were playing both ends against the middle, it would not be wise to just ride over there with one of their buddies draped belly-down across his saddle. On the other hand, Cord had to be notified.

Smoke headed for the Box T. On the way, he ran into Hardrock and sent him over to the Circle Double C to get Cord.

The old gunfighter had looked close at the dead man.

"You know him, Hardrock?"

"Only by his rep. His name is Black. Call him Blackie. He's a back-shooter. Was."

"Keep this quiet at the ranch. Speak to only Cord."

"Right."

Smoke rode on over to the bunkhouse and relieved the horse of its burden and saddle, letting the animal water and feed and roll. Fae came out of the house, accompanied by her brother.

Smoke explained, ending with, "Something's up. I think we'd better get set for a hard wind."

"And a violent one," Parnell added, grimacing at the smell of the dead gunny.

"You better get a gun, Parnell," Smoke told him.

"I will not have one of those abominable things in my possession!"

"Suit yourself. But I have a hunch you're gonna change your mind before this is all over."

"Never!" Parnell stood his ground.

"Uh-huh" was all Smoke said in reply to that.

Parnell's sister had plenty to say about her brother. Smoke could but stand in awe and amazement at the words rolling from her mouth.

"I don't understand this," Cord said, after viewing the dead man.

"I didn't think you would. But the big question is this: was the sniper working as a lone wolf, perhaps just to gain a reputation for killing me, or was he part of a larger scheme?"

"Involving the gunhands from both ranches?"

"Yes."

Cord's sigh was loud in the hot stillness of Montana summer. "I don't know. My first thought is: yes. My next thought is: I've got to get Dooley to talk to me; bury the hatchet before this thing goes any further."

"Forget it," Smoke said bluntly. "The man is crazy. He's kill-crazy. I've heard he's making all sorts of wild claims and charges and plans. He's going to take over the whole area and be king. Keep a standing army of a hundred gunhawks—all sorts of wild talk."

"He's damn near got a hundred," Cord said glumly. "If what we're both thinking is true."

"Close to fifty if they all get together," Smoke added it up.

"And if I go back and fire all of those drawing fighting wages . . . ?" Cord left it hanging.

"We'd know where they stand. And you and your family would probably be safer. But if we're wrong, it would leave you wide open, 'cause for sure the gunnies you fire would just hire on at the D-H."

Cord cursed softly for a few seconds. "I'm stuck between that much-talked-about rock and a hard place."

"Whichever way you decide to go, watch your back."

"Yeah." He looked at the blanket-covered body of the sniper. "What about him?"

"We'll bury him. And don't mention it, Cord. Just let the others wonder what happened—if there really is some sort of funny business going on."

"There is some grim humor in all of this, Smoke. If this thing goes on for any length of time, both Dooley and me will go broke paying fighting wages."

"Maybe that's what the gunhands want. Maybe that's why they're hanging back, for the most part."

Cord shook his big head. It appeared that the man's hair had grayed considerably since Smoke had first seen him, only a few weeks back. "This thing's turnin' out to have more maybe's and what-if's than a simple man can understand."

Smoke motioned for Charlie and Spring to come over. "Let's get him in the ground, boys. Well away from the house and unmarked. Spring, you can have that .44-40. It's a whale of a rifle. Dusted my butt proper," he added.

"I'll go through his pockets," Charlie said. "See if there is some address for his family."

Smoke nodded. "Take his horse and turn him loose. He'll find his way back to the ranch. We'll keep the rig. That'll add even more doubt in the minds of the gunslicks." He turned to Cord. "You 'bout caught up at your place, Cord?"

"Yeah. Why?"

"Pull a couple of your best men off the range. Keep them close by at all times. When you ride, take one of them with you and let the other stay around the house."

"Good idea. But at night I don't worry much." He smiled a father's smile. "Ever'time I look up, the Moab Kid is over there sparkin' my daughter."

Smoke chuckled. "She could do worse. Beans is a good man."

"At first, I told her she couldn't see him. That made about as much impression on her as a poot in a whirlwind. I finally told her to go ahead and see him. She told me that she'd never stopped. Daughters!"

"You keepin' a tight rein on your boys?"

"I'm trying. Lord, I'm trying. I've got them working just as far away from D-H range as possible. But they told me last night they think they're being watched. Stalked was the word Max used. That gives me an uneasy feelin'."

"It might be wise to pull them in and keep them around the house." He smiled. "Tell you what; do this: Tell the gun-hands to start workin' the range."

Cord thought about that for a moment, then burst out laughing. "*Hell,* yes! That'll make them earn their pay and keep them away from the house."

"Or it'll put them on the road."

The men shook hands and Cord rode back to his ranch. Fae came to Smoke's side. "Now what?"

"We sell some cows to the Army. And wait."

The buyer for the Army had already looked over the cattle and agreed to a price. When he returned, a couple of days after Smoke's misunderstanding with the sniper, he brought drovers with him. Smoke and the buyer settled up the paperwork and the bank draft was handed over to Fae. The two men leaned up against a corral railing and talked.

"You know about the battle looking at us in the face, don't you?" Smoke asked.

"Uh-huh. And from all indications it's gonna be a real cutter."

"What would it take to get the Army involved?"

"Not a chance, Jensen. The Army's done looked this situation over and, unofficially, and I didn't say this, they decided to stay out of it. It'd take a presidential order to get them to move in here."

It was as Smoke had guessed. All over the fast-settling West little wars were flaring up; too many for the authorities or the Army to put down, so they were letting them burn themselves out. Here, they would be on their own, whichever way it went.

The buyer and his men moved the cattle out and the range was silent.

Smoke wondered for how long.

TWELVE

"You tellin' me you're not gonna work cattle?" Cord faced the gunslick.

"I'm paid to fight, not herd cattle," Jason Bright told him.

"You're not being paid to do either one after this moment. Pack your kit and clear out. Pick up your money at the house."

Jason's eyes became cloudy with hate. "And if I don't go?"

"Then one of us is going to be on the ground."

Jason laughed. "Are you challengin' me, old man?"

Cord was far from being an old man. At forty-five he was bull-strong and leather-tough. And while he was no fast gun, there was one thing he was good at. He showed Jason a hard right fist to the jaw.

Flat on his back, his mouth leaking blood, Jason grabbed for his gun, forgetting that the hammer thong was still on it. Cord stomped the gunfighter in the belly, reached down while Jason was gasping for breath, and jerked the gun out of leather, tossing it to one side. He backed up, his big hands balled into fists.

"Catch your breath and then get up, you yellow-bellied pup. Let's see how good you are without your gun."

A dozen gunhawks ran from the bunkhouse, stopping

abruptly as Cord's sons, his daughter, his wife, and four regular hands appeared from both sides of the house and on the porch, rifles and sawed-off shotguns in their hands.

"It's going to be a fair fight, boys," Alice McCorkle said, her voice strong and calm. She held a double-barreled shotgun in her hands. "Between two men; and my husband is giving Mr. Bright a good ten or fifteen years in age difference. Boys, I was nineteen when I killed my first Indian. With this very shotgun. I've killed half a dozen Indians and two outlaws in my day, and anytime any of you want to try me, just reach for a gun or try to break up this fight—whichever way it's going—and I'll spread your guts all over this yard. Then I'll make your gunslinging buddies clean up the mess."

She lifted the shotgun, pointing the twin muzzles straight at Pooch Matthews.

"Lord, lady!" Pooch hollered. "I ain't gonna interfere."

"And you'll stop anyone who does, right, Mr. Matthews?"

"Oh, yes, ma'am!"

Jason was on his feet, his eyes shiny with hate as he faced Cord.

"Clean his plow, honey," Alice told her husband.

Cord stepped in and knocked Jason spinning, the gunfighter's mouth suddenly a bloody smear. Like so many men who lived by the gun and depended on a six-shooter to get them out of any problem, Jason had never learned how to use his fists.

Cord gave him a very short and very brutal lesson in fistfighting.

Cord gave him two short hard straight rights to the stomach then followed through with a crashing left hook that knocked the gunfighter to the ground. Normally, Cord would have kicked the man in the face and ended it. No truly tough man, who fights only when hard-pushed, considers that "dirty" or unfair fighting, but merely a way to get the fight over with and get back to work. In reality, there is no such thing as a "fair fight." There is a winner and a loser. Period.

But in this case, Cord just wanted the fight to last a while. He was enjoying himself. And really, rather enjoying showing off for his wife a little bit.

Cord dropped his guard while so pleased with himself and Jason busted him in the mouth.

Shaking his head to clear away the sparkling confusion, for Jason was no little man, Cord settled down to a good ol'-fashioned rough-and-tumble, kick-and-gouge brawl.

The two men stood boot to boot for a moment, hammering away at each other until finally Jason had to give ground and back up from Cord's bull strength. Jason was younger and in good shape, but he had not spent a lifetime doing brutally hard work, twelve months a year, wrestling steers and digging postholes and roping and branding and breaking horses.

Jason tried to kick Cord. Cord grabbed the boot and dumped the gunhawk on the ground, on his butt. That brought several laughs from Jason's friends, all standing and watching and being very careful not to let their hands get too close to the butts of their guns.

Jason jumped to his boots, one eye closing and his nose a bloody mess, and swung at Cord. Cord grabbed the wrist and threw Jason over his hip, slamming him to the ground. This time Jason was not as swift getting to his feet.

Cord was circling, grinning at Jason, but giving the man time to clear his head and stand and fight.

But this time Jason came up with a knife he'd pulled out of his boot.

"No way, Jason!" Lodi yelled from the knot of gun-slingers. "And I don't give a damn how many guns is on me. Drop that knife or I'll shoot you personal."

With a look of disgust on his face, Jason threw the knife to the ground.

Cord stepped in and smashed the man a blow to the jaw and

followed that with a wicked slash to Jason's belly, doubling him over. Then he hit him twice in the face, a left and right to both sides of the man's jaw.

Jason hit the ground and did not move.

Cord walked to a water barrel by the side of the house and washed his face and soaked his aching hands for a moment. He turned and faced the gunslicks.

"I want Jason out of here within the hour. No man disobeys an order of mine. Any of you who want to stay, that's fine with me. But you'll take orders and you'll work the spread, doing whatever Del tells you to do. Make up your mind."

"Hell, Mister McCorkle . . ." a gunhawk said. He looked at the ladies. "I mean, heck. We come here to fight, not work cattle. No disrespect meant."

"None taken. But the war is over as far as I'm concerned. Any of you who want to ride out, there'll be no hard feelings and I'll have your money ready for you at the house."

All of them elected to ride.

"See me on the porch for your pay," Cord told them.

When the last gunslick had packed his war bag, collected his pay, and ridden out, Del sat down beside Cord on the front porch.

"Feels better around the place, Boss. But if them gunnies hire on with Hanks, we're gonna be hard up agin it."

"I know that, Del. Tell the men that from this day on, they'll be receiving fighting wages." He held up a warning finger. "We start nothing, Del. Nothing. We defend home range and no more. I won't ask that the men stay out of Gibson; only that they don't go in there looking for trouble. Send Willie riding over to the Box T and tell Smoke what I've done. He needs to know."

"Sure got the crap pounded out of you," Lanny said, looking at the swollen and bruised face of Jason Bright.

Jason lay on a bed in the bunkhouse of the D-H spread. "It ain't over," he mush-mouthed the words past swollen lips. "Not by no long shot, it ain't."

Dooley Hanks had eagerly hired the gunslicks. He was already envisioning himself as king. And he wanted to kill Cord McCorkle personally. In his maddened mind, he blamed Cord for everything. He'd worked just as hard as Cord, but had never gained the respect that most people felt toward McCorkle. And this just wasn t right. King Hanks. He sure liked the way that sounded.

"It's just going to make matters worse," Hanks's wife was telling their daughter.

Rita looked up from her packing. "Papa's crazy, Mother. He's crazy as a lizard. Haven't you seen the way he slobbers on himself? The way he sits on the porch mumbling to himself? Now he's gone and hired all those other gunfighters. Worse? For who? I'll tell you who: everybody. Everything from the Hound to the Sixteenmile is going to explode."

"And you think you'll be safer over at the Box T?"

"I won't be surrounded by crazy people. I won't be under guard all the time. I'll be able to walk out of the house without being watched. Are you going to tell on me, Mother?"

She shook her head. "No. You're a grown woman, Rita. Your father has no right to keep you a prisoner here. But I don't know how you're going to pull this off."

Rita smiled. "I'll make it, Mother." She kissed her mother's cheek and hugged her. "This can't last forever. And I won't be that far away."

"Have you considered that your father might try to bring you back by force?"

"He might if I was going to Sandi's. I don't think he'll try with Smoke Jensen."

The mother pressed some money into the daughter's hand. "You'll need this."

"Thank you, Mother. I'll pretend I'm going to bed early. Right after supper. Then I'll be gone."

After her mother had left the room, Rita laid out her clothes. Men's jeans, boots, a man's shirt. She had one of her brother's old hats and a work jacket to wear against the cold night. She picked up the scissors. Right after supper she would whack her hair short.

She believed it would work. It had to work. If she stayed around this place, she would soon be as nutty as her father and her crazy brothers.

"Peaceful," Cord said to Alice. "Like it used to be."

They sat on the front porch, enjoying the welcome coolness of early evening after the warm day.

"If it will only last, Cord."

"All we can do is try, honey. That's all a mule can do, is try."

"Tell me about this Smoke Jensen. I've met him, but never to talk with at length."

"He's a good man, I believe. A fair man. Not at all like I thought he'd be. He's one of those rare men that you look at and instantly know that this one won't push. I found that out very quickly." His last comment was dry, remembering that first day he'd yelled at Smoke, in Gibson, and the man had looked at him like he was a bug.

"It sounds like you have a lot of respect for the man."

"I do. I'd damn sure hate to have him for an enemy."

From inside the house, they heard the sounds of Sandi's giggling. She was entertaining her young man this evening, as she did almost every evening. The Moab Kid was fast becoming a fixture around the place.

Cord and Alice sat quietly, smiling as they both recalled their own courting days.

* * *

Smoke leaned against a corral railing and thought about Sally and the babies. He missed them terribly. One part of him wanted this little war to come to a head so he could go home. But another part of him knew that when it did start, there would be a lot of people who would never go home . . . except for six feet of earth. And he might well be one of them.

Charlie Starr walked up and the men stood in silence for a moment, enjoying the peaceful evening. Charlie was the first to break the silence.

"I'd like to have seen that fight 'tween Cord and Jason."

Smoke smiled, then the smile faded. "Jason won't ever forget it, though. The next time he sees Cord, Cord better have a gun in his hand."

"True."

They stood in silence for another few moments. Both men rolled an after-supper cigarette and lit up.

"You were in deep thought when I walked up, Smoke. What's on your mind?"

"Oh, I had a half dozen thoughts going, Charlie. I was thinking about my wife and our babies; how much I miss them. And, I was thinking just what it's going to take to blow the lid off this situation here."

"What don't concern me as much as when."

"Tonight."

Charlie looked at him. "What are you, one of them fortune-tellers?"

"I feel it in my guts, Charlie. And don't tell me you never jumped out of a saddle or spun and drew on a hunch."

"Plenty o' times. Saved my bacon on more than one occasion, too. That's what you're feelin'?"

"That's it." Smoke dropped his cigarette butt and ground it out with the heel of his boot. "It's always something you least expect, too."

"I grant you that for a fact. Like that time down in Taos this here woman crawled up in bed with me. Like to have scared the longhandles right off of me. Wanted me to save her from her husband. Didn't have a stitch on. I tell you what, that shook me plum down to my toenails."

"Did you save her?"

Charlie chuckled softly. "Yeah. 'Bout two hours later. I've topped off horses that wasn't as wild as she was."

THIRTEEN

Rita had cropped her hair short, hating to do it, but she had always been a tomboy and, besides, it would grow back. She had turned off the lamp and now she listened at her bedroom door for a moment, hearing the low murmur of her mother talking to her father. The front door squeaked open and soon the sound of the porch swing reached her. She picked up her valise and swung out the window, dropping the few feet to the ground. She remained still for a long moment, checking all around her. She knew from watching and planning this that her guards were not on duty after nine o'clock at night. It had never occurred to her father that his daughter would attempt to run away.

Sorry, Pa, Rita thought. But I won't be treated like a prisoner.

Rita slipped away from the house and past the corral and barn. She almost ran right into a cowboy returning from the outhouse but saw him in time to duck into the shadows. He walked past her, his galluses hanging down past his knees. The door to the bunkhouse opened, flooding a small area with lamplight.

"Shut the damn door, Harry!" a man called.

The door closed, the area once more darkened. But

something primeval touched Rita with an invisible warning. She remained where she was, squatting down in her jeans.

"It's clear," a man's voice said.

Rita recognized it as belonging to the shifty-eyed gunslinger called Park. And the men were only a few yards away.

Rita remembered something else, too: she had heard that voice before. The sudden memory was as hot and violent as the act that afternoon. While she was being raped.

Fury and cold hate filled the young woman. Her father's own men had done that to her. She thought about returning to the house and telling her father. She immediately rejected that. She had no proof. And her father would take one look at her close-cropped hair and lock her up tight, with twenty-four-hour guards.

She touched the short-barreled .44 tucked behind her belt. She was good with it, and wanted very badly to haul it out and start banging.

She fought back that feeling and waited, listening.

"When?" the other man asked.

"Keep your britches on," Park said. "Lanny gives the orders around here. But it'll be soon, he tole me so hisself."

"I'd like to take my britches off with Rita agin," the mystery man said with a rough chuckle.

And I'd like to stick this pistol . . . Rita mentally brushed away the very ugly thought. But it was a satisfying thought.

"You reckon Hanks is so stupid he don't realize what his boys is up to?"

"He's nuts. He don't realize them crazy boys of his'n would kill him right now if they thought they could get away with it."

Rita crouched in the darkness and wanted to cry. Not for herself or for her father—he had made the boys what they were today, simply by being himself—but for her mother. She deserved so much better.

"It better be soon, 'cause the boys is gettin' restless."

"It'll be soon. But we gotta do it all at once. All three ranches. There can't be no survivors to tell about it. They got to be kilt and buried all in one night. We can torture the widows till they sign over the spreads to us."

"We gonna keep the young wimmen alive for a time, ain't we? 'Specially that Fae Jensen. I want her. I want to show her a thing or two."

"I don't know. Chancy. Maybe too chancy. It's all up to Jason and Lanny."

"Them young wimmen would bring a pretty penny south of the border."

"Transport them females a thousand miles! You're nuts, Hartley."

"It was jist a thought."

"A bad one. Man, just think of it: the whole area controlled by us. Thousands and thousands of acres, thousands of cattle. We could be respectable, and you want to mess it all up because of some swishy skirts. Sometimes I wonder about you, Hartley."

"I'm sorry. I won't bring it up no more."

"Fine."

The men walked off, splitting up before entering the bunkhouse.

Rita felt sick to her stomach; wanted to upchuck. Fought it back. Now more than ever, she had to make it to the Box T. She waited and looked around her, carefully inspecting each dark pocket around the ranch, the barn and the bunkhouse. She stood up and moved out, silently praying she wouldn't be spotted.

Once clear of the ranch complex, Rita began to breathe a little easier. She slung her valise by a strap and could move easier with it over her shoulder. She headed southwest, toward the Box T.

* * *

The restlessness of the horses awakened Smoke. He looked at his pocket watch. Four o'clock. Time to get up anyway. But the actions of the horses bothered him. Dressed and armed, he stepped out of the ranch house just as the bunkhouse door opened and Lujan stepped out, followed by the other men. Smoke met them in the yard. They all carried rifles.

"Spread out," Smoke told them. "Let's find out what's spooking the horses."

"Hello the ranch!" the voice came out of the darkness. A female voice.

"Come on in," Smoke returned the call. "Sing out!"

"Rita Hanks. I slipped away from the house about eight o'clock last night. You might not recognize me, 'cause I cut off my hair to try to fool anyone who might see me."

"Come on in, Rita," Smoke told her, then turned to Beans. "Wake up those in the house; if they're not already awake. Get some coffee going. As soon as Hanks finds out his girl is gone, we're going to have problems."

She was limping from her long walk, and she was tired, but still could not conceal her happiness at finally being free of her father. Over coffee and bacon and eggs, she told her story while Fae and Parnell and all the others gathered around in the big house and listened.

When she was finished, she slumped in her chair, exhausted.

"I wondered why the gunnies were holding back," Hardrock said. "This tells it all."

"Yes," Lujan said. "But I don't think they came in here with that in mind. No one ever approached me with any such scheme. And both sides offered me fighting wages."

"I think this plan was just recently hatched, after several others failed. Rita's attack did not produce the desired effect; Hanks didn't attack Cord. Blackie failed to kill me. So they came up with this plan."

Smoke looked at Rita. The young woman was asleep, her head on the table.

"I'll get her to bed," Fae said. "You boys start chowing down. I think it's going to be a very long day."

"Yeah," Beans agreed. "'Cause come daylight, Hanks and his boys are gonna be on the prowl. If this day don't produce some shootin', my name ain't Bainbridge."

Silver Jim looked at him and blinked. "Bainbridge! No wonder they call you Beans. Bainbridge!"

Hanks knocked his wife sprawling, backhanding her. "You knew, damn you!" he yelled at her. "You heped her, didn't you? Don't lie to me, woman. You and Rita snuck around behind my back and planned all this."

Liz slowly got to her feet. A thin trickle of blood leaked from one corner of her mouth. She defiantly stood her ground. "I knew she was planning to leave, yes. But I didn't know when or how. You've changed, Dooley. Changed into some sort of a madman."

That got her another blow. She fell back against the wall and managed to grab the back of a chair and steady herself. She stared at her husband as she wiped her bloody mouth with the back of her hand.

"Where'd she go?" Hanks yelled the question. "Naw!" Dooley waved it off. "You don't have to tell me. I know. She went over to Cord's place, didn't she?"

"No, she didn't," Liz's voice had calmed, but her mouth hurt her when she spoke.

"You a damn liar!" Dooley raged. "A damn frog-eyed liar. There ain't no other place she could have gone."

Outside, just off the porch, Lanny was listening to the ravings.

"This might throw a kink into things," Park spoke softly.

"Maybe not. This might be a way to get rid of Cord and his

boys in a way that even if the law was to come in, they'd call it a fair shootin'. Man takes another man's kid in without the father's permission, that's a shootin' offense."

"I hadn't thought of that. You right."

"If she did go to the Double Circle C," Lanny added.

"Where else would she go? Her and that damn uppity Sandi McCorkle is good friends."

"Rita is no fool. She just might have gone over to the Box T. But we won't mention that. Just let Hanks play it his way."

"I'm gonna tell you something, woman," Hanks pointed a blunt finger at his wife. "I find out you been lyin' to me, I' gonna give you a hidin' that you'll remember the rest of your life."

"That would be like you," she told him. "Whatever you don't understand, you destroy."

"What the hell does that mean?" Dooley screamed at her, slobber leaking out of his mouth, dribbling onto his shirt and vest.

She turned her back to him and started to leave the room.

"Don't you turn your back to me, woman! I done put with just about all I'm gonna take from you."

She stopped and turned slowly. "What are you going to Dooley? Beat me? Kill me? It doesn't make any difference. Love just didn't die a long time ago. Your hatred killed it. Your hatred, your obsession with power. You allowed our sons to grow up as nothing more than ignorant savages. You . . ."

"Shut up, shut up, shut up!" Dooley screamed, spittle flying from his mouth. "Lies, all lies, woman. I'm ridin' to get my kid back. And when I get her back here, I'm gonna take a buggy whip to her backside. That's something I shoulda done a time ago. And I just might take it in my head to use the whip on you."

Liz stared hard at him. "If you ever hit me again, Dooley. I'll kill you." Dooley recoiled as if struck with those words.

"And the same goes for Rita. But you've lost her. She'll never come back here; don't worry about that. I'll tell you where she's gone, Dooley. She's gone to the Box T."

"Lies! More lies from you. Cord planned with you all on this, and you know it. He's conspired agin me ever since we come into this area. He'd do anything to get at me. He's jealous of me."

His wife openly laughed at that.

Dooley's face reddened and he took a step toward his wife, his hand raised. She backed up and picked up a poker from the fireplace.

"You were warned," she told him. "You try to hit me and I'll bash your head in."

He stood and cursed her until he ran out of breath. But she would not lower the poker and even in his maddened state he knew better than to push his luck.

"I'll deal with you later," he said, then turned and stalked out the door.

She leaned against the wall, breathing heavily, listening to him holler for his men to saddle up and get ready to ride. She did not put down the poker as long as he was on the front porch. Only when she heard him mount up and the thunder of hooves pound away did she lower the poker and replace it in the set on the hearth.

She walked outside to stand on the porch, waiting for the dust to settle from the fast-riding men. She noticed Gage and several of the other hands had not ridden with her husband.

The foreman walked over to the porch and looked up at the still attractive woman. There was open disgust in his eyes as he took in the bruises on her face.

"I ain't got no use atall for a man who hits a woman," Gage said.

"That's not the man I married, Gage."

"Yeah, it is, Liz. It's the same man I been knowin' for years. You just been deliberately blind over the years, that's all."

"Maybe so, Gage." She sighed. She knew, of course, that Gage had been in love with her for a long, long time. And her feelings toward the foreman had been steadily growing stronger with time. She cut her eyes toward him. "You're not riding with him?"

"Me and the boys punch cows, Liz. I made that plain to him the other day. He still has enough sense about him to know that someone has to work the spread."

"What would you say if I told you I was going to leave him?"

"Then me and you would strike out together, Liz."

She smiled. "And do what, Gage?"

"Get married. Start us a little spread a long ways from here."

"I'm a married woman, Gage. It's not proper to talk to a married woman like that."

"I don't see you turnin' around and walkin' off, Liz."

She looked hard at him. "Mister Hanks and I will be sharing separate bedrooms from now on, Gage. I would appreciate if you would stay close as much as possible."

"I would consider that an honor, Liz."

"Would you like to have some coffee, Gage?"

"I shore would."

"Make yourself comfortable on the porch, Gage. I'll go freshen up and hotten the coffee. I won't be a minute."

"Take your time, Liz. I'll be here."

She smiled. Her hair was graying and there were lines in her face. But to the foreman, she was as beautiful as the first day he'd laid eyes on her. "I'm counting on that, Gage."

FOURTEEN

Cord heard the riders coming long before he or any of his men could spot them. It was a distant thunder growing louder with each heartbeat.

"Load up the guns, Mother," he told his wife. "I believe it's time." He walked to the dinner bell on the porch and rang it loudly, over and over. Del and four hands came on the run, carrying rifles, pistols belted around them.

"Stand with me on the porch, boys. Mother, get your shotgun and take the upstairs."

"I'm up here with a rifle, Daddy!" Sandi called.

"Good girl."

Rifles were loaded to capacity. Pistols checked. A couple of shotguns were loaded up and placed against the porch railing.

Thirty riders came hammering past the gate and up to the picket fence around the ranch house, Hanks in the lead.

"I don't appreciate this, Dooley," Cord raised his voice. "You got no call to come highballin' up to my place."

"I got plenty of call, Cord. Where's my daughter?"

Cord blinked. "How the hell do I know? I haven't seen her in days."

"You're a damn liar, McCorkle!"

Cord unbuckled his gun belt and handed it to Dell. He

swung his eyes back to Hanks. "You'll not come on my property and call me names, Dooley. Git out of that saddle and let's settle this feud man-to-man."

"Goddamn you! I want my daughter!"

"I ain't got your daughter! But what I will have is your apology for callin' me a liar."

"When hell freezes over, McCorkle!"

Two upstairs windows were opened. A shotgun and a rifle poked out. Sandi's voice said, "The first man to reach for a gun, I kill Lanny Ball." The sound of a hammer being eared back was very plain.

The sounds of twin hammers on a double-barreled shotgun was just as plain. "And I blow the two Mexicans out of the saddle," Alice spoke.

Diego and Pablo froze in their saddles.

"Dooley," Cord's voice was calm. "Would you like to step down and have some coffee with me? You can inspect the house and the barn and the bunkhouse . . . after you tell me your anger overrode your good sense when callin' me a liar."

Hanks's eyes cleared for a moment. Then he looked confused. "I know you ain't no liar, Cord. But where'd she go?" There was a pleading note in the man's voice.

"I don't know, Dooley. I didn't even know she was gone."

But the moment was gone, and Jason Bright and Lanny Ball and most of the others knew it. There would be no gunfire this day.

"The Box T," Dooley said. "Liz wasn't lyin'."

"Dooley," Cord said, "You go over there a-smokin', and if she is there, she's liable to catch a bullet. 'Cause Smoke Jensen and them others are gonna start throwin' lead just as soon you come into range.'

"She's my daughter, dammit, Cord!" Some of the madness reappeared.

"She's also a grown woman," Alice called from the second floor.

Hanks slumped in his saddle. The fire had left him . . . for the moment. "She don't want my hearth and home, she can stay gone. I don't have no daughter no more." He looked at Cord. "It ain't over, Cord. Not between us. The time just ain't right. There'll be another day."

"Why, Dooley? Tell me that. Your spread is just as big as mine. I made peace with Fae Jensen. She ain't botherin' nobody. Let's us bury the hatchet and be friends. Then you can fire these gunslicks and we can get on with livin'."

Dooley shook his head. "Too late, Cord. It's just too late." He wheeled his horse and rode off, the gunnies following.

"Did you see his eyes, Boss?" Willie asked. "The man is plumb loco."

"I'm afraid you're right, Willie. Question is, when will it take control of him . . . or rather, when will he lose control?"

"One thing for certain, Boss," Del said. "When he does go total nuts, we're all going to be right smack dab in the big fat middle of it."

"Something is rotten," Cord spoke softly. "Something is wrong with this whole setup."

"Riders coming, Boss," Fitz said.

As the dot on the landscape grew larger, Del squinted his eyes. "Smoke Jensen and the Moab Kid."

Sandi smiled and Alice said, "I'll make fresh coffee."

Beans sniffed the air. "Lots of dust in the air."

"I think Cord's had some visitors," Smoke replied. "Look at the hands gathered around the house."

The men swung down and looped the reins around the hitchrail. Cord shook hands with them both and introduced Smoke to those punchers he had not met.

"Fancy seeing you, Beans," Cord said, a twinkle in his eyes. "It's been so long since you've come callin'. Hours, at least."

Beans just grinned.

"Gather your men, Cord," Smoke told the man. "This is something that everybody should hear."

Cord's three sons had just ridden in. His other four punchers were out on the range. Everybody gathered around on the porch and listened as Smoke related what Rita had told him.

"Damn!" Max summed it up, then glanced at his mother, who was giving him a warning look for the use of profanity.

"Let's kick it around," Smoke said. "Anybody got any suggestions?"

"Take it to them 'fore they do it to us," Corgill said.

"No proof," Cord said. "Only the word of Rita and she didn't even see the men; just heard them talkin'."

"If we don't do something," Cal said, "we're just gonna be open targets, and they'll pick us off one at a time."

Cord shook his head. "Maybe, but I don't think so. I think they got to do everything all at once. At night. If what Rita says is true—and I ain't got no reason to doubt it—they'll split their people and hit us at the same time. And they can't leave any survivors."

"I've got people bunching the cattle and moving them to high graze," Smoke said. "They'll scatter some, but they can be rounded up. From now on, we stay close to the ranch house."

Cord nodded his head and looked at Willie. "Ride on out, Willie. Tell the boys to start moving them up toward summer graze. Get as much as you can done, and then you boys get on back here. We're gonna lose some to rustlers, for a fact. But it's either that or we all die spread out." He glanced at Smoke. "When do you think they'll hit us?"

Smoke shook his head. "Tonight. Next week. Next month. No way of knowing."

Cord did some fancy cussing, while his wife listened and looked on with a disapproving frown on her face. "We may end up taking to the hills and fighting defensively."

"I'm thinking that we will," Smoke agreed.

"You mean leave the house?" Sandi protested. "But they'll just move in!"

"Can't be helped, girl," her father told her. "We can always clean up and rebuild."

"Or just go on over and kill Dooley Hanks," Rock McCorkle said grimly.

"Rock!" his mother admonished.

Cord put a big hand on her shoulder. "It may come to that, Alice. God help me, I don't want it, but we may have no choice in the matter."

"Here comes Jake," Del said. "And he's a-foggin' it."

The puncher slowed up as he approached the house, to keep the dust down, and walked his horse up to the main house, dismounting.

"What's up, Jake?" the foreman asked.

"I just watched about fifteen guys cut across our range, comin' from the northeast. Hardcases, ever' one of them. They was headin' toward Gibson."

Alice handed the puncher a cup of coffee and a biscuit, then looked at her husband. He wore an increasingly grim expression.

"The damn easterners talk about law and order," Cord said. "Well, where is it when it comes down to the nut-cuttin'?"

Smoke pulled out his right-hand Colt and held it up for all to see. "Right here, Cord. Right here."

"The Cat Jennings gang," Charlie said. He had been to town and back while Smoke was talking with the men and women of the Double Circle C. "He's been up in Canada raisin' Cain for the past few years."

"This here thing is shapin' up to be a power play," Pistol said.

"Yeah," Lujan agreed. "With us right in the middle of it."

"Damn near seventy gunslingers," Silver Jim mused. "And the most we can muster is twenty, and that's stretchin' it."

"One thing about it," Smoke stuck some small humor into a grim situation, "we've sure taken the strain off of a lot of other communities in the West."

"Yeah," Hardrock agreed. "Ever' outlaw and two-bit pistol-handler from five states has done converged on us. And it wouldn't do a bit of good to wire for the law. No badge-toter in his right mind would stick his face into this situation."

"Must be at least a quarter of a million dollars' worth of reward money hanging over them boys' heads," Silver Jim said. "And that's something to think about."

"Yeah, it shore is," Pistol said. "Why, with just a little dab of that money, we could retire, boys." There was a twinkle in his hard eyes.

"Now, wait just a minute," Smoke said.

The old gunfighters ignored him. "You know what we could do," Charlie said. "We could start us up a retirement place for old gunslingers and mountain men."

"You guys are crazy!" Lujan blurted out the words. "You are becoming senile!"

"What's that mean?" Hardrock asked.

"It means we ain't responsible for our actions," Charlie told him.

"That's probably true," Hardrock agreed. "If we had any sense, none of us would be here." He looked at Lujan. "And that goes for you, too."

Lujan couldn't argue with that.

"Cat backed up from me a couple of times," Charlie said. "This time, I think I'll force his hand."

Smoke and Beans had stepped back, letting the men talk it out.

"Peck and Nappy is gonna be with him, for sure," Pistol said. "That damn Nappy got lead in a friend of mine one time. I been lookin' for him for ten year. And that Peck is just a plain no-good."

"No-Count George Victor's got ten thousand on his head," Silver Jim mused. "And he don't like me atall."

"Insane old men!" Lujan muttered.

"Well, I damn shore ain't gonna try to stop them," Beans made that very clear. "I ain't real sure I could take any of them . . . even if I was a mind to," he added.

Smoke stepped back in. "You boys ride for the Box T," he reminded them. "You took the lady's money to ride for the brand. Not to go off headhunting. You all are needed here. Now when the shootin' starts, speaking for myself, you can have all the reward money."

"Same for me," Beans and Lujan agreed.

"Aw, hell, Smoke," Charlie said, a bit sheepishly. "We was just flappin' our gums. You know we're stickin' right here. But Cat Jennings is mine."

"And Peck and Nappy belong to me." Pistol's tone told them all to stand clear when grabbin'-iron time came.

"And No-Count George Victor is gonna be lookin' straight at me when I fill his belly full of lead," Silver Jim said.

Hardrock said, "Three-Fingers Kerman and Fulton kilt a pal of mine over to Deadwood some years back. Back-shot him. I didn't take kindly to that. So them two belongs to me."

"You men are incorrigible!" Parnell finally spoke.

"Damn right," Pistol said.

"Whatever the hell that means," Hardrock muttered.

Fae walked out to join them. "Rita's up, having breakfast."

"How's she feeling?" Smoke asked.

"Aside from some sore feet—she's not used to walking in men's boots—she's doing all right. I think she's pretty well resigned that her father is around the bend. I told her what you said about Dooley saying he no longer had a daughter. It hurt her. But not as much as I thought it would. I think she's more concerned about her mother."

"She should be. There is no telling what that crazy bastard is liable to do," Silver Jim summed it up.

FIFTEEN

He had looked into their bedroom and came stomping out. "Where is all your clothes, Liz?" Dooley demanded, his voice hard.

"I moved them out. I no longer feel I am married to you, Dooley."

"You don't . . . *what?*"

"I don't love you anymore. I haven't for a long time. Years. I cringe when you touch me. I . . ."

He jumped at her and backhanded her, knocking her against a wall. She held back a yelp of pain. She didn't want Gage to come storming in, because she knew that she had absolutely no rights as a married woman. She owned nothing. Could not vote. And in a court of law, her husband's word was next to God's. And if Gage were to kill Dooley during a domestic squabble, he would hang.

She leaned against the wall, staring at Dooley as the front door opened, her sons stomping in.

Conrad, the youngest of the boys, grinned at her. "You havin' a good time while Pa's usin' you for a punchin' bag?"

Sonny and Bud laughed.

Dooley grabbed Liz by the arm and flung her toward the kitchen. "Git in there and fix me some dinner. I don't wanna hear no more mouth from you."

Liz walked toward the kitchen, her back straight. I won't put up with this any longer, she vowed. I'll follow Rita, just as quickly as I can.

A plan jumped into her head and she smiled at the thought. It might work. It just might work.

She began putting together dinner and working out the plan. It all depended on what Gage said. And the other hands.

She had gone out to gather eggs in the henhouse. Dooley and her sons had left the house without telling her where they were riding off to. As usual. All the hired guns were in town, drinking. Gage had ambled over, as he always did, to carry her basket. She told him of her plan.

"I like it, Liz. Go in the house and pack a few things while ever'body is gone. I'll get the boys."

She stared at him, wide-eyed. "You mean . . . ?"

"Right now, Liz. Let's get gone from this crazy house 'fore Dooley gets back. Move, Liz! '

She went one way and Gage trotted to the bunkhouse. He sent the only rider in the bunkhouse out to tell the others to meet him at the McCorkle ranch.

"We quittin', Gage?"

"I am."

"I'm with you. And so will the others. Hep me pack up their stuff, will you? I'll tote it to them on a packhorse. How about ol' Cook?"

"He'll go wherever Liz goes. He came out here with them."

The hand cut his eyes at the foreman and grinned. "Ahh! OK, Gage."

Working frantically, the two men stuffed everything they could find into canvas and lashed it on a packhorse. "I'll tell Cook to hightail it. Move, Les. See you at the Circle Double C."

Ol' Cook was right behind Les. He packed up his war bag

and swung into the saddle just as Liz was coming out of the house, a satchel in her hand.

"You want me to hitch up the buckboard, Gage?"

"No time, Cook."

"Wal, how's she fixin' to ride then? We ain't got no side-saddle rigs."

"Astride. I done saddled her a horse."

Ol' Cook rolled his eyes. "Astride! Lord have mercy! Them sufferingetts is gonna be the downfall of us all." He galloped out.

Gage led her horse over to the porch. "Turn your head, Gage. I don't quite know how I'm going to do this. I have never sat astride in my life."

Gage turned his head.

"You may look now, Gage," she told him.

He had guessed at the stirrup length and got it right. She sure had a pretty ankle "Hang on, Liz. We got some rough country and some hard ridin' to do."

"Wherever you ride, I'll be with you," she told him, adding, "Darling."

Gage blushed all the way down to his holey socks.

"I'll kill ever' goddamn one of them!" Dooley screamed. "I'll stake that damn Gage out over an anthill and listen to him scream." Dooley cussed until he was red-faced and out of breath.

"This ain't good," Jason said. "I'm beginnin' to think we're snake-bit."

"I don't know." Lanny scratched his jaw. "It gives the other side a few more guns, is all."

"Seven more guns."

"No sweat."

Inside the house, Dooley was still ranting and cussing and roaring about what he was going to do to Gage and to his wife. The men outside heard something crash against a wall. Dooley had picked up a vase and shattered it.

The sons were leaning against a hitchrail, giggling and scratching themselves.

"Them boys," Jason pointed out, "is as goofy as their dad."

"And just as dangerous," Lanny added. "Don't sell them short. They're all cat-quick with a gun."

"About the boys . . . ?"

"We'll just kill them when we've taken the ranches."

"Of course you can stay here, Liz," Alice told her. "And stop saying it will be a bother." She smiled. "You and Gage. I'm so happy for you."

"If we survive this," Liz put a verbal damper on the other woman's joy.

"We'll survive it. Oh, Liz!" She took the woman's hands into hers. "Do you remember how it was when we first settled here? Those first few years before all the hard feelings began. We fought outlaws and Indians and were friends. Then . . ." She bit back the words.

"I know. I've tried to convince myself it wasn't true. But it was and is. Even more so now. Dooley began to change. Maybe he was always mad; I don't know. I know only that I love Gage and have for a long, long time. From a distance," she quickly added. "I just feel like a great weight has been lifted from me."

"You rest for a while. I'll get supper started."

"Pish-posh! I'm not tired. And I want to do my share here. Come on. I've got a recipe for cinnamon apple pie that'll have Cord groaning."

Laughing, the two women walked to the kitchen.

Outside the big house, Cord briefed Gage and the other men from the D-H about the outlaws' plans.

Gage shuddered. "Kill the women! God, what a bunch of

no-goods. Well, we got out of that snake pit just in time. Cord, me and boys will hep your crew bunch the cattle." He cut his eyes to Del. "You 'member that box canyon over towards Spitter Crick?"

Del nodded. "Yeah. It's got good graze and water that'll keep 'em for several weeks. That's a good idea. We'll get started first thing in the morning. Smoke said him and his boys will be over at first light to hep out. They done got their cattle bunched and safe as they could make 'em."

"I sent a rider over to tell them about y'all," Cord told him. "I 'magine Rita will be comin' over to stay with her momma. Smoke's already makin' plans to vacate the Box T. We both figure that'll be the first spread Dooley will hit, and Smoke ain't got the men to defend it agin seventy or more men."

"No, but them men that he's got was shore born with the bark on," Gage replied. "I'd shore hate to be in that first bunch that tackles 'em.

"They'll cut the odds down some, for sure," Del said. "You know," he reminisced, "I growed up hearin' stories about Pistol Le Roux and Hardrock and Silver Jim . . . and Charlie Starr. Lord, Lord! Till Smoke Jensen come along, I reckon he was the most famous gun-handler in all the West. Hardrock and Pistol and Silver Jim . . . why, them men must be nigh on seventy years old. But they still tough as wang leather and mean as cornered grizzlies. It just come to me that we're lookin' at history here."

"Let's just hope that we all live to read about it," Cord said drily.

"I think they'll try us tonight, Smoke," Charlie said. "My old bones is talkin' to me."

"I agree with you."

"I done tossed my blankets over yonder in that stand of

trees," Pistol said, pointing. "I never did like to sleep all cooped up noways. I like to look at the stars."

"We'll all stay clear of the house tonight," Smoke said. "Fill your pockets with ammunition, boys, and don't take your boots off. I think tonight is gonna be interesting."

Bob was in the loft of the barn. Spring and Pat stayed in the bunkhouse, both of them armed with rifles. Lujan was in the barn, lower level. Pistol, Silver Jim, Charlie, and Hardrock were spread around the house. Smoke elected to stay close to the now-empty corral. The horses had been moved away to a little draw; Ring was with them. Beans had slipped into moccasins and was roaming. Parnell was in the house with the women. Rita and Fae were armed with rifles. Parnell refused to take a gun.

About a quarter of a mile from the ranch complex, Beans knelt down in the road and put his ear to the hard-packed earth. He smiled grimly, then stood up. "Coming!" he shouted to Silver Jim, who was the closest to him. "Sounds like a bunch of them, too."

Silver Jim relayed the message and then settled in, earing back the hammer on his Winchester.

Beans was the first to see the flames from the torches the gunnies carried. "They're gonna try to burn us out!" he yelled.

Then the hard-riding outlaw gunslingers were thundering past Beans's position. At almost point-blank range, Beans emptied his six-shooter into the mass of riders, then holstered his pistol and picked up his Winchester. He put five fast rounds into the outlaws, then shifted positions when the lead started flying around him.

Beans knew he'd hit at least three of the riders, and two of them were hard hit and on the ground.

Silver Jim got three clean shots off, with one outlaw on the ground and the other two just hanging on, gripping the saddle horn. Not dead, but out of action.

Bob took his time with his Winchester and emptied two

saddles before Lujan hollered, "Another bunch coming behind us, Bob. Shift to the rear."

Smoke stood by the corral, a dim figure in the torchlit night, with both hands full of long-barreled Colts, and picked his targets. His aim was deadly true. He knocked two to the ground and knew he'd hit several more before being forced to run for cover

A rider threw his torch through a window—only two windows were not shuttered, front and back, giving the women a place to fire from—and the torch landed on the couch. The couch burst into flames and Parnell went to work with buckets of water already filled against such an action. He managed to keep the fire confined to the couch.

The barn was not so lucky. While Lujan and Bob were fighting at the rear of the barn, a rider tossed a torch into the hayloft. That action got him a bullet from Smoke that cut his spine and shattered his heart, but there was no saving the barn. Bob and Lujan fought inside until it became too difficult to see and breathe and they had to run for cover amid a hail of lead.

The small band of defenders of the Box T were now having to fight against range-robbers on all sides. One outlaw made the mistake of finding the horses and thinking he was going to set them free.

One second he was in the saddle, the next second he was on the ground. The last thing he would remember hearing on this earth was a deep voice rumbling, "I do not like people who are mean to nice people."

Huge hands clamped around the man's head and with one quick jerk, Ring broke the gunny's neck and tossed him to one side, his head flopping from side to side. Ring got the rifle from the outlaw's saddle boot, made sure it was full, and waited for some more action.

The area around the ranch house was now brightly lighted from the flaming barn; too bright for the outlaws' taste, for the accuracy of the defenders was more than they had counted on.

"Let's go!" came the shout.

No one bothered to fire at or pursue the outlaws. All ran into the yard to form a bucket line to wet down the roof of the house so sparks from the burning barn could not set it on fire. The men worked frantically, for already there were smoldering spots on the roof.

It did not take long for the barn to go; soon there was nothing left except a huge mound of glowing coals.

The men sat down on the ground where they were, all of them suddenly tired as the adrenaline had slowed.

"Fae!" Parnell said. "Give up this madness. Let us leave this barbaric country and return to civilization."

Fae walked toward him, her gloved hands balled into fists. Her face was sooty and her short hair disheveled and she was mad clear through. When she got within swinging distance she let him have it, giving him five in the mouth and dropping him to the ground.

Parnell lay flat on his butt, blood leaking out of a busted lip, looking up at his baby sister. He wore a hurt expression on his face. He blinked and said, "I suppose, Sister, that is your quaint way of saying no?"

Smoke and the others burst out laughing. The laughter spread and soon Fae and Rita were laughing. No one paid any attention to the bodies littering the yard and the areas all around the ranch complex.

Parnell sat up and rubbed his jaw. "I, for one, fail to see the humor in this grotesque situation."

That caused another round of laughter. They were still laughing as Ring walked up, leading several horses, one with the body of the neck-broke outlaw draped across the saddle.

"Crazy folks," Ring said. "But nice folks."

Sixteen

"This ain't worth a damn!" Jason summed up the night's action. "Nine dead and six wounded. Couple more nights like this and we might as well hang it up."

"Shore got to change our plans," Lanny agreed. "We should have hit McCorkle first."

"Well, you can bet they all is gonna be on the alert after this night," No-Count Victor said. "Hell, let's just go on and kill that stupid Dooley and his sons and settle for this spread."

"No!" Lanny stopped that quick. "It's got to be the whole bag or nothing. Think about it. You think Cord and Smoke would let us stay in this area, on this spread? And what about Dooley's wife; you forgettin' about her?"

"I reckon so," Cat said sullenly.

Both Jason and Lanny had been admiring Cat's matched guns since he'd arrived. They were silver-plated, scroll-engraved, with ivory grips. Smith & Wesson .44s, top break for easier loading. They both coveted Cat's guns. Both of them had thought, more than once: When this is over, I'll kill him and take them fancy guns.

Honor extended only so far.

A wounded man moaned in restless unconsciousness on his bloody bunk. Before he had passed out, he had drunk a full bottle of laudanum to ease the pain in his chest. Pink froth was bubbling past his lips. Lung shot, and all knew he wasn't going to make it.

"You want me to shoot him, Jason?" Nappy asked.

"Naw. He'll be gone in a few hours. If he's still alive come the mornin', we'll put a piller over his face and end it that-away. It won't make so much noise."

Smoke stepped out before first light, carrying his rifle, loaded full. It had come to him during the night, and if it came to the range-robbers, the small band of defenders would be in trouble. They could starve them out; a few well-placed snipers could keep them pinned down for days. He hated to tell Fae, but Smoke felt it would be best to desert the ranch and head for Cord's place. If they stayed here, it was only a matter of time before they were overrun.

He looked around the darkness. Before turning in, they had stacked the bodies of the outlaws against a wall of a ravine. At first light, they would go through their pockets in search of any clues to family or friends. They would then bury the men by collapsing dirt over the stiffening bodies. There would be no markers.

Smoke smelled the aroma of coffee coming from the bunkhouse, the good odors just barely overriding the smell of charred wood from the remnants of the barn. Smoke walked to the bunkhouse, faint lantern light shining through the windows.

"Comin' in," he announced just before reaching the door.

"Come on," ol' Spring called. "Got hot coffee and hard biscuits."

Before Smoke poured his first cup of coffee of the day, he noticed the men had already packed their war bags and rolled their slim mattresses.

"You boys read my mind, hey?"

"Figured you'd be wantin' to pull out this mornin'," Hardrock said, gumming a biscuit to soften it. He had perhaps four teeth left in his mouth. "What about the cattle?"

Smoke took a drink of the strong cowboy coffee before replying. "Figured we'd drive them on over to Cord's."

"Them no-goods is gonna fire the cabin soon as we're gone," Silver Jim said. "After they loot it." He grinned nastily. "We all allow as to how we ought to leave a few surprises in there for them."

Smoke, squatting down, leaned back against the bunkhouse wall and smiled. "What you got in mind?"

Hardrock kicked a cloth sack by his bunk. The sack moved and buzzed. "I gleamed me a rattler nest several days back. 'Fore I snoozed last night I paid it a visit and grabbed me several. I figured I'd plant 'em in the house 'fore we left, in stra-teegic spots." He grinned. "You like that idee?"

"Oh, yeah!"

"Thought you would. Soon as Miss Fae and that goosy brother of her'n is gone we'll plant the rattlers."

Smoke chewed on yesterday's biscuit and took a swallow of coffee. "You reckon any varmits got to the bodies last night?"

"Doubtful," Charlie said. "Ring stayed out there, close by. Said he didn't much like them people but it wouldn't be fitten to let the coyotes and wolves chew on them. Strange man."

Pistol looked toward the dusty window. "Gettin' light enough to see. I reckon we better get to it whilst it's cool. Them ol' boys is gonna get plumb ripe when the sun touches 'em."

The men put on their hats, hitched up their britches, and turned out the lamps. "I'd hate to be an undertaker," Hardrock said. "Hope when I go I just fall off my horse in the timber."

"By that time, you'll be so old you won't be able to get in the saddle," Silver Jim needled him.

"Damn near thataways now," Hardrock fired back.

* * *

They kept the outlaws' guns and ammunition and put what money they had in a leather sack to give to Fae. Then they caved in the ravine wall and stacked rocks over the dirt to keep the varmints from digging up the bodies and eating them. By the time they had finished, it was time for breakfast.

Fae and Rita had fixed a huge breakfast of bacon and eggs and oatmeal and biscuits. The men dug in, piling their plates high. Conversation was sparse until the first plates had been emptied. Eating was serious business; a man could talk anytime.

After eating up everything in sight—it wasn't polite to leave any food; might insult the cook—the men refilled their coffee cups, pushed back their chairs, and hauled out pipes and papers, passing the tobacco sack around.

"We're leaving, aren't we?" Fae asked, noticing how quiet the men were.

"Till this is over," Smoke told her. "It's a pretty location here, Cousin, but it'd be real easy for Hanks's men to pin us down."

"They'll destroy the house."

"Probably. But you can always rebuild. That beats gettin' buried here. Take what you just absolutely have to have. We can stash the rest for you. Spring, you and Pat stay here and keep a sharp eye out. We'll go bunch the cattle and start pushing them toward Cord's range. We'll cross the Smith at the north bend, just south of that big draw. Let's go, boys."

The cattle were not happy to be leaving the lush grass of summer graze, but finally the men got the old mossyhorn lead steer moving and the others followed. Smoke and Hardrock rode back to the ranch house. Hardrock went to the bunkhouse to get his bag of goodies for the outlaws. Ring had bunched the horses and with Pat's help was holding them just off the road. Spring was driving the wagon. Both Rita and

Rae were riding astride; Parnell was in his buggy. He had a fat lip from his encounter with his sister the night past. He didn't look at all happy.

"I'll catch up with y'all down the road," Hardrock told Smoke.

"What is in the sack?" Parnell inquired.

"Some presents for the range-robbers. It wouldn't be neighborly to just go off and not leave something."

Parnell muttered something under his breath about the strangeness of western people while Smoke grinned at him.

The caravan moved out, with Smoke riding with his rifle across his saddle horn. Smoke did not expect any trouble so soon after the outlaw attack the past night, but one never knew about the mind of Dooley Hanks. The man didn't even know his own mind.

The trip to the Smith was uneventful and Spring knew a place where the wagon and the buggy could get across with little difficulty. A couple of Cord's hands were waiting on the west side of the river to point the way for the cattle. Smoke rode on to the ranch with the women and Parnell. Cord met them in the front yard.

"The house and barn go up last night?" he asked. "We seen a glow."

"Just the barn. I imagine the house will be fired tonight." He smiled. "After they try to loot it. But Hardrock left a few surprises for them." He told the ranch owner about the rattlesnakes in the bureau drawers and in other places.

Cord's smile was filled with grim satisfaction. "They'll get exactly what they deserve. Your momma's in the house, Rita." He stared at her. "Girl, what *have* you done to your hair?"

"Whacked it off." Rita grinned. "You like my jeans, Mister Cord?"

Cord shook his head and muttered about women dressin' up in men's britches and ridin' astride. Rita laughed at him as

Sandi came out onto the porch. She squealed and the young women ran toward each other and hugged.

"The women been cleaning out the old bunkhouse all mornin', Smoke. It ain't fancy, but the roof don't leak and the bunks is in good shape and the sheets and blankets is clean."

"Sounds good to me. I'll go get settled in and get back with you."

"Smoke?"

He turned around to face Cord. The man stuck out his big hand and Smoke took it. "Good to have you with us in this thing."

"They done pulled out!" Larado reported back to Jason and Lanny. "They moved the cattle toward the Smith this mornin'. I found where they caved a ravine in on top of them they kilt last night. And it looks like the house is nearabouts full of good stuff."

"One down," Lanny said with a grin. "Let's take us a ride over there and see what we can find in the house. If they left in a hurry, they prob'ly didn't pack much."

The range-robbers rode up cautiously, but already the place had that aura of desertion about it. Lanny and Jason were feeling magnanimous that morning and told the boys to go ahead, help themselves to whatever they could find in the house.

A dozen gunnies began looting the house.

"Hey!" Slim called. "This here box is locked. Gimme that there hammer over yonder on the sill." He hammered the lock off while others squatted down, close to him, ready to snatch and grab should the box be filled with valuables. Slim opened the lid. Two rattlesnakes lunged out, one of them taking Slim in the throat and the other nailing a bearded gunny on the cheek and hanging on, wrapping around the gunny's neck, striking again and again.

One outlaw dove through a window escaping the snakes; another took the back door off its hinges. A gunny known only as Red fell over the couch, knocking a bureau over. A rattler slithered out of the opened drawer and began striking at the man's legs, while Red kicked and screamed and howled in agony.

Larado ran from the house in blind fear, running into Lanny, who was running toward the house. Lanny fell back into Jason, and all three of them landed in the dust in a heap of arms and legs.

Ben Sabler rode up with his kin just in time to see Red crawl from the house and scream out his misery, the rattlesnake coiled around one leg, striking again and again at Red's stomach.

Ben did not hesitate. He jerked iron and shot Red in the head, putting him out of his agony, and then shot the snake, clipping its head off with deadly accuracy.

The bearded gunny staggered out the door, dying on his feet. Venom dripped from his face. He stood for a moment, and then fell like a tree, face-first in the dirt. The rattler sidewinded toward Larado, who jerked out his pistol and emptied it into the rattler.

"Burn this damn place!" Lanny shouted.

"Slim's in there!"

Lanny looked inside. Slim was already beginning to swell from the massive amount of venom in his body. Lanny carefully backed out. "Slim's dead," he announced. "Damn Smoke Jensen. The bassard ain't human to do something lak this."

"I heard that he was from hell, myself," a gunny called Blaine said. He sat his horse and looked at the death house. "I knowed a man said Jensen took lead seven times one day some years back. Never did knock him down. He just kept on comin'."

"That ain't no story," Ben Sabler said. "I was there. I seen it."

Lanny looked at Ben. "I'll kill him. And that's a promise."

"I gotta see it." Ben didn't back down. "I seen his grave-yards. I ain't never seen none of yours."

"Hang around," Lanny told him. He turned his back and shouted the order. "Burn this damn place to the ground!"

SEVENTEEN

They stood in the front yard and watched the smoke spiral up into the sky, caught by vortexes in the hot air and spinning upward until breaking up.

Parnell stood with clenched fists, his eyes on the dark smoke. "I say now, that was unnecessary. Quite brutish. And that makes me angry." He stalked away, muttering to himself.

Fae was on the porch, her face in her hands, crying softly.

"She's a woman after all," Lujan said, so softly only Smoke could hear.

Del worked the handle of the outside pump, wetting a bandanna and taking it to Fae.

Fae looked at the foreman, surprise in her eyes, and tried a smile as she took the dampened bandanna. "Thank you, Del."

"You're shore welcome, ma'am." He backed off a few feet.

"Lujan," Smoke said. "You and me and Beans. We hit them tonight."

"*Sí, señor.*" Lujan's teeth flashed in a smile. "I was wondering when you would have enough of being pushed."

By late afternoon, everyone at the Circle Double C knew the three men were going headhunting. But no one said a word about it. That might have caused some bad luck. And no one took umbrage at not being asked along. This was to be—they guessed—a hit-hard-and-quick-and-run-like-hell operation. Too many riders would just get in the way.

When Smoke threw a saddle on Dagger, the big mean-eyed horse was ready for the trail, and he showed his displeasure at not being ridden much lately by trying to step on Smoke's foot.

The men took tape from the medicine chest and taped everything that might jingle. They took everything out of their pockets that was not necessary and looped bandoleers of ammunition across their chests. They were all dressed in dark clothing.

Just after dusk, Beans and Sandi went for a short walk while Smoke and Lujan squatted under the shade of a huge old tree by the bunkhouse and watched as Cord left the main house and walked toward them.

He squatted down beside them in the near-darkness of Montana's summer dusk. "Nice quiet evenin', boys."

"Indeed it is, señor." Lujan flashed his smile. His eyes flicked over to Beans and Sandi, now sitting in the yard swing. "A night for romance."

Cord grunted, but both men knew the rancher liked the young man called the Moab Kid. "Sandi would be inclined to give me all sorts of grief if anything was to happen to Beans."

When neither Smoke nor Lujan replied, Cord said, "Three against sixty is crappy odds, boys."

"Not the way we plan to fight," Smoke told him. "They'll be expecting a mass attack. Not a small surprise attack."

Again, the rancher grunted. It was clear that he did not like the three of them going headhunting. "We can expect you back when?"

"Around dawn. But keep guards out, Cord. If we do as much damage as I think we will, Dooley is likely to ride against you this night."

"I'll double the guards."

Beans and Sandi had parted, with Sandi now on the lamp-lighted front porch. The Moab Kid was walking toward the three men at the tree. Faint light reflected off the double bandoleers of ammunition crisscrossing his chest.

All three men wore two guns around their waist; a third pistol rested in homemade shoulder holsters. They had each added another rifle boot; with two fully loaded Winchester .44 rifles and three pistols, that meant each man was capable of firing fifty-two times before reloading. And each man carried a double pouch over their saddlebags, each pouch containing a can of giant powder, already rigged with fuse and cap.

The men intended to raise a lot of hell at Dooley's D-H spread.

Smoke and Lujan rose to their boots.

Cord's voice was soft in the night. "See you, boys."

The three men walked toward their horses and stepped into the saddles. They rode toward the east, fast disappearing into the night.

The old gunslingers joined Cord by the tree. "Gonna be some fireworks this night," Silver Jim said. "Pistol, you 'member that time me and you and that half-breed Ute hit them outlaws down on the Powder River?"

Pistol laughed in the night. "Yeah. They was about twenty of them. We shore give them what-for, didn't we?"

"Was that the time y'all catched them gunnies in their drawers?" Hardrock asked.

"Takes something out of a man to have to fight in his long-handles. We busted right up into their camp. Stampeded their horses right over them, with us right behind the horses, reins in our teeth and both hands full of guns. Of course," he added with a smile, "that was when we all had teeth!"

* * *

The men rode slowly, saving their horses and not wanting to reach the ranch until all were asleep. They kept conversation to a minimum, riding each with their own thoughts. They did not need to be shared. Facing death was a personal thing, the concept that had to be worked out in each man's mind. None of the three considered themselves to be heroes; they were simply doing what they felt had to be done. The niceties of legal maneuvering were fast approaching the West, but it would be a few more years before they reached the general population. Until that time, codes of conduct would be set and enforced by the people, and the outcome would usually be very final.

The men forded the Smith, careful not to let water splash onto the canvas sacks containing the giant powder bombs. On the east side of the river, they pulled up and rested, letting their horses blow.

The men squatted down and carefully checked their guns, making sure they were loaded up full. Only after that was done did Lujan haul out the makings and pass the sack and papers around. The men enjoyed a quiet smoke in the coolness of the Montana night and only then was the silence broken.

"We'll walk our horses up to that ridge overlooking Dooley's spread," Smoke spoke softly. "Look the situation over. If it looks OK, we'll ride slow-like and not light the bombs until we're inside the compound. Lujan, you take the new bunkhouse. Beans, you toss yours into the bunkhouse that was used by Gage and his boys. I'll take the main house." He picked up a stick and drew a crude diagram in the dirt, just visible in the moonlight. "We've got about a hundred and fifty rounds between us all loaded up for the first pass. But let's don't burn them all up and get caught short.

"Beans, the corral is closest to your spot; rope the gates and pull 'em down. The horses will be out of there like a shot. We make one pass and then get the hell gone from there. We'll link up just south of that ridge. If we get separated, we'll meet back at the Smith, where we rested. I don't want to bomb the barn because of the horses in there. Ain't no point in hurtin' a good horse when we don't have to."

Lujan chuckled quietly. "I think when the big bangs go off, there will be no need for Beans to rope the gates. I think the horses will break those poles down in a blind panic and be gone."

"Let's hope so," Smoke said. "That'll give us more time to raise Cain."

"And," Beans said, "when them bombs go off, those ol' boys are gonna be so rattled they'll be runnin' in all directions. I'd sure like to have a pitcher of it to keep."

Lujan ground out his cigarette butt under a boot heel and stood up. "Shall we go make violent sounds in the night, boys?"

The men rode deeper into the night, drawing closer to their objective. It was unspoken, but each man had entertained the thought that if Dooley had decided to strike first this night, Cord would be three guns short. If that was the case, and they were hitting an empty ranch, Dooley would experience the sensation of seeing another glow in the night sky.

His own ranch.

The three men left their horses and walked up to the ridge overlooking the darkened complex of the D-H ranch. They all three smiled as their eyes settled on the many horses in the double corral.

Without speaking, Smoke pointed out each man's perimeter and, using sign language, told them to watch carefully. He gave the soft call of a meadowlark and Lujan and Beans nodded their understanding, then faded into the brush.

They watched for over an hour, each of them spotting the locations of the two men on watch. They were careless, puffing on cigarettes. Smoke birdcalled them back in, and they slipped to their horses.

"What'd you think?" Smoke tossed it out.

"Let's swing around the ridge and walk our horses as close in as we can," Beans suggested.

"Suits me," Lujan said.

"Let's do it."

They swung around the ridge and came up on the east side of the ranch, walking their horses very slowly, keeping to the grass to further muffle the sound of the hooves.

"They're either drunk or asleep," Beans whispered.

"With any kind of luck, we can put them to sleep forever," Lujan returned the whisper. He reached back for the canvas sack and took out a giant powder bomb, the others following suit.

They were right on the edge of the ranch grounds when a call went up. "Hey! They's something movin' out yonder!"

The three men scratched matches into flames and lit the fuses. Beans let out a wild scream that would have sent any self-respecting puma running for cover and the horses lunged forward, steel-shod hooves pounding on the hard-packed dirt road.

Smoke reached the house first, sending Dagger leaping over the picket fence. He hurled the bomb through a front window and circled around to the back, lighting the fuse on his second bomb and tossing it into an upstairs window. The front of the house blew, sending shards of glass and splintered pieces of wood flying, just as Smoke was heading across the backyard, low in the saddle, his face almost pressing Dagger's neck. He was using his knees to guide the horse, the reins in his teeth and both hands filled with .44s.

The upstairs blew, taking part of the roof off just as the bunkhouses exploded. All the men knew that with these black powder bombs, as small as they were, unless a man was directly in the path of one, or within a ten-foot radius, chances of death were slim. Injury, however, was another matter.

The first blast knocked Dooley out of bed and onto the floor. The second blast in the house went off just as he was getting to his feet, trying to find his boots and hat and gun belt. That blast went off directly over his bedroom and caved in the ceiling, driving the man to his knees and tearing out the button-up back flap in his longhandles. A long splinter impaled itself to the hilt in one cheek of his bare butt, bringing a howl of pain from the man.

One of his sons fell through the huge hole in the ceiling and landed on his father's bed, collapsing the frame and folding the son up in the feather tick.

"Halp!" Bud hollered. "Git me outta here. Halp!"

Conrad came running, saw the hole in the ceiling too late, and fell squalling, landing on his father, knocking both men even goofier than they were already were.

Outside, Smoke leveled a six-shooter and fired almost point-blank at a gunny dressed in his longhandles, boots, and hat—with a rifle in his hands. Smoke's slug took the man in the center of the chest and dropped him.

Dagger's hooves made a mess of the man's face as Smoke charged toward a knot of gunnies, both his guns blazing, barking and snarling and spitting out lead.

He ran right through and over the gunnies, Dagger's hooves bringing howls of pain as bones were broken under the steel shoes.

Lujan knee-reined his horse into a mass of confused and badly shaken gunslicks. He fired into the face of one and the man's face was suddenly slick with blood. Turning his horse, Lujan knocked another gunslick sprawling and fired his left-hand gun at another, the bullet taking the man in the belly.

Smoke was suddenly at his side, and both men looked around for Beans, spotting him, and with a defiant cry from Lujan's throat, the two men charged toward the Moab Kid. They circled the Kid, holstering their pistols and pulling Winchesters from the boots. The three of them charged the yard, firing as fast as they could work the levers of their seventeen-shot Winchesters. In the darkness, they could not be sure they hit anything, but as they would later relate, the action sure solved blocked bowel-movement problems any of the gunnies might be suffering from.

The horses from the corral were long gone, just as Lujan had predicted, stampeding in a mad rush and tearing down the corral gates after the explosion of the first bomb.

"Gimme a bomb!" Smoke yelled over the confusion.

At a full gallop, Beans handed him a bomb and Smoke circled the house, screaming like a painted-up Cheyenne, while Lujan and Beans reined up and began laying down a blistering line of fire. Smoke lit the bomb and tossed it in a side window.

"Let's go!" he yelled.

Screaming like young bucks on the warpath, the three men gave their horses full rein and galloped off into the dusty night. Smoke took one look back and grinned.

Dooley was getting to his feet for the third time when the bomb blew. The blast impacted with Dooley, turning him around and sending him, door, and what was left of his long-handles, right out the bedroom window. Dooley landed right on top of Lanny Ball, the door separating them, both of the men knocked out cold.

"Lemme out of here!" Bud squalled. "Halp! Halp!"

Eighteen

There had been no pursuit. It would take the gunnies hours to round up their horses. But come the dawning, all three men knew the air would be filled with gunsmoke whenever and wherever D-H riders met with Circle Double C men.

Several miles from the house, the men stopped and loosened cinch straps on their horses, letting them rest and blow and have a little water, but not too much; this was no time for a bloated horse.

Smoke, Lujan, and Beans lay belly-down beside the little creek and drank alongside their horses, then sat down on the cool bank and rolled cigarettes, smoking and relaxing and unwinding. They had been very, very lucky this night, and they all knew it.

Suddenly, Beans started laughing and the laughter spread. Soon all three were rolling on the bank, laughing almost hysterically.

Gasping for breath, tears running down their tanned cheeks, the men gripped their sides and sat up, wiping their eyes with shirtsleeves.

"Sabe Dios!" Lujan said. "But I will never see anything so funny as that we witnessed tonight if I live to be a hundred!"

"Man," Beans chuckled, "I never knew them fellers was so ugly. Did you ever see so many skinny legs in all your life?"

"I saw Dooley blown slap out of the house," Smoke said. "He looked like he was in one piece, but I couldn't tell for sure. He was on a door, looked like to me. Landed on somebody, but I couldn't tell who it was, 'cept he wasn't wearing longjohns, had on one of those short-pants lookin' things some men have taken to wearing. Come to think of it, it did sorta resemble Lanny Ball. He had his guns belted on over his drawers."

That set them off again, howling and rolling on the ground while their horses looked at the men as if they were a bunch of idiots.

After a few hours' sleep, Smoke rolled out of his blankets, noting that Lujan and Beans were already up. Smoke washed his face and combed his hair and was on his first cup of bunkhouse coffee—strong enough to warp a spoon—when Cord came in.

"I just got the word," the rancher said. "You and the boys played Billy-Hell last night over to the D-H. Doc Adair was rolled out about three this morning. So far there's four dead and two wounded who ain't gonna make it. Several busted arms and legs and heads. Dooley took a six-inch-long splinter in one side of his butt. Adair said the man has gone slap-dab nuts. Just sent off a wire to a cattle buyer to sell off a thousand head for money to hire more gunslicks . . . or rather, he sent someone in to send the wire. Dooley can't sit a saddle just yet." Try as he did, Cord could not contain his smile.

"Hell, Cord," Smoke complained. "There *aren't* any more gunfighters."

"Dad Estes," Cord said, his smile fading.

Smoke stood up from the rickety chair. "You have got to be kidding!"

"Wish I was. They been hiding out over in the Idaho wilderness. Just surfaced a couple of weeks ago on the Montana border."

"I haven't heard anything about Dad in several years. Not since the Regulators ran them out of Colorado."

Cord shook his head. "I been hearin' for some time they been murderin' and robbin' miners to stay alive. Makin' little forays out of the wilderness and then duckin' back in."

"How many men are we talking about, Cord?"

Cord shrugged his shoulders. "Don't know. Twenty to thirty, I'd guess."

"Then all we're doing is taking two steps forward and three steps back."

"Looks like."

"Did you get a report on damage last night?"

"One bunkhouse completely ruined, the other one badly damaged. The big house is pretty well shot, back and front. Smoke, Dooley has given the word: shoot us on sight. He says Gibson is his and for us to stay out of it."

"The hell I will!"

"That's the same thing everybody else around here told me . . . more or less."

"Well, it was funny while it lasted." Smoke's words were glum.

Cord poured a cup of coffee. "Personally, I'd like to have seen it. Beans and Lujan has been entertaining the crews for an hour. Did Lanny Ball really have his guns strapped on over his short drawers?"

Smoke laughed. "Yeah. That was right before the door hit him."

Both men shared a laugh. Cord said, "Would it do any good to wire for some federal marshals?"

"I can't see that it would. It would be our word against theirs. And they'd just back off until the marshals left, then we'd still have the same problem facing us. If I had the time, I could probably get my old federal commission back . . . but what good would it do? Dooley's crazy; the gunslicks he's buyin' are playing a double-cross and Dooley's so nuts you'd never convince him of it. I think we'd just better resign ourselves that we're in a war and take it from there."

"The wife says we need supplies in the worst way. We've got to go into town."

"Then we'll go in a bunch. This afternoon. We've got to show Dooley he doesn't run the town."

"Sorry, Mister McCorkle," Walt Hillery said primly. "I'm completely out of everything you want."

"You're a damn liar!" Cord flushed. "Hell, man, I can see most of what I ordered."

"All that has been bought by the D-H spread. They're coming in to pick it up this afternoon."

"Jake!" Cord yelled at his hand driving the wagon. "Pull it around back and get ready to load up."

"Now, see here!" Leah's voice was sharp. "You don't give us orders, Mister Big Shot!"

"Dooley's bought them," Smoke said quietly. He stood by a table loaded with men's jeans. He lifted his eyes to Walt. "You should have stayed out of this, Hillery." He walked to the counter and dug in his jeans pocket, tossing half a dozen double eagles onto the counter. "That'll pay for what I pick out, and Cord's money is layin' right beside mine. If Dooley sets up a squall, you tell him to come see me. Load it up, Jake."

The sour-faced and surly Walt and Leah stood tight-lipped, but silent as Jake began loading up supplies.

"Grind the damn coffee, Walt," Cord ordered. "As a matter of fact, double my order. That way I won't have to look at your prissy face for a long time."

"I hope Mister Hanks kills you, McCorkle!" Leah hissed the verbal venom at him. "And I hope you die hard!"

Cord took the hard words without changing expression. "You never have liked me, Leah, and I never could understand why."

She didn't back down. "You don't have the mental capability to appreciate quality people, McCorkle . . . like Dooley Hanks."

"Quality people? What in the name of Peter and Paul are you talking about, Leah?"

But she would only shake her head.

"Money talks, Cord," Smoke told him. "Especially with little-minded people like these two fine citizens. They're just like Dooley: prideful, envious, spiteful, hateful . . . any and all of the seven deadly sins." He walked around the counter and stripped the shelf of all the boxes of .44 and .45 rounds. "Tally it up, storekeeper."

Cord walked around the general store, filling a large box with all the bandages and various balms and patent medicines he could find. "Might as well do it right," he muttered.

If dark looks of hate could kill, both Cord and Smoke would have died on the spot. Not another word was exchanged the rest of the time spent in the store except for Walt telling the men the amount of their purchases. All the supplies loaded onto the wagon, both Cord and Smoke experienced a sense of relief when they exited the building to stand on the boardwalk.

"Quality people?" Cord said, shaking his head, still not able to get over that statement.

"Forget them," Smoke said. "They're not worth worrying about. When this war is over, and we've won—and we will win, count on it—those two will be sucking up to you as if nothing had happened."

"What they'll do is do without my business," Cord said shortly.

The men walked over to Hans for a cup of coffee and a piece of pie. Beans and Lujan, with Charlie Starr and his old gunslinging buddies, had dropped into the Pussycat for a beer. There were half a dozen horses wearing the D-H brand, among others, at the hitchrail in front of the Hangout.

"You any good with that six-gun?" Smoke asked the rancher.

"Contrary to what some believe, I'm no fast gun. But I hit what I aim at."

"That counts most of all in most cases. I've seen so-called fast guns many, many times put their first shot in the dirt. They didn't get another shot." Then Smoke added, "Just buried."

They sipped their coffee and enjoyed the dried apple pie with a hunk of cheese on it. They both could sense the tension hanging in and around the small town; and both knew that a shooting was more than likely looking them in the face. It would probably come just before they tried to leave Gibson.

Nothing stirred on the wide street. Not one dog or cat could be seen anywhere. And it was very hot, the sun a bubbling ball in a very blue and very cloudless sky. A dust devil spun out its short frantic life, whipping up the street and then vanishing.

Hilda refilled their cups. "And how is Ring?" she inquired, blushing as she asked.

"Fine." Smoke smiled at her. "He sends his regards."

She giggled and returned to the kitchen.

Smoke looked at Cord as he scribbled in a small tally book most ranchers carried with them. "Eighteen dead," the rancher muttered. "Near as I can figure. May God have mercy on us."

"They'll be fifty or sixty dead before this is over. If Dooley doesn't pull in his horns."

"He won't. He's gone completely around the bend. And you know," Cord said thoughtfully, some sadness in his voice, "I don't even remember what caused the rift between us."

"That's the way it usually is. Your rider who talked to Doc Adair, he have any idea when Dad Estes and his bunch will be pulling in?"

"Soon as possible, I reckon. They'll ride hard gettin' over here. And I'd be willing to bet they'd already left the wilderness and was waitin' for word; and I'd bet it was Jason or Lanny who put the bug about them into Dooley's ear."

"Probably right on both counts."

Both men looked up as several riders rode into town, reining up in front of the Hangout.

"You know them, Smoke?"

"Some of No-Count Victor's bunch."

"Daryl Radcliffe and Paul Addison are ze zwo in der front," Hans rumbled from behind the counter. "Day vas pointed out to me when day first come to zown."

"I've heard of them," Smoke said. "They're scum. Bottom of the barrel but good with a pistol."

"Maybe ve vill get lucky and day will all bite demselves und die from der rabies," Hans summed up the feelings of most in the town.

They all heard the back door open and close and Hans turned as Olga came to his side and whispered in his ear. She disappeared into the kitchen and Hans said, "Four men she didn't know have hitched dere horses at der far end of town and are valking dis vay. All of dem vearing zwo guns."

"Is that our cue?" Cord asked.

"I reckon. But I'm going to finish my pie and coffee first."

"You always this calm before a gunfight?"

"No point in getting all worked up about it. Stay as calm as you can and your shootin hand stays steady."

"Good way to look at it, I suppose." Cord finished his pie and took a sip of coffee. "I hate it that we have to do this in town. A stray bullet doesn't care who it hits."

Smoke drained his coffee cup and placed it carefully in the saucer. "It doesn't have to be on the street if you're game."

"I'm game for anything that'll keep innocent people from getting hurt."

"You ready?"

"As I'll ever be. Where are we going?"

"Like Daniel, into the lion's den. Or in this case, the Hangout. Let's see how they like it when we take it to them."

Nineteen

Beans and Lujan and Charlie Starr and his old buddies were waiting on the boardwalk.

"The beer is on me, boys," Smoke told them. "We'll try the fare at the Hangout."

"I hope they have tequila," Lujan said. "They didn't a couple of weeks ago. I have not had a decent drink in months."

"They probably do by now, with Diego and Pablo hanging around in there. But the bottles might be reserved for them."

"If they have tequila, I shall have a drink," Lujan replied softly, tempered steel under the liltingly accented words.

The men pushed through the batwing doors and stepped inside the saloon. For all but Lujan and Cord, this was their first excursion into the Hangout. The men fanned out and quickly sized up the joint.

They realized before the first blink that they were out-numbered a good two to one. Surprise mixed with irritation was very evident on the faces of the D-H gunfighters. This move on the part of the Circle Double C had not been an-ticipated, and it was not to their liking. For in a crowded barroom, gunfights usually took a terrible toll due to the close range.

Smoke led the way to the bar, deliberately turning his back

to the gunslicks. The barkeep looked as if he really had to go
to the outhouse. "Beer for me and the Moab Kid and Mister
McCorkle, please. And a bottle of whiskey for the boys and
a bottle of tequila for Mister Lujan."

The barkeep looked at the "boys," average age about sixty-
five, and nodded his head. "I got ever'thing 'cept the tequila.
Them bottles is reserved for my regular customers."

"Put a bottle of tequila on the bar, partner," Smoke told
him. "If a customer can see it, it's for sale."

"Yes, sir," the barkeep said, knowing he was caught between a rock and a hard place. But who the hell would have
ever figured this bunch would come in *here*?

Smoke and his men could watch the room of gunfighters
in the mirror behind the bar, and they could all see the D-H
hired guns were very uncertain. It showed in their furtive
glances at one another. Smoke kept a wary eye on Radcliffe
and Addison, for they were known to be backshooters and
would not hesitate to kill him should Smoke relax his guard
for just a moment.

Several D-H guns had been standing at the bar. They had
carefully moved away while Smoke was ordering the drinks.

"Diego finds out you been suckin' at his tequila bottle," a
gunny spoke, "you gonna be dead, Lujan."

"One day is just as good as the next day to meet the Lord,"
Lujan replied, turning to face the man. "But since Diego is
not present, perhaps you would like to attempt to fill his
boots, *puerco*."

"What'd you call me?" the man stood up.

Lujan smiled, holding his shot glass in his left hand.
"A pig!"

Radcliffe and Addison and half a dozen others stood up,
their hands dangling close to their guns.

The town's blacksmith pushed open the batwings, stood
for a moment staring at the crowd and feeling the tension in

the room. He slowly backed out onto the boardwalk. The sounds of his boots faded as he made his exit.

"No damn greasy Mex is gonna call me a pig!" the gunny shouted the words.

Lujan smiled, half turning as he placed the shot glass on the bar. He expected the D-H gunny to draw as he turned, and the man did. Lujan's Colt snaked into his hand and the beery air exploded in gunfire. The D-H gunny was down and dying as his hand was still trying to lift his pistol clear of leather.

Radcliffe and Addison grabbed for iron. Smoke's right hand dipped, drew, cocked, and fired in one smooth cat-quick movement. A second behind his draw, Cord drew and fired. Radcliffe and Addison stumbled backward and fell over chairs on their way to the floor.

The room erupted in gunsmoke, lead, and death as Beans and the old gun-handlers pulled iron, cocked it back, and let it bang.

Two D-H riders, with more sense than the others, jumped right through a saloon window, landing on the boardwalk and rolling to the street. They were cut in a few places, but that beat the hell out of being dead.

The bartender had dropped to the floor at the first shot. He came up with a sawed-off ten-gauge shotgun, the hammers eared back, and pointed it at Pistol's head. Cord turned and shot the man in the neck. The bartender jerked as the bullet took him, the barrels of the shotgun pointed toward the ceiling. The shotgun went off, the stock driving back from the recoil, smashing into the man's mouth, knocking teeth out.

Cord felt a hammer blow in his left shoulder, a jarring flash of pain that turned him to one side for a painful moment and rendered his left arm useless. Regaining his balance and lifting his pistol, the rancher fired at the man who had shot him, his bullet taking the man in his open mouth and exiting out the man's neck.

Beans felt a burning sensation on his cheek as a slug grazed him, followed by the warm drip of blood. He jerked out his second pistol and added more gunsmoke and death to the mounting carnage.

Lujan twisted as a slug tore through the fleshy part of his arm. Cursing, he lifted his Colt and drove two fast rounds into the belly of the D-H gunhawk who stood directly in front of him, doubling the man over and dropping him screaming to the floor.

The barroom was thick with gunsmoke, making it almost impossible to see. The roaring of guns was near-deafening, adding to the screaming of the wounded and the vile cursing of those still alive.

Smoke jerked as a bullet burned his leg and another slug clipped the top of his ear, sending blood flowing down his face. He stumbled to one side and picked up a gun that had fallen from the lifeless fingers of a D-H gunslick. It was a short-barreled Colt Peacemaker .45. Smoke eared the hammer back and let it snarl as he knelt on the floor, his wounded leg throbbing.

The old gunfighters seemed invincible as they stood almost shoulder to shoulder, hands filled with .44s and .45s, all of them belching fire and smoke and lead. This was nothing new to them. They had been doing this since the days a man carried a dozen filled cylinders with him for faster reloading. They had stood in barrooms from the Mississippi to the Pacific Ocean, and from Canada to the Mexican border and fought it out, sometimes with a tin star pinned to their chests, sometimes close to the outlaw trail. This was as familiar to them as to a bookkeeper with his figures.

Several D-H hired guns stumbled through the smoke and the blood, trying to make it to the boardwalk, to take the fight into the streets. The first one to step through the batwings was flung back into the fray, his face missing. Hans had blown it off with a sawed-off shotgun. The second D-H gunny had his legs knocked out from under him from the other barrel of Hans's express gun.

Through the thick choking killing haze, Smoke saw a man known to him as Blue, a member of Cat Jennings's gang of no-goods and trash. Blue was pointing his Smith & Wesson Schofield .45 at Charlie.

He never got to pull the trigger. Smoke's Peacemaker roared and bucked in his hand and Blue felt, for a few seconds, the hot pain of frontier justice end his days of robbing and murdering.

The gunfire faded into silence, broken only by the moaning of wounded gunslingers.

"Coming in!" Hans shouted from the boardwalk.

"Come on, partner," Hardrock said, punching out empties and filling up his guns.

Hans stepped through the batwings and coughed as the acrid smoke filled his nostrils. His eyes widened in shock at the human carnage on the floor. Widened further as he looked at the wounded men leaning up against the bar. "I vill get the doctor." He backed out and ran for Doc Adair's office.

While Charlie and Pistol kept their guns on the moaning gunslicks on the floor, Smoke and Lujan walked among them, silently determining which should first receive Adair's attentions and who would never again need attention.

Not in this life.

Smoke knelt down beside a young man, perhaps twenty years old. The young man had been shot twice in the stomach, and already his dark eyes were glazing over as death hovered near.

"You got any folks, boy?" Smoke asked.

"Mother!" the young man gasped.

"Where is she?"

"Arkansas. Clay County. On the St. Francis. Name's . . . name's Claire . . . Shelby."

"I'll get word to her," Smoke told him as that pale rider came galloping nearer.

"She always told me . . . I was gonna turn out . . . bad." The words were very weak.

"I'll write that your horse threw you and you broke your neck."

"I'd . . . 'preciate it. That'd make her . . . feel a bunch better." He closed his eyes and did not open them again.

"I thought you was gonna kiss him there for a minute, Jensen," a hard-eyed gunslick mocked Smoke. The lower front of the man's shirt was covered with blood. He had taken several rounds in the gut.

"You got any folks you want me to write?" Smoke asked the dying man.

The gunslick spat at Smoke, the bloody spittle landing close to his boot.

"Suit yourself." Smoke stood up, favoring his wounded leg. He limped back to the bar and leaned against it, just as the batwings pushed open and Doc Adair and the undertaker came in.

Both of them stopped short. "Jesus God!" Adair said, looking around him at the body-littered and blood-splattered saloon.

"Business got a little brisk today, Doc," Smoke told him, accepting a shot glass of tequila from Lujan. "Check Cord here first." He knocked back the strong mescal drink and shuddered as it hit the pit of his stomach.

The doctor, not as old as Smoke had first thought—of course he'd been sober now for several weeks, and was now wearing clean clothes and had gone back to shaving daily—knew his business. He cleaned out the shoulder wound and bandaged it, rigging a sling for Cord out of a couple of bar towels. He then turned his attention to Lujan, swiftly and expertly patching up the arm.

Smoke had cut open his jeans, exposing the ugly rip along

the outside of his leg. "It ought to be stitched up," Adair said. "It'll leave a bad scar if I don't."

"Last time my wife Sally counted, Doc, I had seventeen bullet scars in my hide. So one more isn't going to make any difference."

"So young to have been hit so many times," the doctor muttered as he swabbed out the gash with alcohol. Smoke lifted himself out of the chair as the alcohol cleaned the raw flesh. Adair grinned. "Sometimes the treatment hurts worse than the wound."

"You've convinced me," Smoke said as his eyes went misty, then went through the same sensation as Adair cleaned the wound in his ear.

"How 'bout us?" a gunfighter on floor bitched. "Ain't we get no treatment?"

"Go ahead and die," Adair told him. "I can see from here you're not going to make it."

Charlie and his friends had walked around the room, gathering all the guns and gun belts, from both the dead and living.

"Always did want me a matched set of Remingtons," Silver Jim said. "Now I got me some. Nice balance, too."

"I want you to lookee here at this Colt double-action," Charlie said. "I'll just be hornswoggled. And she's a .44-40. Got a little ring on the butt so's a body could run some twine through it and not lose your gun. Ain't that something, now. Don't have to cock it, neither. Just point it and pull the trigger." He tried it one-handed and almost scared the doctor half to death when Charlie shot out a lamp. "All that trigger-pullin'-the-hammer-back does throw your aim off a mite, though. Take some gettin' used to, I reckon."

"Maybe you 'pposed to shoot it with both hands," Hardrock suggested.

"That don't make no sense atall. There ain't no room on there for two hands. Where the hell would you put the other'n?"

"I don't know. Was I you, I'd throw the damn thing away. They ain't never gonna catch on."

"I'm a hurtin' something fierce!" a D-H gunhawk hollered.

"You want me to kick you in the head, boy?" Pistol asked him. "That'd put you out of your misery for a while."

The gunhawk shut his mouth.

Adair finished with Beans and went to work on the fallen gunfighters. "This is strictly cash, boys," he told them. "I don't give no credit to people whose life expectancy is as short as yours."

TWENTY

All was calm for several days. Smoke imagined that even in Dooley's half-crazed mind it had been a shock to lose so many gunslicks in the space of three minutes, and all that following the raid on Dooley's ranch. So much had happened in less than twenty-four hours that Dooley was being forced to think over very carefully whatever move he had planned next.

But all knew the war was nowhere near over. That this was quite probably the lull before the next bloody and violent storm.

"Dad Estes and his bunch just pulled in," Cord told Smoke on the morning of the fourth day after the showdown in the saloon. "Hans sent word they came riding in late last night."

"He'll be making a move soon then."

"Smoke, do you realize that by my count, thirty-three men have been killed so far?"

"And about twenty wounded. Yes. I understand the undertaker is putting up a new building just to handle it all."

"That is weighing on my mind. I've killed in my lifetime, Smoke. I've killed three white men in about twenty years, but they had stole from me and were shooting at me. I've hanged one rustler." He paused.

"What are you trying to say, Cord?"

"We've got to end this. I'm getting where I can't sleep at night! That boy dying back yonder in the saloon got to me."

"I'm certainly open to suggestions, Cord. Do you think it didn't bother me to write that boy's mother? I don't enjoy killing, Cord. I went for three years without ever pulling a gun in anger. I loved it. Then until I got Fae's letter, I hadn't even worn both guns. But you know as well as I do how this little war is going to be stopped."

Cord leaned against the hitchrail and took off his hat, scratching his head. "We force the issue? Is that what you're saying?"

"Do you want peace, Cord?"

"More than anything. Perhaps we could ride over and talk to . . . ?" He shook his head. "What am I saying? Time for that is over and past. All right, Smoke. All right. Let me hear your plan."

"I don't have one. And it isn't as if I haven't been thinking hard on it. What happened to your sling?"

"I took it off. Damn thing worried me. No plan?"

"No. The ranch, this ranch, must be manned at all times. We agreed on that. If not, it'll end up like Fae's place. And if we keep meeting them like we did back in town, they're going to take us. We were awfully lucky back there, Cord."

"I know. So . . . ?"

"I'm blank. Empty. Except for hit-and-run night fighting. But we'll never get as lucky as we did the other night. Count on that. You can bet that Dooley has that place heavily guarded night and day."

"Wait them out, then. I have the cash money to keep Gage and his boys on the payroll for a long time. But not enough to buy more gunslicks . . . if I could find any we could trust, that is."

"Doubtful. Must be half a hundred range wars going on out here, most of them little squabbles, but big enough to keep a lot of gunhawks working."

"I've written the territorial governor, but no reply as yet."

"I wouldn't count on one, either." Smoke verbally tossed cold water on that. "He's fighting to make this territory a state; I doubt that he'd want a lot of publicity about a range war at this time."

Cord nodded his agreement. "We'll wait a few more days; neither one of us is a hundred percent yet . . ." He paused as a rider came at a hard gallop from the west range.

The hand slid to a halt, out of the saddle and running to McCorkle. "Saddle me a horse!" he yelled to several punchers standing around the corral. "The boys is bringin' in Max, Mister Cord. Looks like Dooley done turned loose that back-shootin' Danny Rouge. Max took one in the back. He's still able to sit a saddle, but just barely. I'll ride into town and fetch Doc Adair." He was gone in a bow-legged run toward the corral.

Cord's face had paled at the news of his oldest son being shot. "I'll have Alice get ready with hot water and bandages. She's a good nurse." He ran up the steps to the house.

Smoke leaned against the hitchrail as his eyes picked up several riders coming in slow, one on either side helping to keep the middle rider in the saddle. Smoke knew, with this news, all of Cord's willingness to talk had gone right out the window. And if Max died . . . ?

Smoke pushed away from the hitchrail and walked toward the bunkhouse. If Max died there would be open warfare; no more chance meetings between the factions involved. It would be bloody and cruel until one side killed off the other.

"Might as well get ready for it," Smoke muttered.

"All we can do is wait," Adair said. "I can't probe for the bullet 'cause I don't know where it is. It angled off from the entry point. It missed the kidney and there is no sign of excessive internal bleeding; so he's got a chance. But don't move him any more than you have to."

Smoke and several others stood listening as Doc Adair spoke with Cord and Alice.

"His chances . . . ?" Cord asked, his voice tired.

"Fifty-fifty." Adair was blunt. "Maybe less than that. Don't get your hopes up too high, Cord. Have someone close by him around the clock. We'll know one way or the other in a few days."

"Did you get him?" Dooley asked the rat-faced Danny Rouge.

"I got him." Danny's voice was high-pitched, more like a woman's voice.

"Good!" Dooley took a long pull from his whiskey bottle, some of the booze dribbling down his unshaven chin. "One less of that bastard's whelps."

He was still mumbling and scratching himself as Danny walked from the room and stepped outside. Dooley's sons were on the porch, sharing a bottle.

"Did he squall when you got him?" Sonny asked, his eyes bright from the cruelty within the young man.

"I 'magine he did," Danny told him. "But I couldn't hear him; I was a good half mile away." Danny stepped from the porch and walked toward the one bunkhouse that was still usable. With the coming in of Dad Estes and his bunch, tents had been thrown up all over the place, the ranch now resembling a guerrilla camp.

The other gunhawks avoided Danny. No one wanted anything to do with him, all feeling that there was something unclean about the young man, even though Danny was as fastidious as possible, considering the time and the place. He was considerate of his personal appearance, but his mind resembled anyone's concept of hell. Danny was a cold-blooded killer. He enjoyed killing, the killing act his substitute for a woman. He would kill anybody: man, woman, or child. It did not make one bit of difference to Danny. Just as long as the price was right.

He went to his bunk and carefully cleaned his rifle, returning it to the hard leather case. Then he stretched out on the bunk and closed his eyes. It had been a very pleasing day. He knew he'd gotten a good clean hit by the way the man had jerked and then slumped in the saddle, slowly tumbling to the ground, hitting the ground like a rag doll.

It was a good feeling knowing he had earned his pay. A day's work for a day's pay. Made a man feel needed. Yes, indeed.

At the Circle Double C, the men sat, mostly in small groups, and mostly in silence, cleaning weapons. The hands, not gunfighters, but just hard-working cowboys, were digging in war bags and taking out that extra holster and pistol, filling the loops of a spare bandoleer. They rode for the brand, and if a fight was what Dooley Hanks wanted, a fight would be what he would get.

The hands who had come over to Cord's side from the D-H did not have mixed feeling about it. They had been shoved aside in favor of gunhawks; they had seen Dooley and his ignorant sons go from bad to savage. There was not one ounce of loyalty left among them toward Dooley. They knew now that this was a fight to the finish. OK. Let's do it.

Just before dusk, Cord walked out to the bunkhouse, a grim expression on his face. "I sent Willie in for the doctor. Max is coughin' up blood. It don't look good. I can't stand to sit in here and look at my wife tryin' to be brave about the whole damn thing when I know that what she really wants to do is bust out bawlin'. And the same goes for me."

Then he started cussing. He strung together some mighty hard words as he stomped around the big room, kicking at this and that; about every fourth and fifth word was Dooley Hanks. He traced the man's ancestry back to before Adam and Eve, directly linking Dooley to the snake in the Garden.

He finally sat down on a bunk and put his face in his hands. Smoke motioned the men outside and gently closed the door, leaving Cord with his grief and the right for a man to cry in private.

"It's gonna be Katy-bar-the-door if that boy dies," Hardrock said. "We just think we've seen a little shootin' up to now."

"I'm ready," Del said. "I'm ready to get this damn thing over with and get back to punchin' cows."

"It's gonna be a while 'fore any of us gets back to doin' that," Les said, one of the men who had come from the D-H.

"And some of us won't," Fitz spoke softly.

Someone had a bottle and that got passed around. Beans pulled out a sack of tobacco and that went the way of the bottle. The men drank and smoked in silence until the bottle was empty and the tobacco sack flat as a tortilla left out in the sun.

"Wonder how Dooley's ass is?" Gage asked, and the men chuckled softly.

"I hope it's healed," Del said. "'Cause it's shore about to get kicked hard."

The men all agreed on that.

Cord came out of the bunkhouse and walked to the house, passing the knot of men without speaking. His face bore the brunt of his inner grief.

Holman got up from his squat and said, "I think I'm gonna go write my momma a letter. She's gettin' on in years and I ain't wrote none in near'bouts a year."

"That's a good idea," Bernie said. "If I tell you what to put on paper to my momma, would you write it down for me?"

"Shore. Come on. I print passable well."

They were happy-go-lucky young cowboys a few weeks ago, Smoke thought. Now they are writing their mothers with death on their minds.

That ghostly rider would be saddling up his fire-snorting stallion, Smoke mused. Ready for more lost souls.

"What are you thinking, *amigo*?" Lujan asked him.

Smoke told him.

"You are philosophical this evening. I had always heard that you were a man who possessed deep thoughts."

Smoke grunted. "My daddy used to say that we came from Wales—years back. Jensen wasn't our real name. I don't know what it was. But Daddy used to say that the Celts were mysterious people. I don't know."

"I know that there is the smell of death in the air," the Mexican said. "Listen. No birds singing. Nothing seems to be moving."

The primal call of a wolf cut the night air, its shivering howl touching them all.

"Folks cut them wolves down," Del spoke out of the darkness. "And I've shot my share of them when they was after beeves. But I ain't got nothing really agin them. They're just doing what God intended them to do. They ain't like we're supposed to be. They can't think like nothin except what they is. And you can't fault them for that. Take a human person now, that's a different story. Dooley and them others, and I know that Dooley's done lost his mind, but I think his greed brung that on. His jealousy and so forth. But them gunning over yonder. They coulda been anything but what they is. They turned to the outlaw trail 'cause they wanted to. What am I tryin' to say anyways?"

Silver Jim stood up and stretched. "It means we can go in smokin' and not have no guilty conscience when we leave them bassards dead where we find them."

Lujan smiled. "Not as eloquently put as might have been, but it certainly summed it up well."

Cord stepped out on the porch just as Doc Adair's buggy pulled up. The men could hear his words plain. "Max just died."

TWENTY-ONE

Max McCorkle, the oldest son of Cord and Alice, and brother to Rock, Troy, and Sandi, was buried the next day. He was twenty-five years old. He was buried in the cemetery on the ridge overlooking the ranch house. Half a dozen crosses were in the cemetery, crosses of men who had worked for the Circle Double C and who had died while in the employment of the spread.

Sandi stood leaning against Beans, softly weeping. Del stood with Fae. Ring stood with Hilda and Hans and Olga. Gage with Liz. Cord stood stony-faced with his wife, a black veil over her face. Parnell stood with Smoke and the other hands and gunfighters. And Smoke had noticed something: the schoolteacher had strapped on a gun.

The final words were spoken over Max, and the family left while the hands shoveled the dirt over the young man's final resting place on this earth.

Parnell walked up to Smoke. "I would like for you to teach me the nomenclature of this weapon and the proper way to fire it."

A small smile touched Smoke's lips, so faint he doubted Parnell even noticed it. "You plannin' on ridin' with us, Cousin?"

The man shook his head. "Regretfully, no. I am not that

good a horseman. I would only be in the way. But someone needs to be here at the ranch with the women. I can serve in that manner."

Smoke stuck out his hand and the schoolteacher, with a surprised look on his face, took it. "Glad to have you with us, Parnell."

"Pleased to be here, Cousin."

"We'll start later on this afternoon. Right now, let's wander on down to the house. Mrs. McCorkle and the others have been cookin' all morning. Big crowd here. I 'spect the neighbors will be visitin' and such all afternoon."

"Funerals are barbaric. Nothing more than a throwback to primitive and pagan rites."

"Is that right?

"Yes. And dreadfully hard on the family."

Weddings and funerals were social events in the West, often drawing crowds from fifty to seventy-five miles away. It was a chance to catch up on the latest gossip, eat a lot of good food—everybody brought a covered dish—and see old friends.

"We got the same thing goin' on up on the Missouri," Smoke heard one man tell Cord. "Damn nesters are tryin' to grab our land. Some of the ranchers have brung in some gunfighters. I don't hold with that myself, but it may come to it. I writ the territorial governor, but he ain't seen fit to reply as yet. Probably never even got the letter."

Smoke moved around the lower part of the ranch house and listened. Few knew who he was, and that was just fine with him.

"Maybe we could get Dooley put in the crazy house," a man suggested. "He's sure enough nuts. All we got to do is find someone to sign the papers."

"No," another said. "There's one more thing: findin' someone stupid enough to serve the papers when Dooley's got hisself surrounded by fifty or sixty gunslicks."

"I wish I could help Cord out, but I'm shorthanded as it is. The damn Army ought to come in. That's what I think."

Smoke heard the words "vigilante" and "regulators" several times. But they were not spoken with very much enthusiasm.

Smoke ate, but with little appetite. Cord was holding up well, but his two remaining sons, Rock and Troy, were geared up for trouble, and unless he could head them off, they would be riding into disaster. He moved to the boys' side, where they stood backed up against a wall, keeping as far away from the crowd as possible.

"You boys best just snuff out your powder fuse," Smoke told them. "Dooley and his bunch will get their due, but for right now, think about your mother. She's got enough grief on her shoulders without you two adding to it. Just settle down."

The boys didn't like it, but Smoke could tell by the looks on their faces his words about their mother had hit home. He felt they would check-rein their emotions for a time. For how long was another matter.

Having never liked the feel of large crowds, Smoke stayed a reasonable time, paid his respects to Cord and Alice, and took his leave, walking back to the bunkhouse to join the other hands.

"When do we ride?" Fitz asked as soon as Smoke had walked in.

"Don't know. Just get that burr out from under your blanket and settle down. You can bet that Dooley is ready and waiting for us right this minute. Let's don't go riding into a trap. We'll wait a few days and let the pot cool its boil. Then we'll come up with something."

Fine words, but Smoke didn't have any plan at all.

They all worked cattle for a few days, riding loose but ready. In the afternoons, Smoke spent several hours each day with Parnell and his pistol. Parnell was very fast, but he couldn't hit anything but air. On the third day, Smoke concluded that the man never would be able to hit the side of a barn, even if he was standing inside the barn. Since they had plenty of rifles, Smoke decided to try the man with a Winchester. To his surprise, Parnell turned out to be a good shot with a carbine.

"You can tote that pistol around if you want to, Parnell," Smoke told him. "But you just remember this: out here, if a man straps on a gun, he best be ready and able to use it. Don't go off the ranch grounds packing a short gun, 'cause somebody's damn sure going to call your hand with it. Stick with the rifle. You're a pretty good shot with it. We got plenty of rifles, so keep half a dozen of them loaded up full at all times."

"I need to go in and get some books and papers from the school."

"I wouldn't advise it, Cousin. You'd just be askin' for trouble. Tell me what you need, and I'll fetch it for you."

"Perhaps," the schoolteacher said mysteriously, and walked away.

Smoke had a feeling that, despite his words, the man was going into town anyway. He'd have to keep an eye on him. He knew Parnell was feeding on his newly found oats, so to speak, and felt he didn't need a baby-sitter. But Smoke had a hunch that Parnell really didn't know or understand the caliber of men who might jump him, prod him into doing something that would end up getting the schoolteacher hurt, or dead.

Smoke spread the word among the men to keep an eye on Parnell.

"Seems to me that Rita's been lookin' all wall-eyed at him the last couple of days," Pistol said. "Shore is a bunch of spoonin' goin' on around here. Makes a man plumb nervous."

"Wal, you can relax, Pistol," Hardrock told him. "No

woman in her right mind would throw her loop for the likes of you. You too damn old and too damn ugly."

"Huh!" the old gunfighter grunted. "You a fine one to be talkin'. You could hire that face of yours out to scare little children."

Smoke left the two old friends insulting each other and walked to the house to speak with Cord, who was sitting on the front porch, drinking coffee.

Cord waved him up and Smoke took a seat.

"I'm surprised Dooley hasn't made a move," the rancher said. "But the men say the range has been clear. Maybe he's counting on that Danny Rouge to pick us off one at a time."

"I doubt that Dooley even knows what's in his mind," Smoke replied. "I've been thinking, Cord. If we could get a judge to him, the judge would declare him insane and stick him in an institution."

"Umm. Might be worth a shot. I can send a rider up to Helena with a letter. I know Judge Ford. Damn! Why didn't I think of that?"

"Maybe he'd like to come down for a visit?" Smoke suggested. "Has he been here before?"

"Several times. Good idea. I'll spell it all out in a letter and get a man riding within the hour. I'll ask him if he can bring a deputy U.S. marshal down with him."

"We just might be able to end this mess," Smoke said, a hopeful note in his voice. "With Dooley out of the picture, Liz could take over the running of the ranch, with Gage to help her, and she could fire the gunslicks."

"It sounds so simple."

"All we can do is try. Have you seen Parnell and Rita?"

"Yeah. They went for a walk. Can't get used to the idea of that schoolteacher packin' iron. It looks funny."

"I warned him about totin' that gun in town."

"And I told Rita not to go into town. However, since I'm not her father, it probably went in one ear and out the other.

Dooley and me told those girls fifteen years ago not to see one another. Did a hell of a lot of good, didn't it? Both those girls are stubborn as mules. Did Parnell get his back up when you warned him?"

"I . . . think perhaps he did. I tell you, Cord, he can get that six-shooter out of leather damn quick. He just can't hit anything with it."

The men chatted for a time, then Smoke left the rancher composing the letter he was sending to Judge Ford. The rider would leave that afternoon. Smoke saddled up and rode out to check on Fae's cattle. As soon as he pulled out, Parnell and Rita left in the buggy, heading for town.

"I shan't be a moment, Rita," Parnell said as they neared Gibson. "I only need to gather up a few articles from the school."

Rita put a hand on Parnell's leg and almost curled his toenails. "Take as long as you like. I'll be waiting for you . . . darling."

Parnell's collar suddenly became very tight.

He gathered up his articles from the school and hurried back to the buggy.

"Would you mind terribly taking me over to Mrs. Jefferson's house, Parnell? I have a dress over there I need to pick up."

"Not at all . . . darling."

Rita giggled and Parnell blushed. He clucked the horse into movement and they went chatting up the main street of Gibson. They did not go unnoticed by a group of D-H gunslicks loafing in front of the Hangout, the busted window now boarded up awaiting the next shipment of glass.

"Yonder goes Miss Sweety-Baby and Sissy-Pants," Golden said, sucking on a toothpick.

"Let's us have some fun when they come back through," Eddie Hart said with a wicked grin.

"What'd you have in mind?"

"We'll drag Sissy-Britches out of that there buggy and strip him nekkid right in the middle of the street; right in front of Pretty-Baby."

They all thought that would be loads of fun.

Golden looked at an old rummy sitting on the steps, mumbling to himself. "What the hell are you mumbling about, old man?"

"I knowed I seed that schoolteacher afore. Now it comes to me."

"What are you talkin' about, you old rum-dum?"

"'Bout fifteen year ago, I reckon it was. Back when Reno was just a sandy collection of saloons and hurdy-gurdy parlors. They was a humdinger of a shootin' one afternoon. This kid come riding in and some hombres decided they'd have some fun with him. In 'bout the time hit'd take you to blink your eyes four times, they was four men in the street, dead or dyin'. The kid was snake quick and on the mark. He disappeared shortly after that." The old man pointed toward the dust trail of the buggy. "That there, boys, is the Reno Kid!"

TWENTY-TWO

"The *Reno Kid*!" Golden hissed, as his front chair legs hit the boardwalk.

"He's right!" Gandy, a member of Cat Jennings's gang almost shouted the words. "I was there! I seen it! That there is shore nuff the Reno Kid. He's all growed up and put on some weight, but that's him!"

"Damn right!" the wino said. "I said it was, din I? I was thar, too."

"That's why he don't never pack no gun," another said. "Who'd have thought it?"

"He's mine," Golden said.

"We'll both take him," Gandy insisted. "Man lak 'at you cain't take no chances with."

"But he ain't packin' no iron!" another said. "Hit'd be murder, pure and simple."

Golden said a cuss word and leaned back in his chair.

"Here they come!" Gandy looked up the street. "To hell with it. I'll force his hand and call him out. Make him git a six-gun."

"I'll keep you covered in case he's packin' a hideout gun," Golden told him.

Both men stood up, Gandy stepping out into the wide street, directly in the path of the buggy.

Parnell whoaed the horse and sat glaring at the gunslick.

Gandy glared back.

"Will you please remove your unwashed and odious presence from the middle of the street, you ignorant lout!" Parnell ordered.

"Whut the hale did you say to me, Reno?"

Parnell blinked and looked at Rita, who was looking at him.

"I'm afraid you have me confused with someone else," Parnell said. "Now kindly step out of the way so we may proceed on our journey."

"Git outta that thar buggy, Reno! I'm a gonna kill you."

"He thinks you're the Reno Kid." Rita gripped Parnell's arm.

"Who, or what, is the Reno Kid?"

"A legendary gunfighter from the Nevada Territory. He'd be about your age now. No one has seen him in fifteen years."

"What the hale-far is y'all whisperin' about?" Gandy hollered. "What'd the matter, Reno, you done turned yeller?"

"I beg your pardon!" Parnell returned the shout. "Begone with you before I give you a proper hiding with a buggy whip, you fool!"

No one seemed to notice the tall, lean, darkly tanned stranger standing in the shadows of the awning in front of the Pussycat. He was wearing a gun, but then, so did nearly every man. He stood watching the goings-on with a faint twinkle of amusement in his dark eyes.

If it got out of hand, he would interfere, but not before.

"Y'all heard it!" Gandy shouted. "He called me a fool! Them's fightin' words, Reno. Now get out of that there buggy."

"I most certainly will not, you . . . you . . . hooligan!"

"I think I'll just snatch your woman outta there and lift her petticoats. Maybe that'll narrow that yeller stripe a-runnin' down your back."

Before he even thought about the consequences, Parnell

stepped from the buggy to the street. His coat was covering his pistol. "I demand you apologize to Miss Rita for that remark, you brute!"

"I ain't a-gonna do no sich of a thing, Reno."

"My name is not Reno and oh, yes, you will!"

"Your name shore as hell is Reno and I will not!"

Gandy could not see most of Parnell for the horse. Parnell brushed back his coat and put his hand on the butt of his gun, removing the leather thong from the hammer and stepping forward, drawing as he walked.

Gandy saw the arm movement and grabbed iron. Parnell stubbed his toe on a rock in the street and fell forward, pulling the trigger. The hammer dropped, the slug striking Gandy right between the eyes and knocking him down, dead before he hit the dirt.

Shocked at what he'd done, Parnell turned, the muzzle pointing toward Golden just as Golden jerked his gun out of leather.

Parnell instinctively cocked and fired, the bullet slamming into Golden's stomach and doubling him over. By this time, Rita had jerked a Winchester out of the boot and eared the hammer back.

"That's it, Reno!" Eddie Hart hollered. "We don't want no more trouble."

Parnell looked at the dead and dying men. He felt sick at his stomach; fought back the nausea as he climbed back into the buggy, first holstering his pistol. He picked up the reins and clucked the mare forward, moving smartly up the street.

"I feel quite ill," Parnell admitted.

"You're so brave!" Rita threw her arms around his neck and gave him a wet kiss in his ear.

Parnell almost lost the rig.

"I seen some fancy shootin' in my days, boys," Pooch Matthews said. "But I ain't never seen nothing like that. Damn, but that Reno is fast."

"Like lightnin'," another said. "Smoke's been holding an ace in the hole all this time."

The stranger walked back into the Pussycat and up to the bar. "You got rooms for rent upstairs?"

"Sure do. Bath's out back. That was some shootin', wasn't it?"

"Yes," the stranger chuckled. "I will admit I have never seen anything like it. I'll take a room; might be here several days."

"Fix you right up. Even give you a clean towel. Them sheets ain't been slept in but once or twice. Maybe three times. Clean sheets'll cost you a quarter."

The stranger laid a quarter down on the bar. "Clean ones, please."

"We ain't got no registry book. But I'm nosy. You ain't from around here, are you?"

"No."

"If you gonna hire on with Dooley, the room is gonna cost you fifty dollars a night."

"I never heard of anyone called Dooley. I'm just tired of riding and would like to rest for a few days."

"Good. Fifty cents a night, then. The schoolteacher is really the Reno Kid. Dadgum! How about that? Where are you from, mister?"

"Oh, over Nevada way."

"Dammit, Parnell!" Smoke grabbed the reins behind the driving bit. "I told you not to go into town wearin' that gun."

"He's the Reno Kid!" Rita shouted, and everybody within hearing range turned and came running. "I just watched him beat two gunnies to the draw and kill them both. Right in front of the Hangout."

Smoke looked at Parnell, shock in his eyes. "You *hit* something? With a pistol?"

"I stubbed my toe. The gun went off. I am not the Reno Kid."

"He ain't the Reno Kid!" Charlie said. "I been knowin' Reno for twenty years."

Parnell turned to Rita. "You see. I told you repeatedly that I am not the Reno Kid."

"Oh, I know that, honey. But I sure got everybody's attention, didn't I?" She hopped from the buggy and raced over to Sandi to tell her story.

"Reno changed his name about fifteen years ago and went to ranchin' up near the Idaho border." Charlie cleared it up. "But he shore left a string of bodies while he was gun-slingin'."

Smoke turned back to Parnell. "You really got them both?"

"One was hit between the eyes. I'm sure he's dead. The lout called Golden took a round in the stomach. If he isn't dead, he'll certainly be incapacitated for a very long time."

"What the hell is in-capassiated?" Hardrock muttered.

"Beats me," Pistol said. "Sounds plumb awful, though."

Parnell climbed down from the buggy and Corgill led the rig to the barn. Smoke faced the man. "All right, Parnell. You're tagged now. There'll be hundred guns looking for you . . ."

"That is perfectly ridiculous!" Parnell cut in. "I am not the Reno Kid!"

"That don't make no difference," Silver Jim told him. "This time tomorrow the story will be spread fifty miles that the Reno Kid has surfaced and is back on the prowl. By this time next week it'll be all over the territory and they'll be no tellin' how many two-bit punks and would-be gunhawks comin' in to make their rep. By killin' you. Welcome to the club, Schoolteacher," he added bitterly.

Charlie patted Parnell on the back. "You go git out of them town duds, Parnell. The four of us is gonna take you under our wing and teach you how to handle that there Colt."

Parnell stood with his mouth open, unable to speak.

"But Parnell don't sound like no gunfighter's name to me," Silver Jim said. "Where was you born, Parnell?"

"In Iowa. On the Wolf River."

"That's it!" Charlie exclaimed. "You ain't the Reno Kid, so from now on, your handle is Wolf."

"Wolf!" Parnell stared at the man. "Have you taken leave of your senses?"

"Nope. Wolf, it is. The Wolf is on the prowl. I like it."

"This is madness!" Parnell yelled.

"Go on now, Wolf," Hardrock told him. "Git you some jeans and boots. Strap on and tie down that hogleg. We'll set up a target range."

"See you in a few minutes, Wolf." Pistol grinned at him.

"This is absurd!" Parnell muttered. He started up the steps, tripped, and fell facedown on the porch. He picked himself up with as much dignity as possible and entered the house.

Charlie shook his head. "We got our work cut out for us, boys."

Golden died that night, cursing the man he believed to be the Reno Kid as he slipped across that dark river. Twenty-four hours later, a dozen men were riding for Gibson, their burning ambition to be the one man who faced the Reno Kid and brought him down. Another twenty-four later, two dozen more punks and tinhorns would be on their way, until those looking to make a reputation by killing the Reno Kid would grow to a hundred. And the news had spread that Smoke Jensen was really in Gibson—nobody had believed it up to now; indeed, many people believed that Smoke Jensen really did not exist, he was such an elusive figure.

Telegraph wires began humming and a dozen big newspapers sent reporters into Montana to cover the story. Within a week, Gibson had a brand-spanking-new hotel and had been added to the stagecoach route.

The stranger from Nevada decided to stay, watching all the fuss with amusement in his eyes, spending most of his time sitting in a chair under the awning in front of the Pussycat.

Dooley had pulled in his men, cussing at all the notoriety and knowing this was no time to enlarge the range war. The hate within the man continued to fester, ready to erupt at any moment, spewing blood and violence all over the area.

Judge Ford was at some sort of conference, out of the state, and would be back in about a month.

"Another good idea shot down," Cord said, disgusted at the news.

Four more saloons had been thrown up in Gibson, along with several more stores, including a gunshop, a dress shop—for a lot of ladies of the evening were coming in—an apothecary shop, and another general store.

A lot had happened in a week.

Thanks to the Reno Kid, aka Parnell.

"We found out what was wrong with Wolf not bein' able to shoot worth a damn," Charlie told Smoke.

Smoke closed his eyes for a few seconds and shook his head. "Wolf," he muttered. "What a name. What was wrong with him, Charlie?"

"He's scared of guns! Pistols 'specially."

"Good God! Charlie, there's about a hundred people in Gibson—new people—with one thought in mind: to kill the Reno Kid, real name Parnell, now called Wolf. He's a schoolteacher, Charlie. Not a gunfighter. The poor man is a walking target."

Hardrock grinned. "But we come up with something, Smoke. Lookee here." He held up the ugliest and most awesome-looking rig Smoke had ever seen.

"What in God's name . . . !"

The old gunfighters had taken two double-barreled

shotguns and sawed the barrels down to about ten inches long. They had then fashioned a pistol-type butt for the terrible weapons.

"Those things would break a man's arm!" Smoke said, eyeballing the rigs.

"Not Wolf's arm. For a schoolteacher, he's powerful strong. And he's just as fast with these here things as he is with a pistol," Silver Jim said with a nearly toothless grin.

"That's all the booming I been hearing."

"Right! Man, Wolf is plumb awesome with these here things," Pistol said. "We got 'um loaded up with rusty nails and ball bearin's and raggedly little rocks and the like. We done loaded up near'bouts a case of shells for him. He's ready to go huntin' him a rep."

"Pistol, Parn . . . Wolf doesn't want a rep," Smoke said.

Charlie grinned. "You ain't seen much of him for a week, Smoke. You gonna be ass-tonished at the change. Come on."

Smoke was more than astonished. He didn't even recognize the man. Parnell had grown a mustache, and that had completely changed his appearance. He was dressed all in black, from his hat down to his polished boots. He looked very capable and very tough.

"I gotta see him draw and cock and fire these hand cannons," Smoke said.

"With pleasure, Cousin." Parnell strapped on the weapons.

"You watch this," Charlie said, as Cord and several others gathered around.

Pistol and Silver Jim rolled several full water barrels out and backed away.

"They's a-facin' you, Wolf!" Charlie said, excitement in his voice. "Watch 'um now. Watch they eyes. That'll give 'em away ever time."

Parnell tensed, his hands hovering over the butts of the terrible weapons.

"They's about ready to make their play!" Hardrock called out. "You got to take out the man on your left first, he's the bad one."

"Now!" Silver Jim yelled.

Parnell's right hand dipped and his left hand came across to support the sawed-off shotgun. One barrel exploded in a roar of gunsmoke, the second barrel was shattered as Parnell let loose the second charge. As fast as anything Smoke had ever seen—considering the cumbersome weapons he was using—Parnell dropped the first sawed-off to the ground and drew the left-hand shotgun. The third barrel was reduced to splinters.

"I'm impressed," Smoke said.

"I'm proud of you, Brother!" Fae said.

"I love you!" Rita yelled.

Hardrock looked close at Parnell and shook his head. "Furst time I ever seen a wolf blush!"

TWENTY-THREE

"Feel like trying out the new general store?" Cord asked Smoke.

"I thought you'd never ask. I forgot to pick up some tobacco last time in."

"Ah . . . Parnell wants to go along. I refuse to call him Wolf. I just can't!"

Smoke laughed. "I can't either. Sure, if he wants to come along. I notice he's been in the saddle for the last week. He's turned out to be a pretty good rider."

"Man is full of surprises. And speaking of surprises, I'm told that we're all in for a surprise when we see what's happening, or has happened, to Gibson."

"Yeah. I hear there's even a paper."

"*The Gibson Express*. I want to pick up a copy."

"How about your boys?"

"I ordered them to stay close to their ma. They'll obey me."

"I'll put on a clean shirt and meet you out front."

Cord, Smoke, Parnell, Lujan, Beans, Del, Charlie, and Ring rode into Gibson. A wagon rattled along behind them to carry the supplies back, Cal at the reins. At the edge of town, they reined up and stared in disbelief. The once tiny and sleepy little town was now a full three blocks long and several blocks deep on either side. Many of the new stores were no more than knocked-together sideboards with canvas tops, but it was still a very impressive sight.

"This spells trouble, gentlemen," Lujan said.

"Yeah," Charlie agreed, standing up in his stirrups for a moment. "You bet your boots it does."

"I fail to see how the advancement of civilization, albeit at first glance quite primitive in nature, could be called trouble," Parnell stated.

"That town ain't filled with nothin' but trash," Charlie told him. "Hurdy-gurdy girls, tinhorn hustlers and pimps, two-bit gunslingers, slick-fingered gamblers, and the like. It's dyin' while it seems to be growin'. As soon as this war is settled, one way or the other, ninety-nine percent of them down yonder will pull up stakes and haul their ashes. Town will be right back where it started from."

"How about the one percent that will stay?" Parnell questioned.

"Good point," Charlie agreed. "Wolf, you stay on top of things down yonder in that town. They's gonna be a bunch of people eyeballin' ever move you make. And you gonna get called out. Bet on it."

"I am aware of that," the schoolteacher turned gunfighter said. "I am ready to confront whatever comes my way."

"Me and you, Parnell," Beans said, "will have us a cool beer in one of them new saloons. Check things out."

Parnell glanced at him. "I detest the taste of beer. However, I might have a sarsaparilla."

The Moab Kid returned the glance. "You go sashayin' up in a saloon in the middle of a bunch of hardcases and order sodee pop, Parnell, you better be ready for trouble, 'cause it's shore gonna be comin' at you."

"I am aware of that, too."

"Let's go," Smoke said.

The men rode slowly toward the now-crowded street of the

West's newest boomtown. The news of their arrival spread as quickly as a prairie fire across dry grass. In less than a minute, the wide street had emptied. No one wanted to be caught in the middle of a gunfight, and that was something that everybody knew might be, probably was, only a careless word away.

As the men rode past the Pussycat, Charlie cut his flint-hard eyes to a stranger sitting on the boardwalk, his chair tilted back. Charlie smiled faintly.

Gonna get real interestin' around here, Charlie thought.

Ring reined up in front of Hans and dismounted. "I shall be visiting Hilda," he told them. "I will come immediately if there is trouble."

Cord, Del, and Cal pulled up in front of the new general store. "Which one of those new joints are you boys going to try?" Cord asked.

"How about Harriet's House?" Parnell asked. "That sounds quite congenial."

"Oh, I'm sure it will be," Beans said. "Harriet always runs a stable out back."

"Well, then, that will be a convenient place for our horses."

"A stable of wimmin, Parnell," Beams told him. "For hire."

"You mean . . . I . . . ladies who sell their . . . ?"

"Right, Parnell."

Smoke dismounted and almost bumped into a small man wearing a derby hat and a checkered vest. The man's head struck Smoke about chest-high.

"Horace Mulroony's the name, sir. Owner and editor of *The Gibson Express*. And you would be Smoke Jensen?"

"That's right."

Horace stuck out his hand and Smoke took it, quickly noticing that the hand was hard and calloused. He cut his eyes just for a flash and saw that the stocky man's hands were thick with calluses around the knuckles. A Cornish boxer sprang into Smoke's mind. Not very tall, but built like a boxcar. Something silently told him that Horace would be hard to handle.

"And your friends, Mister Jensen?"

Smoke introduced the man all around, pointing them out. "Charlie Starr, Lujan, the Moab Kid, Parnell Jensen."

"The man they're calling the Reno Kid."

"I am not the Reno Kid."

"Name's Wolf," Charlie said shortly. He didn't like newspaper people; never wanted any truck with them. They never got anything right and was always meddlin' in other folks' business.

"I see," Horace scribbled in his notebook. "That is quite an unusual affair strapped around your waist, Wolf."

"I would hardly call two sawed-off shotguns an affair, Mister Mulroony. But since this is no time to be discussing proper English usage, I will let your misunderstanding of grammer be excused—for now."

Mulroony laughed with high Irish humor. "You sound like a schoolteacher, Wolf."

"I am."

"Ummm. Are you gentlemen going to have a taste in Miss Harriet's saloon?"

"We was plannin' on it," Charlie said. "The sooner the better. All this palaverin' is makin' me thirsty."

"Do you mind if I join you?"

"Could we stop you?" Charlie asked.

"Of course not!" Horace grinned. "After you, Mister Starr." He waved at a man toting a bulky box camera and the man came at a trot. Horace grinned at the gunfighters. "One never knows when a picture might be available. I like to record events for posterity."

Charlie grunted and pushed past the smaller man, but not before he saw the stranger leave his chair in front of the Pussycat and walk across the street, toward the saloon they were entering.

Charlie had a hunch the stranger was thinking about joining the game. He knew from experience that the man was a sucker for the underdog.

The saloon was filled with hardcases, both real and imagined. Smoke's wise and knowing eyes immediately picked out the real gunslingers from the tinhorn punks looking for a reputation.

Smoke knew a few of the hardcases in the room. Several from Dad Estes's gang were sitting at a table. A few that had left Cord's spread were there. A couple of Cat Jennings's bunch were present. They didn't worry Smoke as much as the young tinhorns who were sitting around the saloon, their guns all pearl-handled and fancy-engraved and tied down low.

The known and experienced gunhandlers had stiffened when their eyes touched the awesome rig belted around Parnell's waist. Nobody in their right mind wanted to tangle with a sawed-off shotgun, since a buckshot load at close range would literally tear a man in two. Even if a man could get lead into the shotgun toter first, the odds were, unless the bullet struck him in the brain or the heart, that he could still pull a trigger.

"Beer," Smoke said.

"Tequila," Lujan ordered.

Beans and Charlie opted for whiskey.

Horace ordered beer.

Parnell, true to his word, looked the barkeep in the eyes and ordered sarsaparilla.

Several young punks seated at a nearby table started laughing and making fun of Parnell.

Parnell ignored them.

The barkeep served up the orders.

"What's the matter with you, slick?" a young man laughed the question. "Cain't you handle no real man's drink?"

Parnell took a sip of his sarsaparilla and smiled, setting the bottle down on the bar. He turned and looked the young man in the eyes. "Does your mother know where you are, junior?"

The punk's eyes narrowed and he opened his mouth to retort just as the batwings swung open and the stranger entered.

There is an aura about really bad men, and in the West a bad man was not necessarily an outlaw. He was just a bad man to fool with. The stranger walked between the punk and Parnell, his hands hanging loosely at his side. He wore one gun, a classic Peacemaker .45, seven-and-a-half-inch barrel. It was tied down. The man looked to be in his mid-to-late thirties, deeply tanned and very sure of himself. He glanced at Parnell's drink and a very slight smile creased his lips.

Walking to Charlie's side, he motioned to the barkeep. "A sarsaparilla, please."

Another loudmouth sitting with the punk started giggling. "Another sissy, Johnny. You reckon they gonna kiss each other?"

"I wouldn't be surprised."

The barkeep served up the stranger's drink and backed away, to the far end of the bar. When they had entered, the bar had been full. Now only the seven of them remained at the long bar.

The stranger lifted his bottle. "A toast to your good health," he said to Charlie.

Charlie lifted his shot glass and clinked it against the bottle. "To your health," he replied. If the man wanted to reveal his real identity. That was up to him. Charlie would hold the secret.

"Hey, old man!" Johnny hollered. "You with them wore-out jeans on."

Charlie sipped his whiskey and then turned to face the mouthy punk. "You talkin' to me, boy?"

"I ain't no boy!"

"No," Charlie said slowly, drawling out the word. "I reckon you ain't. Strappin' on them guns makes you a man. A loud-mouth who ain't dry behind the ears yet. And if you keep flappin' them lips at me, you ain't never gonna be dry behind your dirty ears."

Johnny stood up, his face flushed red. "Just who the hell do you think you are, old man?"

"Charlie Starr."

The words were softly offered, but they had all the impact of a hard slap across Johnny's face.

Johnny's mouth dropped open. He closed it and swallowed hard a couple of times. Beads of sweat formed on his forehead.

Charlie spoke, his words cracking like tiny whips. "Sit down, shut your goddamned mouth, or make your play, punk!"

The experienced gunhandlers had noticed first off that the men at the bar had entered with the leather thongs off their hammers.

"You cain't talk to me lak 'at!" Johnny found his voice. But it was trembly and high-pitched.

"I just did, boy."

Johnny abruptly sat down. He tried to pick up his beer mug but his hand was shaking so badly he spilled some of it on the tabletop.

Charlie turned his back to the mouthy punk and picked up his shot glass in his left hand.

But there wasn't a man or woman in the bar who thought it was over. The punk would settle down, gulp a few more drinks to boost his nerve, and would have to try Charlie, or leave town with his tail tucked between his legs.

"Been a long time, Charlie," the stranger said.

"Near'bouts ten years, I reckon. You just passin' through?"

"I was. I decided to stay."

"What name you goin' by nowadays?"

"Same name that got hung on me seventeen-eighteen years ago."

Being a reporter—Charlie would call it being a snoop, among other things—Horace leaned around and asked, "And what name is that, sir?"

The stranger turned around, facing the crowd of punks and tinhorns, loudmouths and barflys, hurdy-gurdy girls, gamblers, and gunfighters, who were all straining to listen. He let his eyes drift around the room. "I never did like a lopsided fight, Charlie. You recall that, I suppose." It was not posed in question form.

"I allow as to how I do. I 'member the time me and you stood up to a whole room filled to the rafters with trash and cleaned it out." He chuckled. "That there was a right good fight." Charlie held up his shot glass in salute and the stranger clinked his sarsaparilla bottle to the glass.

"I got my other gun in my kit over to the roomin' house. reckon I best go on over and get it and strap it on. Looks like got some house-cleanin' to do."

"I couldn't agree more."

Smoke was smiling, nursing his beer. He'd already figured who the stranger was.

One of Cat Jennings's men lifted his leg and broke wind. "That's what I think about you, stranger."

"How rude!" Parnell said.

"Sissy-pants," the man who had made the coarse social comment stood up. "I think I'll just kill you. 'Cause I don't believe you're the Reno Kid."

"Of course, he isn't," the stranger said. "I am!"

TWENTY-FOUR

That news broke the spirit of a couple of men who had already been toying with the idea of rattling their hocks. They stood up and walked toward the door. Charlie Starr and them old gray-headed he-cougars with him was bad enough. Add the Moab Kid and Lujan to that mixture and you was stirrin' nitro too fast with a flat stick. Smoke Jensen was the fastest gun in the West. Now here comes the Reno Kid, and there goes anybody with a lick of sense.

The batwings squeaked and two gunnies were gone.

The gunhand facing Parnell didn't back down. Without taking his eyes from Parnell, he said, "Did anybody pull your chain, Reno?"

"Nope," Reno answered easily.

"You gonna fight Sissy-pants's battles for him?"

"Nope."

"You ready to die, Sissy-pants?"

"Oh, I think not." Parnell had turned, facing the man, his right hand hovering near the butt of the holstered sawed-off. "But I do have a question?"

"Ax it!"

"What is your name?"

"Readon. What's it to you?"

"I just wondered what to have carved on the marker over your grave."

"Draw, damn your eyes!" the man shouted, and grabbed for his six-gun.

Parnell was calm and quick. Up came the awesome weapon, the right-side hammer eared back. Across went his left hand in a practiced move, gripping the short barrels. The range was no more than twelve feet and the booming was enormous in the beery, smoky room. The ball bearings and rusty nails and ragged rocks hit the gunhand in the belly and lifted him off his boots while the charge was tearing him apart. He landed on a table several feet away from where he had been standing, smearing the tabletop with crimson and collapsing the table. He had never even cleared leather.

The hurdy-gurdy girls began squalling like hogs caught in barbed wire and ran from the room, their short dresstails flapping as they ran.

Parnell, seeing that no one was going to immediately take up the fight, but sensing that was only seconds away, broke open the shotgun pistol and tossed aside the empty, loading it up full. He snapped it shut and eared back both hammers.

The gunhand Smoke had first seen at that little store down on the Boulder stood up. "Me and Readon had become pals, Jensen," Dunlap said. "You a friend of that shotgun-toter, so that makes you my enemy. I think I'll just kill you."

He grabbed for his guns.

Smoke shot Dunlap in the chest just as his hands gripped the butts of his guns. Dunlap looked puzzled for a moment, coughed up blood, and sat down in the chair he should never have gotten out of. He slowly put his head on the tabletop and sighed as that now-familiar ghost rider came galloping up, took a look around, and grinned in a macabre fashion. He

decided to stick around. Things were quite lively in this
little town.

The ghost rider put a bony hand on another's shoulder as
half the men in the barroom grabbed for iron and Lujan shot
one between the eyes.

Mulroony jumped behind the bar and landed on top of
the barkeep, who was already on the floor. He'd been a bartender in too many western towns not to know where the
safest place was.

Parnell's sawed-off shotgun-pistol roared again, the charge
knocking two gunnies to the floor. Johnny picked that time
to make his move. Just as he was reaching for his guns, Parnell stepped the short distance as he was reversing the weapon.
Using it like a club, he hit Johnny in the mouth. Teeth flew in
several directions and Johnny was out cold. Parnell dropped
to the floor and once more loaded up.

The Reno Kid was crouched by the bar, coolly and carefully picking his shots.

Charlie had dropped two before a bullet took him in the
shoulder and slammed him against the bar. He did a fast
border-roll with his six-gun and kept on banging. When his
gun was empty, Lujan grabbed the older man and literally
slung him over the bar, out of the line of fire.

The Moab Kid took a round in the leg and the leg buckled
under him, dropping him to the floor, his face twisted in pain.

But it was Parnell who was dishing out the most death
and destruction. Firing and loading as fast as he could, the
schoolteacher did the most to clear out the room and end
the fighting.

The gunnies and tinhorns gave it up, one by one dropping their still-smoking six-guns and raising their hands in
the air. Cord, Del, Ring, and Cal stepped through the batwings, pistols drawn and cocked, Ring with his double-barrel
express gun.

"Get Doc Adair," Smoke said, his voice husky from the thick gunsmoke in the saloon.

Cal was gone at a bow-legged trot to fetch the doctor.

Lujan helped Charlie to a chair. The front of the old gunslinger's shirt was soaked with blood.

"Did I get the old bassard?" a gunhawk moaned the question from the floor. He had taken half a dozen rounds in the chest and stomach and death was standing over him, ready to take him where the fires were hot and the company not the best.

"You got lead in me," Charlie admitted. "But I'm a long ways from accompanyin' you."

"If not today, then some other time. So I'll see you in hell, Starr," the gunny grinned the words, his mouth bloody. He started to add something, but the words would not form on his tongue. His eyes rolled back in his head and he mounted up behind the ghost rider.

Smoke had reloaded. He stood by the bar, his hands full of Colts, his eyes watching the gunnies who had chosen to give up the fight.

Johnny moaned on the floor and rolled over on his stomach, one hand holding his busted mouth. The other hand went to his right-hand gun. But it was gone.

"Are you looking for these?" Parnell asked, holding out the punk's guns in his left hand. His right hand was full of twelve-gauge sawed-off blaster.

Johnny mumbled something.

"Your diction is atrocious," Parnell told him. He looked at Smoke and smiled. "My, Cousin, but for a few moments, it was quite exhilarating."

Smoke grinned and shook his head. "Yeah, it was, Parnell. I'll stand shoulder to shoulder with you anytime, Cousin."

Mulroony had crawled from behind the bar and waved his photographer in. The man set up his bulky equipment and sprinkled the powder in the flashpan. "Smile, everyone!" he hollered, then popped his shot, adding more smoke to the already eye-smarting air.

Beans had cut his jeans open to inspect the wound, and it was a bad one. "Leg's busted," he said tightly. "Looks like I'm out of it."

The flashpan popped again, the lenses taking in the bloody sprawl of bodies and the line of gunhawks standing against a wall, their hands in the air, their weapons piled on a table.

While Doc Adair tended to Charlie and Beans, Smoke faced the surrendered gunhandlers. His eyes were as cold as chips of ice and his words flint-hard.

"You're out of it. Get on your horses and ride. If I see any of you in this area again, I'll kill you! No questions asked. I'll just shoot you. And no, you don't pack your truck, you don't get your guns, you don't draw your pay—you ride! Now! Move!"

They needed no further instrucitons. They all knew there would be another time, another place, another showdown time. They rushed the batwings and rattled their hocks, leaving in a cloud of dust.

"You tore up my place!" a woman squalled, stepping out of a back room.

"Howdy, Harriet," Beans called. "Right nice to see you again."

"You!" she hollered. "I might have known it'd be you, Moab." Her eyes flicked to the Reno Kid. "You back gunhandlin', Reno?"

"I reckon."

She looked at Smoke. Took in his rugged good looks and heavy musculature. "Remember me, big boy?"

"I remember you, Harriet. You were one of the smart ones who left Fontana early."

"Did you kill Tilden Franklin?"

"I sure did."

"Man ever deserved killin', that one did. You gonna run me out of Gibson?"

"I didn't run you out of Fontana, Harriet."

"For a fact. See you around, baby." She turned and pushed through a door.

"He can't sit a saddle," Adair said, standing up from working on Beans's leg. "And I'd rather he didn't for a few days." The doctor pointed to Charlie.

"I'll put some hay in the wagon," Cal said, and left the saloon.

The undertaker and his helper, both of them trying very hard to keep from smiling, entered the saloon and walked among the dead and dying, pausing at each body to go through the pockets.

"Does I get my guns back?" Johnny pushed the words through mashed lips and broken teeth.

Parnell looked at Smoke. Smoke nodded his head. "Give them to the punk. He'd just find some more. One of us is gonna have to kill him sooner or later."

The flashpan belched once again.

"What a story this will make!" Horace chortled, rocking back and forth on his feet. "I shall dispatch it immediately to New York City."

"Do try to be grammatically correct," Parnell reminded him.

Horace gave him a smile. A very thin smile.

Sandi hollered and bawled and carried on something fierce when she saw Beans in the back of the wagon but then brightened up considerably when she realized he'd be laid up for several weeks and she could nurse him.

Reno had checked out of his room and rode back to the

Circle Double C with the men. He had strapped on his other
Peacemaker and was in the fight to the finish.

Charlie bitched about having to be bedded down in the
main house so the ladies could take proper care of his wound.
Hardrock told him to shet his mouth and think about what a
relief it would be to the others not to have to look at his ugly
face for a spell.

"It works both ways," Charlie popped back, smiling as the
ladies fussed over him.

Parnell had taken a slight bullet burn on his left arm. But
the way Rita acted a person would have thought he'd been
near killed. She insisted on spoon-feeding him some hot soup
she fixed—just for him.

"What did we accomplish?" Cord asked Smoke.

"Damn little," he admitted. "Seems like every time we run
off or kill a gunhawk, there's ten to step up, taking his place."

Cord added some more numbers in his tally book and
shook his head at the growing number of dead and wounded.
"Why did the Reno Kid toss in with us, Smoke? Charlie says
he's married, with several children."

"So am I," Smoke reminded the man.

Something good did come out of the gunfight inside
Harriet's saloon: many of the hangers-on decided to pull out;
the fight was getting too hot for many of the tinhorns and
would-be gunfighters. They'd go back to their daddy's farms
and be content to milk the cows and gather the eggs, their
guns hanging on a peg.

But it left the true hardcases, many of them on no one's
payroll. Like buzzards, they were waiting to see the outcome
and perhaps pick up a few crumbs of the pie.

Johnny and his punk sidekick, Bret, were still in town,
swaggering around, hanging on the fringes of the known

gunslingers, talking rough and tough and lapping up the strong beer and rotgut and snake-head whiskey served at most of the newer saloons.

Crime had increased in Gibson, with foot-padders and petty thieves plying their trade on the unsuspecting men and women who had to venture out after dark. And the hardcases were getting surly and hard to handle, craving action.

There were several minor run-ins among the gunhawks, provoked by recklessness and restlessness and booze and the urge to kill and destroy. The leaders of the gangs had to step in and calm the situation, reminding the outlaws that their fight was not with each other, but with the Double Circle C.

"Then gawddammit!" Lodi snarled. "Let's *make war* on them!"

The Hangout, jammed full of hired guns, shook with the roars of approval.

Dad Estes did his best to shout his boys down while Jason Bright and Cat Jennings and Lanny Ball tried to calm their people.

They were only half successful.

The leaders looked at each other and shrugged their shoulders. Dad jerked his head toward the boardwalk and the men stomped outside, to stand in the night.

"We got to use them or lose them," Dad summed it up. "My boys ain't gonna stand around here much longer twiddlin' their thumbs."

The others agreed with Dad.

"So you got some sort of a plan, Dad?"

"We hit them, tonight."

"What does Dooley have to say about that?" Jason asked.

"I ain't discussed it with him."

The others smiled, Dad continuing, "Look here, we could turn this into a right nice town, and if we was all big landowners, why, we'd also own the sheriff and deputies and the like."

"We got to kill Dooley and them first," he was reminded by Cat Jennings.

Dad shifted his chewing tobacco to the other side of his mouth. He took out an ornate pocket watch and clicked it open. "Well, boys, I got some people doin' that little thing in about an hour."

TWENTY-FIVE

Dooley came awake, keeping his eyes closed. The slight creaking of the hall door had brought him awake. He had drank himself to sleep, sitting in the big chair just inside the living room. The first time he'd ever done that. Now wide awake, he sat very still in the darkness and opened his eyes.

"I tole you to oil that door!" his oldest boy, Sonny, hissed the words.

"Shet your mouth," Bud whispered. "The old fool was prob'ly so drunked up when he went to bed a shotgun blast wouldn't wake him up."

Conrad giggled. "A shotgun blast is what we're goin' to give him!"

Cold insane fury washed over the father as he froze still in his chair. If he'd had a gun in his hand, he'd have killed all three of them right this minute. But his gun belt was hanging on the peg in the hall.

Sonny shushed his brothers. "Stay here and keep watch, Conrad. Me and Bud will do the deed."

"I don't wanna keep no watch! I wanna see it when the buckshot hits him. And what the hell is I gonna be watchin' for anyways? There ain't nobody here but us. The others is all back in town."

"Do what I tell you to do."

Dooley carefully drew his feet up under the chair, hiding them from view should any of his traitorous offspring look into the living room. The sorry sons of bitches.

The dark humor and irony of that thought almost caused him to chuckle.

The stillness of the house was shattered by twin shotgun blasts.

Then he remembered he hadn't made up his bed from the past night; the pillows and covers must have fooled the boys into thinking their dad was lying in bed.

Boots ran up the hall. "Got the old nut-brain!" Sonny shouted. "The ranch is ourn. Let's go join the other boys and finish the deed."

The front door slammed shut.

What deed? Dooley thought.

The thunder of hooves hammered past the house. Dooley moved to the window and watched his bastard sons gallop out of sight.

That damn Cord put them up to this! Dooley's fevered brain quickly reached that conclusion. He jerked on his boots and ran into the hall, pausing to yank his gun belt from the peg and belt it around his waist. He ran to the kitchen and filled a gunnybag with cans of food, a side of bacon, some hardtack. He took a big canteen and filled that at the kitchen pump. Then he ran to the study and quickly opened his safe, stuffing a money belt full of cash money he'd just received from the army cattle buyer. He belted the money bag around his middle. In his bedroom, he rolled up some clothes in a blanket and slipped out the back of the house, stopping only once, to fill his pockets with .44 rounds and pick up a small coffeepot and skillet.

Dooley saddled a horse and stuffed the saddlebags full of supplies. He hung the canteen and bag on the saddle horn and took off into the timber of the Little Belt Mountains. When his boys come back, they'd find that what they'd shot was only a bed, and they'd come lookin' to kill their pa.

"Come on, you miserable whelps," Dooley muttered, talking to his horse. His best horse. His favorite horse. Dooley could sleep in the saddle and his horse would never falter. The horse also knew where Dooley was going as soon as Dooley guided the way toward the old Indian trail that wound in a circuitous route to the base of Old Baldy, the highest peak in the Little Belts, which ran for some forty miles from southeast of Great Falls to the Musselshell. Dooley and his horse had come here often, just to think—to let the hate fester over the past few years.

"Goddamn you, Cord," Dooley muttered. "You heped take my woman from me and now you done turned my sons agin me. I'm a-gonna kill ever' one of you. Ever' stinkin' one of you!"

"Here they come!" the shout from Smoke was only seconds before the mass of riders entered the Circle Double C ranch complex. But it was enough to roust everybody out of bed.

Smoke's shout was followed by a war whoop from Hardrock that echoed across the draws and hollows and grazing land of the ranch.

"Hep me clost to that winder." Charlie told Parnell. "I'll take it from there. I can shoot jist as good with my left hand as I can with my right."

Across the hall, Beans told Sandi, "Get some help and shove my bed to that window and hand me my rifle. Then you and Rita get on the floor."

The girls positioned the bed and reached for their own rifles.

"Cain't you wimmin take orders?" Beans asked over the thunder of hooves.

"We stand by our men," Sandi told him. "Now shut up and shoot!"

"Yes, dear," Beans said, just as a bullet from an outlaw's gun knocked a pane of glass out of the window.

Before Beans could sight the rider in, Parnell's sawed-off blaster roared, the charge lifting the man out of the saddle and hurling him to the ground, his chest and throat a bloody mess.

"Give 'em hell, baby!" Rita shouted her approval.

"You curb that vulgar tongue, woman!" Parnell glared at her.

"Yes, dear," Rita muttered.

From the bunkhouse, Ring was deadly with a rifle, knocking two out of the saddle before a round misfired and jammed the action. Ring turned just as a man was crawling in through a rear window. Reversing the Winchester, Ring used the rifle like a club and smashed the outlaw on the forehead with the butt. The sound of a skull cracking was evident even over the hard lash of gunfire. Ring grabbed up the man's Colts and moved to a window. He wasn't very good with a pistol, but he succeeded in filling the night with a lot of hot lead and made the evening very uncomfortable for a number of outlaws.

Smoke and the Reno Kid had grabbed up rifles and bandoleers of ammunition and raced to the barn and corral, knowing that if the outlaws succeeded in stampeding their horses they were doomed. Reno climbed into the loft, with Jake and Corgill. Fitz, Willie, and Ol' Cook stayed below, while Smoke and Gage remained outside, behind watering troughs by the corral.

The outlaw, Hartley, who was wanted for murder down in the Oklahoma Nations, tried to rope the corral gates and bring them down. Smoke leveled his pistol and the hammer fell on an empty chamber. Running to the man, Smoke jerked him off his horse and smashed the man in the face with a balled right fist, then a left to the man's jaw. He jerked Hartley's pistol from leather and rapped the outlaw on the head-bone with it. Hartley lay still in the dirt.

Smoke stuck both of Hartley's pistols behind his belt, reloaded his own .44s, and climbed onto Hartley's horse, a big dun. He would see how the outlaws liked the fight taken to them.

Smoke charged right into the middle of the confusing dust-filled fray. He saw the young punk gunslick Twain and shot him out of the saddle; one of Twain's boots caught in the stirrup. Twain's horse bolted, dragging the wounded and screaming young punk across the yard. His screaming stopped when his head impacted against a tree stump.

Smoke stayed low in the saddle, offering as little target as possible for the outlaws' guns. He slammed the horse's shoulder into an outlaw's leg. The gunny screamed in pain from his bruised leg and then began screaming in earnest as the horse lost its balance and fell on him, breaking the outlaw's other leg. The horse scrambled to its feet, the steel-shod hooves ripping and tearing flesh and breaking the outlaw's bones.

Cat Jennings rammed his big gelding into Smoke's horse and knocked Smoke to the ground. Rolling away from the hooves of the panicked horse, Smoke jumped behind a startled outlaw, stuck a pistol into the man's side, and pulled the trigger. Shoving the wounded man out of the saddle, Smoke slipped into the saddle, grabbed up the reins, and put his spurs to the animal's sides, turning the horse, trying to get a shot at Cat.

But the man was as elusive and quick as his name implied, fading into the milling confusion and churning dust. Smoke leveled his pistol at Ben Sabler and missed him clean as the man wheeled his horse. The bullet slammed into another outlaw. The outlaw was hard hit, but managed to stay in the saddle and gallop out of the fight.

"Back! Back!" Lanny Ball screamed, his voice faint in the

booming and spark-filled night. "Fall back and surround the place."

Smoke tried to angle for a shot at Lanny and failed. Jumping off his horse, Smoke rolled behind a tree in the front yard of the main house, and with a .44 in each hand, emptied the guns into the backs of the fast-retreating outlaws. He saw several jerk in their saddles as hot lead tore into flesh and one man fell, the back of his head bloody.

Smoke ran to the house. Jumping on the front porch, he saw the body of Willie, draped over the porch railing. On the other side of the porch, Holman was sprawled, a bloody hole in his forehead.

"Damn!" Smoke cursed, just as Cord pushed open the screen door and stepped out.

Cord's face was grim as he looked at the body of Willie. "Been with me a long time," the rancher said. "He was a good hand. Loyal to the end."

"Man can't ask for a better epitaph," Smoke said. "Cord, you take the barn and I'll run to the bunkhouse. Tell the men to fortify their positions and fill up every canteen and bucket they can find." He cut his eyes as Liz and Alice came onto the porch. "You ladies start cooking. The men are going to need food and lots of it. We might be pinned down here for days."

Cord said, "I'll have some boys gather up all the guns and ammo from the dead. Pass them around." He stepped off the porch and trotted into the night.

"Larry!" Smoke called, and the hand turned. "Get the horses out of the corral and into the barn. Find as much scrap lumber as you can and fortify their stalls against stray lead."

The cowboy nodded and ran toward the corral, hollering for Dan to join him.

Smoke and Parnell carried the bodies of Holman and Willie away from the house, placing them under a tree; the shade would help as the sun came up. The men covered them with blankets and secured the edges with rocks.

Snipers from out in the darkness began sending random rounds into the house and the outbuildings, forcing everyone to seek shelter and stay low.

"This is going to be very unpleasant," Parnell said, lying on the ground until the sniping let up and he could get back to the house.

"Wait until the sun comes up and the temperature starts rising," Smoke told him. "Our only hope is that cloud buildup." He looked upward. "If it starts raining, I plan on heading into the timber and doing some headhunting. The rain will cover any sound."

"Do you think prayer would help?" Parnell said, only half joking.

"It sure wouldn't hurt."

There were seven dead outlaws, and all knew at least that many more had been wounded; some of them were hard hit and would not live.

But among their own, Corgill and Pat had been wounded. Their wounds were painful, but not serious. They could still use a gun, but with difficulty.

Smoke and Cord got together just after first light and talked it out, tallying it up. They were badly outnumbered, facing perhaps a hundred or more experienced gunhandlers, and the defenders' position was not the best.

They had plenty of food and water and ammunition, but all knew if the outlaws decided to lie back and snipe, eventually the bullets would seek them out one by one. The house was the safest place, the lower floor being built mostly of stone. The bunkhouse was also built of stone. The wounded had been moved from the upstairs to the lower floor. Beans, with his leg in a cast, could cover one window. Charlie Starr, the old warhoss, had scoffed off his wound and dressed, his right arm in a sling, but with both guns strapped around his lean waist.

"I've hurt myself worser than this by fallin' out of bed," he groused.

Parnell had gathered up a half dozen shotguns and loaded them up full, placing them near his position. The women had loaded up rifles and belted pistols around their waists.

Silver Jim almost had an apoplectic seizure when he ran from the bunkhouse to the main house and put his eyes on the women, all of them dressed in men's britches, stompin' around in boots, six-guns strapped around their waists. He opened his mouth and closed it a half dozen times before he could manage to speak. Shielding his eyes from the sight of women all dressed up like men, with their charms all poked out ever' whichaway, he turned his beet-red face to Cord and found his voice.

"Cain't you do something about that! It's plumb indecent!"

"I tried. My wife told me that if we had to make a run for it, it would be easier sittin' a saddle dressed like this."

"Astride!" Silver Jim was mortified.

"I reckon," Cord said glumly.

"Lord have mercy! Things keep on goin' like this, wimmin'll be gettin' the vote 'for it's over."

"Probably," Parnell said, one good eye on Rita. There was something to be said about jeans, but he kept that thought to himself.

"Wimmin a-voting'?" Silver Jim breathed.

"Certainly. Why shouldn't they? They've been voting down in Wyoming for years."

The old gunfighter walked away, muttering. He met Charlie in the hall. "What's the matter, that bed get too much for you?"

"'Bout to worry me to death. Layin' in there under the covers with nothing on but a nightgown and wimmin comin' and goin' without no warning. More than a body can stand."

"Where are you fixin on shootin' from?"

"I best stay here with these folks. Come the night they'll be creepin' in on us."

"Gonna rain in about an hour. My bones is talkin' to me."

"Then Smoke is gonna be goin' headhuntin'. Preacher taught him well. He'll take out a bunch."

"You reckon some of us ought to go with him?"

"Nope. You know Smoke, he likes to lone-wolf it."

"He's been diggin' in his war bag and he's all dressed up in buckskin, right down to his moccasins. He was sittin' on a bunk, sharpenin' his knife, when I left."

Charlie's grin was hard. "Them gunhandlers is gonna pay in blood this afternoon. Bet on that, old hoss."

"Who's gonna pay in blood?" Cord asked, walking up to the men.

"Them mavericks out yonder. Smoke's fixin' to go lookin' for scalps come the rain."

"Sounds dangerous to me," the rancher shook his head.

Silver Jim laughed. "Oh, it will be." He jerked his thumb toward the hills. "For them out there."

TWENTY-SIX

The sky darkened and lightning began dancing around the high mountains of the Little Belt, thunder rolling ominously. Then the sky opened and began dumping torrents of rain. With his rifle slung over his shoulder with a strap, hanging barrel down, and his buckskin shirt covering his six-guns and a long-bladed Bowie knife sheathed, Smoke slipped out into the rain on moccasin-clad feet. He kept low to the ground, utilizing every bit of natural cover he came to. He moved swiftly but carefully and made the timber and brush without drawing a shot.

Once in the brush, he paused, studying every area in his field of vision before moving out. He had shifted his long-bladed knife to just behind his right-hand .44.

He froze still as a mighty oak at the sound of voices. Clad in buckskins, with the timber dark and gloomy as twilight, Smoke would be hard to spot unless he was right on top of a man.

And he was just about was!

"I shore wants me a crack at that Sandi McCorkle," the voice came to him very clear, despite the driving rain and gusts of wind.

"We'll use all them pretty gals 'fore we kill them," a second voice was added. "You see anything movin' down yonder?"

"Naw. They all shet up in the buildings."

"I be back, Tabor. I got to . . ." His words were drowned out by a clap of thunder. ". . . Must have been somethang I et."

Slowly Smoke sank down behind a bush as a red-and-white checkered shirt stood and began moving toward him. The pair must be Tabor and Park. Two thoroughly tough men. When Park passed the bush, Smoke rose up like a brown fog, his Bowie in his right hand. He separated Park's head from his shoulders with one hard slash, catching the headless body before it could come crashing to the ground and alert Tabor.

Easing the body to the wet earth, Smoke picked up the head and placed it in a gunnybag he'd tucked behind his belt.

Then he went looking for Tabor.

Circling around to come in behind the Oklahoma outlaw, Smoke laid his bloody-bottomed sack down on a rock and Injuned up to Tabor, coming in slowly and making no sound.

Tabor never knew what happened. The big-bladed and heavy knife flashed in the stormy light and another head plopped to the earth. That went in the sack with Park's head.

Smoke moved on through the rain and spots of fog that clung low to the ground, swirling around his moccasined feet, as silent as his footsteps.

Someone very close to him began firing—not at Smoke, for at the sound of the hammer being eared back, Smoke had bellied on the gound—but at the house. More guns were added to the barrage and Smoke added his .44 to the man-made thunder, his bullet striking a gunman in the head.

"Hey!" a man shouted, his voice just audible over the roar of rifles. "Pete's hit!" He stood up, an angry look on his face, sure that someone on his side was getting careless.

Smoke shot him between the eyes and the man fell back with a thud that only Smoke could feel as he lay on the ground.

Smoke worked his way back into the timber, climbing up the hill as he moved. Behind a thick stand of timber, he paused for a break and squatted down, the bloody sack beside him. He hadn't made up his mind what to do with the heads, but an idea was formed.

He ate a biscuit and cupped his hands for a drink of rainwater. He did not have one ounce of remorse or regret for what he was doing. He knew only too well that to fight the lawless, one must get down and wallow in the muck and the crud and the filth with them, using the same tactics, or worse, that they would use against an innocent. To win a battle, one must understand the enemy.

Rested, Smoke moved out, staying above the positions of the outlaws. He circled wide, wanting to hit them at widely separated spots, wanting them to know they had not been alone and had been attacked by someone who had walked among them with the stealth of a ghost.

A hard burst of gunfire came from the house, the bullets hitting the rocks and the rain-soaked earth several hundred feet below Smoke's position. As the outlaws returned the fire, Smoke leveled his Winchester and counted more coup, his fire covered by the outlaw's own noise. The lone outlaw— Smoke did not know his name and did not recall ever seeing him before—slumped forward, his rifle sliding from lifeless hands, a bloody hole in the man's back.

Smoke slipped down to the man's position and left the bloody bag of heads by the dead man's side. He added his ammunition to that he'd gathered from the others and moved on.

He had planned on sticking the heads up on poles but decided this way would be just as effective.

He continued his circling, which would eventually bring him out on the north end of the ranch complex. He caught just a glimpse of the Hanks boys. Bellying down, he started working his way to their position, freezing log-still as two gunslicks, wearing canvas ponchos, stepped out of the timber and headed in his direction. They were so sure of themselves they were not expecting any trouble and were not checking their surroundings. Smoke could catch only a few of the words that passed between them.

". . . Never thought them boys would do it . . ."

". . . Didn't like my old man, but I don't think I'd have had the . . . kill him with a shotgun."

". . . Be gettin' ripe layin' up in that bed . . . Sonny pulled the trigger, I reckon."

". . . All three of um's crazy as a bessy-bug."

The outlaws moved out of earshot and Smoke lay for a moment, putting some sense into what he'd heard. The Hanks boys had killed their father with a shotgun, probably as he lay sleeping in bed.

Smoke broke off his headhunting and began making his way back to the ranch. If the news was true, and he had no reason to doubt it, for the Hanks boys were as goofy as their father, that meant that part of the outlaws' plans had been accomplished. And everyone at the Circle Double C had to die for the outlaws' planned takeover to succeed.

Smoke moved quickly, always staying in the brush and timber. As he was approaching the ranch complex, he heard a horrified shout from the hills and knew that the bag of heads had been found . . . either that or the headless bodies of the outlaws.

Smoke began moving cautiously, for at this point he was open to fire from either side. Closer to the house, he began a meadowlark's call. Charlie waited for a moment and then returned the call. When a human gives a birdcall, a practiced ear can pick up the subtle difference, no matter how good the caller is.

Smoke ran the last few hundred feet, zigging and zagging

to offer a hard target. But if the outlaws saw him, they did not fire; probably they were too busy searching the ridges for the unknown headhunter. On the back porch, Liz and Alice had towels for him, a change of clothes—Cord's long underwear and jeans and shirt—and a mug of coffee, for Smoke was soaked and cold.

Smoke broke the news to a horrified audience.

Liz shook her head but shed no tears for her husband or sons. And neither did Rita.

"Killed their own father!" Cord was visibly shaken by the news. "Good God!"

Parnell was the first to put the upcoming horror into words. "Then we—all of us—have to die if their plans are to succeed."

The women looked at each other. They knew that for them, it would not be a quick bullet. They would be used, and used badly, until the outlaws tired of them. Only then would death bring relief.

"Reno comin' at a run," Charlie said, looking out the window. "He's been out eyeballin' the situation close to home."

The gunfighter was as soaked as Smoke had been. The women shooed him into a room and handed him towels and dry clothing. When he emerged, they had coffee waiting for him.

He took a gulp of the strong hot coffee. "They blocked off the road leading south and have men waiting in the passes. They have so many men it was no problem to seal us off. Any bust-out is gonna be difficult, if not downright impossible."

"And walking out will be tough with the wounded," Smoke added. "But if we stay here, they'll eventually overrun us by their number. Or they'll burn the buildings down around us. Beans is gonna have to be carried out of here. Pat and Corgill can walk out with him. I'm going to suggest that the women leave with them." He looked at Parnell. "Parnell, you and Gage, Del and Bernie will spell each other with the litter. Me and Reno will make the litter right now. You people pack some food and blankets; make a light backpack and get ready to move out at dark. Let's do it."

All knew that Smoke had casually but deliberately chosen the men to accompany the women. Then he irritated the hell out of Charlie Starr by suggesting that he accompany the foot party.

"I'll be damned if I will!" the old gunfighter flared up.

"Charlie . . . ," Smoke put a hand on his friend's shoulder. "They need you. They need your experience in guiding them and they need your gun."

"Well . . ." Charlie calmed down. "If you put it that way. All right. But I hate like hell to miss out on this here fight."

"Damned ol' rooster with a busted wing." Hardrock told him. "You look after them folks, now, you hear me, you old coot?"

"I've told them to head for the old Fletcher gold mine in the Big Belt," Cord said. "It's been abandoned for years and we cache supplies there. From there, they can angle back East and make it into Gibson. But it's gonna be a long hard haul for them all."

"You just get me in a saddle!" Beans groused. "I ain't never seen the day I couldn't sit on a hurricane deck."

"Oh, hush up!" Lujan told him. "Just lay back and enjoy the trip. *Amigo,* you injure that leg again, and you'll be a cripple for the rest of your life. It's better this way and you know it."

Beans did some fancy cussing, but finally agreed to shut up about it and accept his fate.

Smoke pulled Cord to one side. "How do you feel about leaving your ranch to those jackals out there on the ridges?"

"I don't like it. But I think it's gonna happen. See if my plan agrees with yours: We give them walkin' out a full twenty-four hours. Then we saddle up, put sacks on the horses' hooves, and lead them out a'ways. Then we all hit one spot just as hard as we can."

"That's it. We'll get the foot party moving just after dark and pray that this rain doesn't let up. They're going to be wet and cold and miserable, but I think they've got more of a chance out there than staying here."

Cord nodded his big head. "I'll pass the word to the hands. You sure you don't want a diversion?"

"No. That would be a sure tipoff that we're up to something. Anyway, I think they'll hit us at full dark. That'll be enough."

The afternoon wore on with only a few shots being exchanged from each side. Those in the house knew that the outlaws would be cold, soaking wet, and miserable, and their patience would be growing thin with each sodden hour that passed.

And those in the ranch compound also knew, some more than others, that after finding the sack of bloody heads and several more of their kind shot to death, most of the outlaws would be wanting revenge in the worst sort of way, for they would know it had been Smoke stalking them silently on the ridges.

Smoke looked out onto the gray dripping afternoon. Twenty-four hours. They had to hold out for twenty-four hours.

Reno seemed to read his thoughts. "We'll hold, Smoke. Some of them might breach the house, but it'll be a death trap for them. One thing in our favor, they damn sure can't burn the place down . . . at least not this night."

"From the outside," Smoke stuck an amendment to that. "A couple of torches tossed inside, though . . ."

Cord heard it. "I've got some lumber out in the shed.

Rock, Troy, you boys fetch the lumber while we get some nails and hammers. We'll board up windows we're not shooting from. On both levels of the house." He began ripping down curtains and drapes to lessen the fire hazard.

As the sounds of the muffled hammering began drifting to the outlaws on the ridges, the gunfire picked up, forcing the men to work more carefully, without exposing themselves. Those inside the house didn't have to worry about breaking a window with all the hammering; all the windows were already shot out.

Those windows not being used as shooters' positions boarded up, Smoke went to find Fae.

He put his arm around her shoulders and kissed her cheek. "I'm headin' back outside, Fae. I like to be outside when the action goes down." He looked at the other women. "You ladies watch your step this night. We'll see you all in a couple of days."

He shook hands with the men who were leaving that night. "You boys enjoy your stroll. As soon as it gets full dark, take off. And good luck."

He walked back into the living room, leaving Cord to say his goodbyes to wife and daughter.

"I'm going to pull Ring and Hardrock, Silver Jim, and Pistol in the house with you and Cord and the boys," he told Reno. "The rest of us will be in the bunkhouse and the barn." He looked outside. "Be dark shortly. I'm heading out yonder. The others will be showing up one at a time about five minutes apart. Good luck tonight."

"Luck to you, Smoke."

There was nothing left to say. The two famed gunhandlers looked at each other, nodded their heads, and Smoke slipped out onto the stone and wood porch. He knew the chances of his being seen from several hundred yards away were practically nonexistent, but he stayed low from force of habit.

Smoke darted off the porch and to a tree in the yard, then over the fence and a foot race to the corral. Then, as he got set for the run to the bunkhouse, a cold voice spoke from behind him.

"I'll be known as the man who kilt Smoke Jensen. Die, you meddlin' bastard!"

TWENTY-SEVEN

Smoke threw himself to one side just as the pistol roared. He could feel the heat of the bullet as it passed his arm. He twisted his body in the air and hit the muddy ground with a .44 in his hand, the muzzle spitting fire and smoke and lead.

Hartley took the first slug in his chest and Smoke fired again, the force of his landing lifting his gun hand, the second slug striking the gunhawk in the throat. Hartley, with a knot plainly visible on his rain-slicked head, the hair matted down, leaned up against a corral rail and lifted his six-gun, savage all the way to the grave.

A .44-40 roared from the bunkhouse and Spring's aim was true. Hartley's head ballooned from the impact of the slug and he pitched forward, into a horse trough.

Riflemen from the ridges and the hills opened up, not really sure what they were shooting at, but filling the air with lead. Smoke lay where he was, as safe there as anywhere in the open expanse between house and bunkhouse. When the fire from the outlaws slacked up; Smoke scrambled to the bunkhouse and dove headfirst into the building, rolling to his feet.

"Thanks, Spring," he told the old hand. "Hartley must have laid out there in the corral all covered up with hay since I conked him on the noggin last night."

"Hell, he was dead on his feet when I shot him," the old hand said. "I just like some in'shorence in cases like that."

He poured Smoke a cup of coffee and returned to his post by a window.

Smoke drank the strong hot brew and laid out the plans. One by one, the old gunfighters began leaving the bunkhouse, heading for the house. Ring was the last to stand in the door. He smiled at Smoke.

"You always bring this much action with you when you journey, Smoke?"

"It sure seems like it, Ring," Smoke said with a laugh.

The big man returned the laugh and then slipped out into the rapidly darkening day, the rain still coming down in silver sheets.

"I got to thinkin' a while back," Spring said. "After Ring asked me how it was nobody come to our aid. Smoke, they's sometimes two, three weeks go by don't none of us go to town. Ain't nobody comin' out here."

"And even if they did come out, what could they do? Nothing," he ansered his own question. "Except get themselves killed. It'd take a full company of Army troops to rout those outlaws."

There had been no fire from the ridges, so the men had safely made the house. Darkness had pushed aside the day. Those walking out would be leaving shortly, and they had a good chance of making it, for the move would not be one those on the ridges would be expecting. To try to bust out on horseback, yes. But not by walking out. Not in this weather.

When the wet darkness had covered the land for almost an hour, Smoke turned to Spring. He could just see him in the gloom of the bunkhouse.

"I don't think they'll try us on horseback this night, Spring. They'll be coming in on foot."

"You right," Donny whispered from the far end of the

bunkhouse. "And here they come. You want me to drop him now or let them come closer?"

"Let them come on. This rain makes for deceptive shooting."

A torch was lighted, its flash a jumping flame in the windswept darkness. The torch bobbed as the carrier ran toward the house. From the house, a rifle crashed. The torch stopped and fell to the soaked earth, slowly going out as its carrier died.

All around the compound, muzzle flashes pocked the gloom, and the dampness kept the gunsmoke low to the ground as an acrid fog.

A kerosene bomb slammed against the side of the bunkhouse, the whiskey bottle containing the liquid smashing. The flames were slow to spread and those that did were quickly put out by the driving rain. Spring's pistol roared and spat sparks. Outside, a man screamed as the slug ripped through flesh and shattered bone. He lay on the wet ground and moaned for a moment, then fell silent.

Smoke saw a moving shadow out of the corner of his eyes and lifted his pistol. The shadow blended in with the night and Smoke lost it. But it was definitely moving toward the bunkhouse. It was difficult, if not impossible, to hear any small sounds due to the hard-falling rain and the crash of gunfire. Smoke left the window and moved to the door of the bunkhouse, standing some six feet away from the door. Spring and Donny and two other hands kept their eyes to the front, occasionally firing at a dark running shape within their perimeter.

The bunkhouse door had no inner bar; most people didn't even lock their doors when they left for town or went on a trip. If somebody used the house to get out of the weather or to fix something to eat, they were expected to leave it as they found it.

The door smashed open and the doorway filled with men.

Smoke's .44s roared and bucked in his hands. Screaming was added to the already confusing cacophony of battle. More men rushed into the bunkhouse, leaping over the bodies sprawled in the doorway. Smoke was rushed and knocked to the floor. He lost his left-hand gun but jammed the muzzle of his right-hand gun into the belly of a man and pulled the trigger. A boot caught him on the side of the head, momentarily addling him.

Smoke heaved the badly wounded man away and rolled to the far wall. Men were all over him swinging fists and gun barrels. Using his own now-empty pistol as a club, he smashed a face, the side of a head. Jerking the pistol from a man's holster, Smoke began firing into the mass of wet attackers. A bullet burned his side; another slammed into the wooden leg of a bunk, driving splinters into Smoke's face.

Jerking his Bowie from its sheath, Smoke began slashing out, feeling the warm flow of blood splatter his arm and face as the big blade drew howls of pain from his attackers.

He slipped to one side and listened to the cursing of the outlaws still able to function. Lifting the outlaw's pistol, Smoke emptied it into the dark shapes. The bunkhouse became silent after the battle.

"You hit, Smoke?" Spring called.

"Just a scratch. Donny?"

The young cowboy did not reply.

"I'll check," Fitz spoke softly. He walked to the cowboy's position and knelt down. "He rolled twelve," Fitz's voice came out of the darkness.

"Damn!" Smoke said.

Another attack from the outlaws had been beaten back, but Donny was dead and Cal had been wounded. Smoke's wounds were minor but painful. No one in the house had been hurt.

They had bought those walking out some time and distance.

By this time, if they had not been discovered, they were clear. Clear, but facing a long, cold, wet, and slow march into the Big Belts. The house, the barn, and the bunkhouse were riddled with bullet holes. They had lost two horses, having to destroy them after they'd been hit by stray bullets. And no cowboy likes to shoot a horse.

The rain slacked and the clouds drifted away, exposing the moon and its light. With that, the outlaws slipped away into the shadows and made their way back to the ridges overlooking the ranch.

The moonlight cast its light upon the bodies of outlaws sprawled in death on the grounds. Some of those with wounds not serious tried to crawl away. Cord and Smoke and the others showed them no mercy, shooting them if they could get them in gunsights.

After the intitial attack had been beaten back, the outlaws fired from the ridges for several hours, finally giving it up and settling down for some rest.

The moonlight was both a blessing and a curse, for it would make their busting out a lot more difficult.

Smoke ran to the house to confer with Cord.

"I figure just after sunset," the rancher said. "After the moon comes up, it'll be impossible."

"All right. We'll head in the opposite direction of those walking out. We'll start out like we're trying to bust through the roadblock, then cut east toward the timber. That sound all right to you?"

"Suits me."

Dooley had changed his mind about heading farther into the mountains, turning around when he was about halfway to Old Baldy. He rode slowly back toward Gibson.

At dawn of the second day of the attack on the Circle Double C, he was standing in front of the newly opened stage offices, waiting for the station agent. He plopped down his money belt.

"Stash that in your big safe and gimme a receipt for it," he told the agent.

That taken care of, Dooley walked over to the new hotel and checked in. He slept for several hours, then carefully bathed in the tub behind the barber shop, shaved, and dressed in clean clothes. He was completely free of the effects of alcohol and intended to remain that way. Nuts, but sober.

He walked over to Hans and enjoyed a huge breakfast, the first good meal he'd eaten in days. Hans and Olga and Hilda eyeballed the man suspiciously.

"Vere is everybody?" Hans broke the silence.

"I ain't got no idea," Dooley told him, slurping on a mug of coffee. "I ain't been to the ranch in two-three days." Really, he had no idea how long he'd been gone. Two days or a week. Time meant nothing to him anymore. He had only a few thoughts burning in his brain: to kill Cord McCorkle and then turn his guns on his traitor sons and watch them die in the muddy street. And if he didn't soak up too much lead doing that, and he could find her, he wanted to shoot his wife.

That was the sum total of all that was in Dooley Hanks's brain. He paid for his meal and took a mug of coffee with him, sitting in a chair on the boardwalk in front of the café. He would wait.

He sat in his chair, watching the town wake up and the people start moving around. He drank coffee and rolled cigarettes, smoking them slowly, his eyes missing nothing.

He watched as two very muddy and tired-looking riders rode slowly up the street, coming in from the north. Dooley set his coffee mug on the boards and stood up, staying in the morning shadows, only a dark blur to those still in the sunlight. He slipped the thongs from the hammers of his guns. The two riders reined up and dismounted, looping the reins around the hitchrail and starting up the steps to Hans. They stopped and stared in disbelief at the man.

Hector and Rod, two punk gunslicks Dooley had hired, stood with their mouths open.

"You 'pposed to be *dead*!" Hector finally managed to gasp.

"Well, I ain't," Dooley told them. "And I want some answers from you."

"We ain't got no quarrel with you," Rod told him. "All we want is some hot coffee and food."

"You'll get hot lead, boy," Dooley warned him. "Where the hell is my no'count sons?"

"I . . ." Hector opened his mouth. A warning glance from Rod closed it.

"You'd better talk to me, pup!" Dooley barked. "'Fore I box your ears with lead."

Hector laughed at the man. "You ain't seen the day you could match my draw, old man." Hector was all of nineteen. He would not live to see another day.

Dooley drew and fired. He was no fast gunslinger, but he was quick and very, very accurate. The slug struck Hector in the heart and the young man died standing up. He fell on his face in the mud.

Dooley turned his gun toward Rod, the hammer jacked back. "My boys, punk. Where is they?"

"They teamed up with Jason and Lanny and Cat Jennings," he admitted. "I don't know where they is," he lied.

Dooley bought it. He sat down in the chair, his gun still in his hand. He would wait. They would show up. Then he'd kill them. He'd kill them all.

Rod backed up and led his horse across the street, to a little tent-covered café. Horace Mulroony had stood on the boardwalk across the street and witnessed the shooting. He motioned for his cameraman to bring the equipment. They had another body to record for posterity.

"Mister Hanks," he said, strolling up. "I would like to talk to you."

"Git away from me!" Dooley snarled, spittle leaking out of one corner of his mouth.

Horace got.

TWENTY-EIGHT

In the middle of the afternoon, in order to keep suspicion down, Smoke risked a run to the barn and began saddling all the horses himself. He laid four gunnybags or pieces of ripped-up blankets in front of each stall, to be used to muffle the horses' hooves when they first pulled out. Smoke went over each saddle, either taping down or removing anything that might jingle or rattle.

That done, he climbed up into the warm loft to speak to the men. Lujan was reclining on some hay. He opened his eyes and smiled at Smoke.

"At full dark, *amigo*?"

"At full dark. If you know any prayers, you best be saying them."

The gunfighter grinned. "Oh, I have!"

The other men in the loft laughed softly, but in their eyes, Smoke could see that they, too, had been calling—in their own way—for some heavenly guidance.

He climbed back down and decided to stay in the barn until nightfall. No point in drawing unnecessary gunfire from the ridges. He lay down on a pile of hay and closed his eyes. Might as well rest, too. It was going to be a long night.

* * *

Gage and Del had led the party safely past the gunmen on the ridges. An hour later they were deep in the timber and feeling better. It was tough going, carrying Beans on the stretcher, but by switching up bearers every fifteen minutes, they made good time.

Dawn found them miles from the Circle Double C. But instead of following Cord's orders, Del had changed directions and was heading toward Gibson. He had not done it autocratically, but had called for a vote during a rest period. The vote had been unanimous: head for town.

By midafternoon they were only a few miles from town, a very tired and footsore group.

Late in the afternoon, they came staggering up the main street of Gibson. People rushed out of stores and saloons and houses to stand and stare at the muddy group.

"Them wimmin's wearin' men's britches!" a man called from a saloon. "Lord have mercy. Would you look at that."

Gage quickly explained what had taken place and why they were here, Dooley listening carefully.

Rod stood on the boardwalk and stared at the group, his eyes bugged out. Parnell felt the eyes on him and turned, his hot gaze locking with Rod's disbelieving eyes. Parnell slipped the thongs from his blasters and walked toward the young man.

"I ain't skirred of you!" Rod shouted.

"Good," Parnell said, still walking. "A man should face death with no fear."

"Huh! It ain't me that's gonna die."

"Then make your play," Parnell said, and with that he became a western man.

Rod's hands grabbed for iron.

Parnell's blaster roared, and Rod was very nearly cut in two by the heavy charge. It turned him around and tossed him through the window and into the café, landing him on a table, completely ruining the appetite of those having an early supper.

Beans had been keeping a good eye on Dooley; a good eye and his gun. Crazy as Dooley might be, he wasn't about to do anything with Beans holding a bead on him.

Dooley stood up slowly and held out his hand as he walked up to Gage. With a look of amazement on his face, Gage took the offered hand.

"You got a good woman, Gage. I hope you treat her better than I did." He turned to Liz and handed her the receipt from the stage agent. "Money from the sale of the cattle is over yonder in the safe. I'm thinkin' straight now, Liz. But I don't know how long it's gonna last. So I'll keep this short. Them boys of ourn took after me. They're crazy. And they got to be stopped. I sired them, so it's on my shoulders to stop them." Then, unexpectedly, and totally out of character for him, he took off his hat and kissed Liz on the cheek.

"Thank you for some good years, Liz." He turned around, walked to his horse, and swung into the saddle, pointing the nose of the horse toward the Circle Double C.

"Well, I'll just be damned!" Gage said. "I'd have bet ever' dollar I owned—which ain't that many—that he was gonna start shootin.'"

Liz handed him the receipt. "Here, darling. You'll be handling the money matters from now on. You might as well become accustomed to it."

"Yes, dear," the grizzled foreman said meekly. Then he squared his shoulders. "All right, boys, we got unfinished business to take care of. Let's find some cayuses and get to it."

Their aches and pains and sore feet forgotten, the men checked their guns and turned toward the hitchrails, lined with horses. "We're takin' these," Del said. "Anybody got any objections, state 'em now."

No one had any objections.

Hans rode up on a huge horse at least twenty hands high. He had belted on a pistol and carried a rifle in one big paw. "I ride vit you," he rumbled. "Friends of mine dey are, too."

Horace came rattling up in a buggy, a rifle in the boot and a holstered pistol on the seat beside him. "I'm with you, boys."

More than a dozen other townspeople came riding up and driving up in buggies and buckboards, all of them heavily armed.

"We're with you!" one called. "We're tired of this. So let's ride and clean it out."

"Let's go, boys!" Parnell yelled.

"Oohhh!" Rita cooed. "He's so manly!"

"Don't swoon, child," her mother warned. "The street's too muddy."

Del leaned out of the saddle and kissed Fae right on the mouth, right in front of God and everybody.

Parnell thought that was a good idea and did the same with Rita.

The hurdy-gurdy girls, hanging out of windows and lining the boardwalks, all applauded.

Olga and Hilda giggled.

Gage leaned over and gave Liz a good long smack while the onlookers cheered.

Then they were gone in a pounding of hooves, slinging mud all over anyone standing close.

Dooley rode slowly back to his ranch. He looked at the buckshot-blasted bed and shook his head. Then he fixed a pot of coffee and poured a cup, taking it out to sit on the front porch. He had a hunch his boys would be returning to the ranch for the money they thought was still in the safe.

He would be waiting for them.

* * *

"I don't like it," Jason told Lanny, with Cat standing close. "Something's wrong down there. I feel it."

"I got the same feeling," Cat spoke. "But I got it last night while we was hittin' them. It just seemed like to me they was holdin' back."

Lanny snapped his fingers. "That's it! Them women and probably a few of the men walked out durin' the rain. Damn them! This ain't good, boys."

Cat looked uneasily toward the road.

Jason caught the glance. "Relax, Cat. There ain't that many people in town who gives a damn what happens out here." Then he smiled. "The town," he said simply.

Lanny stood up from his squat. "We've throwed a short loop out here, boys. Our plans is busted. But the town is standin' wide open for the takin'."

But Cat, older and more experienced in the outlaw trade, was dubious. "There ain't nobody ever treed no western town, Lanny. We done lost twenty-five or so men by the gun. Them crazy Hanks boys left nearabouts an hour ago."

"Nobody ever tried it with seventy-five-eighty men afore, neither. Not that I know of. 'Sides, all we've lost is the punks and tinhorns and hangers-on."

"He's got a point," Jason said.

"Let's ride!"

Dooley Hanks sat on his front porch, drinking coffee. When he saw his sons ride up, he stood up and slipped the thongs from the hammers of his guns. The madness had once more taken possession of his sick mind, leaving him with but one thought: to kill these traitor sons of his.

He drained his coffee mug and set the mug on the porch railing. He was ready.

The boys rode up to the hitchrail and dismounted. They were muddy and unshaven and stank like bears after rolling in rotten meat.

"If you boys come for the money, you're out of luck," Dooley called. "I give it to your momma. Seen her in town hour or so back."

The boys had recovered from their initial shock at seeing their father alive. They pushed through the fence gate and stood in the yard, facing their father on the porch. The boys spread out, about five feet apart.

"You a damn lie, you crazy old coot!" Sonny called. "She's over to Cord's place. Trapped with the rest of them."

"Sorry, boys." Dooley's voice was calm. "But some of 'em busted out and walked into town, carrying the Moab Kid on a stretcher. Now they's got some townspeople behind 'em and is headin' back to Cord's place. Your little game is all shot to hell."

Sonny, Bud, and Conrad exchanged glances. Seems like everything that had happened the last several days had turned sour.

"Aw, hell, Daddy!" Bud said, forcing a grin. "We knowed you wasn't in that there bed. We was just a-funnin' with you, that's all. It was just a joke that we made up between us."

"Yeah, Daddy," Sonny said. "What's the matter, cain't you take a joke no more?"

"Lyin' scum!" Dooley's words were hard, verbally tossed at his sons. "And you knowed who raped your sister, too, didn't you?"

The boys stood in the yard, sullen looks on their dirty and unshaved faces.

"Didn't you?" the father screamed the question at them. "Damn you, answer me!"

"So what if we did?" Sonny asked. "It don't make no difference now, do it?"

A deadly calm had taken Dooley. "No, it doesn't, Sonny. It's all over."

"Whut you mean, Daddy?" Conrad asked. "Whut you fixin' to do?"

"Something that I'm not very proud of," the father said. "But it's something that I have to do."

Bud was the first to put it together. "You can't take us, Daddy. You pretty good with a gun, but you slow. So don't do nothing stupid."

"The most stupid thing I ever done was not takin' a horse-whip to you boys' butts about five times a day, commencin' when you was just pups. It's all my fault, but it's done got out of hand. It's too late. Better this than a hangman's noose."

"I think you done slipped your cinches agin, Pa," his oldest told him. "You best go lay down; git you a bottle of hooch and ponder on this some. 'Cause if you drag iron with us, you shore gonna die this day."

Dooley shot him. He gave no warning. He had faced men before, and knew what had to be done, so he did it. His slug struck Sonny in the stomach, doubling him over and dropping him to the muddy yard.

Bud grabbed iron and shot his father, the bullet twisting Dooley, almost knocking him off his boots. Dooley dragged his left-hand gun and got off a shot, hitting his middle son in the leg and slamming the young man back against the picket fence, tearing down a section of it. The horses at the hitchrail panicked, breaking loose and running from the ugly scene of battle.

Conrad got lead in his father before the man turned his guns loose on his youngest boy. Conrad felt a double hammer-blow slam into his belly, the lead twisting and ripping. He began screaming and cursing the man who had fathered him. Raising his gun, the boy shot his father in the belly.

But still Dooley would not go down.

Blood streaming from his chest and face, the crazed man

took another round from his second son. Dooley raised his pistol and shot the young man between the eyes.

As the light began to dim in Dooley's eyes, he stumbled from the porch and fell to the muddy earth. He picked up one of Sonny's guns just as the gut-shot boy eared back the hammer on his Colt and shot his father in the belly. Dooley jammed the pistol into the young man's chest and emptied it.

Dooley fell back, the sounds of the pale rider's horse coming closer.

"Daddy!" Conrad called, his words very dim. "Help me, Daddy. It hurts so bad!"

The ghost rider galloped up just in time to see Dooley stretch his arm out and close his fingers around Conrad's hand. "We'll ride out together, boy."

The pale rider tossed his shroud.

TWENTY-NINE

"They're pullin' out!" Lujan yelled from the loft.

Smoke was up and running for his horse as the men streamed out of the bunkhouse, all heading for the barn.

"Why?" Reno asked.

"That damn crazy Del led 'em into town!" Cord said, grinning. "We got help on the way. Bet on it."

In the saddle, Smoke said, "That means the town is gonna get hit. That's the only thing I can figure out of this move."

"Let's go, boys!" Cord yelled the orders. "They'll hit that town like an army."

The men waited for a few minutes, to be sure the outlaws had really pulled out, then mounted up and headed for town. They met the rescue party halfway between the ranch and Gibson.

Smoke quickly explained and the men tore out for Gibson.

"There she is, boys," Lanny pointed toward the fast-growing town. "We hit them hard, fast, grab the money, and get gone."

"I gotta have me a woman," one of Cat Jennings's men said. "I can't stand it no more."

"Mills," Cat said disgustedly. "You best start thinkin' with your brain instead of that other part. You can always find you a woman."

"A woman," Mills said, his eyes bright with his inner cruelty.

"Let's go." Jason spurred his horse.

Some seventy strong, the outlaws hit the town at a full gallop, firing at anything that came into sight. They rampaged through on the first pass, leaving several dead in the muddy main street and that many more wounded, crawling for cover.

At the end of the street, the men broke up into gangs and began looting the stores and terrorizing the citizens. Mills blundered into Hans's café and eyeballed Hilda.

"You a fat pig, but you'll do," he told the woman, walking toward her.

Hilda threw a full pot of boiling coffee into the man's face.

Screaming his pain and almost blind, Mills stumbled around the café, crashing into tables and chairs, both hands covering his scalded face.

Olga ran from the upstairs, carrying two shotguns. She tossed one to Hilda and eared back the hammers of her own, leveling the double-barrel twelve-gauge at Mills. She gave him both barrels of buckshot. The outlaw was slung out the window and died on the boardwalk.

Mills's buddy and cohort in evil, Barton, ran into the café, both pistols drawn. He ran right into an almost solid wall of buckshot. The charges blew him out of one boot and sent him sailing out of the café, off the boardwalk, and into a hitchrail. Barton did a backflip and landed dead in the mud.

Hilda and Olga picked up his dropped pistols and re-loaded their shotguns, waiting for another turkey to come gobbling in.

Harriet and her hurdy-gurdy girls had armed themselves and already had accounted for half a dozen outlaws, the bodies littering the floor of the saloon and the boardwalk out front a clear warning to others not to mess with these short-skirted and painted ladies.

The smithy, a veteran of the War Between the States and several Indian campaigns, stood in his shop with a Spencer .52 and emptied several saddles before the outlaws decided there was nothing of value in a blacksmith shop anyway.

Some of Dad Estes's men had charged the general store and laid a pistol upside Walt Hillery's head, knocking the man unconscious. They then grabbed his sour-faced wife, Leah, dragging her to the storeroom and having their way with her.

Leah's screaming brought Liz and Alice and Fae on the run, the women armed with pistols and rifles. Sandi and Rita were at the doctor's office with the wounded men.

Fae leveled her .45 at a man with his britches down around his boots and shot him in the head just as Alice and Liz began pulling the trigger and levering the action, clearing the store-room of nasties.

Liz tossed a blanket over the still-squalling and kicking and pig-snorting Leah and gave her a look of disgust. "They must have been hard up," she told the shopkeeper.

Leah stopped hollering long enough to spit at the woman. She stopped spitting when Liz balled her right hand into a fist and started toward her.

"You wouldn't dare!" Leah hissed.

"Maybe you'd like to bet a broken jaw on it?" Liz challenged.

Leah pulled the blanket over her head, leaving her bony feet sticking out the other end.

The agent at the stagecoach line had worked his way up the ladder: starting first as a hostler, then a driver, then as a guard on big money shipments from the gold fields. He didn't think this stop would be in operation long, but damned if a bunch of outlaws were going to strip his safe.

When some of No-Count George Victor's bunch shot the

lock off the door, the agent was waiting behind the counter, with several loaded rifles and shotguns and pistols. With him were his hostler and two passengers waiting for the stage, all heavily armed.

The first two outlaws to step through the door were shot dead, dying on their feet, riddled with bullet holes. Another tried to ride his horse through the big window. The animal, already frightened by all the wild shooting, resisted and bolted, running up the boardwalk. The outlaw, just able to hang on, caught his head on the side of an awning and left the saddle, missing most of his jaw.

Beans was sitting next to an open window of the doctor's office, a rifle in his very capable hands. He emptied half a dozen saddles.

And Charlie Starr was calmly walking up the boardwalk, a long-barreled Colt in his hand. He was looking for Cat Jennings. One of Cat's men, a disgustingly evil fellow who went by the name of Wheeler, saw Charlie and leveled his pistol at him.

Charlie drilled him between the eyes with one well-placed shot and kept on walking.

A bullet slammed into Charlie's side and turned him around. He grinned through the pain. Doc Adair had seen the lump pushing out of Charlie's side and their eyes had met in the office.

"Cancer," Charlie had told him.

Charlie lifted his Peacemaker, and another outlaw went on that one-way journey toward the day he would make his peace with his Maker.

"Cat!" Charlie called, and the outlaw wheeled his horse around.

Charlie shot him out of the saddle.

Cat came up with his hands full of Colts, the hate shining in his eyes.

Charlie took two more rounds, both of them in the belly,

but the old gunfighter stayed on his feet and took his time, carefully placing his shots. Cat soaked up the lead and kept on shooting.

Charlie border-rolled his second gun just as he was going to his knees in the muddy street. He could hear the thunder of hooves and something else, too: singing. It sounded like a mighty choir was singing him Home.

Charlie lifted his Peacemaker and shot Cat Jennings twice in the head. Propped up on one elbow, the old gunfighter had enough strength to make sure Cat was dead, then slumped to the ground.

Hardrock and Silver Jim and Pistol LeRoux had seen Charlie go down, and they screamed their rage as they jumped off their horse, their hands full of guns.

Silver Jim stalked up the boardwalk, holding his matched set of Remington .44s, looking for No-Count George Victor. Hardrock was by his side, his hands gripping the butts of his guns, his eyes searching for Three-Fingers Kerman and his buddy, Fulton. Pistol had gone looking for Peck and Nappy.

The Sabler brothers, Ben, Carl, and Delmar, were waiting at the edge of town, waiting for Lujan.

Diego, Pablo, and a gunfighter called Hazzard were waiting to try Smoke.

Twenty or more gunslicks had already hauled their ashes out of town. They had realized what the townspeople already knew: nobody hog-ties and trees a western town.

The Larado Kid had teamed up with several more punks, including Johnny and his buddy, Bret, and the backshooter, Danny Rouge. They had turned tail and galloped out of town. There would be another day. There always was. Besides, Johnny had him a plan. He wanted to kill Smoke Jensen. And he knew this fight was just about over. Smoke would be heading home. And a lot could happen between Montana and Colorado.

"No-Count!" Silver Jim yelled, his voice carrying over the

din of battle, the screaming of the wounded, and the sounds of panicked horses.

No-Count whirled around, his hands full of pistols. Silver Jim drew and fired as smoothly as he had forty years back, when he had cut the flap off a soldier's holster and tied it down.

Both the old gunfighter's slugs struck true and No-Count squatted down in the muddy alley, dropped his pistols, and fell over face-first in the mud.

Hardrock felt a numbing blow striking him in the shoulder, staggering him. He turned, falling back up against a building front, his right-hand gun coming up, his thumb and trigger finger working as partners, rolling thunder from the muzzle.

Three-Finger Kerman went down, the front of his shirt stained with blood. Fulton fired at Hardrock and missed. Hardrock grinned at the outlaw and didn't miss.

Pistol Le Roux rounded a corner and came face-to-face with Peck and Nappy. Pistol's guns spat fire and death before the two so-called badmen could react. Pistol looked down at the dead and damned.

"Pikers!" he snorted, then turned and walked into one of the new saloons, called the Pink Puma, and drew himself a cool one from the deserted bar. He could sense the fight was over. He had already seen Dad Estes and his gang hightail it out of town.

Damn! but he hated that about Charlie. Him and Charlie had been buddies for nigh on . . . Hell, he couldn't remember how many years.

He drew himself another beer, sat down, and propped his boots up. It could be, he mused, he was getting just too old for this type of nonsense.

Naw! he concluded. He looked up as Hardrock came staggering in, trailed by Silver Jim.

"What the hell happened to you, you old buzzard?" he asked Hardrock.

"Caught one, you jackass!" Hardrock snapped. "What's it look like—I been pickin' petunias?"

"Wal, sit down." He shoved out a chair. "I'll fetch you a beer and then try to find the doctor. If I don't, you'll probably whine and moan the rest of the day." He took his knife and cut away Hardrock's shirt. "Bullet went clear through." He got Hardrock a beer and picked up a bottle of whiskey. "This is gonna hurt you a lot more than it is me," he warned.

Hardrock glared at him.

Pistol poured some whiskey on the wounds, entrance and exit, and took a reasonably clean bar towel that Silver Jim handed him and made a bandage.

"You'll keep. Drink your beer."

"Make your play, gentlemen," Lujan told the Sabler brothers.

Parnell stood by Lujan's side, smiling faintly.

The sounds of battle had all but ceased.

The Sablers grabbed for iron.

Lujan's guns roared just a split second before Parnell's blasters boomed, sending out their lethal charges. In the distance, a bugle sounded. Someone shouted, "The Army's here!"

Ben, Carl, and Delmar Sabler lay on the muddy bloody ground. Ben and Carl had taken slugs from Lujan. Delmar had taken a double dose from Parnell's blasters. He was almost torn in half.

Lujan holstered his guns and held out his hand. "My friend, you can stand shoulder to shoulder with me anytime you like. You are truly a man!"

Parnell blushed.

"Thank you, Lujan." He shook the hand.

"Come on, *amigo*. Let's go have us a . . . sarsaparilla."

THIRTY

The commander of the Army contingent, a Captain Morrison, met with Cord, Smoke, and a few others in what was left of the Hangout, while the undertaker and his helper roamed among the carnage.

"A lot of bad ones got away," Smoke told the young captain. Smoke's shirt was stiff from sweat and dirt and blood. "I expect I'll meet up with some of them on the trail home."

"Are you really Smoke Jensen?" The captain was clearly in awe.

"Yes."

Horace's photographer popped another shot.

The captain sighed. "Well, gentlemen. This is not an Army matter. I will take a report, certainly, and have it sent to the sheriff. But I imagine it will end there. I'm new to the West; just finished an assignment in Washington. But during my short time here, I have found that western justice is usually very short and very final."

"I don't understand part of what you just said," Cord leaned forward. "You mean you weren't sent in here?"

"No. We were traveling up to Fort Benton and heard the gunfire. We just rode over to see what was going on."

Smoke and Cord both started laughing. They were still laughing as they walked out of the saloon.

"The strain of battle," Captain Morrison spoke the words in all seriousness. "It certainly does strange things to men."

A grizzled old top sergeant who had been in the Army since before Morrison was born shifted his chew of tobacco to the other side of his mouth and said, "Right, sir."

Smoke went to the tubs behind the barber shop and took a long hot bath. He was exhausted. He dressed in clean clothes purchased at the new general store and walked over to Hans for some hot food. The bodies of the outlaws were still being dragged off the street.

Hans placed a huge platter of food before the man and poured him a cup of coffee. Smoke dug in. Cord entered the café and sat down at the table with Smoke. He waved away the offer of food and ordered coffee.

"We have a problem about what to do with the wounded, Smoke."

"I don't have any problem at all with it. Treat their wounds and when they're well, try them."

"We don't have a jail to hold them."

"Build one to hold them or hang them or turn them loose."

"Captain Morrison is leaving a squad here to see that we don't hang them."

"Sounds like a real nice fellow to me. Very much law and order."

"You're being sarcastic, Smoke."

"I'm being tired, is what I am. Sorry to be so short with you. Is it OK to have Charlie buried out at the ranch?"

"You know it is," the rancher replied, his words softly spoken. "I wouldn't have it any other way."

"Any reward money goes to Hardrock and Silver Jim and Pistol."

"I've already set that in motion." He smiled. "You really think they're going to open a home for retired gunfighters?"

"It wouldn't surprise me at all."

"I tell you what: I'd hate to have them for enemies."

The men sat and watched as wagons pulled up to the four new saloons and began loading up equipment from Big Louie's, the Pink Puma, The JimJam, and Harriet's House.

"I'll be glad to see things get back to normal," Cord said.

"It won't be long. I been seeing that fellow who opened up the new general store makin' trips to Walt and Leah's place. Looks like he's tryin' to buy them out."

Cord's smile was not of the pleasant type. "Liz and Alice paid Walt and Leah a visit. They convinced Walt that it would be the best thing if they'd sell out and get gone. Parnell is buyin' their house. Him and Rita will live there after they're married."

"Beans?"

"I told him he was my new foreman. He's gonna file on some sections that border my spread."

Smoke finally smiled. "Looks like it's going to be a happy ending after all."

"A whole lot of weddin's comin' up next week. You are goin' to stay for them, aren't you?"

"Oh, yeah. I couldn't miss those." He looked up at Hans, smiling at them from behind the counter. "Hilda and Ring gonna get hitched up, Hans?"

The man bobbed his big head. "*Ja.* Ever'boody vill be married at vonce."

Smoke looked out at the muddy, churned-up street. All the bodies had been toted off.

"I reserved all the rooms above the saloon," Cord said. "The hands are back at the ranch, cleaning it up and repairing the damage. Bartender has your room key."

Smoke stood up, dropped some money on the table, and put on his hat. "I think I'll go sleep for about fifteen hours.

* * *

Bob and Spring and Pat and some hands from the D-H and the Circle Double C began rebuilding Fae's burned-down house and barn. Smoke, Hardrock, Silver Jim, and Pistol began driving the cattle back onto Box T range.

The legendary gunfighter, Charlie Starr, was buried in a quiet ceremony in the plot on the ridge above the ranch house at the Circle Double C. His guns were buried with him. He had always said he wanted to be buried with his boots on. And he was; a brand-new pair of boots.

Dooley Hanks and his sons were buried in the family plot on the D-H.

Horace Mulroony said he would stay around long enough to photograph the multiple weddings and then was going to open a paper up in Great Falls. Things were just too quiet around Gibson.

"How about you, Lujan?" Smoke asked the gunfighter.

"Oh, I think that when you pull out I might ride down south with you. I have talked it over with Silver Jim and the others. They're coming along as well." He lit a long slender cigar and looked at Smoke. "You know, *amigo,* that this little war is far from over."

"I think they'll wait until we're out of Montana Territory to hit us."

"Those are my thoughts as well."

"We'll hang around until Hardrock's shoulder heals up. Then we'll ride."

Lujan smiled. "The first of the reward money has arrived. The old men said I would take a thousand dollars of it or we'd drag iron. I took the money. It will last a long time. I am a simple man and my needs are few."

"I'd hate to have to drag iron against those old boys," Smoke conceded. "They damn sure don't come any saltier."

Lujan laughed. "They have all bought new black suits and boots and white dusters. They present quite a sight."

Parnell packed away his double-barreled blasters. But his reputation would never quite leave him. He would teach school for another forty years. And he would never have any problems with unruly students.

Walt and Leah Hillery pulled out early one morning in a buckboard. They offered no goodbyes to anyone, and no one lifted a hand in farewell. It was said they were going back East. They just weren't cut out to make it in the West.

Several of the wounded outlaws died; the rest were chained and shackled and loaded into wagons. They were taken to the nearest jail—about a hundred miles away—escorted by the squad of Army troops.

The brief boomtown of Gibson settled back into a quiet routine.

Young Bob drew his time and drifted, as Smoke had predicted he would. The hard-eyed young man would earn quite a name for himself in the coming years.

Then came the wedding day, and the day could not have been any more perfect. Mild temperatures and not a cloud in the sky.

Del and Fae, Parnell and Rita, Liz and Gage, Ring and Hilda, and Beans and Sandi got all hitched up proper, with lots of fumbling around for rings and embarrassed kisses and a big hoo-rah right after the weddings.

Beans took time out after the cake-cuttin' to speak to Smoke.

"When you pullin' out, partner?"

"In the morning. I'm missin my wife and kids. I want to get back to the Sugarloaf and the High Lonesome. Reno is pullin' out today; headin' back to Nevada."

"Them ol' boys is gonna be comin' at you, you know that, don't you?"

"Oh, yes. Might as well get it over with, 'way I look at it. No point in steppin' around the issue."

"You watch your backtrail, partner."

Smoke stuck out his hand and Beans took it. "We'll meet again," Smoke told him.

"I'm countin' on it."

As was the western way, there were no elaborate or prolonged goodbyes. The men simply packed up and mounted up before dawn and pointed the noses of their horses south, quietly riding down the main street of Gibson, Montana Territory, without looking back.

"Feels good to be movin'," Pistol said. "I git the feelin' of being all cooped up if I stay too long in one place."

"Not to mention the fact that your face was beginnin' to frighten little children," Hardrock needled him. "All the greenbacks you got now you ought to git you a bag special-made and wear it over your head."

Smoke laughed and put Dagger into a trot. It did feel good to be on the trail again.

They followed the Smith down to the Sixteenmile and then followed an old Indian trail down to the Shields—the trail would eventually become a major highway.

The men rode easily, but always keeping a good eye out for trouble. None of them expected it until they were out of the territory, but it never hurt to be ready.

They began angling more east than south, crossing the Sweetgrass, taking their time, enjoying some of the most beautiful scenery to be found. They would stop early to make camp, living off the land, hunting or fishing for their meals, for the most part avoiding any towns. They ran out of coffee and sugar and bacon just north of the Wyoming line and stopped in a little town to resupply.

The man behind the counter of the general store gave Smoke and the others a good eyeballing as they walked into the store. The men noticed the clerk seemed awfully nervous.

"Feller's got the twitchies," Hardrock whispered to Silver Jim.

"I noticed. I'll take me a stroll down to the livery; check out the horses there."

"I'll go with you," Hardrock said. "Might be walkin' into something interestin'."

"You Smoke Jensen, ain't you?" the clerk asked.

"Yes."

"You know some hard-lookin gents name of Eddie Hart and Pooch Matthews? They travelin' with several other gents just as hard-lookin'."

"I know them."

"They here. Crost the street in the saloon. My boy—who earns some pennies down to the stable—heared them talkin'. They gonna kill you."

"They're going to try." Smoke gave the man his order and then took a handkerchief and wiped the dust from his guns. Hardrock stepped back into the store.

"Half a dozen of them ol' boys in town, Smoke."

"I know. They're over at the saloon."

As the words were leaving his mouth, the town marshal stepped in.

"Jackson Bodine!" Hardrock grinned at the man. "I ain't seen you in a coon's age."

"Hello, Hardrock." The marshal stuck out his hand and Hardrock gripped it.

"When'd you take up lawin'?"

"When I got too old to do much of anything else." He looked at Smoke. "I don't want trouble in my town, Mister-whoever-you-are."

"This here's Smoke Jensen, Jackson," Hardrock said.

The marshal exhaled slowly. "I guess a man don't always get his wishes," he said reluctantly.

"I don't want trouble in your town or anybody else's town, marshal. But I'm afraid this is something those men over in the saloon won't let me sidestep." Briefly, he explained what had taken place over the past weeks.

The marshal nodded his head. "Give me ten minutes before you call them out, Smoke. That'll give me time to clear the street and have the kids back at home."

"You can have as much time as you need, Marshal."

The marshal smiled. "I never really knew for sure whether you were real or just a made-up person. They's a play about you, you know that?"

"No, I didn't. Is it a good one?"

The marshal laughed. "I ain't seen it. Folks that have gone to the big city tell me they got you somewheres between Robin Hood and Bloody Bill Anderson."

Smoke chuckled. "You know, Marshal, they just may be right."

Jackson Bodine left the store to warn the townspeople to stay off the streets.

"He's a good man," Hardrock said. "Come out here 'bout, oh, '42 or '43, I reckon. Preacher knows him. 'Course, Preacher knows just about ever'body out here, I reckon."

Silver Jim stepped inside. "I could have sworn we dropped Royce back yonder at the ranch," he said. "But he's over yonder, 'live and well and just as ugly as ever."

"Anybody else?" Lujan asked.

"Lodi, Hazzard, Nolan . . ." His eyes touched Lujan's unblinking stare. "And Diego and Gomez. Three or four more I know but can't put no names to."

The Chihuahua gunfighter grunted. "Well, gentlemen, shall we cross the street and order us a drink?"

"I am a mite thirsty," Hardrock said. "Boredom does that to me," he added with a smile.

THIRTY-ONE

The men walked across the dusty street, all of them knowing the gunfighters in the saloon were waiting for them, watching them as they crossed the street.

Smoke was the first to push open the batwings and step inside, moving to one side so the others could follow quickly and let their eyes adjust to the dimmer light.

The first thing Smoke noticed was that Diego and Gomez were widely separated, one standing clear across the room from the other. It was a trick they used often, catching a man in a crossfire.

Smoke moved to the bar, his spurs jingling softly with each step. He walked to the far end of the bar while Lujan stopped at the end of the bar closest to the batwings. The move did not escape the eyes of Diego and Gomez. Both men smiled knowingly.

Only Smoke, Lujan, and Hardrock were at the bar. Pistol and Silver Jim positioned themselves around the room, and that move made several of the outlaws very nervous.

Smoke decided to take a chance and make a try for peace. "The war is over, boys. This doesn't have to be. You're professionals. Dooley is dead. You're off his payroll. There is no profit in dying for pride."

A very tough gunfighter that Pistol knew only as Bent

sighed and pushed his chair back. "Makes sense to me. I don't fight for the fun of it." He walked out the batwings and across the boardwalk, heading for the livery.

"One never knows about a man," Diego spoke softly. "I was certain he had more courage than that."

"I always knowed he was yeller," Hazzard snorted.

"Maybe he's just smart," Smoke said.

Diego ignored that and stared at Lujan. "The noble Lujan," he said scornful "Protector of women and little children." He spat on the floor.

"At least, Diego," Lujan said, "I have that much of a reputation for decency. Can you say as much?"

"Who would want to?" the gunfighter countered. "Decency does not line my pockets with gold coins."

There was no point in talking about conscience to the man—he didn't have one.

Lujan flicked his dark eyes to Smoke. No point in delaying upcoming events, the quick glance seemed to say.

Smoke shot the Mexican gunfighter. He gave no warning; just drew, cocked, and fired, all in a heartbeat. Lujan was a split second behind him, his slug taking Gomez in the belly.

Hardrock took out Pooch Matthews just as Smoke was pouring lead into Eddie Hart, and Silver Jim and Pistol had turned their guns on the others.

Royce was down, hanging onto a table. Dave and Hazzard were backed up against a wall, the front of their shirts turning crimson. Blaine and Nolan were out of it, their hands empty and over their heads, total shock etched on their tanned faces.

Diego raised his pistol, the sound of the cocking loud in the room.

"Don't do it, Diego," Smoke warned him.

The gunfighter cursed Smoke, in English and in Spanish, telling him where he could go and in what part of his anatomy he could shove the suggestion.

Smoke shot him between the eyes just as Lujan was putting the finishing touches to Gomez.

The batwings pushed open and Jackson Bodine walked in, carrying a sawed-off double-barrel express gun.

"There might be re-ward money for them two," Hardrock said, pointing to Blaine and Nolan. "You might send a telly-graph to Fort Benton."

Hazzard finally lost the strength to hang onto the table and he fell to the floor. Dave hung on, looking at Smoke through eyes that were beginning to lose their light.

"We was snake-bit all through this here job," he said, coughing up blood. "Didn't nothin' turn out right." The table tipped over under his weight and he fell to the floor. He lay amid the cigar and cigarette butts, cursing Smoke as life left him. Profanity was the last words out of his mouth.

"Anyone else gunnin' for you boys?" the marshal asked.

"Several more," Smoke told him.

"I sure would appreciate it if y'all would take it on down the road. This is the first shootin' we've had here in three years."

Hardrock laughed at the expression on the marshal s face. "I swear, Jackson. I do believe you're gettin' crotchety in your old age."

"And would like to get older," the marshal replied.

Hardrock slapped his friend on the back. "Come on, Jackson, I'll buy you a drink."

The men rode on south, crossing the Tongue, and rode into the little town of Sheridan, Wyoming. There, they took their first hot soapy bath since leaving Gibson, got a shave and a trim, and enjoyed a café-cooked meal and several pots of strong coffee.

The sight of five of the most famous gunslingers in all the West made the marshal a tad nervous. He and some of the locals, armed with shotguns, entered the café where Smoke and his friends were eating, positioning themselves around the room.

"I swanny," Silver Jim said. "I do believe the town folks is a mite edgy today." He eyeballed the marshal. "Ain't it a bit early for duck-huntin'?"

"Very funny," a man said. "We heard about the shootin' up North. There ain't gonna be no repeat of that around here."

"I shore hope not," Hardrock told him. "Violence offends me turrible. Messes up my di-gestive workin's. Cain't sleep for days. I'm just an old man a-spendin' his twilight years a-roamin' the countryside, takin' in all the beauty of nature. Stoppin' to smell the flowers and gander at the birds."

"Folks call me Peaceful," Silver Jim said, forking in a mouthful of potatoes and gravy. "I sometimes think I missed my callin'. I should have been a poet, like that there Long-britches."

"Longfellow," Smoke corrected.

"Yeah, him, too."

"I think you're all full of horse hockey," the marshal told them. "No trouble in this town, boys. Eat your meal and kindly leave."

"Makes a man feel plumb unwanted," Pistol said.

They made camp for the night a few miles south of town. Staying east of the Bighorns, they pulled out at dawn. They rode for two days without seeing another person.

Over a supper of beans and bacon, Smoke asked, "Where do you boys pick up the rest of your reward money?"

"Cheyenne," Silver Jim replied.

"You best start anglin' off east down here at the Platte."

"That's what we was thinkin'," Pistol told him. "But I just don't think it's over, Smoke."

"You can't spend the rest of your life watching my back-trail." He looked across the fire at Lujan. "How about you, Lujan?"

"I'll head southwest at the Platte." He smiled grimly. "My services are needed down on the Utah line."

Smoke nodded. "Are you boys really going to start up a place for old gunfighters and mountain men?"

"Yep," Hardrock said. "But we gonna keep quiet about it. Let the old fellers live out they days in peace and quiet. Soon as we get it set up, we'll let you know. We gonna try to get Preacher to come and live thar. You think he would?"

"Maybe. You never know about that old coot. He's nearabouts the last mountain man."

"No," Silver Jim drawled the word. "The last mountain man will be ridin' the High Lonesome long after Preacher is gone."

"What do you mean?"

"You, boy. You be the last mountain man."

The men parted ways at the Platte. They resupplied at the trading post, had a last drink together, and rode away; Lujan to ply his deadly trade down on the Utah line; Silver Jim and Pistol Le Roux and Hardrock to get the bulk of their reward money and find a spot to build a home for old gunfighters. Smoke headed due south.

"We're goin' home, boy," he spoke to Dagger, and the horse's ears came up. "It'll be good to see Sally and the babies."

Smoke left the trail and took off into the wild, a habit he had picked up from Ol' Preacher. He felt in his guts that he was riding into trouble, so he would make himself as hard to find as possible for those wanting to kill him.

He followed the Platte down, keeping east of the Rattlesnake Hills, then crossing the Platte and making his way south, with Bear Mountain to his east. He stayed on the west side of the Shirley Mountains and rode into a small town on the Medicine Bow River late one afternoon.

He was clean-shaven now, having shaved off his mustache before leaving Gibson, although he did have a stubble of beard on his face, something he planned to rectify as soon as he could get a hot bath and find a barber.

He was trail-worn and dusty, and Dagger was just as tired as he was. "Get you rubbed down and find you a big bucket of corn, boy," Smoke promised the horse. "And me and you will get us a good night's sleep."

Dagger whinnied softly and bobbed his head up and down, as if to say, "I damn well hope so!"

Smoke stabled Dagger, telling the boy to rub him down good and give him all the corn he could eat. "And watch my gear," he said, handing the boy a silver dollar.

"Yes, *sir*!"

Slapping the dust from his clothes, Smoke stopped in the town's only saloon for a drink to cut the dry from his throat.

He was an imposing figure even in faded jeans and worn shirt. Wide-shouldered and lean-hipped, with his arms bulging with muscle, and cold, emotionless eyes. The men in the saloon gave him a careful once-over, their eyes lingering on the guns around his waist, the left gun butt-forward. Don't see many men carrying guns thataway, and it marked him immediately.

Gunfighter.

"Beer," Smoke told the barkeep and began peeling a hard-boiled egg.

Beer in front of him, Smoke drank half of the mug and wiped his mouth with the back of his hand and then ate the egg.

"Passin' through?" the barkeep asked.

"Yeah. Lookin' for a hot bath and a shave and a bed."

"Got a few rooms upstairs. Cost you . . ."

"He won't be needin' no bath," the cold voice came from the batwings. "Just a pine box."

Smoke cut his eyes. Jason Bright stepped into the room, which had grown as silent as the grave.

Smoke was tired of killing. Tired of it all. He wanted no

trouble with Jason Bright. But damned if he could see a way out of it.

"Jason, I'll tell you the same thing I told Diego, just before I killed him."

Chairs were pushed back and men got out of the line of fire. Diego dead? Lord have mercy! Who was this big stranger anyways?

"Speak your piece, Jensen," Jason said.

Smoke Jensen! Lordy, Lordy!

"The war is over," Smoke spoke softly but firmly. "Nobody's paying you now. There are warrants all over the place for you. Ride out, man."

"You queered the deal for me, Smoke. Me and a lot of others. They scattered all around, from here to Colorado, just waitin' for a shot at you. But I think I'll just save them the trouble."

"Don't do it, Jason. Ride on out."

The batwings were suddenly pushed inward, striking Jason in the back and throwing him off balance. Smoke lunged forward and for the second time in about a month, Jason Bright was about to get the stuffing kicked out of him.

Smoke hit the gunfighter in the mouth and floored him, as the man who had pushed open the batwings took one look inside and hauled his freight back to the house. He didn't need a drink noways.

Smoke jerked Jason's guns from leather and tossed them into a man's lap, almost scaring the citizen to death.

"I'm tired of it, Jason," Smoke told the man, standing over him like an oak tree. "Tired of the killing, tired of it all."

Jason came up with the same knife he once tried to use on Cord. Smoke kicked it out of his hand and decked the man with a hard right fist. He jerked Jason up and slammed him against the bar. Then Smoke proceeded to hammer at the man's midsection with a battering-ram combination of lefts and rights. Smoke both felt and heard ribs break under the hammering. Jason's eyes rolled back in his head and Smoke let him fall to the floor.

"You ought to go on and kill him, Smoke," a man called from the crowd. "He ain't never gonna forget this. Someday he'll come after you."

"I know," Smoke panted the words. "But I'm tired of the killing. I don't want to kill anybody else. Ever!"

"We'll haul him over to the doc's office for you, Smoke," a man volunteered. "He ain't gonna be ridin' for a long time to come. Not with all them busted ribs. And I heard 'em pop and crack."

"I'm obliged to you." He looked at the bartender. "The tub around back."

"Yes, sir. I'll get a boy busy with the hot water right away."

"Keep anybody else off me, will you?"

Several men stood up. "Let us get our rifles, Mister Jensen. You can bathe in peace."

"I appreciate it." He looked down at Jason. "You should have kept ridin', Jason. You can't say I didn't give you a chance.'

THIRTY-TWO

Dagger was ready to go when Smoke saddled up the next morning. Not yet light in the east. He wanted to get gone, get on the trail home. He would stop down the road a ways and fix him some bacon to go with the bread he'd bought the night before. But he would have liked some coffee. He looked toward the town's only café. Still dark. Smoke shrugged and pointed Dagger's nose south. He had his small coffeepot and plenty of coffee. No trouble to fix coffee when he fixed the bacon.

About an hour after dawn, he stopped by a creek and made his fire. He fixed his bacon and coffee and sopped out the pan with the bread, then poured a cup of coffee and rolled a cigarette.

The creek made happy little sounds as it bubbled on, and the shade was cool. Smoke was reluctant to leave, but knew he'd better put some miles behind Dagger's tail.

Jason's words returned to him: "They scattered all around, from here to Colorado, just waitin' for a shot at you."

He thought back: Had there been a telegraph wire at that little town? He didn't think so. And where would the nearest wire office be? One over at Laramie, for sure. But by the time he could ride over there and wire Sally to be on the lookout, he could be almost home.

He really wasn't that worried. The Sugarloaf was very isolated, and unless a man knew the trails well, they'd never come in from the back range. If any strangers tried the road, the neighbors would be instantly alerted.

Smoke made sure his fire was out, packed up his kit, and climbed into the saddle. He'd make the northernmost edge of the Medicine Bow Range by nightfall. And he'd stay in the timber into Colorado, doing his best to avoid contact with any of the outlaws. Ol' Preacher had burned those trails into his head as a boy. He could travel them in his sleep.

Nightfall found him on the ridges of the Medicine Bow Range. It had been slow going, for he followed no well-traveled trails, staying with the trails in his mind.

He made his camp, ate his supper, and put out his fire, not wanting the fire's glow to attract any unwanted gunslicks during the night. Smoke rolled up in his blankets, a ground sheet under him and his saddle for a pillow.

He was up before dawn and built a hat-size fire for his bacon and coffee. For some reason that he could not fathom, he had a case of the jumps this morning. Looking over at Dagger, he could see that the big horse was also uneasy, occasionally walling his eyes and laying his ears back.

Smoke ate his breakfast and drank his coffee, dousing the fire. He filled his canteens from a nearby crick and let Dagger drink. Smoke checked his guns, wiping them free of dust, and then loaded up the chamber under the hammer, usually kept empty. He checked his Winchester. Full.

Then, on impulse, he dug out a bandoleer from the saddle-bags and filled all the loops, then added a handful of cartridges to his jacket pocket.

He would be riding into wild and beautiful country this day and the next, with some of the mountains shooting up past twelve thousand feet. It was also no country to be caught up high in a thunderstorm, with lightning dancing all around you. That made a fellow feel very small and vulnerable.

And it could also cook you like a fried egg.

The farther he rode into the dark timber, the more edgy he became. Twice he stopped and dismounted, checking all around him on foot. He could find nothing to get alarmed about, but all his senses were working hard.

Had he made a mistake by taking to the timber? The outlaws knew—indeed, half the reading population of the States knew—that Smoke had been raised in the mountains by Preacher, and he felt more at home in the mountains.

He pressed on, slowly.

He came to a blowdown, a savage-appearing area of about thirty or forty acres—maybe more than that—that had suffered a ravaging storm, probably a twister touchdown. It was a dark and ominous-looking place, with the trees torn and ripped from the earth, piled on top of each other and standing on end and lying every which-a-way possible.

He had dismounted upon sighting the area, and the thought came to him that maybe he'd better picket Dagger and just wait here for a day, maybe two or three if it came to that. He did not understand the thought, but his hunches had saved his life before.

He found a natural corral, maybe fifty by fifty feet, with three sides protected by piled-up trees, the front easily blocked by brush.

He led Dagger into the area and stripped the saddle from him.

There was plenty of grass inside the nature-provided corral, so he covered the entrance with brush and limbs and left Dagger rolling; soon he would be grazing. There were pools where rainwater had collected, and that would be enough for several days.

Taking a canteen and his rifle, Smoke walked several

hundred yards from where he left his gear, reconnoitering the area.

Then he heard a horse snort, another one doing the same. Faint voices come to him.

"Lost his damn trail back yonder."

Smoke knew the voice: Lanny Ball.

"We'll find it," Lodi said. "Then we'll torture him 'fore we kill him. I done had some of that money spent back yonder till he come along and queered it for us."

Smoke edged closer, until he could see the men as they passed close by. Cat Jennings's gang were in the group.

"Hell, I'm tarred," a man complained. "And our horses are all done in. We gonna kill them if we keep on. And we got a lot of rough country ahead of us."

"Let's take a rest," Lodi said. "We can loaf the rest of the day and pick up the trail tomorrow."

"Damn good idee," an outlaw named Sutton said. "I could do with me some food and coffee."

"All right," Lanny agreed. "I'm beat myself."

Smoke kept his position, thinking about this new pickle he'd gotten himself into.

It was only a matter of time—maybe minutes or even seconds—before Dagger caught the scent of other horses and let his presence be known. Then whatever element of surprise Smoke had working for him would be gone.

There were few options left for him. He could back-track and saddle up, hoping Dagger didn't give his position away, and try to ride out. But he knew in his heart that was grabbing at straws.

His other option was to fight.

But he was body and soul sick of fighting. If he could ride out peacefully and go home and hang up his guns and never strap them on again he would be content. God, but that would be wonderful.

The next statement from the mouth of a outlaw drifted to

him, and Smoke knew this fight had to be ended right here and now.

"They tell me that Jensen's wife is a real looker. When we kill him, let's ride on down to Colorado. I'd like to have me a taste of Sally Jensen. I like it when they fight." Then he said some other things he'd like to do to Sally. The filth rolled in a steady stream from his mouth, burning deep into Smoke's brain. Finally he stood up, the verbal disgust fouling the pure clean mountain air.

Smoke lifted his Winchester and shot the man in the belly.

Smoke shifted position immediately, darting swiftly away. He was dressed in earth colors, and had left his hat back at the corral. He knew he would be nearly impossible to spot. And after hearing the agreeing and ugly laughter of the outlaws at the gut-shot man's filthy, disgustingly perverted suggestions, Smoke was white-hot angry and on the warpath.

He knelt behind a thick fallen log, all grown around with brush, and waited, his Winchester at the ready, hammer eared back.

Movement to his right caught his eyes. He fired and a wild shriek of pain cut the air. "My elbow's ruint!" a man wailed.

Smoke fired again into the same spot. The man with the ruined elbow stood up in shock and pain as the second bullet slammed into him. He fell forward onto his face.

As the lead started flying around him, thudding into the fallen logs and still-standing trees, Smoke crawled away, working his way around the outlaws' position, steadily climbing uphill.

He swung wide around them, moving through the wilderness just as Ol' Preacher had taught him, silently flitting from cover to cover, seething mad clear through; but his brain was clear and cold and thinking dark primal thoughts that would have made a grizzly back up and give him room.

In the West, a man just didn't bother a good woman—or even a bad woman for that matter. Or even say aloud the things the now-dead outlaw had mouthed. Molest a woman, and most western men would track that man for days and either shoot him or hang him on the spot.

Smoke caught a glimpse of color that did not fit into this terrain. He paused, oak-tree still, and waited. The man's impatience got the better of whatever judgment he possessed, and he started to shift positions.

Smoke lifted his rifle and drilled the outlaw, the bullet entering his right side and blowing out the left side.

Smoke thought the man's name was Sweeney; one of Cat Jennings's crud.

Lead splattered bark from a tree and Smoke felt the sting of it. He dropped to one knee and fired just under the puff of gunsmoke drifting up from the outlaw's position, working the lever just as fast as he could, filling the cool air with lead.

A crashing body followed the spray of bullets.

"He ain't but one man!" a harsh voice shouted. "Come on, let's rush him."

"You rush him, Woody" was the reply. "If you so all-fired anxious to get kilt."

"I'm gonna kill you, Jensen!" Woody hollered. "Then drag your stinkin' carcass till they ain't nothing left for even the varmits to eat."

Smoke remained still, listening to the braggard make his claims.

"I'll take him," a high thin voice was added to the brags.

Danny Rouge.

The only thing that moved was Smoke's eyes. He knew he couldn't let Danny live, couldn't let Danny get him in gunsights, for the punk's aim was deadly true.

There, Smoke's eyes settled on a spot. That's where the voice came from. But was the back-shooter still there? Smoke doubted it. Danny was too good to speak and then remain in the same spot. But which direction did he take?

There was only one direction that was logical, at least to Smoke's mind. Up the rise.

Smoke sank to the cool moist earth that lay under the pile of storm-torn and -tossed logs. As silent as a stalking snake he inched his way under a huge pile of logs and paused, waiting.

"Well, dammit, boy!" Woody's voice cut the stillness, broken only by someone's hard moaning, probably the gut-shot outlaw. "What are you waitin' on, Christmas?"

But Danny was too good at his sneaky work to give away his location with a reply.

Smoke lay still, waiting.

Someone stepped on a dry branch and it popped. Smoke's eyes found the source and he could have easily killed the man. He chose to wait. He had the patience of an Indian and knew that his cat-and-mouse game was working on the nerves of the outlaws.

"To hell with you people!" a man spoke. "I'm gone. Jensen ain't no human person."

"You git back here, Carlson!" Lanny shouted.

Carlson told Lanny, in very blunt and profane language, where to go and how to get there.

That would be very painful, Smoke thought, allowing himself a thin smile.

He heard the sound of horses' hooves. The sound gradually faded.

Rifle fire slammed the air. A man cursed painfully. "Dammit, Dalton, you done me in."

A rifle clattered onto wood and fell to the earth with a dull thud. The outlaw mistakenly shot by one of his own men fell heavily to the earth. He died cursing Dalton.

Still Smoke did not move.

"Smoke? Smoke Jensen? It's me, Jonas. I'm gone, man. Pullin' out. Just let me get to my hoss and you'll never see me agin."

"Jonas, you yeller rabbit!" Lanny yelled. "Git back here."

But the fight had gone out of Jonas. He found his tired horse and mounted up. He was gone, thinking that Smoke Jensen was a devil, worser than any damn Apache that ever lived.

Smoke sensed more than heard movement behind him. But he knew that he could not be spotted under the pile of tangled logs, and he had carefully entered, not disturbing the brush that grew around and over the narrow entrance.

For a long minute the man, Danny, Smoke felt sure, did not move. Then to Smoke's surprise, boots appeared just inches from his eyes. Danny had moved, and done so with the stealth of a ghost.

He was good, Smoke conceded. Very good. Maybe too good for his own good.

Very carefully, Smoke lifted the muzzle of his rifle, lining it up about three feet above the boots. The muzzle followed the boots as they moved silently around the pile of logs, then stopped.

Smoke caught a glimpse of a belt buckle, lifted the muzzle an inch above it, and pulled the trigger.

Danny Rouge screamed as the bullet tore into his innards. Smoke fired again, for insurance, and Danny was down, kicking and squalling and crying.

"I'm the bes'," he hollered in his high, thin voice. "I'm the bes' they is."

Wild shooting drowned out whatever else Danny was saying. But none of the bullets came anywhere near to Smoke's location. None of the outlaws even dreamed that Smoke had shot the back-shooter from almost point-blank range.

Danny turned his head and his eyes met those of Smoke, just a couple of yards away, under the pile of logs.

"Damn you!" Danny whispered, his lips wet with blood. "Damn you to hell!" He closed his eyes and shivered as death took him.

Smoke waited until the back-shooter had died, then took

a thick pole and shoved the body downhill. It must have landed near, or perhaps on, an outlaw, for the man yelped in fright.

"Lanny, let's get out of here," a man called. "We ain't gonna get Jensen. The man's a devil."

"He's one man, dammit!" Lanny yelled. "Just one man, that's all."

"Then you take him, Lanny." The outlaw's voice had a note of finality in it. "'Cause I'm gone."

Lanny cursed the man.

"Jensen, I'm hauling my freight," Hayes called. "I hope I don't never seen you no more. Not that I've seen you this day," he added wearily.

Another horse's hooves were added to those already riding down the trail, away from this devil some called the last mountain man.

Smoke remained in his position as Lanny, Woody, and a few more wasted a lot of ammunition, knocking holes in trees and burning the air.

Smoke calmly chewed on a piece of jerky and waited.

THIRTY-THREE

Smoke had carefully noted the positions of those left. Five of them. He had heard their names called out. Woody, Dalton, Lodi, Sutton, and Lanny Ball.

The outlaws had tried to bait Smoke, cursing him, voicing what they were going to do to his wife and kids. Filthy things, inhuman things. Smoke lay under the jumble of logs and kept his thoughts to himself. If he had even whispered them, the white-hot fury might have set the logs blazing.

After more than two hours, Sutton called, "I think he's gone, Lanny. I think he suckered us and pulled out and set up a new position."

"I think he's right, Lanny," Woody yelled. "You know his temper; all them things we been sayin' about his wife would have brought him out like a bear."

Sutton abruptly stood up for a few seconds, then dropped to the ground. Lodi did the same, followed by the rest of them, and cautiously, tentatively, the outlaws stood up and began walking toward each other. Lanny was the last one to stand up.

He began cursing the rotten luck, the country, the gods of fate, and most of all, he cussed Smoke Jensen.

Smoke emptied his rifle into Lodi, Sutton, Dalton, and Woody, knocking them spinning and screaming to the littered earth.

Lanny hit the ground.

Smoke had dragged Danny's fancy rifle to him with a stick. Dropping his empty Winchester, Smoke ended any life that might have been left in the quartet of scum, then backed out of his hiding place and stretched his cramped muscles, protected by the huge pile of logs.

Smoke carefully checked his Colts, wiping them free of dirt with a bandanna. "All right, Lanny!" he called. "You made your brags back in Gibson. Let's end this madness right here and now. Let's see if you've got the guts to face a man. You sure have been real brave telling me what you planned to do with my wife."

"You know I wouldn't do that to no good woman, Jensen. That was just to make you mad."

"You succeeded, Lanny."

"Let's call it off, Smoke. I'll ride away and you won't see me no more."

"All right, Lanny. You just do that little thing."

"You mean it?"

"I'm tired of this killing, Lanny. Mount up and get gone."

"You'll back-shoot me, Jensen!" There was real fear in the outlaw's voice.

"No, Lanny. I'll leave that to punks like you."

Lanny cursed him.

"I'm steppin' out, Lanny." This was to be no fast-draw encounter. Smoke knew Lanny was going to try to kill him any way he could. Smoke's hands were full of Colts, the hammers eared back.

At the edge of the piled-up logs, Smoke started running. Lanny fired, missed, and fired again, the bullet burning Smoke's side. He turned and began pulling and cocking, a thunderous roar in the savage blowdown.

Lanny took half a dozen rounds in his upper torso, the force of the striking slugs driving him back against a huge old stump. He tried to lift his guns. He could not. His strength was gone. Smoke walked over to him, reloading as he walked.

"You ain't human," Lanny coughed up the words. "You a devil."

"You got any kin you want me to write?"

"You go to hell!"

Smoke turned his back to the man and walked away.

"You ain't gonna leave me to die alone, is you?" Lanny called feebly.

Smoke stopped. With a sigh, he turned around and walked back to the outlaw's side. Lanny looked up as the light in his eyes began to dim. Smoke rolled a cigarette, lit it, and stuck it between Lanny's lips.

"Thanks."

Smoke waited. The cigarette fell out of Lanny's lips. Smoke picked it up and ground it out under the heel of his boot.

"Least I can go out knowin' it wasn't no two-bit tinhorn who done me in," were Lanny's last words.

Smoke returned to the natural corral and saddled up. He wanted no more of this blown-down place of death. And from Dagger's actions, the big horse didn't either. Smoke rode out of the Medicine Bow Range and took the easy way south. He crossed the Laramie River and made camp on the shores of Lake Hattie.

He crossed over into Colorado the next morning and felt he was in home territory, even though he had many, many hard miles yet to go.

He followed the Laramie down into the Medicine Bow Mountains, riding easy, but still with the smell of sudden and violent death seeming to cling to him. He wanted no more of it. As he rode he toyed with the idea of selling out and pulling out.

He rejected that almost as quickly as the thought sprang into his brain.

The Sugarloaf belonged to Smoke and Sally Jensen. Fast gun he might be, but he wasn't going to let his unwanted reputation drive him away. If there were punks and crud in the world who felt they just had to try him . . . well, that was their problem. He had never sought the name of Gunfighter; but damned if he was going to back down, either.

The West was changing rapidly. Oh, there would be a few more wild and woolly years, but probably no more than a decade before law and order settled in. Law and order was changing everything and everybody west of the Mississippi. Jesse James was dead, killed in 1882. Clell Miller had been dead for years. Clay Allison had died a very ignoble death back in '77. Sam Bass was gone. Curley Bill Brocius had been killed by Wyatt Earp in Tombstone in '82. John Wesley Hardin was in a Texas prison. Rowdy Joe Lowe had met his end in Denver, killed in a gunfight over his wife. Mysterious Dave Mather had vanished about a year back and no one knew where he was.

Smoke doubted Dave would ever resurface. Probably changed his name and was living respectable.

Smoke rode the old trails, alive with the ghosts of mountain men who had come and gone years back, blazing the very trails he now rode. He thought of all the gunfighters and outlaws that were gone.

Charlie Storms was dead—and not too many folks mourned his passing. Charlie had been sitting at the table in Deadwood back in '76 when Cross-Eyed Jack McCall walked up behind Wild Bill and blew his brains out. Charlie tried to brace Luke Short in Tombstone back in '81. He rolled twelve.

I've known them all, Smoke mused. The good and the bad and that curious combination of both.

Dallas Stoudenmire finally saw the elephant back in '82.

Ben Thompson had been killed just the year back, Smoke recalled, down in San Antonio. Killed while watching a play.

The list was a long one, and getting longer.

And me? Smoke reflected. How many men have gone down under my guns?

He really didn't know. But he knew the count was awesomely high. He knew that he was rated as the number-one gunfighter in all the West; knew that he had killed a hundred men—or more. Probably more.

He shook those thoughts out of his head. There was no point in dwelling on them, and no point in trying to even think that he could live without his guns. There was no telling how many tinhorn punks and would-be gunslicks would be coming after him after the news of Gibson hit the campfires and the saloons of the West.

He stopped at a small four-store town and bought himself a couple of sacks of tobacco and rolling papers. He cut himself a wedge of cheese and got him a pickle from the barrel and a sackful of crackers. He went outside to sit on the porch of the store to have his late-afternoon snack.

"That there's Smoke Jensen." The words came to him from inside the store.

"No!"

"Yeah. He's killed a thousand men. Young, ain't he?"

"A thousand men?"

"Yeah. 'Course, that ain't countin' Indians."

Small children came to stand by the edge of the store to stare at him through wide eyes. Smoke knew how a freak in a carnival must feel. But he couldn't blame the kids. He'd been written about so much in the penny dreadfuls and other books of the time that the kids didn't know what to think of him.

Or the adults, either, for that matter.

Damn! but he was tired. Tired both physically and mentally.

Once he got back to Sally and the Sugarloaf, he didn't think he'd ever leave her side until she got a broom and ran him off.

He offered a cracker to a shy little girl and she slowly took it.

"Jeanne!" her mother squalled from a house across the dusty street. "You get away from him!"

Jeanne smiled at Smoke, grabbed the cracker and took off.

Smoke looked up at the sounds of horses walking toward him. He sighed heavily. The two-bit punk who called himself Larado and that pair of no-goods, Johnny and Brett, were heading his way.

He slipped the thongs off his hammers and called over his shoulder, "Shopkeep! Get these kids out of here—right now!"

Within half a minute, the street was deserted.

Smoke stood up as the trio dismounted and began walking toward him.

"Back off, boys!" Smoke called. "This doesn't have to be."

Larado snorted. "What's the matter, Jensen? You done turned yeller on us?"

"Don't be a fool!" Smoke's words were hard. "I'm tryin' to make you see that there is no point to this."

"The point is, Mister Big-Shot," Johnny said, and Smoke could smell the whiskey from all them even at this distance, "we gonna kill you."

Smoke shook his head. "No, you're not, boys. If you drag iron, you're dead. All of you." He started walking toward them.

Bret's eyes widened in fear. Johnny and Larado wore looks of indecision on their young faces.

"Well!" Smoke snapped, closing the distance. "At this range we're all going to die, you know that, don't you, boys?"

They knew it, and it literally scared the pee out of Bret.

Smoke slapped Larado with a hard open palm, knocking the young man's hat off and bloodying his mouth. He backhanded Johnny with the same hand and drove his left fist into Bret's stomach.

Reaching out, he tore the gunbelt from Larado and hit the young man in the face with it, breaking his nose and knocking him to the ground.

Smoke tossed the gunbelt and pistols into a watering trough. He looked down at the young men, lying on the ground.

"It's not as easy as the books make it out to be, is it, boys?" Smoke asked them. He expected no reply and got none.

Smoke reached down and jerked guns from leather, tossing them into the same trough.

"You can keep your rifles. Keep them and ride out. Go on back home and learn you a trade. Go to school; make something out of yourselves. But don't ever brace me again. For if you do, I'll kill you without hesitation. I'm giving you a chance. Take it."

The young men slowly picked themselves up off the ground and mounted up. They rode out without looking back.

"Mighty fine thing you done there, Mister Smoke," a man said. "Mighty fine. You could have killed them all."

Smoke looked at the citizen. "I'm tired of killing. I know that I'll have to kill again, but I'm not looking forward to it."

"The wife is fixin' a pot roast for supper. We'd be proud to have you sit at our table. She's a good cook, my old woman is. And the kids would just be beside themselves if you was to come on over. Don't a home-cooked meal sound good to you?"

A smile slowly creased Smoke's lips. "It sure does."

Smoke did not leave the Sugarloaf for a week. He got reacquainted with Sally every time she bumped into him . . . and she bumped into him a lot.

He rolled on the floor with the babies and acted a fool with them, making faces at them, letting him ride his back like a horse, and in general, settling back into the routine of being a husband, father, and rancher.

On the morning that he decided to ride into town, Sally's voice stopped him in the door.

"Aren't you forgetting something, Smoke?"

He turned. She was holding his guns in her hands.

He stared at her.

"I know, honey," she said. "I've known for a long time that you're tired of the killing."

"It just seems like a man ought to be able to ride into town without strapping on a gun."

"I don't know whether that day will ever come, honey. As long as you are Smoke Jensen, the last mountain man, there will be people riding to try you. And you know that." She came to him and pressed against him. "And speaking very selfishly, I kind of like to have you around."

Smoke smiled and took the gunbelt, hooking it on a peg.

She looked up at him, questions in her eyes.

He whispered in her ear.

She laughed and bumped into him again.

TRIUMPH OF THE
MOUNTAIN MAN

ONE

Once a week, a Sugarloaf hand rode into Big Rock, Colorado, to pick up the mail. Lost Ranger Peak brooded over the town, its 11,940-foot summit covered by a mantle of white year-round. Often the journey proved to be nothing more than an excuse to spend an hour or two in the Bright Lights saloon. With the exception of Sally Jensen's sporadic correspondence with a few old school friends, scant mail ever came to the home of the fabled gunfighter Smoke Jensen. On a fine morning in late April, then, Ike Mitchell, the Sugarloaf foreman, expressed his surprise when Smoke Jensen announced that he reckoned he would be the one to ride into Big Rock.

Ike hastened to relieve his employer of the burden. "No need to trouble yourself, Mr. Jensen. One of the boys can make the mail run."

"No trouble, Ike. I really feel like I ought to go." Smoke brushed at his reddish blond hair and gazed across the pastures of the Sugarloaf with his oddly gold-cast eyes. "There's some little—something—nagging me to make the ride into town."

Ike chuckled behind a big, work-hardened hand. The wings of gray hair at his temples waved in a light breeze. "Needin' a little time away from Miz Sally, eh?"

"Not exactly, Ike. Though I'll admit I would enjoy a good card game and a few schooners of beer with friends."

With a knowing wink, Ike encouraged Smoke. "You'll have time enough for that, like as not. Not many people know where the Sugarloaf is, let alone how to reach it by mail. Enjoy your day, Mr. Jensen."

"I will Ike. Anything I can bring you from town?"

Ike removed his black, low-crowned Stetson and scratched his head. "The missus could use a bottle of sulphur elixir to treat the young'uns for spring."

Smoke involuntarily made a face at the memory of that medical treatment. It had not been one of the things he missed when separated from his family and taken in by Preacher. "I'll get it, then. Only, don't tell your brood who it was brought it."

Amorous meadowlarks whistled to prospective mates as Smoke Jensen rode over the wooden bridge that spanned the Elk River. and entered Big Rock. He kept his Palouse stallion, Cougar, at a gentle walk. In spite of the chill in the air, the sun felt warm on his shoulders. He had left his working chaps behind, and wore a rust-colored pair of whipcord trousers, a green yoke shirt, and a buckskin vest. Around his narrow waist he carried his famous—or infamous, according to some—pair of .45 Colt Peacemakers. The right-hand one was slung low on his leg, the left in a pouch holster high on the cartridge belt, the butt pointed forward. Several writers of dime novels, Ned Buntline included, had made such a getup known to millions as a "gunfighter's rig."

Smoke looked on it as a practical necessity. The same as the .45-70-500 Winchester Express rifle in the saddle scabbard. While not expecting trouble, Smoke had learned long ago that it paid to come prepared at all times. As his legendary mentor, Preacher, had said, "It tends to increase a feller's life span."

"Morning," Smoke greeted a teamster who struggled with the ten-up team hauling a precarious-looking load of logs on a bedless, cradle wagon. The man gave a wave as Smoke rode on.

Farther into town, the streets became more populous. Women in gingham dresses and bonnets, their shopping baskets clutched in gloved hands, clicked the heels of their black, high-button shoes on the boardwalk of the main street. Horses stood, hip-shot, outside the saddle maker's, the bank, three saloons and the general store. A couple of empty buckboards rattled in from another direction, while one was being loaded by a harassed-looking teenager in a white apron. A typical Saturday in Big Rock, Smoke allowed. He nosed Cougar toward the hitch rail in front of the general mercantile. There he dismounted and climbed to the plank walk.

Inside the store, Nate Barber, the owner, greeted Smoke warmly. "Not often enough we see you, Mr. Jensen. You sure picked a day for it. Got near a whole mail bag full for you."

Smoke raised a yellow-brown eyebrow. "That so? I wonder what the occasion might be?"

"Catalogue time again," the postmaster/merchant advised, then added a familiar complaint. "Those mail-order outfits are going to be the ruin of stores like mine."

Smoke nodded and went to the caged counter, behind which ran a ceiling-high rank of pigeon-hole boxes to hold the mail. His, he noted, bulged with envelopes. Barber went into his small post office and bent to retrieve a stack of bound, soft-cover volumes. "Here you are, Mr. Jensen. I'll get those letters for you, too."

Smoke went quickly through the catalogues. He found the latest Sears issue for Sally, another for musical instruments by mail order, and one for himself, from a saddle and tack manufacturer. That might prove useful, he reasoned. Anything made of leather eventually wore out, and no manner of patching could salvage it in the end. Some of the breaking saddles used on the Sugarloaf had begun to look rather shabby. If the prices were lower for this outfit in San Angelo, Texas, than in Denver, he might order four new ones. Among the correspondence he found a creamy, thick envelope of obvious high quality, addressed to him in a rich, flowery script that denoted that the writer had learned his letters in a language other than English. The return address was Rancho de la Gloria, Taos, New Mexico Territory. Don Diego Alvarado, Smoke recognized at once.

Smoke had come to know Diego Alvarado several years ago, when he had been in New Mexico briefly on a cattle-buying trip. The gentlemanly, reserved Don Diego was the grandson of an original Spanish grandee, who had the patent of the King of Spain for roughly a thousand acres of high, mountainous desert to the west of Taos. His father had retained title to the land through service to the Mexican government after independence and had added to the family holdings. Steeped in the traditions of his ancestors' culture, Alvarado was a superb host who loved to entertain. Smoke had soon discovered that Diego's facade of reserve quickly vanished with a glass of tequila in one hand and a slice of lime in the other. The "little feast" put on for Smoke and his hands had turned out to be a three-day extravaganza of food and drink. They had paid for their lavish keep before leaving, however. Smoke and his men had joined the *vaqueros* of Rancho de la Gloria in fighting off a band of renegade Comanches who swarmed up out of the Texas panhandle.

Barber interrupted his speculation. "Need any supplies today, Mr. Jensen?"

"No, Nate, I didn't bring a wagon along. Say, do you happen to have any of that sulphur elixir?"

Nate Barber nodded. "Just happens I do, now that I bought out old Doc Phillips's stock from the apothecary shop. How many bottles?"

Smoke chuckled. "Ike's got six youngsters out there. Might as well make it two bottles."

"Sure thing."

The merchant produced the corked, seamless glass bottles and wrapped each in paper. Smoke noticed that the packaging material appeared to be printed pages. "Advertising your place now, Nate?"

Nate glanced down, then smiled as he cut his eyes to Smoke. "Nope. Discarded catalogues. Some folks find 'em a bother and toss 'em away."

Smoke nodded his understanding, paid for his purchase and took his mail and the medicine along. Outside, he stowed it all in his saddlebags, swung into the saddle, and directed Cougar toward his next stop. Monte Carson would no doubt be downing his twelfth cup of coffee about now.

"Smoke! How'er you doin'?" Monte Carson bellowed as Smoke entered the office portion of the jail. Smoke and the sheriff had been friends for many long years, ever since the time when Smoke foreswore the dangerous life of a gun-fighter-for-hire and stood back-to-back with Monte to rid the streets of Big Rock of some mighty nasty gunhawks and saddle trash. They had done a fair job of cleaning up all of Routt County for that matter. Smoke Jensen wore a badge for the first time in his life then, and had done so often since. Not that Smoke had been an outlaw in the truest sense of the word. He had never stolen anything, nor had he taken money for killing a man. Yet, it was always a close thing for a gun-fighter to prove self-defense in a shoot-out. Being fully and permanently on the side of the law had a good feeling. Smoke had Monte to thank for that.

He poured coffee for himself and used the toe of one boot

to hook a captain's chair over by a rung. Seated, he faced Monte. "Well, Monte, I came in on the mail run."

"You expectin' somethin' important?"

"No, but it appears I got it anyway." He went on to tell Monte about the letter from Don Diego Alvarado.

"Why don't you open it up and find out what it is?" Monte asked. "Might be an invite to the wedding of one of his sons."

Smoke shook his head. "I doubt that. Last I heard, Alejandro was already married. Xavier is down in Mexico at some seminary, studying to become a priest. Pablo would be a mere boy in his teens. Lupe could be only eight or so, and Miguel was born not three years ago."

Always curious, Monte prompted his friend. "So? Open the dang thing up and get a look."

"I will. But, being it's near noon, I thought you'd like to join me for a schooner or two of beer and some of Hank's free lunch over at the Bright Lights."

Monte grinned and, coming to his boots, nodded his head in eagerness. "You buyin'?"

"Of course. Although I wouldn't want it to be considered bribing an officer of the law. I don't want to be a guest of the county for even half an hour."

Monte reached for a drawer. "Well, then, hang a deputy's badge on yer vest and we'll call it a treat among brother lawmen. You know I'll bend heaven and earth to get a free beer."

They laughed together as they left the office. It was a short enough walk, only across the street, Smoke left Cougar tied off in front of the jail. The bar of the Bright Lights was crowded when they entered, so they took a table near the back of the room. The resinous odor of fresh sawdust perfumed the saloon. Smoke and Monte ordered beer and then built sandwiches of thick-sliced country ham, Swiss cheese, and boiled buffalo tongue, all on home-baked bread. They added fat dill pickles and hard-boiled eggs to their plates and carried them to where they would sit.

After taking a bite and chewing thoroughly, Smoke asked Monte about the town. The lawman responded eagerly.

"Let me tell you about these two drifters who tried to rob Nate's general mercantile," Monte began around a bite of his huge sandwich. "This happened about a week ago. They went in with bandannas pulled up over their noses and six-guns out. Well, Nate had no mind to try to stop them. One of the saddle trash growled at him about giving up all the money. Nate did, and put it in a paper bag, like they asked. The one who took the bag must have had a sweet tooth, 'cause right then he spied a jar of rock candy on the counter. Like a kid who only gets to town once in six months, he set the bag full of money aside and made for that jar. He stuffed his shirt pockets full of candy, and the ones in his vest, too. Then he grabbed up the cash and started to back out the door with his partner.

"What he didn't know," Monte went on, fighting back laughter, "is that he set that paper sack on top of the pickle barrel. It was a new, unopened one, but the lid had sprung. The bottom of the bag got soaked, and the weight of the money caused it to fall through. Coins went ever which a way. Right then, Nate grabbed up his shotgun while the robbers gaped at the fluttering bills that still fell from the sack. He had 'em disarmed and hands in the air when a passerby saw what was happenin' and came over to get me."

Smoke joined Monte's chuckles. "They don't make desperados like they used to. That all the excitement you've had?"

"Nope. Mrs. Granger had another baby, her eighth. Her husband swore he thought they were both too old for that to happen. A boy. That makes five boys and three girls."

"And all living?" Smoke inquired.

"Yep. By some miracle. Oh, yeah, how'd you fare out at the Sugarloaf in that thunderstorm middle of last week?"

"Not bad. Barely a shower there."

Monte frowned. "A lot more around here. A regular

goose-drownder. The Elk River went over its banks all along the valley. We had tree trunks and driftwood floating down Tom Longley Street for two days."

Smoke bit, chewed, and swallowed before remarking, "I thought it looked a mite damp along there."

"'Damp' don't get it by about three feet, Smoke. Had some of the merchants writin' to the governor to ask for help in cleanup and repair. Hell, any fool knows the government ain't got any money. Only that they take from the people in taxes."

Smoke nodded agreement. "And I remember the time when a decent man wouldn't ask for a handout when he could make do for himself."

Monte put on a poker face. "But I reckon times they are a-changin'. It's gettin' too civilized around here."

Smoke slapped a big palm on one thigh. "Don't get me started on that. Any other urgent news?"

"Only that my chief deputy, Sam Barnes, was sparking the young widow Phillips last Sunday at the church box supper social."

"You mean the pretty young thing that some gossips are saying put old Doc Phillips in an early grave?"

"The same. A man's shy some gravy for his grits when he brings one home that's not half his age. Mind, I don't know about their home life and have no desire to speculate. She's a looker, though."

"That she is, Monte." In silence, they returned to their food.

Ace Banning paused to extinguish a quirley before he entered the bank in Big Rock. Few people remained in the lobby this close to noon. The bank would close in five minutes, according to the oak-cased wall clock that hung on the far wall. He waited behind a weighty dowager at one teller cage, and when his turn came, he asked for change for a twenty-dollar gold double eagle. All the while, his eyes shifted, taking note of the layout of the establishment. Would they shut the vault at noon? He doubted it. There were two armed guards. That made Ace think of his friends waiting outside.

Shem Turnbull and George Cash lounged in front of the Bucket O' Suds saloon, two doors down from the bank. As noon neared, the street began to clear of people. Most of the shops closed over the dinner hour. Carefully they eyed passersby. Many of the men were armed. Those who were going home would be no trouble. Already a line had formed outside the eatery on the corner, and those would have to be closely watched. Shem turned to George.

"We shoulda brought another gun. Three fellers is not enough to carry this off."

"Oh, I don't know, Shem. They won't be expectin' anything, and their minds will be on their dinners. Ace can handle it real good."

"Not without a little help from you," Ace Banning declared as he walked up to his friends. "Shem, I want you inside with me. There's two armed guards. We've got only a minute, so let's move."

Smoke Jensen downed the last of his second schooner of beer, pushed back his chair, and dug in his pocket for a cartwheel dollar. "I'll walk over to the office with you, but then I have to head right back. I've got three mares who are due to foal at any time."

"You never opened that letter from Alvarado," Monte complained good-naturedly.

"That's right. I'll have to read it when I get home." Then reading his friend's expression, he added, "I'll let you know what Don Diego wrote about."

They had reached the tall, double doors with the painted

glass inserts when the sound of a gunshot came from the direction of the bank. A woman's scream followed. Smoke turned that way at once, to be stopped when Monte laid a hand on his shoulder.

"I'll take care of this, Smoke. No need for you to stick your neck out."

Smoke cut his eyes to his friend and growled, "Even if I want to?"

Monte shook his head. "Not this time."

He set off for the bank. Monte made it halfway down the block before the outside man saw him coming and fired his six-gun from the lawman's blind side. The bullet struck Monte in the chest. Deflected as it punched through a rib, the slug cut a path through his lung from front to rear and buried itself in the thick muscle of his back. Shock took Monte off his boots. At once, Smoke started for him.

"Watch it, there's one over there somewhere." A pink froth formed on Monte's lips, and his voice came out far weaker than he expected.

Smoke reached his friend, his .45 Colt in hand, and glanced in the direction Monte had pointed before the sheriff lost consciousness. Smoke saw his man instantly. A cruel grimace distorted the outlaw's mouth as he raised his revolver for another shot at the lawman. Smoke fired first. His round pinwheeled the man, punched through his sternum and tore apart his aorta. Charged up on adrenaline and action, he bled to death before he hit the boardwalk.

Kneeling, Smoke examined his fallen friend. Monte's face had grown pale, with a tinge of green around his lips, his breathing shallow and rapid. Smoke could hear a faint gurgle. If that bastard's killed him . . . he thought in a flash of anger. The thought came to him then. The first shot had been muffled; it had to have come from inside the bank. At once, he started that way.

* * *

It began going wrong the moment they entered the bank with bandannas tied over their faces. The employees and customers of the bank had no doubt what the masked men intended. Shem Turnbull headed for the teller cages, and Ace Banning shoved through the low swinging gate in the wall that divided the lobby from the working area. At once, the tellers raised their hands. Shem gestured with his gun barrel.

"That's right, keep 'em up until I tell you otherwise. You, get a money bag and start filling it," he told the nearest teller.

Ace concentrated on the portly, balding man in a glassed-in cubicle. "Step out here and come over to the vault. We want all the hard money and all the greenbacks you can load in those sacks."

Rosemont Faulkner knew better than to make vain protests about the robbers not getting away with it. He left his desk and hastened across the floor to the door of the vault. There, instead of stooping to load the bank's precious capital into a canvas money sack, he swiftly grabbed the heavy door and gave it a hefty swing. It clanged shut, and he spun the deadbolt wheel. Defiantly he put hands on his hips and spoke with relish.

"That's a time lock. It won't open again until eight o'clock tomorrow morning."

That's when Ace Banning, already strained beyond control by the presence of two armed guards who were presently out of his sight, lost it.

"You bastard!" he screamed as the hammer fell on a cartridge, and Ace shot the bank president through the heart. A woman behind him began to scream. He spun on one boot heel and strode to the tellers.

"All right, Shem, grab everything they have and let's get out of here."

Two minutes went by with the outlaws holding bags in one hand and tellers stuffing them. Then a loud report came from outside. Ace nodded to the door. "That's George, let's go."

Quickly they reached the door, and Shem Turnbull flung it open. They stepped out into the presence of an angry Smoke Jensen.

"Hold it right there," Smoke growled.

Two men stood before him, crowded into the open double doors of the bank. Each held three bulging canvas bags. They also gripped identical Smith & Wesson .44 Americans. Smoke followed his command with sizzling lead. Ace Banning dropped flat as the Colt in Jensen's hand bucked. The slug slammed into the pane of the bank door, and it shattered; shards flew inward to the chorus of screams from the three women inside. Ace fired wildly as the musical tinkle of glass sounded behind him.

His slug flew between Smoke's outspread legs. Already the last mountain man had moved his point of aim and triggered a shot that took Shem Turnbull in the thick meat of his side. He clapped a hand against it and discharged his Smith & Wesson. The .44 bullet cracked past Smoke's left ear and struck the banister post of the balcony across the street. Smoke moved then, as Ace fired again. His third shot struck the prone Ace Banning in his shoulder, snapped the collarbone, and bored down into his lung.

At once, Ace began to gag and fight for air. His hand went slack on the revolver, and it dropped from his fingers. Smoke Jensen changed position again and fired a safety shot. Due to the small target, it gouged the back of Ace Banning. He cried out as the slug plowed along his spine and entered his right buttock. Beside him, Shem fired again.

A hot crease burned along the outer point of Smoke's left shoulder. Twisting with the impact, Smoke lined up on the bank robber and fired again. His bullet ripped into Shem's middle and punched a hole in his liver. As massive shock stole over him, he sagged back against the wall and released his hold on the money bags and six-gun. Slowly, he slid down to a sitting position. Peacemaker leading the way, Smoke Jensen walked up to them and kicked the gun away from Ace, then Shem. Years of experience told him that both would die within an hour. One of the bank guards came to the door.

"Go get Doc Simpson," Smoke commanded the astonished man.

Ace groaned and looked up at Smoke. "Th-thank you, mister. Ah—who—who are you?"

Smoke kept it cold. "I didn't send for the doctor to treat you. You'll be dead before an hour's gone by. And, I'm known as Smoke Jensen."

Greater misery washed over the pale face of Ace Banning. "We—ah—we didn't think you were still alive. And a lawman at that."

His last sentence did not make much sense to Smoke, so he ignored it and replied to the first. "Your mistake."

Dr. Hiram Simpson entered the outer treatment room of his office wiping his hands on a towel. "Let's take a look at you, Mr. Jensen."

"First tell me, how is Monte?"

Doc Simpson sighed tiredly "It was close. I had to clean the wound channel first off. Then, when I got the bullet hole plugged, and closed the two holes in his lung, the Almighty musta smiled on me, 'cause the lung reinflated. He's healthy. he should heal that up in good time. I've given him enough laudanum that he will sleep through to evening. That should aid the healing process. But, the bullet is lodged in the thick muscle only a fraction of an inch from his spine. After having to open his chest to work on his lung, no one can go in there after it right now."

"When can you?"

Doc Simpson read the strain in Smoke's voice. "Provided

the sheriff heals as expected, I'd say someone could operate within six weeks, if that lead don't shift and paralyze him in the meantime."

"That could happen?"

With a hesitant nod Simpson replied, "I'm not a master surgeon, but right or wrong, it is taught in medical school that foreign objects in the body can shift under certain circumstances. That's why I don't want to operate on him. I'll send for a special surgeon from Denver."

That information did not sit well with Smoke. While Dr. Simpson worked on him, he kept at the physician to give a more accurate description of what damage had been done to Monte Carson. He remained dissatisfied when the doctor cut the last piece of tape and handed him two laudanum pills.

"Take half of one of these now. If the pain persists, take another half every six hours."

"I don't think I'll be needing them, Doctor," Smoke informed him, handing back the medicine. "How much do I owe you?"

"The county will pay for it. You were working as a deputy at the time."

With that settled, Smoke shrugged into his bloodied shirt, put on his vest and hat and headed to the door. It would be a long, uncomfortable ride back to the Sugarloaf.

Two

Halfway back to the Sugarloaf, Smoke started to regret his rash decision to reject the opium-based medicine. He also thought darkly about the morning's events. Why did it have to be Monte Carson who caught that bullet? Although Monte had the constitution of an ox, he was nearing sixty. People didn't heal so quickly then. Smoke knew from experience that a lung shot often led to pneumonia, which more often killed the victim than the bullet itself. In his moody thoughts, Smoke castigated himself for not having gone along with Monte. Better still, gone in his place.

No, Smoke admitted to himself, Monte had too much pride. It would have robbed him of his self-respect to acknowledge that age might be slowing his gunhand, delaying the proper read of a situation. Yet, the results spoke for themselves. Monte lay unconscious in the small infirmary off Doc Simpson's office. Smoke had a slight bullet burn on his shoulder. They had both gone about it wrong. Admitting it did not mollify Smoke in the least.

Once he had turned Cougar into the corral, in the hands of Bobby Jensen to cool him out, Smoke took the mail to the main house. Sally greeted him with a spoon dripping melted lard in one hand. "Hello, handsome. I'm fixing a batch of doughnuts. My, what a lot of mail."

"Yep. There's a Sears catalogue for you."

Sally clapped her hands. "Oh, goody, I get to buy things."

Smoke answered her with a sidelong glance. "No, you don't. And a letter from a woman named Mary-Beth Gittings."

"Who?"

"That's what it says. I'll give it to you inside."

Seated at the kitchen table, Smoke distributed the mail into neat piles. While Sally chattered on and added more lard to the heated deep skillet for the doughnuts, he turned his attention to the intriguing letter from New Mexico. He opened it to find a disturbing difference in his old friend. Instead of the usual bubbling enthusiasm of this jovial grandee, who so loved to entertain, it was a gloomy account of growing difficulties. High in the Sangre de Cristo range of the Rocky Mountains, things were not right, Don Diego Alvarado informed Smoke Jensen. He went on to illustrate:

> There is an Anglo named Clifton Satterlee who covets all of the land around Taos. He is powerful and wealthy. He has a hacienda outside Santa Fe and is believed to have the ear of many of his fellow Anglos in the territorial government. It is also said that he has many interests and much influence in the East. He has surrounded himself with some most unsavory men, who aid him in achieving his goals by any means necessary. Amigo, [the letter went on] there have been some incidents of violence. Men have been driven out, Anglos as well as Mejicanos.

Absently Smoke reached to the plate holding the doughnuts. He let go of one quickly enough the moment he touched it. "They're hot," Sally reminded him with a laugh.

Smoke went back to the letter for the final paragraph.

No one here seems capable of dealing with the man. So, forgive my presumption in asking this, old friend, but I feel that I must appeal to you to come out here and get the feel of what is going on. Only reluctantly, it seemed to Smoke, did Don Diego add his personal difficulties. *I, myself, have lost some cattle and the lives of some of my vaqueros.* His missive concluded with some of his usual flourish. Smoke put it aside in thoughtful silence.

They rode up quietly, five beefy, hard-faced, tough men, and tied off their horses to a stone-posted tie rail outside the high-walled hacienda on Calle Jesus Salvador in Taos, New Mexico Territory. Beyond the wall they could see the red tile roof of a Spanish colonial-style two-story house. Nestled in a large valley, surrounded by the Sangre de Cristo range, the residence had an air of peacefulness. That was quickly broken when the leader, Whitewater Paddy Quinn, spoke to his henchmen.

"Remember, we ain't here to break him up, just to get him to sign."

One of the thugs, a man named Rucker, responded with a snigger. "Right, boss."

"Sure, I mean that, Rucker. Not a bruise. Now, let's get in there."

Quinn stepped up to a human-sized doorway inset in the tall, double gate, and raised a large brass knocker. The striker plate bolted to the portal gave off a hollow boom as he rapped it. He kept at it until a short, swarthy servant in a white cotton pullover shirt and trousers opened the door. *"¿Sí, señores?"*

"We're here to see Mr. Figueroa."

"¿Qué? Lo siento, no hablo Ingles."

Paddy Quinn struggled to put his request into Spanish. *"Es necesario a hablamos con Señor Figueroa."* His grammar might not be perfect, but he conveyed the idea.

Figueroa's majordomo brightened. *"Ay, sí! Vengan."* His leather sandals made soft, scraping noises as he led the visitors across the cobbled courtyard to the main entrance.

Through a wrought-iron gate and a pair of tall double doors, a tunnellike passageway led to a lushly planted open square. A large saguaro cactus filled one corner. In the center, a fountain splashed musically. Standing beside it was a slim gentleman of medium height, his white hair combed straight back in two large wings from his temples. He wore the costume of another age, tight, black trousers, trimmed with gray stripes along the outer seams, matching cutaway coat with gray lapels. His shirt was snowy, with a blizzard of lace and a wing collar. Calf-length boots had been burnished until they shone like polished onyx. From beyond him, practice scales on a piano tinkled from an open, curtained window. He turned at their entrance, and a dark scowl quickly replaced the smile of welcome he had prepared.

"You are not welcome in this house," he declared.

Paddy Quinn put a wide smile on his Irish face. "Sure, I'm sorry you see it that way, Mr. Figueroa. We will try to be brief, we will. I have come to arrange for the sale of this property to Mr. Satterlee."

Figueroa glowered at him. "Then you have come on a mistaken mission, señor. I have no intention of selling."

Beaming happily, Quinn ventured to disagree. "Oh, yes, you do."

"No, I do not. I have told you that five times before. I have not changed my mind. Now, leave or I shall send for some of my retainers."

At that, Paddy Quinn gave a signal to two of his henchmen. They crossed the space separating them from Ernesto Figueroa and grabbed the elderly gentleman by the arms. Quinn gestured toward the open window. With little effort, they frog-marched him to the lace-curtained window from which the music came. Quinn came up behind and shoved

Figueroa's head through the opening. The scales had given over to a piece by Mozart now, played by a sweet-faced little girl.

"A nice girl, your granddaughter, she is," Quinn observed. "Lovely, innocent, vulnerable. You'd not be wanting anything to happen to her, now would you?"

A shudder of revulsion passed through Figueroa a moment before the thugs abruptly swung him around to face their leader. He fought for the words. "You wouldn't dare."

Quinn gave him a smile. "You're right, I would not. But I cannot account for every minute of my men's time. Come, señor. You will be more than generously compensated, an' that's a fact. You can take your lovely, expensive furniture and possessions elsewhere, anywhere you wish, and live to see her grow to womanhood. And a lovely figure she will make, it is."

Wincing from the painful grip on his arms, Ernesto Figueroa remained defiant. "What will happen if I still refuse?"

Paddy Quinn's face changed from beaming benignity to harsh evil. "Then I will let my men have their way with her and kill her before your eyes. But not you," he went on. "We'll be leaving you to live with what your stubbornness caused. Think about it, bucko."

Ernesto Figueroa hesitated only a scant two seconds before his head sagged in resignation and he made a hesitant gesture to indicate he would accept. Paddy Quinn handed him the papers and even produced a travel pen and brass inkwell so the defeated man could sign.

After due consideration, Smoke Jensen decided to go to Taos. His reasoning was simple. The foaling season, from February through April, was over and the first of May not far away. Besides, he owed Diego Alvarado. He left the hands busy with the new colts and went to talk it over with Sally.

"I expected this since you first told me what the letter contained. I'll not beg you to stay here, Smoke. I know better, and you would be disappointed in me if I did. How long do you expect to be gone?"

Smoke considered it. "Ten days. Two weeks at the most."

Sally's chuckle held a hint of irony. "I've heard that before. How are you going to travel, Smoke?"

"I'll take the Denver and Rio Grande south to Raton, then go by horseback through the Palo Flechado Pass to Taos."

A light of mischief glowed in Sally's eyes as though she particularly liked the thought that burst on her. "That sounds easy enough. I think I'll come with you; it will be nice to see Don Diego again."

Smoke shook his head, rejecting the idea. "Who'll run the ranch and look out for Bobby?"

"Ike can run the ranch, and Bobby is grown enough to bunk with the hands and take care of himself."

Smoke remained unconvinced. "Think about what you just said."

"About Ike running the ranch?"

"No. About Bobby. He's thirteen, Sally. Do you remember what our others were like at that age?"

Fresh worry lines formed on Sally's forehead. "Yes . . . unfortunately I do."

"I think you should reconsider."

Sally stood in silence a long two minutes, leaning shoulder to shoulder with Smoke. "All right, you win this one. I'll be realistic and not start to worry until three weeks have gone by."

"Nice of you," Smoke jested, giving her a swift hug. "I will write you when I reach Taos."

"Send a telegram instead. It will get here sooner."

"All right."

"Now, let me ask only one thing. What are you going to do

when you have to keep your promise to that boy about taking him along on one of these trips?"

Smoke affected a groan. "I'll figure that out when the time comes. Now, dear wife, will you pack me something suitable to wear at Diego Alvarado's?"

With an impatient twist to his lips, Clifton Satterlee gazed from the narrow window of the mud wagon stagecoach that rattled and swayed along the narrow dirt roadway that led from Santa Fe to Taos. "One would think," he muttered under his breath, "that since our nation has conquered this country, the government would put down proper paving stones." If they did not reach the relay station soon, he swore he would leave his breakfast on the floor of the coach. Across from him, his chief partner in C. S. Enterprises, Brice Noble, sat beside Satterlee's bodyguard, Cole Granger. To the increase of his discomfort, Satterlee realized that Granger actually liked this trip. He seemed to thrive on the discomfort. Suddenly Clifton's stomach lurched, and a fiery gorge rushed up his throat. He turned sideways and hastily flung aside the leather curtain.

"Oh, God," Satterlee groaned as he thrust his head out the window. With explosive force, he vomited into the rising plume of dust that came from under the iron-tired right front wheel. He could feel Granger's amused gaze resting on him. Damn the man!

When he recovered himself, Clifton Satterlee crawled limply back inside. Cole Granger held out a canteen for him, which he took eagerly, and he rinsed his mouth. Then Granger extended a silver flask. "Here you go, Mr. Satterlee. It's some of your fine, French brandy."

Irritation crackled in Satterlee's voice. "It's cognac, Cole. C-O-G-N-A-C."

Hastily, Satterlee seized the container and swallowed

down a long gulp. Immediately his stomach spun like a carousel. Then the warm, soothing property of the liquor kicked in, and his nausea subsided somewhat. From outside, above on the box, came a welcome cry.

"Whoa, Tucker, whoa, Benny, whoa-up, Nell. Wheel right." He called out the rest of the team, and the momentum of the stagecoach slackened.

Satterlee addressed the rest of the occupants. "About damned time. You know, that little upset of mine has left me ravenously hungry. Or maybe it is the cognac." He took another swig.

Cole Granger checked the stage itinerary. "There'll be a meal stop here, Mr. Satterlee."

Brice Noble looked balefully out the window. "I certainly hope the food will be better than we had this morning. That must have been what caused your discomfort, Cliff."

Satterlee nodded his gratitude for his partner's cover-up of his motion sickness. He hated any sign of weakness, as did Noble. Clifton Satterlee studied his partner. A man in his late forties, ten years senior to himself, Brice Noble had a bulldog face with heavy jowls. For all his youth, Noble was completely gray, his hair worn in long, greasy strands. Shorter by three inches, Noble weighed around one hundred seventy pounds and had the hard hands of a working cowboy, although Satterlee knew he had been a wealthy man for a long time. Brice had never given up his habit of carrying a brace of revolvers, in this instance, Merwin Hulbert .44s. Satterlee knew only too well how good he could be with them. His pale blue eyes had a hard, silver glint when angered.

For his own part, Clifton made certain he never infuriated Brice. Even at six feet, two inches with longer, once stronger, arms and barrel chest, Satterlee readily acknowledged that he was no match for Noble. He sighed as he glanced down at the beginnings of a potbelly. He would have to get out and do more riding, Satterlee admonished himself. Although he was a lean man, Satterlee's left armpit felt chafed by the shoulder holster he wore there, and more so from the weight of the .44 Colt Lightning double-action that fitted it. Recalling its presence brought a laugh to the lips of Clifton Satterlee. He had not had occasion to draw it in anger or even self-defense in the three years since he bought it.

"What's funny, Cliff?"

"I was thinking about my gun, Brice. Do you realize I have not used it, except for practice, in the past three years?"

Noble nodded to Granger. "That's what Cole is here for. But, I can tell you I'm looking forward to whatever food they have for us."

With a shriek of sand caught between brake shoe and wheel, the stage jolted to a stop. The station agent brought out a four-step platform with which the passengers could dismount. "Welcome to Española, folks. We've got some red chili, chicken enchiladas, and beans inside for you."

"Sounds good," Cole Granger told him with a big smile.

Clifton Satterlee saw it differently. "By all that's holy, don't you have any white man's food?"

"Nope. Not with a big, fat Mexican cooking for me. She cooks what she knows how to."

Satterlee appealed to his partner. "Do you know what that will do to my stomach, Brice?"

"Fill it, no doubt." Then, to the agent, "Do you have any flour tortillas?"

"Yep. An' some sopapillas with honey to finish off with."

Stifling a groan, Clifton Satterlee instructed, "I'll start with those."

Inside, over savory bowls of beef stewed with onions, garlic, and red chili peppers, corn tortillas stuffed with chicken, onions, black olives, cheese, and sauce, the driver and guard joined in demolishing the ample food laid out for the occupants of the coach. Satterlee morosely doused the fried dough in an amber pool of honey. After devouring four of the sopapillas, he spoke low to Noble.

"I want you to stay a few days, up to a week, in Taos. Look around, make contact with our people. Make certain they are getting things done. My wife and I will return to Santa Fe two days from now."

Brice Noble chewed on the flavorful cubes of meat. He washed them down with beer that had been cooled in the well. "What do you propose doing next?"

"Our people have to accelerate their efforts. We need that timber and damned soon. Our whole lumber business depends upon it. Go after those blasted savages."

Smoke Jensen stopped in on Monte Carson the next day, before he took the afternoon train south to Denver, where he would change for the run to Raton. He could have taken the AT&SF to Santa Fe, but he wanted to catch what word there might be running up and down the trail. Monte was awake when Smoke entered the infirmary. His skin held a pallor, and his response when he turned his head and saw Smoke was weak.

"Smoke, good you came. Maybe you can talk sense to the man."

"What's that about?"

"That croaker, Simpson, says I have to stay here for two, maybe three weeks. Then some kind of operation by a doctor from Denver."

Smoke nodded. "You've got a bullet in you, Monte. I'll tell you what he probably won't. It's near your spine. There's the chance . . . for permanent injury."

Monte cut his eyes away from Smoke. "Damn. If that happens, I won't be fit for anything. Old before my time and stove up. Not a fittin' end."

"No," Smoke agreed. "At least you would be alive."

"You call that alive? Ask me, it'd be nothin' more than livin' hell."

Smoke decided on a change of subject. "I came to tell you what was in that letter from Don Diego."

That brightened the lawman somewhat. "Really? What did the old grandee have to say?"

Smoke's fleeting frown framed his words. "There's trouble brewing out in the Sangre de Cristo. Some feller named Satterlee has it in mind to build himself a little empire. According to Don Diego, he's not shy about the sort of persuasion his men use to get what he wants. Alvarado's lost some stock and some cowboys. He asked if I'd come take a look."

"And are you?"

Smoke nodded. "Leavin' today, Monte. Train to Raton, then trail it from there. But I feel bad about leaving you here all bunged up."

Monte tried to make little of it. "Not much happens in Big Rock anymore. My deputies can handle it."

"After that list you gave me yesterday, and what we ran into, I'd say your 'not much' is a bit of an exaggeration." Smoke tipped back the brim of his Stetson. "Well, I have to get to the depot. Look out for yourself, Monte. And do what the doctor says."

Monte scowled, then gave a feeble wave. "Watch yer back trail."

Smoke turned for the door. "I have a feelin' I'm going to have to."

THREE

On the train south, Smoke Jensen settled into his Pullman car with a copy of the Denver *Dispatch* and sat in the plush seat that would become part of his sleeping berth. The editorial page contained the usual harangue about the lawlessness of the miners and smelter workers. Someone named Wilbert Clampton had a piece on the subject of temperance. According to him, Demon Rum was soaking the brains and inflaming the passions of the lower classes. Until Denver banned liquor, the depredations chronicled elsewhere in the newspaper would only continue and increase. A moderate man in his drinking habits, Smoke could not find the energy to get worked up over Clampton's cry for abstinence. After twenty minutes and a dozen miles had gone by, Smoke put the paper aside. Immediately he noticed an attractive young woman seated in the same car.

She smiled in his direction with her eyes as well as her lips, then dabbed at her mouth with a dainty square of white linen. Her heart-shaped face was framed by a nest of small, blond curls. That and her expensive clothes added to her allure. Fiercely loyal to his beloved Sally, Smoke made only the lightest of passing acknowledgment to her discreet flirtation. The rail carriage swayed gently as the train rolled through the high mountains. Up ahead, Smoke knew, his two horses, a sturdy pack animal and Cougar, would be comfortable in padded stalls in a special car. The expense of such travel conveniences had grown steeply over the past few years. Yet, he could afford it. Blooded horses brought good money. Far more so than cattle. Smoke went back to his newspaper.

There was talk again of building a canal across Central America to speed ship passage. More for cargo, Smoke knew, than passengers. With the nation linked from coast to coast with steel rails, the hazards of a sea voyage could be easily abandoned for the more secure railroads. At least with the James gang out of business, there seemed little possibility of robberies like those of the past. After completing the speculations on a canal, Smoke reached into an inner coat pocket and removed a twisted-tip Marsh Wheeling cigar and came to his boots.

When he walked past the young woman, on his way to the vestibule for his smoke, she spoke in a melodic, honeyed voice. "Good day."

Smoke touched fingertips to the brim of his hat. "Yes, it is."

He had barely gotten in four satisfactory puffs when she appeared in the doorway to their car. With a hesitant smile, she came forward. "Excuse me. My name is Winnefred Larkin. Forgive me if this sounds too brazen. But, I'm traveling alone, you see, and I wish to ask you if you would be so kind as to escort me to the dining car later this evening."

Smoke hid his smile behind his cigar. "Not at all, Miss Larkin. My name is Jensen, Smoke Jensen. I would be delighted to be your escort."

"Thank you. I am so relieved. Smoke . . . Jensen. What an odd name."

"It's sort of a handle other folks hung on me. My given name is Kirby." *Now why did he say that?* Smoke wondered. He hated that name.

Winnefred made a small moue of her pretty lips. "Then I shall call you Smoke. First call for dinner is at five. Or is that too early for your liking?"

"Yes, it is, a bit," Smoke allowed.

"Would seven be better?" Without conscious intent, Winnefred appeared coy.

"Perfect. I'll present myself to you then," Smoke replied, working out of himself a gallantry he rarely had cause to display.

"Then, I shall leave you to your cigar. And again, my sincerest thanks."

When Smoke Jensen entered the dining car with Winnefred Larkin on his arm, it turned heads all up and down both sides of the aisle. They made a striking couple. Smoke led her to a vacant table and seated her, then drew up his own chair opposite. A rather recent addition, these rolling restaurants had been designed, like the sleeping cars, by George Mortimer Pullman. They had proven quite successful, much to the chagrin of the Harvey House chain of depot-based eating establishments. Smoke examined the menu, printed in flamboyant style, bold black on snowy white.

"What sounds good to you?" Winnefred asked after a few silent moments of study. "Everything seems so strange to me."

Smoke nodded understanding. "I gather you are from the East, Miss Larkin? When one gets this far west, the larder on these dining cars is stocked from locally available food for the most part. See? There's rainbow trout listed, though I don't know what *amandine* means. Bison tongue, elk steak, and beef stew."

"Please, make it Winnie. And, *amandine* means the fish is done with an almond and lemon sauce. Quite the rage in

Philadelphia. Perhaps you would choose for the both of us, Smoke?"

Never a fancy eater, Smoke Jensen concentrated to select something that he believed would please Winnie and yet not be too out of his ordinary fare. He selected cold, sliced bison tongue in a mildly hot sauce for an appetizer, then followed with elk steak, new potatoes and peas, cold pickled lettuce, and hot bread. Winnie Larkin seemed enchanted with the choices. Their waiter, a large, smiling, colored man in a short, white jacket and black trousers, suggested a bottle of wine. At Smoke's insistence, Winnie made the selection.

For once it all turned out right, and even Smoke enjoyed the meal. Cut from the rib eye, the elk steak was juicy and tender. The California claret went well with it. Fortuitously, Smoke had asked that the cook withhold the green pepper-corn sauce from the meat. It was rich and thick, and to the way Smoke thought, if a piece of meat was poor in quality, one could dump all the sauce in the world on it and not make it the least bit better. This time it was decidedly not needed.

While they ate, Winnie kept up a light, fanciful banter about her travels in the West. She found New Orleans charming, Texas rough and exhilarating, Denver a cultural oasis in the midst of near-barbarism. Now she looked forward to Santa Fe. She had heard somewhere that the territorial governor had written a most popular book.

"Yes," Smoke informed her. "It's called *Ben-Hur.* Surely you have read it?"

"Oh! Then General Lew Wallace is *Governor* Wallace? And, yes, I have read that book. It is so . . . uplifting."

When she learned Smoke was involved in breeding blooded horses, she waxed ecstatic over her childhood desire to have a papered horse. All her parents had, Winnie lamented, were a pair of plodding dray horses. She spoke of riding lessons as a girl in her teens and how she still longed to own a Thoroughbred of her own.

Smoke quickly disabused her of that ambition. "I don't raise Thoroughbreds. They are for racing and fancy shows back east. Mine are Palouse and Morgans and Arabians. Those of lower quality I sell to the army as remounts. Arabians are show horses, but a lot of military officers want, and can afford, them for parade horses. The Morgans are great for carriages as well as saddle stock. Since the Nez Perce have been forced onto a reservation, their breed, the Palouse, has all but died out. I am trying to recover it."

Winnie looked entirely helpless. "Oh, dear, that sounds incredibly complicated. It must be rewarding to see all those horses thriving, though."

"Yes, it is, Winnie. I used to raise cattle. They are stupid, intractable animals. They also eat a lot and are vulnerable to the harsh winters in the mountains. Horses aren't much brighter, but they survive better and do useful work. Did you know that wolves are the smartest animals in the wild?"

Winnie shuddered. "Wolves? How awful. They're killers."

"No. Not how you mean. A wolf will not attack a human, even a child, unless cornered or they believe their young to be threatened. They have a structured society, with strict rules and a pecking order. They care for their pups until they are able to fend for themselves. They even have intricate tactics for hunting."

"See, that's what I mean. They are relentless killers."

Masking a flare of impatience with a straight face, Smoke tried to explain. "Wolves prey on the weakest animals of a herd. By doing so, they improve the breed. You might say that what I do for horses by record keeping and selective breeding, they do by instinct."

Tiny frown lines appeared on Winnie's high, smooth brow. "I've never heard anything like that before."

"Not likely that you will. People have been bad-mouthing wolves since the Middle Ages. Wolves are the most misunderstood animals on the frontier. I have counted up to eight in one pack running on my ranch, and I have never lost a foal." He paused, then produced a rueful grin. "Of course, I wouldn't want one living under the same roof with me. They are still wild animals."

Winnie's eyes grew wide. They went on talking amiably through dessert and coffee. Gradually the car emptied of occupants. The waiters began to clear the tables and turn down kerosene lamps. Only a balding, portly man and his buxom wife remained when Smoke stood and went around the table to help Winnie from her chair. Smoke had noticed earlier that the fusty busybody had been giving them a jaundiced eye throughout the meal and had even restrained her husband when he made to leave earlier. With a silent snigger at those with nothing better to do, he pushed the incident out of his mind, took Winnie by the elbow, and escorted her to the door.

They found their Pullman bunks made up and ready. Smoke and Winnie said their goodnights, and Smoke went on back to the smoking car for a cigar. He struck up a conversation with a man near his own age about the severe storms of the previous winter. When their stogies had burned down to short stubs with long, white ash, Smoke excused himself and went on back to his bed.

A shrill scream punctured the peaceful silence of the sleeping car.

It seemed to Smoke Jensen that he had only just laid down his head, yet light streamed around the pull-down shade as he opened his eyes to the continued wailing that came from up the aisle.

"She's dead! She's dead! My God, it's horrible. Blood everywhere."

Smoke swiftly pulled on his trousers and boots, shrugged into a shirt and slipped a .45 Colt Peacemaker into his waistband. A middle-aged woman stood in the aisle, hands to her pasty white cheeks as she continued to shriek. Smoke reached her in four long strides. He took her by one shoulder and shook her gently.

"Who is dead? What do you mean?"

She pointed with a suddenly palsied hand, and her voice quavered. "In—in there. Th—the y-y-y-young woman you took to dinner last night. W-w-we h-had an arrange—arrangement for breakfast this morning. Only her Pullman was still closed. I called out, then looked in." This time she covered her face and spoke through broken sobs. "Her—her eyes were staring right at me, but I could tell they held no life. Sh-sh-she's covered with blood." Suddenly she broke off and stared with horror at the hands of Smoke Jensen, as though expecting to see splashes of crimson.

Speaking firmly to maintain control, Smoke directed, "Sit down over there. I will go get the conductor."

He returned three minutes later with a worried man in a dark blue uniform trimmed with silver braid. At Smoke's urging, the conductor looked in the closed Pullman. He recoiled in aversion. "Lordy, what a sight. When did this happen?"

Smoke shook his head. "I don't know. The woman over there found her about . . ." He plucked his watch from the small pocket in his trousers. "Four minutes ago. Her screaming woke me up."

By then, a crowd had gathered, and Smoke noted five heads poking out of curtained bunks. The conductor examined them with disapproval. Then he waved the people away with small shooing motions as though dispersing a flock of chickens.

"There has been an unfortunate accident. Everyone who does not have a seat in this car, please leave. Those who belong here, take your seats and remain there." Then he turned to Smoke. "You'll likely want to get into your coat. Then I would like to talk to you at length. I'll send for the train crew to take care of the body."

Wise in the ways of trail crafts, Smoke knew how many bits of information could be gained from a study of all signs. "No, I don't think that's a good idea. I want to get a thorough look in there before anything is moved, including Miss Larkin."

Face twisted with distaste, the conductor responded indignantly. "We can't just leave a—a *dead body* lying here. People will blame the line."

Smoke spoke firmly, convincingly. "You can leave it until a peace officer examines the area around her."

"But that won't be until Walsenburg. And, oh, dear, everyone on the train will have to be questioned."

"As to your first observation, that is not necessarily so. Come with me, I have something to show you."

Still dithering, the conductor followed along in the wake of Smoke Jensen. At Smoke's bunk, he reached in and retrieved a small leather wallet from his valise. He used his back to block view of it from the rest of the car and opened the fold. The silver shield of a deputy U.S. marshal shined up at the conductor.

"I have jurisdiction in Colorado. Inasmuch as you have a mail car on this train, I also have jurisdiction over any crime that occurs on it, if I choose to exercise it. What I would like you to do is lock the doors to each car and contain the occupants while you put this train on a siding somewhere along the line, close to here, then have your express agent use his key to send ahead to Walsenburg that you have an emergency and are on the siding and identify which one. That's when we can conduct our own investigation."

Testily, the conductor removed his visored cap and scratched at a balding spot on the crown of his head. "That's a tall order, Marshal—ah—"

"Jensen. Smoke Jensen."

"Jesus, Mary and Joseph! You're *the* Smoke Jensen?" At Smoke's nod, he went on in a rush. "I'm Martin Stoddard, folks call me Marsh. I'll try to do everything I can to see that you get what you want. We'll put men out once we've stopped to watch and make sure no one tries to get away from the train."

"Good thinking, Mr. Stoddard—er—Marsh. I'll naturally come with you. We will need to set up a place to question everyone. Say the smoking and bar car? But first, I want to take a look at the body."

Rail coaches squealed and jolted to a stop beyond the southernmost switch of a siding. The switchman threw the tall cast-iron lever that opened the switch and signaled to the engineer. Huge gouts of black smoke billowed from the fat stack as the engineer reversed the drive and the big wheels spun backward. Slowly the observation platform on the smoking car angled onto the parallel rails of the siding and swayed through the fog. With creeping progress, the other carriages followed. When the cowcatcher cleared, the mobile rails slid back to the normal position. The train braked.

At once, members of the crew dismounted. Armed with rifles and shotguns taken from the conductor's compartment, they took position to observe the entire length of both sides of the train. From the express car came a short, slender, balding man with a green eyeshade fitted to his brow. He carried a portable telegraph key with a length of wire attached.

Smoke Jensen and Marsh Stoddard joined him at the base of a pole. The express agent nodded toward the upright shaft.

"I ain't gonna try climbin' that. Not a man of sixty, fixin' to retire."

Smoke turned to him. "Do you have climbing spikes and a belt in the express car?"

"Sure do."

"Fetch them for me, will you, please," Smoke requested.

Quizzically, the grizzled older man cut his eyes to Smoke. "D'ya mean you can do Morse code?"

Smoke nodded. "Among my lesser accomplishments I did happen to learn it. I may be a bit rusty, but I can manage. If need be, I'll have you write the message out for me in dots and dashes and simply follow along."

"Now that's a good idea. 'Sides, you'll need the identity code for Walsenburg."

"It is WLS, isn't it?" Smoke asked.

Surprise registered on the old-timer's face. "Wall I'll be danged, you do know something about it after all." Then he cut Smoke a shrewd look. "What about the train signal?"

"I'll bet it's DLX."

"Right as rain; Daylight Express." Nodding eagerly, the express agent started for the car. "Be jist a minute."

While Smoke Jensen fitted himself with the climbing gear, the agent wrote out the message, as dictated by Marsh Stoddard, in plain English and handed it and the key to the last mountain man. Smoke ascended the pole with ease. He settled himself comfortably at a level with the wires and fastened the bare ends of the lead to the proper one. Then he tightened the wing nut that fed power from the battery pack slung over one shoulder and freed the striker. Eyes fixed on the message form, Smoke tapped out the words.

After two long minutes, acknowledgment came back along with a question. "DLX whose fist is that(q) It is not Eb(x)"

Smoke sent back, "No(x) Eb did not want to climb the pole(x) This is US Marshal Smoke Jensen(x)"

That brought a flurry of questions. "What is a marshal doing on the train(q) What is the nature of your emergency(q) How long will you be delayed(q)"

Smoke's reply must have electrified them. "There has been a murder(x) Notify the law in WLS(x) We will be at least two hours(x)"

With that Smoke detached the lead and descended the pole. "Now, Marsh, I suggest we set up to question the good folks on this train."

Naturally enough, Smoke Jensen began by questioning the people from the car where the murder had occurred. He had passed through ten of them, including the still upset woman who had found the body, when he came face-to-face with the nosy dowager from the dining car. Mrs. Darlington Struthers—Hermione—proved to be a woman of strong opinions and downright regal condescension to those she considered her inferiors. With small, gloved fists on her ample hips she stood before the table where Smoke interrogated the passengers.

"I will tell you nothing, young man. The very idea that an upstart the likes of you can commandeer this train, halt it on a siding, and pry into the affairs of its passengers is a matter I shall have my husband take up with the directors of the line. Darlington Struthers has considerable influence, as I am sure you shall learn to your regret."

Smoke eyed her with ice glinting off the gold flecks in his eyes. "Are you quite through? This is a murder investigation. You will please answer my questions, or you will spend a few days at the tender mercies of the sheriff in Walsenburg."

Hermione's face grew bright red. "The nerve . . ."

"I assure you it is not nerve. Now, where are you seated in relation to the dead woman?"

"You are not the law, and I do not have to answer your questions."

Smiling, Smoke produced his badge folder. "Oh, but I am. Deputy U.S. Marshal. First, let me say that your evasions and bluster make you sound more like the guilty party than a mere fellow passenger. With that in mind, let me ask again: Where are you seated?"

Testily, Hermione Struthers answered. Smoke asked if she had seen or heard anything unusual during the night. Her face took on the expression of a dog passing a peach pit when she snapped her answer in the negative. Smoke tried another tack.

"Well, now, I might be just a hick lawman from the high lonesome, but I do have some smarts about me. From where you would have been in your bunk, it is impossible not to have heard any sounds of struggle. And believe me, from the looks of that Pullman berth, there was considerable struggle. Even the window shade is torn."

"I am a sound sleeper."

Smoke could not resist the barb. "A little too much claret, eh?"

Indignation rose to balloon the face of Hermione Struthers. "I am a teetotaler, I'll have you know."

Smoke considered her stubbornness. She knew something, of that he was sure. Yet, he could not use force to learn it. And right now, his guile was wearing thin. "So, you heard nothing. Did you see anything, anyone around there?"

"I am not in the habit of spying on others."

I'll bet you're not, Smoke thought silently. "Hmm. We'll let that pass for the moment. If you heard nothing and saw nothing during the night, what about early this morning, when people began to rise for the day?"

"Again, nothing. Not the least thing."

"Very well. You may go, ma'am. But I may want to talk to you again."

Hermione turned to the door and spoke over her shoulder. "Do as you will. You will get nothing from me." With a smug, tight expression she opened the portal and stepped across the threshold.

That's when Smoke Jensen launched his final arrow. "Oh, so there is . . . something?"

Outside in the vestibule between the smoking car and the rearmost Pullman, Hermione Struthers unloaded her bile on Marsh Stoddard, her voice loud and cawing. "Mr. Conductor, there is something you should know about that so-called marshal in there. To my certain knowledge, he is the last person to have seen the late Miss Larkin alive. They were carrying on scandalously in the dining car."

FOUR

For two blistering minutes, Hermione Struthers belabored Marsh Stoddard with a highly fanciful account of an imagined torrid liaison between Smoke Jensen and Winnefred Larkin. What she lacked in imagination, she made up for in viciousness. She concluded with a demand, hot with vehemence.

"I insist that you put this train in motion at once and proceed on our way. I'll have you know that my husband is an associate of the president of the line and well known to the board of directors. I intend to bring your dereliction to the attention of Mr. Struthers. Your future employment may depend upon your prompt obedience."

Stoddard tipped the billed cap to her and spoke softly. "Somehow I doubt that."

"What did you say?" Hermione demanded.

"I said, I don't doubt that."

"As well you shouldn't. I shall return to my car, and I want immediate entrance." She started for the vestibule steps.

Stoddard hurried to intervene. "I wouldn't do that, ma'am. One of the crew might take a potshot at you."

"What do you mean?"

"Marshal's orders, ma'am. All vestibule doors are to be

kept locked, and no one is to leave the train until the killer is unmasked."

Hermione's face drained of color. "But I have already told you. *He* is the murderer. That false marshal in there."

Stoddard kept a tight rein on his expression. "Very well, ma'am, I'll take care of it right away. First, come with me and I will see you to your car."

Stoddard came back and entered the smoking car. "That damned woman. Claims you are the killer. Once she's got her steam up, she'll blow it off to everyone who will listen, and a good many who won't."

Smoke considered that a moment. "That could complicate matters a little."

"D'you have any more of an idea of who it might be?"

"None, so far. But I am convinced that officious old hen knows something she's not telling. I think I'll have her back in here after I've gone through all the others. Bring the next one, if you will, please."

During the next three-quarters of an hour, Smoke interviewed the train's porters and every one of the passengers, with the exception of four people. Those who had come from the car that housed Hermione Struthers cast nervous, suspicious glances at Smoke when they thought he was not watching them. So much for the old bag. Finally, one of that group blurted out his apprehension.

"Mrs. Struthers says she has positive proof that you are the killer."

"Well, Mr. Paddington, tell me this. When's the last time you saw a Poland China sail past overhead?"

Paddington looked confused a moment, then angry. "That's all stuff and nonsense. Ain't never been a Poland China that could fly."

"That's my point. You can believe whatever that woman

says the day pigs start to fly. Now, would you tell me if you saw or heard anything out of the ordinary during the night?"

"Uh—uh well, nothing you'd call unusual, all considered."

"Meaning what?"

"Ain't unusual for young folks to do some sparkin' on a train at night. They think it's romantic."

That grabbed Smoke's attention at once. "And you saw something like that?"

"Yes, I did. I didn't see 'em actually clingin' to one another like soul mates, but I reckon that had come right before." Again, Paddington paused irritatingly.

"Before what?" Smoke pressed.

"Jist before I saw this young man leave our car. He come from down the direction of that poor young woman's berth."

"Could you recognize him?"

For once, Paddington did not hesitate. "Not for certain. His head was all in shadows. An' he seemed in a hurry. I was gettin' up to visit the slop jar an' he like to knocked me back into my bunk."

Smoke listed physical characteristics in an attempt to spark memory. "Was he tall? Short? Heavy? Thin? What did he wear?"

Paddington mused on it. "He was about my height, five-nine, slightly built, I'd say, and had a suit on. Seemed to me the shirt was of two colors, dark and light."

"Could that have been black and white?"

Surprise wrathed Paddington's face. "Say, yer right, marshal. It sure could have been."

"Are you aware that in very low lamplight, or moonlight, blood looks black?" There had been a lot of blood.

"Ohmygod! If only I'd seen his face."

Yes, if only, Smoke thought with disappointment.

That had been fifteen minutes earlier, and Smoke was now ready to start on the last four. He ruled out the first to enter at sight of the man. He was short, fat and wore spectacles that would rival the bottom of a wine bottle. Smoke questioned him anyway.

No. No one had passed through the chair car where he had been trying to sleep. He had heard nothing. At least not until some woman screamed bloody murder early in the morning. Could hear her clear up in his coach. Smoke excused him and asked Stoddard to bring in the next.

A slender man in his early twenties entered the smoking car. He had shifty eyes, and his palms were notably wet and unexpectedly cold when Smoke shook his hand. Smoke let him sweat in silence for two minutes after giving his name.

"Now, Mr. Reierson, in order to save time, we'll start this off the hard way. I am a deputy U.S. marshal, empowered to investigate the murder that happened on this train last night. I'm going to ask you some questions and I expect truthful answers."

"Why, of course. Any—" Reierson's voice caught. "Anything I can do to help."

While Smoke went through his routine questions, Reierson developed a nervous tic at the corner of his left eye. His trepidation increased the harder Smoke probed. More so when Smoke pointed out that his answers did not hold up with the observations of others.

Reierson tried bluster. "That's preposterous. I know where I was and what I did. They must be mistaken."

Smoke rounded on him suddenly, his voice a soft purr. "No they aren't. You did it, all right. What I don't know is why. What made you kill that lovely young woman?"

"I didn't! Y-you're falsely ac-accusing an innocent man."

"No, I'm not, Reierson. You did it, right enough. How did it happen? Did she resist your demands? Struggle? Maybe claw at you with those long fingernails?"

His face alabaster with fright, Reierson made to bolt for the door. Smoke Jensen reached him in two swift strides. He grabbed Reierson by one shoulder, spun him around, and shoved him into a chair. Panicked, the pathetic specimen of a craven killer groped under his coat and whipped out a small, four-shot, "clover-leaf" pocket revolver.

"Yes, I killed her, goddamn you. And I'll kill you, too." Sobbing in frustration, he fired wildly.

Smoke Jensen was a lot faster and much more accurate.

Stoddard burst through the vestibule door. "What happened?"

"He confessed. After he drew a gun on me. I'll write up a complete report and you can give it—and the bodies—to the law in Walsenburg."

Soft music floated through the huge dining room of a hill-top mansion outside Taos, New Mexico Territory. A string quartet in formal black sawed away at an opus by Brahms. Clifton Satterlee sat at the head of a long, shining, cherrywood table that would easily seat eighteen. A wide strip of white linen ran the length of the ruddy, glowing surface. Brice Noble sat to Clifton Satterlee's right; to his left, Clifton's wife, Emma. Noble's wife, Mildred, sat to her husband's right. At the far end were Patrick Quinn and a young woman of his acquaintance, Lettie Kincade. The other women at the table would have been scandalized and highly offended if they knew that until ensnaring the attentions of Quinn, Lettie had been the inmate of a deluxe Santa Fe bordello.

Soft, yellow light from three silver candelabra flattered the complexions of the older women, smoothing out wrinkles, while it put a light of naughty mischief into the pale blue eyes of Lettie Kincade. Cole Granger stood in front of the high double doors that gave into a high-ceilinged, vaulted corridor. Dinner had concluded and the last of the dishes cleared away.

At a sign from her husband, Emma stood and addressed the other women.

"Ladies, I suggest that we retire to my sitting room for coffee and sweets. If you gentlemen will excuse us?"

Clifton nodded blandly, and all of the men came to their boots as the women left the room. When the side door closed behind them, Satterlee turned to the butler. "Pour cognac around, if you will, Ramón, then you are excused."

Soft clinking followed while Ramón Estavez poured from a crystal decanter into three glasses. When he finished his task and lighted cigars for all three, he soundlessly departed from the room. Satterlee lifted his glass in a toast and mockingly paraphrased Shakespeare.

"We grow . . . we prosper. Now, gods, stand up for bastards." They all laughed and drank; then Satterlee continued. "First, let me announce that my lovely Emma will be returning to Santa Fe with me the day after tomorrow. Now, Mr. Quinn, we would appreciate a report of your progress."

Rising, Quinn set aside his cigar. "The Bar-Four now belongs to C.S. Enterprises, it does. So does the Obrigon ranch. We completed papers on the Suarez ranch this morning. Two stores on the Plaza de Armas now belong to your development company, with three others likely to fall in line within two days more, an' that's a fact."

"Thank you, Paddy, my friend." Satterlee beamed.

"Ah, but there's more. The title on the Figueroa hacienda cleared the territorial land office late this afternoon."

Satterlee shot to his feet in enthusiasm. "Splendid."

"Hear! Hear!" Brice Noble chimed in. "Though I must say, it was a blasted expensive undertaking. It cost a fortune to buy that mansion. Why not simply kill the old man? After all, the granddaughter could not inherit. The territorial government would appoint an executor to manage it until she reached her majority. And then"—he gestured widely—

"through our connections in Santa Fe we could have gotten it for a song."

Satterlee countered that at once. "To use our bought politicians on so trivial a matter would have unduly compromised them. The time might come when we need their influence much more. Now, let us move on to the next phase of our agenda."

Railroad workers rolled a movable loading chute in place at the door to the stock car that held the horses Smoke Jensen had brought along. The last mountain man stood by patiently as a man led Cougar down the ramp onto solid ground. Smoke had been surprised by how much Raton had grown since he had last been in the northern New Mexico town. Low adobe houses now sprawled out for a good mile from the more settled part of the community near the depot, each with its familiar picket fence of ocotillo cactus rods. Smoke abandoned his reflections when Cougar let out a shrill squall and swayed drunkenly, unaccustomed to not having the surface below his hooves in constant motion. Smoke hurried to the heaving side of the big Palouse stallion.

"Easy, boy. Whoa, Cougar." To the depot worker he added, "He'll get his legs back in a bit. Don't try to walk him around right now."

When both animals had recovered, Smoke saddled them, then strapped the large panniers on the packsaddle. The sudden thought hit Smoke that in the years past, he had never needed a packhorse to accompany him. Nor had he dragged along all the comforts that the pouches of the panniers now contained. He would have laughed at the wrought-iron trestle, cast-iron skillet and Dutch oven, three-legged grill and cooking utensils. A coffeepot and a small, lidded skillet had been all he had ever needed. *Yet, when the years go by,* he mused with regret, *one's needs change.* Mounted on Cougar, Smoke walked his way toward the main intersection, where he would take the east-west trail toward Taos. With the Santa Fe and Denver and Rio Grande both passing through Raton, the usual entrepreneurs and hustlers had flocked into the burgeoning city. Hawkers with carts stood on street corners, touting their wares. Hundreds of people thronged the streets. A low haze of red-brown dust hovered at first-floor level throughout. Stray dogs yapped at the hooves of his packhorse, and the animal snorted its irritation and flicked one iron shoe. A yellow bitch yelped and slunk off. As he passed a saloon, a loud shout attracted Smoke's attention.

"Hey, let me go!" A young man stumbled out onto the street, as though propelled by eager hands.

Following him came three scraggly ruffians who spread out across the thoroughfare. To Smoke they had the seedy look of low-grade wannabes. The one in the middle raised an arm and pointed in a taunting manner. "Yer wearin' a gun, you little shit. Now yer gonna have to use it."

With a start, Smoke Jensen recognized the speaker as Tully Banning, a two-bit gunfighter more renowned for the number of his back shootings than he was for face-to-face shoot-outs. In the next instant, as he reined in, Smoke realized that the challenged youth could not be more than fifteen. A beardless, frightened boy. Smoke quickly sized up the two louts with Banning. What his read gave him he did not like. The boy did not have a chance. Smoke stepped right in the middle of it.

"Banning! Tully Banning."

Banning turned only his head. "Who th' hell wants to know?"

"That's not important. What I want to know is why you don't pick on someone your own age or older?"

Banning uttered a string of curses, and concluded with, "Maybe you'd be interested in taking this punk kid's place. If so, I'll deal with you first, then kill Momma's little boy anyway."

Smoke pulled a face. "I don't think so. Keep your stray curs off me while I step down so I can accommodate you."

"You've got that, old man."

Old man? Smoke never thought of himself as old. He climbed from the saddle and tied off Cougar and his packhorse, Hardy. Then he walked out to stand beside the youth who had been challenged. "Step out of the street, son. You didn't ask for this, and there's no reason you take any harm for it."

With an expression of mingled relief and frustration, the sandy-haired boy angled off the street to stand by Smoke's horses. Then Smoke looked up at Banning. "I'm ready any time you are."

Tully Banning's shoulders hunched, and his right hand twitched; but he did not go for his six-gun at once. It had been a signal, one old and familiar, to his companions. The challenged individual could be expected to focus his attention and anticipation upon the challenger. That's the way it had worked for Tully Banning time and again. So, when the cheat and sneak made the little jerk and arrest movement, his henchmen immediately drew their revolvers.

One small miscalculation marred their perfect ambush. Although the trio had often heard of the exploits of Smoke Jensen, none of them had ever met with him face-to-face. Now that they had, it was entirely too late. Smoke expected some sort of dirty work, so he readied himself accordingly. When all three louts drew, Banning last of all, Smoke already had their demise planned.

Drawing with his usual blinding speed, Smoke killed the one on the left first. Then he swung past Banning in the middle to take on the right-hand gunhawk. The poor soul never had a chance. He did get off one wild shot that split the air high above the head of Smoke Jensen. Then the hammer of Smoke's .45 Peacemaker fell, and a hot slug ripped into the ruffian's gut. It burned a trail of agony through his liver before it ripped out a piece of his spine and tore a hole in his back. Rapidly dying, he went to his knees as Tully Banning attempted to level his six-gun.

To his horror, Tully Banning saw the calm expression and faint smile of the man facing him an instant before flame and smoke spewed from the muzzle of the Colt and a wrenching agony exploded in his chest. Staggered, he took two feeble, uncertain steps to the right and triggered his piece. Banning's slug kicked up dirt between the wide-spread legs of Smoke Jensen.

Then Smoke shot again. Another terrible hammer blow smashed into the chest of Tully Banning. His legs went out from under him, and he dropped on his backside in the dusty street. Dimly he heard the shouts of amazement from the onlookers who had assembled well out of the line of fire. This couldn't be happening. The trap had always worked before. It would take the best gunfighter in the world to best the three of them, Banning's spinning mind fought to reject his mortality.

Blood bubbled on his lips as he asked weakly, "Who are you?"

Smiling that ghost of a smile again, Smoke Jensen told Tully Banning, who turned even whiter before he died. Suddenly, the freckle-faced, sandy-haired boy appeared at Smoke's side. "I didn't recognize you, Mr. Jensen."

"Don't reckon they did, either."

"You sure saved my life. Uh—my name's Ian Mac-Greggor. Most folks call me Mac. It's an honor to meet you. And, thank you, thank you for getting me out of that fix. They never gave me a chance to say no."

Smoke nodded understanding. "Their kind never do. And, they never, ever pick on anyone capable of defending themselves. Remember that."

"Yes, sir, I will. Thank you again."

It took Smoke Jensen an uncomfortable fifteen minutes with the town constable to explain what he had accomplished in two seconds. Given the assurance it would be recorded as self-defense, Smoke at last got on the trail to Taos.

Thick-foliaged palo verde trees made silver-green smoke clouds against the horizon of red earth and cobalt sky. Cattle grazed on the sparse grass of Rancho de la Gloria. Throughout the prairie lands, from Texas to Montana, cattlemen talked of cows per acre. Not so here. Don Diego Alvarado had learned at his father's knee to think in terms of acres per cow. In future times, the elegant Diego Alvarado often told himself, irrigation would make this harsh desert into a veritable garden place. Not in his lifetime, though. So he did not share his dream with his friends and fellow ranchers. His vaqueros knew of it, and believed him. Three of them had been given the assignment of tending a herd of two hundred that grazed through a high meadow on the north end of the ranch property.

They found their work peaceful and pleasing. Not far off lay a connected chain of *tanques* where the beasts would water and they could take their *almuerzo*. Each had a cloth bag in his saddlebag, provided that morning by his wife, that contained a burrito—beans and onion rolled in a flour tortilla—a savory tamale, and fresh, piquant chile peppers to add flavor and spice. Arturo had even brought along some cornmeal sugar cookies baked by his wife. Arturo Gomez and Hector Blanco had promised their younger sons they could bring lunches and join the men at the tanks, the lads taking a noontime swim. That would get them out from under their mothers' feet. The older boys all tended goat herds during the day and could always find ways to get cool and wet. As a newlywed, Umberto Mascarenas, the third vaquero, only dreamed of the day when he would have sturdy sons like his companions. He looked up at the sound of pounding hooves. Could it be the *niños* already?

Caught unaware, Umberto Mascarenas did not hear the first gunshot, or any of those that followed. A bullet struck him in the right side of his head, an inch above his ear, and blew out the other hemisphere. He pitched from his horse in a welter of gore.

"Git them other greasers," a harsh voice shouted.

More gunfire sounded across the plateau. Arturo Gomez returned fire with his Obrigon copy of a .45 Colt and had the satisfaction of watching an Anglo *ladrón* spill from his saddle at the third round. Then pain burned the life from him as three bullets struck him in half a second. To his right, Hector Blanco dismounted and drew his rifle. The Marlin cracked sharply, and the hat flew from another rustler's head. Hector shot again, and the thief threw up his hands and fell backward off his mount.

By that time, the reports of the weapons had registered on the dim brains of the cattle. They reacted at once and broke into a shambling run. Controlling the cattle became the primary objective of the rustlers, yet one took the time to ride down on Hector Blanco and steal his life with a bullet through the brain. Then the killer galloped ahead to join the others in a V-shaped formation in front of the stampeded herd and direct it off Alvarado land toward a waiting holding pen in a blind canyon.

Twenty minutes later, the horrified and grief-stricken sons of Arturo and Hector found the bodies of all three vaqueros. The Whitewater Paddy Quinn gang had struck again.

FIVE

An hour short of sundown, with long, golden and carmine shafts of light spilling through the canyons, Smoke Jensen made night camp on a bluff above the Canadian River. He staked out his horses to graze and prepared a fire ring. Then he gathered dry windfall and laid a fire. With seemingly calm indifference to his surroundings, he went about setting up his cooking equipment. Constantly, though, he kept his ears tuned to the sound of soft footfalls that grew steadily nearer. Smoke's surprise registered on his face when the source of that noise came up within thirty feet of the campsite and hailed him.

"Hello, Mr. Jensen. It's me, Mac."

Smoke looked up from the task of slicing potatoes into a skillet to study the gangly youth. Mac's shoulders were broad and his arms long, the promise of a fair-sized man when he got his growth. He was slim, though, and narrow-hipped, and with that boyish face, he looked a long way from reaching that maturity. Smoke motioned him in.

"Howdy, Mac. What brings you along?"

"Well, Mr. Jensen, I wanted to thank you again for saving my life. Really, though, I sort of got to thinking. I wondered if—if you'd welcome me to ride along with you. Seein' we're headed the same direction, that is."

So much earnestness shone from his freckled face that Smoke had to turn away to keep control of his laughter. He fished an onion from a pan of water and began to slice it onto a tin plate to add to the potatoes. "Now, what direction would that be?"

"Why, to Taos, of course."

Smoke feigned doubtfulness. "I'll have to think on that one. But, step down. Least you can do now is share my eats. I've got some fatback, taters, and I'll make some biscuits."

Memory of the boiled oatmeal, twice a day, that had sustained him between his home and Raton prodded Ian MacGreggor. "Gosh, you sure eat well, Mr. Jensen."

"Call me Smoke, Mac."

Caught off balance by this, Mac gulped his words. "Yes, sir, ah, Smoke."

"Now, to eatin' well, it's only common sense. In this climate, a man has to use up his fresh stuff right at the start. By the time we reach Taos it'll be spare enough." Smoke turned his attention to the food for a while, then asked, "You have family in Taos?"

"No, sir, I'm leavin' home for good. I'm my pap's third son, so there's nothin' for me around the farm. We have a little dirt-scrabble place over in Texas. Whole lot of Scots folks around Amarillo. The farm'll go to my oldest brother, Caleb. Dirk is hot for workin' on the railroad. Wants to be an engineer. The apprenticeship and schoolin' costs money, so there was not much left for me."

"Then, I gather you are looking for work in Taos?"

"That's right, Smoke. I heard there was plenty work being offered out Taos way. There was even a notice in the Amarillo paper. A man named Satterlee. He's lookin' for cowhands, timber fallers, all sorts of jobs."

Smoke's frown surprised Mac. "Ah—Mac, I don't want to disappoint you, but do you know anything about this Satterlee?"

"No, no I don't. What's the matter?"

Smoke did not want the boy to go bad. He seemed to have some promise. So, he told Mac what he knew of Clifton Satterlee from the letter sent by Diego Alvarado. As he spoke, the youngster's eyes grew big, and he produced an angry expression. When Smoke concluded, Mac shook his head.

"I sure don't want anything to do with someone like that. Sounds like he's puredee crook." Then he took on a sad expression. "But now I've burned my bridges, what am I gonna do to make a livin'?"

"Taos is growing. And I have a friend. A man who owns a large ranch. Do you happen to speak Spanish? His name is Diego Alvarado; he's a real Spanish gentleman."

Mac nodded enthusiastically. "Sure do. Learned it from the sons of our hired hand. I growed up with them."

"Then, if Don Diego takes you on, you'll have lots of use for it. All of his ranch hands are Mexican."

Mac frowned. "I don't know much about cows. We planted mostly hay, sold it to the ranchers, put in some wheat, corn. Pap wanted to try watermelons. They grow real good in Texas."

"As I recall, Diego has some fields down by a creek that runs behind his house which he uses to irrigate them. He grows several kinds of melons, as well as corn, onions, beans, chile peppers, and a little cotton. He provides nearly all the needs for the entire ranch."

"How—how big is this place?"

"Three or four thousand acres, I'm not sure which."

Mac looked at Smoke in awe. "That's the biggest spread I ever heard of. All we have is a quarter section."

Smoke took pity on Mac, though not much. "Diego has more land under irrigated cultivation than that. I'm willin' to bet he could use an experienced farmer."

Over their meal, Smoke worried around another idea in his head. When Mac offered to wash up after supper, Smoke poured a cup of coffee and spoke his mind. "If Diego has no need for a farmer, there might be something else you can do. Something for me. Though it might prove risky."

New hope bloomed on Mac's face. "Anything, so long as it's legal, Smoke."

"I assure you it's that. Don Diego asked me to come out and take a look at this Satterlee's operation. I could use some help in doing that."

"How can you poke into something crooked? That's a job for the law."

Smiling, Smoke produced his badge and showed it to Mac. "So happens, I'm a deputy U.S. marshal. What I have in mind is that if Diego does not take you on, you go ahead and take that job with Satterlee. Only, don't break the law yourself. Look around, keep your ears open. See what kind of sign you cut on his operation. Then, make arrangements to report anything you learn to me. You'd get regular deputy marshal pay, provided by the U.S. Marshal's Office. That should give you a good stake after the job is over."

"What about the risk you mentioned?" Mac asked soberly.

No fool this one, Smoke reflected. "If you are caught, Satterlee or one of his henchmen will try to kill you. Or at least hurt you pretty bad."

Mac cut his eyes to the six-gun in the holster on his hip. "I ain't as fast or accurate as you, Smoke. An' I never caught on to the trap of those three in Raton. But I am good with a gun."

"You'll have to be. What d'you say?"

"Okay. I'll do it."

Smoke looked Mac levelly in the clear, blue eyes. "Done, then. But you may not live to regret it," he told the boy ominously.

* * *

A refreshing spring shower had brightened the yellow bonnets of the jonquils and purple-red tulip globes in the wide beds planted at the front of the main house on the Sugarloaf. A rainbow hung on the breast of the Medicine Bow Mountains to the northeast. Sally Jensen gave up on her industrious dusting program at the clatter of narrow, steel-tired wheels on the ranch yard. She removed the kerchief which covered her raven locks, abandoned her smudged rag, and straightened the apron as she walked to the door. She opened the portal to an astonishing sight.

A woman, vaguely familiar, and four children sat on the spring-mounted seats of a sparkling, brightly lacquered carriage. The three boys, their soft, brown hair cut in bang-fringed pageboy style, wore manly little suits of royal blue, Moorish maroon and emerald green, with identical flat-crowned, wide-brimmed hats. The small girl sat primly beside her mother, in a matching crushed velvet cape and gown of a puce hue, feathered bonnets to match. The young males quarreled loudly and steadily among themselves.

Sally took three small steps to the edge of the porch. She paused then as she put a name to the face, remembering the letter she had received three days earlier. Mary-Beth Whipple. No, Sally corrected herself, her married name was Gittings. Obviously when Mary-Beth had written asking to make a brief visit, she had taken for granted that the answer would be yes. How typical of Mary-Beth, Sally thought ruefully.

"Sally, dearest," Mary-Beth burbled happily as she reined in.

"Mary-Beth?" Sally responded hesitantly. "I—didn't expect you so soon."

Mary-Beth simply ignored that and gushed. "It's so good to see you again. You have no idea how much I've missed my dear schoolmate." She raised her arms and flung them wide to encompass the whole of the Sugarloaf. "We're here at last."

"Uh—yes, so you are. Won't you come in?"

"Of course. Right away. Can you get someone to take care of these dreadfully stubborn animals?"

For a moment Sally wondered if she meant the snorting, lathered horses or her three sons. The volume of their altercation had risen to the shouting stage. Sally recalled her school chum only too well. The daughter of a wealthy New England mill owner, she had always been a petulant, spoiled young woman. One who proved woefully empty-headed. Sally had been compelled to drag Mary-Beth's grades upward at the Teachers' Seminary. Worse, she absolutely, positively refused to eat meat. Yet those were not her only eccentricities, Sally recalled as Mary-Beth spoke again.

"These abominable horses, of course. They have made our journey from Denver absolutely miserable. So tedious. Well," she declared, releasing the reins and standing upright in the carriage. "We're here now. And we can look forward to not having to deal with these fractious creatures for a whole month."

A month? Sally thought sinkingly. *That* was Mary-Beth's idea of a brief stay? "I'm afraid we're not . . . prepared for such a long stay."

Mary-Beth's face clouded up, and she produced a girlish pout. "But, we simply must. My husband is doing business-y things in Denver, and it is frightfully boring."

"But . . . my husband is not here. He has been called away."

"Oh, bother the men. They are all alike. Born to neglect. I sometimes regret that I gave birth to even a single male. Little Francine here is all my life."

Her words chilled Sally, who instantly saw the confusion and hurt in the expressions and suddenly flat eyes of the boys. For all of that, Sally's inborn hospitality compelled her to welcome them. She opened her arms in an inviting gesture. "Come on in, then. I'll fix coffee. And I have a sponge cake. Your boys will like that, I'm sure."

Three bright, happy faces shined out on her. "Cake, yah!" they chorused.

Inside, with the boys gulping down slice after slice of the cake Sally had planned to have for herself and Bobby for supper, Mary-Beth returned to her earlier topic. "Ever since you described this heavenly place to me, I've dreamed of visiting. And we simply must stay the whole month. Grantland will be tied up in dull meetings every day for a full thirty days. Lawyers have such a dreary life. Besides, Denver is so depressing, with its heavy pall of smelter smoke hanging over everything. And, such rough, unlettered people swarming everywhere, with absolutely no control over them." Mary-Beth paused and looked at her cup.

"Actually, I prefer tea. Could you arrange to have tea from now on?"

Sally curbed her temper. "I have some tea. When it's gone, it's gone."

Mary-Beth reached over and patted Sally's forearm. "Fine, dear, I understand." She looked over to where her sons had started to squabble noisily over the last slice of cake. "Boys, you go outside with that. You've eaten quite enough. It will spoil your supper."

Grumbling, the three little louts jumped from the table and trudged outside. Mary-Beth picked up again. "At what hour do you serve dinner? We are accustomed to eight."

"Well, Mary-Beth, we are accustomed to six. If you'll pardon me, we will stick to that schedule." Gloomy images of a month of this flashed through Sally's mind.

Bobby Jensen first encountered the newcomers when he came up to the main house from the foaling barn where he had been mucking out stalls. He went directly to the wash house, where he had laid out clean clothes before beginning his task, to clean himself of the stink of blood, manure, and horse urine. Bobby had barely eased himself into the big, brass bathtub and shuddered in pleasure at the feel of the warm water when he heard a sound like rats in the rafters. He looked around and saw nothing, so he went to his ablutions. The sound came again.

Bobby paused in the vigorous scrubbing of his hands and arms and let his gaze slide from corner to corner. Again he could find no source. He ducked his head of white-blond hair below the surface and began to lather it when he came up. The rustling persisted. Bobby rinsed his hair and pushed up on one arm.

"Who's there?" When no reply came to his demand, he gave careful examination to the interior for a third time, then returned to his bath. When he was satisfied with his degree of cleanliness—he had not washed behind his ears—Bobby climbed from the tub and stepped under the sprinkler can nozzle attached to a length of lead pipe. Lukewarm water cascaded down on the crown of his head and his thin shoulders when he pulled a chain attached to a spring valve. While he rinsed, he caught sight of furtive movement over by the chair where he had laid his fresh clothing.

A small, pale white hand reached slowly around the obstruction of the chair and headed for the parrot bill grip of Bobby's .38 Colt Lightning. Bobby took three quick steps toward the hidden person and called out in as hard a voice as he could muster.

"Get your hand off my gun."

Suddenly, a boy somewhat smaller than Bobby popped up behind the chair. His appearance would have made Bobby laugh if he were not so angry. He wore a funny blue suit, with a big old flowery tie done in a bow under his chin, and had hair only a few shades more yellow than Bobby's, done in a sissy cut. Ribbons tied the bottoms of his trouser legs just below the knees. Full, bee-stung lips that were made for pouting formed a soft, Cupid's-bow mouth. He screwed those lips up now and spoke in a snotty, superior tone.

"You can't have a gun. You're only a kid. Besides, nobody has a right to have a gun, except a policeman. And even they shouldn't have them. My mother says."

Although naked as a jaybird, Bobby immediately snapped out his verbal defense. "The hell I can't. Smoke Jensen gave me this six-gun himself. I've got a rifle, too."

"Liar. My mother says no one has the right to a gun. That they are the most evil things on earth."

Bobby bristled further. "You're the liar. You ever hear of the Constitution? Smoke taught me real good. There's a part of it that says, '. . . the right of the people to keep and bear arms shall not be infringed.' So there."

Mary-Beth's eldest, Billy, narrowed his eyes and balled his small fists. "Think you're one of those dirty, back-shootin', coward gunfighters like Smoke Jensen?"

That proved too much for Bobby. He swiftly closed the distance between himself and the other boy and gave his antagonist a two-handed shove to the chest. Rocked off his heels, twelve-year-old Billy stumbled backward. Bobby came right after him. Another push and Billy went sprawling out of the wash house. Bobby watched the other boy flail in the dirt a moment, then turned back and shrugged into his trousers. He came out of the building as Billy scrambled to his feet.

Billy made the mistake of swinging the moment he saw Bobby. Young Jensen ducked and threw a punch of his own. It smacked Billy under the left eye. He cried out at the pain and then rushed Bobby. Bobby sidestepped and tripped Billy. At once, the older boy dropped down on his knees, astraddle the small of Billy's back. Bobby began to drub his opponent on the shoulders. Billy made squealing, yelping sounds and kicked the toes of his boots against the ground. At last he found purchase enough to thrust upward and throw Bobby off him.

"Damn you, you don't fight fair," Billy sobbed, his dirt-smeared cheeks streaked with tears. He dived on Bobby before the older boy could get up.

From there their fight degenerated into a lot of rolling around in the dirt. Bobby got a couple of good punches to Billy's ribs. Then he clouted his opponent on the ear, which brought a howl of agony from Billy. Bobby wrestled himself around on top and began to drive work-hardened fists into Billy's midriff. All pretense of toughness deserted Billy, and he began to wail in a pitiful voice.

"Help me! Momma, help me! Get him off, get him off."

The sudden commotion reached the ears of Sally Jensen and Mary-Beth Gittings where they sat on the porch, sipping at cups of jasmine tea. Mary-Beth's face went blank, then white a moment, and she clutched at her heart. Half rising, she put her cup aside.

"I think that's Billy. Whatever could be happening?"

Sally listened to the uproar a moment and picked out Bobby's voice. "Yer a liar and a trespasser. Git the hell outta here."

Drily she remarked to Mary-Beth, "I think he has met our youngest. We had better go see."

Together they headed in the direction of the wash house. The sight they saw made Sally Jensen ache, though inwardly she burned with pride for her adopted son. Bobby Jensen remained astride Billy Gittings, pounding him rhythmically. Billy was getting his tail kicked right properly. One eye showed the beginnings of a splendid mouse, and his nose had been bloodied. He sobbed wretchedly with each punch Bobby delivered. She could not let that go on, Sally realized at once. She hurried to the boys.

"Bobby, you stop that at once. Get off Billy this instant."

Embarrassment filled Sally Jensen as she dragged Bobby Jensen off Billy Gittings.

Mary-Beth Gittings harbored entirely different emotions. Her voice became accusatory and filled with indignation. Her son and Bobby each gave his version of what had started the fight. Her face red, she turned with hands on hips to lash out at Sally.

"Billy is correct. No one has the right to own a gun except the police. I would certainly never allow a child of mine to have one."

Bobby remained defiant. "Then why did he try to steal mine?"

Surly, though in control of his sobs and tears, Billy answered truculently. "I was gonna take it away from you and do what's right and give it to Mother."

Sally stepped in. "Bobby is correct. Taking another person's property, whether you think he has a right to it or not, is stealing. There will be no more of that around here. Now, both of you go in there and get yourselves washed up. You're a couple of mud balls. And shake hands and try to be nice."

Thoroughly mollified, Bobby put out a hand. "My name's Bobby, what's yours?"

"Billy," the other boy answered, still offended. Then he drew himself up. "William Durstan Gittings. But you can call me Billy."

They released their grip and turned away from the adults. With an arm around each other's shoulders, they walked toward the bath that awaited them. Sally breathed a sigh of relief, only to learn that Mary-Beth had not finished.

"One thing you must accept, dear Sally. My son was right in what he did. He certainly did not deserve anything like the beating he got."

Sally groaned inwardly at the thought of the ensuing month, saddled with this now former friend.

* * *

In a large, adobe mansion outside of Santa Fe, Clifton Satterlee and four of his associates from back east sat in a sumptuous study, two walls lined floor to ceiling with books in neat rows on their shelves. Long, thick, maroon brocade drapes covered the leaded glass windows, with the usual wrought-iron bars covering them from outside. A small, horseshoe-shaped desk occupied the open space directly in front of the limestone casement. That was where Satterlee held court. The tall back of a large, horsehair-stuffed chair loomed over his six-foot-plus height. He wore a blue velvet smoking jacket and open-front shirt of snowy perfection, riding trousers, and calf-length boots. His guests clothed themselves with all the formality of eastern evening wear. Brass lamps provided illumination, and the yellow rays of the kerosene flames struck highlights off the cut crystal decanter and five glasses on a low table around which the visitors sat. The topic of conversation had turned to their plans for the conquest of Taos and its environs.

"We already have a good foothold," Satterlee reminded his associates. "C.S. Enterprises has the timber rights to a thousand acres on the eastern slopes of the Sangre de Cristo range. By selective cutting, we can clear a way to allow passage of the logs we harvest from the land currently held by those Tua vermin. We can pass them off as coming from our legally held property."

Durwood Pringle cocked an eyebrow. "Do you think that will fool any inspectors the Interior Department sends out here?"

"Of course, they are the same kind of trees. We will continue to log off the eastern slopes so that an inspector will see cutting activity. And, we will have ample advance warning of any surprise visit. Besides, when it comes to the local officials, we have already bought them."

Pringle still lacked assurance. "Yes, but are they *honest* politicians?"

Satterlee snorted in impatience. "What do you mean? We paid them off, didn't we?"

"I understand that, Clifton, old fellow, what I mean is that an *honest* politician is one that once he's been bought, he stays bought."

They shared a good laugh at this levity. Then Satterlee moved on to the next subject. "The merchants and residents of Taos remain stubborn for some reason. Although we have added to our cattle holdings recently with two hundred head from the Alvarado ranch."

A frown creased the forehead of Durwood Pringle. "That's excellent, Clifton. But what we want to know is what is being done to encourage these reticent merchants in Taos to sell out?"

Clifton Satterlee took a long pull on his cognac and produced a warm smile. "Have no fear, Durwood. That is being taken care of as we speak."

SIX

Bright orange tendrils of flame coiled through the black night sky over Taos, New Mexico. The intensity of the inferno paled the thin crescent of moon and dampened the starshine. A horse-drawn fire wagon, its bell clanging frantically, sped through the streets. Men in light blue cotton shirts tugged at the suspenders of their bright yellow, water-proof, oil-skin trousers. A cold hand clutched their minds as one. The worst possible disaster had actually happened.

"Where's the blaze, Cap?" a late arrival volunteer fireman asked of his captain.

Captain Taylor pointed to the south. "Couldn't be worse, Clem. The lumberyard is on fire."

Seconds later, their red-and-black lacquered fire engine stormed down the street toward the lumberyard, which had become an orange ball. The chief of the volunteer fire department, Zeke Crowder, directed them to the south side of the block-square enterprise. Flames and showers of sparks shot fifty feet into the air. Zeke Crowder studied this condition with a grim expression. After several seconds, he called his captains together.

"We've got to keep this from spreading to other buildings. Remember what happened in Albuquerque last year. Three blocks in a row wiped out by what started as a small fire in a restaurant kitchen."

"How do we go about it, Chief?" Fire Captain Taylor asked.

Chief Crowder produced a thoughtful expression. "Even though most of these buildings are made of adobe, they all have palm thatch roofs. Dry as it is, if sparks land in that, fire can sweep through as fast as the scorpions and other critters that live there. We have to knock down the flames now to keep that from happening. If we don't, we'll lose half of Taos."

"How we gonna git it done?" another captain persisted.

Chief Crowder did not hesitate. He gestured to the twelve-foot adobe walls that surrounded the lumberyard. "We need to knock down these walls, make 'em fall inward and blow out the flames. Parker, go to the general store. That's the only other source of dynamite in town. Oh, and you might send someone out to the mines. They'll have some. But hurry."

Captain Taylor stated the obvious. "Don't we have to get Mike Sommers' permission to blow up his walls?"

"Yeah, if we can find him. I haven't seen him at all." Chief Crowder paused a second, then directed Taylor. "Find Hub Yates, Mike's foreman. I need to talk to him anyway."

Five minutes later, Capt. Don Taylor returned with Hubbard Yates. "Hub's not seen Mike, either, Chief."

Quickly, Captain Crowder explained the situation to Yates. He concluded with an appeal. "We have to get someone's permission to knock down these walls."

Yates shook his head. "I don't know if I can do that or not."

"If you can't, I do have the authority to do it anyway. Only thing is the city could be charged with the cost of rebuilding. But, if we don't do it, like I said, we can lose half of the town."

Hub Yates looked at the towering column of sparks. "Go ahead, then. I'll take the chance and speak for Mike."

"All right. Don, come with me. We're going to set charges on both sides of the walls. The stronger ones on the inside. You take a crew that knows explosives and put them to it.

And tamp them solid. We want to upend those adobe blocks and drop them inward. The blast should help blow out the flames, too."

While volunteers and onlookers alike labored at the long pumper rails, other firefighters directed inadequate streams of water onto the burning stacks of raw pine and fir. Steam rose in gouts. The core of the fire glowed a dark magenta. Don Taylor and his men took cases of dynamite as they arrived and prepared charges. A shout of alarm rose when the roof of the building nearest the blaze caught fire from sparks and began to burn lustily.

At once, Chief Crowder directed the three hoses of one company onto the new hot spot. Hissing in protest, the flames slowly died. "Keep on wetting that one down," Crowder directed. He sent two runners to instruct the other fire rigs to do the same.

"Why are you giving up?" a bystander demanded.

"We're gonna lose the whole she-bang, that's for certain. All we can hope for is to keep it from spreading."

"I still say you oughta keep on fighting."

Crowder eyed him coldly. "You're not wearing this coal scuttle on yer head, either. Hell, you're not even helping. I'd keep that mouth buttoned up tight, if I were you.

After half an hour, Captain Taylor reported to the chief. "We're all set."

"Then let her rip!"

At a signal from Taylor, fuses were ignited. The solid thump of explosions rippled along the walls, working outward from the center. Thick clouds of dust billowed and obscured the fire. With a muffled rumble, the tiers of adobe blocks leaned inward and began to fall. The initial blasts had dampened the flames considerably. Now, the four-sided curtains of disturbed air from the falling walls snuffed much more. The feeble streams from the hoses began to gain ground. From the far side a cheer went up.

Chief Crowder began an inspection tour of the fire site. He found that through some fluke, the building front had only been slightly charred. Taking two firemen with him, he picked his way gingerly through the smoldering coals and mounds of ash. Near the rear of the store portion, where the fire had been far hotter, he came upon a huddled mound. Crowder brushed at accumulated ash with a gloved hand and revealed a human shoulder.

"Give me a hand here," he commanded.

His firemen bent to the task. Shortly, they recovered and revealed the severely burned corpse of the owner. A sickeningly sweet odor wafted up from the seared flesh. One of the firefighters, who had eaten mutton for supper, turned away and abruptly lost his supper. Fighting back his own rush of nausea, Chief Crowder issued yet another command.

"Get Doc Walters over here right away."

In midmorning of the next day, a visibly troubled Dr. Adam Walters found Zeke Crowder in his saddlery shop. The volunteer fire chief sat at a bench, shaping strips of leather into the skirt of yet another of his excellent saddles. A steaming coffee cup rested to one side. He looked up as the bell over the door jingled and the doctor entered.

"'Morning, Doc. What news on Mike Sommers?"

"Nothing good, I'm afraid, Zeke. That's why I'm here. I also asked Hank Banner to join us. He should be along shortly."

"The sheriff? What for? Mike died in an accident, didn't he?"

"No. The fire was not an accident and Mike did not die from it."

Right then the bell jingled again, and Sheriff Hank Banner entered. "Howdy, Adam, Zeke. Now, what was so all-fired important, Doc?"

Dr. Walters sighed heavily. "Maybe we should all have a

cup of coffee at hand. I brought along some medicinal brandy."

He remained silent while Crowder poured. Then the physician added brandy to all three mugs. He sighed heavily again before he made his revelation. "Mike Sommers was murdered. He had been shot twice. Once in the chest and once in the head. Whoever started that fire figured he would be too badly burned for us to find that out."

"Any idea who might have done it?" the sheriff asked.

Dr. Walters hesitated. "I think you could guess the name I'd give you. Mike told me only last week that he had been approached with an offer to buy him out. He refused. Then three of the ruffians who have been moving into town of late roughed him up some on Saturday night. Now, this fire, and Mike is dead, killed by someone working for Clifton Satterlee, or I'll eat my medical bag."

With a grunt, the sheriff raised a restraining hand. "Be careful about unsubstantiated accusations, Doc. You know that particular gentleman would not hesitate to haul you into court on a slander suit."

"But dang-bust it. What can we do about this? About everything?"

Again Hank Banner urged caution. "I must admit I share your suspicions that Satterlee is behind all that has happened, including the fire and the murder of Mike Sommers. But, I have no proof. Get me something positive and I'll fling him in jail so fast his boots will take a week to catch up. You know, every day I see more hardcases moving into town. I've a feeling this is about to come to a head."

Beyond the first line of trees that screened a small clearing beside the steep, winding grade that formed the eastern upslope to Palo Flechado Pass, Moose Redaker, Gabe Tucker, Buell Ormsley, and Abe Voss watched two riders walk their mounts past their observation point. When the pair, a young wet-behind-the-ears kid and an older man, had ridden well out of hearing range, Moose Redaker elbowed Buell Ormsley in the ribs.

"Didn't I tell you? When I first seed them, I knew that bigger feller was Smoke Jensen. We're lookin' at better than five thousand dollars re-ward on the hoof."

"You sure those flyers are still in force?" Abe Voss, the cautious one, asked.

Moose had a ready reply. "They ain't been tooken up, have they?"

"That don't mean someone will pay up after all this time."

"Sure they will. And even if they don't, killin' that holier-than-thou gunfighter will be pure satisfaction in itself." Moose Redaker beamed at his companions. "He's done collected too many bounties that should have been ours by rights. 'Sides, it'll do a whole lot for our reputation, now ain't that so, Gabe?"

Gabe Tucker showed a grin of crooked, green-fringed, yellow teeth. "Right as rain, Moose. Hey, how'er we goin' about this?"

A shrewd light glowed in the eyes of Moose Redaker. "These flyers all say he's wanted dead or alive, right?" He paused and put a hand to his wide chin, which hung below a lantern jaw. "Do any of you hanker to manhandle a live and kickin' Smoke Jensen?"

Buell Ormsley scratched at his fringe of ginger hair that surrounded his bald crown. "Not this lad. My momma never raised no idiots."

"She come mighty close," Moose Redaker jibed. "Yep, I reckon we'd do best to jist shoot him in the back and haul his body up north, Montana way."

Buell Ormsley squeezed his bulbous nose. "Won't he get to stinkin' a lot, we do that?" He had a valid point.

In his usual manner, Moose had an answer. "Not if we go by train and ice him down."

Abe Voss rubbed his gloved hands together. "Then, let's get at it."

"Don't be in such a hurry. We gotta do up a plan first."

"What about the boy?" Gabe Tucker inquired.

"Kill him an' leave him for the buzzards," advised Moose.

Ian MacGreggor had dropped back to tighten a loose cinch and relieve a swollen bladder. His horse stood stubbornly sideways in the trail as he tried to mount it. When he swung aboard, he got a quick glimpse of four grim-faced men riding toward him at a fast pace. Swiftly, he turned the animal's head and put spurs to its flanks. Behind him, the evil quartet put their mounts into a gallop. Rapid reaction by Moose Redaker prevented Abe Voss from firing a shot at the boy and revealing their presence for certain. As it happened, they might as well have shot anyway.

When Mac came within hailing distance of Smoke, he called out a warning. "Look out, Smoke. Four hard-looking guys headed our way." Then he reined smartly to the side and disappeared behind a large boulder.

Redaker and his crew of ne'er-do-well bounty hunters crested a rise that had separated them from their quarry and found the boy gone from sight. The four of them faced a lone Smoke Jensen. Had their combined intelligence been anywhere near average, that fact might have given them more than a little pause to consider. Since it was not, they blundered on, drawing their six-guns as they came. Smoke waited patiently. The moment the first eager lout came within range, Smoke cut him down with a round from his Winchester Express rifle.

Abe Voss flew from the saddle, while still far out of revolver range. His companions could only curse. The deadly accurate rifle spoke again and a 500-grain .45 slug sped downrange. Moose Redaker had accurately gauged Smoke Jensen's intentions and ducked low at the precise moment. A fraction of a second later, the bullet cracked past in the space formerly occupied by his head. The distance had decreased, which lent encouragement to the bounty hunters. Gabe Tucker jinked to the left and rode into the meadow to that side. He sought to flank Smoke Jensen and get in a good shot. He made it half the distance to his goal when an invisible fist slammed into his right side and knocked him out of the saddle. He hit in a shower of broken turf and rolled to a halt faced away from Smoke Jensen. The burning pain began to fade to the numbness of shock.

On the other side of Moose Redaker, Buell Ormsley angled toward the cluster of boulders. He watched as Smoke Jensen swung the muzzle of the Winchester toward Moose Redaker. When the express rifle bucked in Smoke's grip, Buell swung the nose of his mount back toward the last mountain man and let fly with two fast rounds.

At first, he thought he had hit his target. Smoke Jensen reared back in his saddle and then bent forward. With a start, Buell realized that Smoke had merely put the rifle back in its scabbard. Jensen came up with a six-gun that looked right at him. A wild cry of denial and fright blew from Buell Ormsley's thick lips as Smoke Jensen fired.

At a range of some thirty feet, the bullet had not the power to kill, but it did hurt like hell when it punched through the leather vest Ormsley wore and broke a rib. Reflex action sent him out of the saddle and onto the ground. He landed hard. More pain shot up his spine when his rump made contact with the soil. Temporarily out of the fight, he fought a wave of dizziness. Dimly he saw Moose Redaker close within killing distance of Smoke Jensen.

Smoke remained calm as he waited out his opponent. The only one still astride a horse, the scruffy-looking hill trash presented the only challenge Smoke could see. Both men fired at the same time, and their slugs missed. Smoke's by so narrow a margin that a hot line burned along the rib cage of Moose Redaker. Moose yowled and fired again. The slug punched through the side panel of Smoke's vest. That brought an instant response.

Another .45 round spat from the Peacemaker in Smoke's hand. This one struck Moose in the chest with stunning force. Redaker reeled in the saddle and tried to put his own six-gun into action. A dark red curtain seemed to descend behind his eyes, and the world grew hazy. At last he triggered his Smith American. The .44 slug screamed off a rock and disappeared in the direction of Taos. Then the ground seemed to leap up and smack Moose in the face. He died wondering how that could happen.

Buell Ormsley scooted over the ground toward his dropped six-gun. He had quickly discovered that he had sprained an ankle in his fall from the horse. Buell reached the weapon while Smoke scanned the other three for any sign of continued resistance. Carefully he raised it, and sighted in on the broad back of Smoke Jensen. He eared back the hammer of the Merwin Hulbert .44 and sighted again. Buell heard the beginning of a loud report from a revolver close by an instant before an intense light washed through his brain, as the off side of his skull flew apart in gory shards.

Ian MacGreggor rode out onto the trail, smoke still curling from the barrel of the old Schofield Smith .44 in his left hand. "He was gonna back-shoot you, Smoke."

Smoke masked his surprise and produced a grateful grin. "You done good, Mac. Saved my life, that's for sure. I'm beholdin' to you."

With sincere modesty, Mac made small of it. "You'd a done the same for me."

"Thanks all the same. I wonder if it's worth the effort to

take this trash along and see if there's a bounty on any of them?"

"D'you think there might be?" Mac had not considered such a possibility.

"Never know." Smoke searched the body of Moose Redaker and found the aged, out-of-date posters depicting his own face. Also a letter signed six years earlier giving a commission to one Albert Redaker to seek out wanted miscreants under the auspice of the sheriff of Denton County, Texas. "Still don't mean they're free of any head money."

"I—ah—if it's all the same, I'd just as soon not have them along for company." Smoke noticed that Mac looked a little gray-green around the mouth.

"First time you killed a man?"

"First time I ever shot at one," Mac admitted.

"Take it from me, Mac, it don't get any easier. Only your reaction to it changes. We'd best cover them with rocks and mark 'em so the nearest law can find them."

Back at the Sugarloaf, little Seth Gittings, Mary-Beth's middle boy, had become a particular burden for Sally Jensen. Every bit as much a brat as his elder brother, he chose this afternoon to leave off the severe biting of his fingernails long enough to bite Bobby. His little jaws proved exceptionally strong as he crunched down on Bobby's left forearm. Bobby instantly felt a jolt of hot pain run up his arm and spread in his chest. He wanted to cry out, to even shed a few tears of agony. Yet he shut his mind to such childish things and sought to remedy the situation.

His hard right fist cracked into the side of his tormentor's head. Seth let go with a yowl and an instant flood of tears. "Ow! Owie! Billy, Billy, he hit me. He hit me," quickly followed.

Bobby immediately pursued his advantage. Chin on his chest, shoulders rolled like Smoke had shown him, he waded in. Fast, solid rights and lefts rained on the chest and exposed belly of Seth Gittings. The ten-year-old back-pedaled and flailed uselessly with his stubby arms. Bobby changed his target and felt a flood of satisfaction as blood gushed from Seth's nose. He continued to whale away on Seth until Billy arrived. At once the twelve-year-old took up for his brother and joined the fray in the form of an attack on Bobby Jensen's turned back.

It staggered Bobby for a moment. Then, determined not to be deterred until he had taught them a lasting lesson, Bobby put his back to the outer wall of the bunkhouse and forced them to come at him from the front. His superior size and strength soon began to tell. First Seth, the cause of the altercation, gave up. He ran off, whining and crying, to find their mother. Billy battled on. The pain of his bite had been forgotten. Bobby never gave it thought until droplets of his own blood splashed in his face. Then he shook his arm in the astonished face of Billy.

"See this? See what that brat little brother of yours did to me?"

Stunned by this evidence, Billy gave off fighting with Bobby. "Yeah, he does get sorta wild at times. Bit the hell outta me once."

Bobby, too, stopped exchanging blows. "What did you do?"

"I whipped his butt."

"What do you think I was doin'?"

"Yeah, but he's my brother."

"So? It's me he bit this time."

"Yep, I guess so. Uh—you oughta get that fixed, Bobby."

Quickly as that, the two boys dissolved their animosity. They had their differences amicably ironed out when Mary-Beth Gittings, led by a wailing Seth, and Sally Jensen descended upon them.

"What is the meaning of this, you monstrous, vicious little wretch?" she snarled at Bobby Jensen. Even her son looked shocked at her vehemence. Then she rounded on Sally Jensen. "Sally, you simply must punish that unruly boy."

Mutely, Bobby held up his arm to show the tooth marks and the blood that ran from them. Always slow to anger, Sally suppressed a hot outburst and spoke sweetly. "Since it was two on one, and Seth obviously bit Bobby, perhaps your little darlings share some of the blame."

To the surprise of the Jensens, it was Billy Gittings who came to the defense of Bobby. "He bit me, too, Mother. Remember?"

Mary-Beth pulled an expression of horror. "The very idea!" Thus dismissing her son's revelation, she turned on Sally and snapped, "Seth would never do a thing like that. My precious children are learning such terrible, ruffian ways out here on the frontier. This—this cast-off child of yours is nothing short of a savage. If it weren't so intolerable in Denver, I would return at once."

Oh, do, please do, Sally thought to herself.

SEVEN

On a hill overlooking Taos, New Mexico Territory, Smoke Jensen halted to consider their course of action from this point on. He turned to Ian MacGreggor. "We'll enter town from different directions. Remember, Mac, when you see me, you don't know me. Later, when this is over, I will definitely introduce you to Diego Alvarado."

Somewhat sobered by the shoot-out on the trail, Mac nodded thoughtfully. "I can understand that, Smoke. Only, how do I make contact when I learn anything important?"

"If there is time, send a letter to Paul Jones, care of general delivery in Taos, giving a time and place. If not, break off from Satterlee's men and ride like the wind for town."

Mac pulled a dubious expression, but answered easily. "Sounds simple enough. Why Paul Jones?"

"More likely to slip past anyone Satterlee might have watching the mail."

Mac pursed his lips. "Yeah—yeah, that makes sense. Did you learn all of this to be a marshal?"

Smoke had to chuckle over that. "No. A lot I figured out on my own, some Preacher taught me, and the rest I got from lawmen like our sheriff back in the high lonesome. Monte Carson is mighty savvy about such things." For a moment, recollection of Monte brought a tightness to Smoke's chest. "Now, get on your way. I'll give you twenty minutes and then ride in."

Smoke watched Mac ride away and could not help but reflect on himself at that age. He had been rough-edged, a bit wild and woolly, and had lived about a year with Preacher. The old mountain man—some people called Preacher the *first* mountain man—had proven to be incredibly knowledgeable about every aspect of life in the high lonesome. He could lecture for hours on the habits, love life, construction skills, and market price of the beaver. Add in religion and fighting techniques and he could do the same for a good seven Indian tribes. A complete fascination with such subjects soon smoothed the rough edges, calmed the wildness, and trimmed the wool of young Kirby Jensen.

At fifteen, Mac's age, Smoke had received a special present from Preacher. It was a Colt Model '51 Navy revolver in .36 caliber. With it came grueling hours of drill and instructions in how to load and accurately fire the weapon. He had also learned the speed draw that had made Preacher famous as the first gunfighter. That had not come without a price. More than a dozen times Smoke had discharged blank loads with the revolver still in the pocket. The accidental discharges had burned like hellfire and scarred his leg. Preacher had found it amusing.

Chuckling each time it happened, he had reminded young Kirby, "Boy, you've gotta be quicker on the draw before you work on quick on the trigger."

It had embarrassed the youth, but it made him work harder and become better. In later years, his speed and accuracy with a six-gun would excel even that of his mentor. If Mac was only a quarter as good as Smoke had become, he could for sure hold his own.

* * *

Pablo Alvarado, third son of Diego Alvarado, strolled into the cool interior of the Bajo el Cielo de Mexico cantina in Taos during the busy noon hour. The ever-present muslin sheeting dropped white bellies from the rafters, placed there to prevent unwelcome visits by the scorpions and insects that inhabited the palm thatch roofing. Men lined the bar, gustily drinking down their cellar-cooled beer, while they munched industriously on plates of *taquitos*—rolled corn tortillas filled with roast, shredded goat meat and fried crisp. Others consumed small clay cups of *caldo de camarón,* a thick dark red chile-shrimp soup made of tiny dried shrimp, onions, garlic, tomato paste, and hot chiles. All of them frequently dipped tortilla chips into bowls of fresh-made *pico de gallo* salsa, redolent with the aroma of chopped chiles, garlic, and fresh cilantro. Nearly half of the patrons were Anglos. Pablo joined three vaqueros from his father's *estancia,* Rancho de la Gloria. He soon had a tall, slender glass of beer, called a *tubo,* in one hand. With his other, Pablo lifted a *taquito* from a plate.

His presence was immediately noted by a trio of scruffy saddle trash seated at a corner table. They bent their heads together and the leader, Garth Thompson, spoke in a low voice. "That's one of that stubborn greaser's sons. I think you two ought to arrange a little entertainment for him outside this place."

"That shines, Garth. What sort of party should we figger to throw?" Norm Oppler responded.

Thompson pursed his lips, then spread them in a nasty grin. "One that will leave him definitely hurting."

Hicky Drago, the third hardcase, flashed a toothy smile. "Now that sounds like fun. Do we leave him alive and hurtin'?"

Garth showed his own teeth. "That's entirely up to you."

Both downed their drinks and came to their boots. They

left the busy saloon without attracting any attention. Over at the bar, Pablo gestured to an old woman in a plain polka-dot dress, her head swathed in a black rebozo. *"Una copa de caldo de camarón, por favor."*

Bearing a large, blue granite kettle, the seam-faced woman attendant came over and ladled out a cup of shrimp soup for the young *caballero.* Pablo took it and nodded his appreciation. *"Gracias."* Then he turned to the ranch hands.

"We will have to start back to the ranch after we've eaten. There seems not to be enough hours in the day."

"Especially to get the work done and for you to see Juanita, eh, *patrón?"* one of the cowboys remarked with a smile.

Pablo's eyes twinkled as he thought of his current favorite. "Juanita is . . . worth making time for. We are going to be married. She doesn't know that yet, but I do."

"¡Que romantico!"

Pablo chided him in jest. "Do not mock true love, Arturo. Some day it will overwhelm you."

"What, me? With a fat wife and three little ones?"

Garth Thompson watched them darkly as they laughed over that sally. He had been given his orders by Whitewater Paddy Quinn as to what to do about the family of the stubborn old fool, Diego Alvarado. The rancher refused to sell out, and his Mexican cowboys had already killed three and wounded eight of those sent to harass him. It was time to turn up the heat, Paddy had said. *So be it,* Garth mused. He watched while Pablo and the vaqueros downed a prodigious quantity of food and two glasses each of beer. Then they hitched up their belts and walked toward the door. Silver conchas along the outer seams of their pant legs sparkled even in the low light.

When they stepped outside, Garth strained to hear over the low rumble of conversation and laughter the challenge he expected. It came a moment later in an angry growl from Norm Oppler.

"Hey, watch where you're goin', greaser."

Smoke Jensen walked Cougar and Hardy down the broad eastern avenue that led to the Plaza de Armas in the center of Taos. Palo verde trees had been planted in circular basins all along the residential section. Their pale, wispy, smoky green leaves fluttered in a light breeze, like the fine hair of a young woman. Most houses sat well back from the Spanish tile sidewalks, presenting high, blank walls to the passersby. Some had built-in niches where flowers had been planted or religious figures installed. Red tile roofs peeked over the blue and green shards of broken bottles plastered into the tops of these ramparts. The last block before the central square had been overtaken by shops, restaurants, and cantinas. Smoke had reached the midpoint when a harsh voice called out insultingly.

"Hey, watch where you're goin', greaser."

A handsome, light-complexioned young man of Spanish/Mexican descent took a step back and spoke soft words of apology. Then the import of the insult sank in. His eyes narrowed, and his full lips twisted in offense. "What did you call me?"

"I called you a bean-slurpin', chile-chompin' greaser."

Smoke Jensen reined in to watch the exchange. The youth had a familiar appearance, though Smoke could not place a name with the face. Both men were armed, though the well-dressed Spanish youth chose to use his hands. With a suddenness that spoke well of his ability, he swung a balled fist that smashed into the jaw of the loudmouthed saddle trash with enough force to knock him off his boots.

He hit the tile walk with a flat smack. At once the youth stepped over him. "I'll accept your apology for that insult and there will be no harm done."

"Like hell you will!" shouted the thug as he whipped out his six-gun and fired point-blank into the young man's belly.

At once the other Anglo cleared leather. His bullet cut a searing path across the small of Pablo's back. Smoke Jensen had time only for a hasty shout before his own hand filled with a .45 Colt. "Don't!"

Three dark-complexioned vaqueros with the youth only then reacted, spreading apart with shock and surprise on their faces. One drew a knife. The Colt in the hand of the seated hardcase roared again. He missed his attempt to shoot the knife wielder through the chest. His slug bit flesh out of the vaquero's side.

"Drop the guns, both of you," Smoke demanded.

When the Anglo opponents refused to comply, Smoke tripped the trigger of his Peacemaker and shot the seated one through the shoulder, breaking his scapula. The smoking revolver in his hand flew from his grasp. His companion spun on one boot heel to face Smoke Jensen. He raised his six-gun to shoulder height and took aim as Smoke cocked and fired his .45 a second time. His bullet took the gunman in the center of his chest. Behind Smoke, Hardy whinnied in irritation. Shouts came from inside the saloon. The man Smoke had shot looked down at his chest with a dumb expression of disbelief as he staggered forward. Slowly he released his grip on his weapon. The revolver thudded in the dirt of the street a moment before the body of the dead assailant.

By then, the wounded one seated on the tile walk had recovered his Colt and threw a shot at Smoke that cracked past the head of the last mountain man to bury itself deep in an adobe wall across the street. Without a flinch, Smoke returned fire. Hot lead punched a neat hole in the upper lip of the shooter, exposing crooked, yellowed teeth. He went over backward and twitched violently for a few seconds.

During that time, the three vaqueros recovered their

composure and rushed to the side of their fallen companion. "Pablo, Pablo, can you hear me?" one spoke urgently.

Pablo? Keeping his Colt handy, Smoke Jensen dismounted and crossed to where two of the Mexican cowboys kneeled beside their employer's son. *"¿Con permiso?"* Smoke addressed them in his rusty Spanish. "Is this Pablo Alvarado?"

Dark, angry faces turned toward him. "Why do you ask, *gringo?"*

Smoke answered simply. "I am a friend of his father."

The surly one produced a sneer. *"Ay, sí.* And I am the pope in Rome. What is your name, *gringo?"*

"I am called Smoke Jensen."

Surprise registered on the three faces. Embarrassment warred with it. At last, the angry vaquero spoke in an amiable tone. *"Tengo mucho vergüenza,* Señor Jensen. I should have known. No one else could have handled two gunmen so fast and so effectively. It is only that Don Pablo has been shot, and Ricardo, *tambien.* And it is forbidden us to carry our *pistólas* into town. We could do nothing."

"And naturally that bothered you. That I can understand. One of you had better go for a doctor." Smoke examined the wounded men. "Ricardo has only a scratch. Pablo is still breathing and he has a strong heartbeat," Smoke observed as he examined the young man. "But he still needs help right away, *inmediatamente, comprende?"*

The embarrassed one spoke up. "I am called Miguel Armillita. I will go."

"Good, Miguel. Another of you should ride to the ranch and tell Don Diego."

"Uh—there is a wagon with supplies," a young vaquero blurted.

Smoke spoke decisively. "Ricardo can drive that, after he is patched up. The other take a fast horse and head for Rancho de la Gloria."

The town marshal and the sheriff of Taos County arrived at the same time. Pablo Alvarado remained unconscious, and two of the vaqueros had sped off on their assigned tasks. An angry and shaken Garth Thompson, who had only now come out of the saloon, leaned against the outside adobe wall of Bajo el Cielo de Mexico scowling at Smoke Jensen. When the lawmen pushed through a crowd of the cantina's patrons, he spoke up in angry accusation.

"This stranger came along and shot two of my men for no reason at all. Shot the Mexican kid as well."

"I'll take that iron," the marshal demanded as he and the sheriff drew their weapons. "You've got some tall explaining to do, mister. Since this involves folks from outside town, I'll let you handle it, Hank. I'd better see to a doctor for young Alvarado."

Smoke looked up at them. "I've already sent for a doctor."

Hank Banner, the sheriff, spoke up then. "I'll take that gun, feller, seein' as how you've not handed it over."

Smoke complied, giving the sheriff both of his Colts, but insisted on waiting until a physician arrived. Miguel Armillita came with him and stood back, silent and respectful in the presence of such awesome authority as the marshal and sheriff. After the doctor had arranged to move Pablo to his office and bandaged Ricardo, and Hank Banner had taken Smoke Jensen off to jail, Miguel went to his horse and rode hastily off toward Rancho de la Gloria to inform Don Diego of this turn of events.

"Sit down and tell me something about yourself," Sheriff Banner invited as he gestured to a chair beside his desk. "Do you regularly go around shooting men without the least provocation?"

Smoke Jensen declined the chair for the moment. Being

uncertain as to which side the lawman happened to be on, he did not use his real name nor did he show his U.S. marshal's badge, nor did he use the cover name he had given to Ian MacGreggor.

"Let's get one thing straight first, Sheriff. I did not shoot Pablo Alvarado. My name is Frank Hickman, and I do go around shooting people who shoot friends of mine."

Banner looked skeptical. "You are a friend of the Alvarados?"

"I am."

Now the sheriff leaned forward, his expression turned hard. "Why is it I don't believe you?"

Smoke gave him a cool, indifferent look. "I could give you a couple of reasons."

Banner did not give in. "Try me."

A frown momentarily creased Smoke's forehead. "You could be one of those folks who dislikes people of Spanish or Mexican origin and is unwilling to believe any white man could be friends with them. Or, you could be one of those lawmen who has taken some consideration from a powerful man."

Banner clenched his fists and made to swing on Smoke. Smoke raised a staying hand. "Sit down, Sheriff I apologize for baiting you that way. What is it you want to know?"

"Everything that happened out there. Start from the first."

"I was riding into town when those two provoked a quarrel with Pablo Alvarado. At that time, I didn't recognize Pablo. It has been quite a while since I last saw him."

Banner still had not lost his suspicion. "People don't often change that much."

"They do if they were ten the last time someone saw them."

"Ah—yes, yes, that makes sense. Go on."

Smoke Jensen related the events surrounding the shooting of Pablo Alvarado. Then he described what he did. When he concluded, the two men sat a long while in silence. At last the sheriff spoke up.

"So you intervened in defense of Pablo Alvarado? He was armed, I saw that."

"The one who shot him first didn't even call him out, he just drew and fired away. The other one tried to back-shoot Pablo."

"Yes, you said that. I think I understand. What I don't follow is why you stepped in at all."

Smoke sighed out his irritation. "Because I have a big problem with sneaks and back-shooters. Both of them drew on the boy. Pablo's men were unarmed. I could do something about it, so I did."

"Sheriff?" a squeaky voice called from the open doorway.

Smoke looked over to see a boy of ten or eleven standing there, his head crowned with a thick thatch of sandy brown hair. His gray-green eyes sparkled with intelligence above speckled cheeks and a wide, generous mouth. Oblivious of Smoke's scrutiny, the lad concentrated on the lawman.

"What is it, Wally?"

"Doc Walters says Pablo Alvarado is con—con—awake now. He's ready to make a statement. But you have to come over to Doc's office."

"Thank you, Wally." Banner flipped a nickel to the boy and cut his eyes to Smoke. "I think you should come along. If Pablo can identify you, I'll be satisfied with your account of what happened."

Well, the Frank Hickman name was out of the barn with this, Smoke thought with irritation. He smiled evenly at Banner. "Whatever you say, Sheriff."

Dr. Adam Walters had his office and infirmary on the entire second floor above a men's haberdashery and a women's clothier. Smoke Jensen followed Sheriff Hank Banner up the steep flight of stairs and through a white-painted door. The odor of ether and carbolic acid hung heavily in the still air of the interior. Dr. Walters greeted the men with surgical tools in hand, which he scrubbed at energetically.

"Pablo got lucky this time, Hank. It was a clean, through-and-through shot to the side. Missed his intestines and liver. He got just a scratch across his back. I cleaned the wounds, closed and sutured them. I'd say he's a sure bet to recover. He's awake now and asking for you. Oh, who is this?" The last accompanied a nod toward Smoke Jensen.

"Says he's a friend of the Alvarados."

"He can come in, then."

They found Pablo Alvarado propped up on pillows, the sheet and quilt folded down to his waist. His bare middle was swathed in bandages. He looked up as they entered and broke out a big smile. "Smoke! You came like Papa said you would. Sheriff, it's good to see you."

Smoke Jensen cut his eyes to the lawman and saw genuine affection for Pablo shining in his. Banner gave him a puzzled expression. "Smoke?"

"I'm afraid I wasn't entirely truthful with you, Sheriff. My name is Smoke Jensen."

"The hell. *The* Smoke Jensen?"

"The only one I know. I needed to find out whose side you are on before letting out too much."

Banner nodded. "Everything I've heard about you argues to that. It's a pleasure to meet you. Now, excuse me. What do you have for me, Pablo?"

"I know those *ladrónes* who shot me, Sheriff. They run with the gang led by Paddy Quinn. They didn't give me a chance. They just drew and fired on me."

"How did Smoke Jensen get involved?"

Pablo frowned. "I'm not sure. I was down by then. What's certain is he saved my life. Smoke is an old friend of my father."

Banner remained skeptical. "That may well be, but not every card is on the table as yet. I'll keep Smoke around until everything is straightened out."

"In jail?" Pablo demanded.

With a shrug, Banner replied. "Where else?"

EIGHT

Late in the afternoon, Don Diego Alvarado, accompanied by Miguel Armillita, arrived at the jail. He stormed in and confronted Hank Banner at his desk. The pencil line of black mustache on Diego's upper lip writhed with his agitation.

"What is this that you have my good friend, Smoke Jensen, in jail? I insist that you release him at once."

Banner remained obstinate. "Now, why should I do that? Two men have been killed. Your son has been shot."

"First, because Smoke is a valued friend. I will vouch for him. And because I sent for him to look into the matters we have discussed. Clifton Satterlee owns the judges, half of the legislature, and nearly as many lawmen. If not for you and Marshal Gates, there would be no one opposing him."

Hank Banner came to his boots. "Then he's as free as a bird, *amigo*." Taking his keys, the sheriff went to release Smoke Jensen.

Diego greeted Smoke with an energetic *abrazo*, then turned to Banner. "His *pistólas*? I am sure he will have need of them."

His weapons restored, and with the assurances of Diego Alvarado as to the honesty of Hank Banner, Smoke Jensen at last showed his badge and covered the reason for being in Taos. "I have to ask you to keep this an absolute secret between us, Sheriff."

"You have my word on it. And I wish you luck. Whatever happens, let me advise that you had better not operate outside the law."

"Sheriff, in my world, I've found it wise to always shoot the bear before the critter could wrap arms around me."

Banner eyed him narrowly. "What does that mean?"

Smoke cheerfully mixed his metaphors in his reply. "When a feller is dealing with a rattler, he doesn't pay much attention to any rules that protect the snake."

"I . . . see."

"I hope you do, Sheriff. Now, Don Diego and I have a lot of catching up to do."

Diego went first to see his son. Then he directed Smoke around the town to proudly show off the improvements that had taken place in the absence of the last mountain man. He waved an arm expansively at an adobe building with a second story of clapboard siding. A large bell stood in the bare yard outside.

"We have a new school now. A *secondary* school, *amigo*. In my modest way I contributed to its construction and established an account in the bank, to which others contribute, to provide pay for the teachers." Diego frowned slightly. "There are only four qualified ones now. The other three are volunteers from among the merchants. Alejandro teaches Spanish when he can get away from the rancho. It is all very exciting, no?"

"Of course it is. How are Alejandro and all your other children?"

"Healthy, thanks be to God. To my way of thinking, living in town robs a man of vigor and his years. My next to youngest, Lupe, who is eight, still breaks the thin spring ice from the *riachuelo* to swim, like her brothers before her. *Gracias a Dios,* she will live a long life. I, myself, have fifty-two years."

"I don't believe it, Don Diego," Smoke spoke truthfully.

Diego Alvarado looked far from fifty-two, more like a young forty. His full mane of longish, black hair showed only thin streaks of gray at the temples, and his face remained unlined, save for the effects of sun, wind, and cold. Trim and fit, he could not weigh more than a hundred fifty pounds, Smoke estimated. He wore his *traje corto* on a five-foot-nine frame with an elegance that made others appear common and shabby.

He was dressed all in brown today, and his cordovan sombrero sat his head at a rakish angle. The bolero jacket, adorned with small, silver conchas, rode the midline of a scarlet sash around his waist, above flared-cuff trousers, with wide gussets of satin in matching color to his girdle. A snowy shirt, with lace-trimmed pleats, appeared above his vest. His string tie stood out in starched erectness, rather than the usual limp droop. Altogether he represented a fine rendering of the man Smoke had known ten years earlier.

"I saw all the new houses to the east," Smoke remarked.

Diego looked unhappy. "Yes. So many children being born and so few jobs on the ranches. They come to town to work in the fine homes of the rich *gringos* and Mexicans, and to make more babies."

Smoke shrugged. "Nature has a way of doing such things. What else is new since my last visit?"

"Come, I will show you. We have a *teatro,* an opera house. Opened last year. At last I can hear my beloved music. Handel, Mozart, Bach. And, of course, the classic Spanish composers. We will stop by the theater first. Then we shall stop at La Comida Buena for something to eat before heading to the ranch."

* * *

Seated at a rickety table in the Bloody Hills road ranch outside Taos, Whitewater Paddy Quinn listened in stony silence to the report of his lieutenant, Garth Thompson. Two men killed. Gunned down, according to Garth, by a saddle tramp who looked to be about forty or so. Impossible. He said as much to Garth.

"No. Norm Oppler and Hicky Drago weren't exactly the fastest and best," Garth advised. "I didn't see the shooting myself. I came out of the saloon after it was over. Like to have knocked me out of my boots. He must have called them out with a gun already in his hand. Don't see any other way."

Quinn's eyes narrowed in curious speculation. "Now I'm wonderin', what was it they were doin' to get themselves killed?"

Garth Thompson studied the toes of his boots, uncomfortable with that question. "Young Pablo Alvarado came into the cantina and joined with some of his vaqueros. That Miguel Armillita was amongst them. You know the one?"

Paddy Quinn nodded. "Him that gives those disgusting bullfight demonstrations, is it?" At Garth's nod, he went on. "Bloody damn barbarian, says I. Sure an' cows is for givin' milk and eatin', not for bloody sport."

"You've got to kill a cow to eat it, don't you?" Garth brazened out.

Quinn sighed and cut his eyes to the ceiling. "An' that's a fact, Garth me boy.

"When this Armillita kills a bull, he gives the meat to the sisters at the mission to distribute to the poor. So it's not a waste."

Quinn cocked an eyebrow, and anger lines formed around his mouth. "Yer talkin' like you approve of that deviltry, is it now?"

Thompson hastened to regain the respect of his superior. "No-no, it's only the man's courage that I admire. It takes a lot to stand out on the sand, with nothing but a cloth in yer hands, in front of a half a ton of raging animal that has two-foot-long horns."

A twinkle in the eyes of Paddy Quinn betrayed his true opinion, contrary to that which he spoke. "Cowards, the lot of them greasers."

Secure in his position once more, Garth Thompson hazarded a barb. "Would you do it?"

Quinn did not hesitate. "Hell no! D'ye think me a bloody fool?" Of a sudden, his mood grew serious again. "Still, I want to know what those two were up to."

Garth swallowed. "You said to put pressure on Alvarado. So I sent Oppler and Drago to pick a fight with Pablo. They did, and they shot him, but he didn't die."

"Something has to be done about the shooting of our boys. This stranger has to be taught a lesson, made an example of, don't ye see?"

"I'll send Luke and Grasser to keep an eye on him. I heard before I left town that the sheriff let him out of jail. Seems he's a friend of the Alvarados."

Fire and ice warred in the black eyes of Paddy Quinn. "Sure an' I'd not lose any sleep if something happened to old man Alvarado. Maybe you oughta get together enough of our lads to have a go at the both of them."

Garth Thompson gave a steady look at his boss. Paddy Quinn had a deceptively cherubic Irish face. He was always smiling, even when he killed a man. He was big for a victim of the potato famine, standing 5'10", with about 158 pounds behind his belt. His ears and nose were small, his mouth wide only when he smiled. A shock of glistening black hair hung over a high forehead. Without his brace of .45 Colt Peacemakers and the .38 Smith & Wesson he carried for a hideout, he could easily pass for a shopkeeper. Garth knew better, though.

When on the prod, the fit, trim, hard-muscled Quinn virtually exploded into violent mania, calmed only by a frenzy of bloodletting. Odd, Garth speculated, that Quinn of all people would object to the violence and spectacle of bullfighting. But, then, the man who had hired the gang had a fondness for pussycats. No telling, Garth thought in dismissal of his reflections.

"Where do we wait for them?"

"Here to begin with. Then it depends on what Luke and Grasser report. Get on it, then, bucko."

Smoke Jensen recognized the type the moment Luke Horner and Charlie Grasser tied off their horses at the tie rail outside the saloon across the street from La Comida Buena. As always, Diego Alvarado had shown impeccable taste in his choice of a place to eat. Contrary to usual Mexican custom, the thinly sliced steak turned out to be remarkably tender. It had been marinated and then quickly grilled over charcoal. The *carne asada* had come to their table on platters that held beans and rice, along with a bowl of freshly made *pico de gallo*. The salsa of tomato, onion, garlic, chile peppers, and chopped cilantro was hot enough to blister the mouth of anyone of lesser fortitude than possessed by Smoke Jensen. He heaped it on everything and chewed with obvious enjoyment. Formal dinner, Smoke knew from experience, would come at around nine-thirty that night at the ranch. It would be preceded by a steady flow of tequila and beer, and served with fine wines from Pedro Domecq, a winery located in the high central valley in the Mexican state of Aguas Calientes. His pleasure diminished when the two hardcases arrived. He nodded to the street, and Diego paused in his mastication to look over his shoulder.

"See that pair? That's more trouble on the hoof, or I miss my guess."

"De veras. That's true, my friend. Though they are obviously—how you say?—small fry."

Smoke produced a wry expression. "Where the fingerlings swim, the bigger fishes are close behind."

Worry clouded the face of Diego Alvarado. "Do you think they came to finish with Pablo?"

With a negative shake of his head, Smoke gave his surmise. "No. I think whoever sent the first two has someone else in mind."

"Meaning you?" Diego prompted.

"Yes. And perhaps you. Well, old friend, let's finish up. We don't want to disappoint them."

Smoke Jensen would have liked to follow, and perhaps question, the two hardcases. Proddy, and eager to impress his boss, Luke Horner didn't give them the chance. He leaned against an upright four-by-four post that supported the canopy over the saloon front across from the restaurant where Smoke and Diego had eaten an early supper. Luke swiveled his head constantly, alert for a sight of the familiar figure of Diego Alvarado. When the subject of their surveillance appeared suddenly outside the restaurant, Luke turned his head away and alerted his companion.

"Grasser, there they are. Right across from us. I say we can take them right now. You game?"

Charlie Grasser came upright in the chair made from a small barrel and peered across at the two men. "I'm not so sure, Luke. Didn't Garth say that feller was faster than greased lightning?"

Luke remained unimpressed. "So what? He caught the boys unaware. There's two of us, an' he can't be all that fast.

That old greaser won't be able to shoot very well. I think we oughta do it."

So saying, he pushed away from the post and stepped out into the street. Not nearly so eager, Charlie Grasser separated from his companion and did the same. Luke jabbed an extended left forefinger toward Smoke Jensen, his right hand already on the butt of his six-gun. "Hey, Mister, you killed two friends of mine. I don't take kindly to that. I'm here to make you pay for it."

With that, Luke Horner pulled his Colt.

Smoke Jensen bested him anyway. The .45 Peacemaker appeared in his hand as if by magic, the hammer fully cocked. As the muzzle leveled on the center of Luke's body, Smoke triggered a round. The bullet struck Luke at the tip of his breastbone. He jolted backward and bent double. The barrel of his Colt had not yet cleared the holster. To the surprise of Charlie Grasser, Diego Alvarado had drawn with nearly equal speed.

Don Diego's Obrigon cracked sharply, and the slug chewed a nasty trough across Grasser's left shoulder, after breaking the collarbone. Charlie howled at the pain. To his right, Luke struggled feebly to free his six-gun and get off a shot. Alvarado's .45 spat another chunk of hot lead, which missed Grasser only because he had spun to his left to distance himself from the fight. Diego cocked the Mexican-made weapon again as Grasser made his first long stride toward the welcome void of an alley.

Dying on his feet, Luke Horner managed to draw at last and distracted Diego Alvarado momentarily when he sent a bullet speeding toward the fastidious rancher. It missed, and the air filled with the hiss and crack of hot lead. Smoke Jensen fired a safety shot into the top of Luke Horner's head, which blasted the second-rate gunfighter off this earth for all eternity. By then, Charlie Grasser had found the safety of the alley and sped off to inform Garth Thompson.

A scant minute later, Sheriff Banner arrived and took in the body of Luke Horner. "Shootin' snakes again, Jensen?"

Smoke tipped back his Stetson. "You might say that. One got away."

Diego Alvarado stepped forward, replacing his three expended cartridge casings. "I wounded him. Too bad he could run faster than I could shoot."

"Do either of you think you could identify him?"

Both men nodded, and Diego spoke. "Oh, yes. He'll have his left arm in a sling. I am positive I got him in the collarbone."

Hank Banner listened to their account of how the shoot-out had begun and left them with another admonition. "Remember, you make good and sure that they force the action every time. I'd not like to lock up a friend . . . friends," he amended.

On the road to Rancho de la Gloria, Smoke Jensen and Diego Alvarado discussed the possibility that there would be another personal attack upon them. Diego weighed all Smoke said about these sort of gunhawks and offered a prophesy.

"You are probably right. But, Satterlee has so far kept it rather quiet. He does not seem ready to force the issue. I think it will be some time before any more of his *ladrónes* come after you or I."

Five minutes farther down the trail proved how wrong he had been.

A fine Andalusian, the horse ridden by Don Diego Alvarado shied a fraction of a second before a plume of white powder smoke spurted upward in a thicket of mesquite that had been cut and stacked for burning. In the next fraction of a second, a bullet cracked past so close to the rancher that it clipped the sombrero from his head. Half a dozen more rounds came from the ambush site.

To Diego's right, Smoke had already fisted his .45 Colt and returned fire. He drubbed Cougar's flanks with his round knob spurs and started away from the hidden gunmen, only to find the way blocked by more of their kind. In a swirl of dust, Smoke Jensen released his packhorse, Hardy, and charged the obstruction.

NINE

Men cursed and fired blindly at where Smoke Jensen had been only moments before. They next saw him as he burst through the fog of dust and powder smoke and blazed away at point-blank range. Two men left their saddles in rapid succession. A third yelped a second later and clutched at his suddenly useless right arm. The rifle he had been holding dropped from his grasp, the small of its stock shattered by the bullet that had smashed his shoulder socket.

Smoke did not stop there. He whirled and disappeared into the miasma, to pop out on the flank of the mesquite barricade, flanking the ambush. One hardcase sensed the presence of Smoke Jensen and whirled to fire his weapon. That way, he took the bullet from Smoke's Colt full in the face. He went over backward with a soft grunt. Beyond the dying man, Smoke saw Diego at the opposite end of the hiding place. Alvarado placed his shots carefully, wounding three men. As soon as they could recover enough from their difficulties, they hastily abandoned the fight. With their desertion, the ambush began to quickly dissolve.

But not before Garth Thompson snapped off a round that nicked Diego Alvarado in the fleshy part of his left upper arm. Diego squinted with the pain that shot through him and coolly pumped a round into another of the outlaws. Garth's hammer dropped on an expended cartridge, and he rose in his stirrups.

"Break off! Pull back, boys. Scatter," he bellowed.

Garth's head spun in confusion over the ferocity and speed of the reaction of their targets. It had not been a fluke, or a sucker call, that had downed Oppler and Drago. Whoever this master gun happened to be, he was fast and mean as a hellhound. The man beside Garth fired again at Diego Alvarado and put spurs to his mount. Garth quickly joined him.

At once, Smoke and Diego joined up and went in pursuit of two of the hardcases who had chosen the roadway as the easiest route of escape. Diego hailed Smoke with a big smile on his face. "We have them trapped between us and the ranch. They will not get far, *amigo.*"

"Might be, but will anyone be expecting them?"

"We are close enough that the shots will have been heard. Someone will be watching. It is too bad the others got away."

Smoke thought on that. "Not for long if we get to question these two."

They picked up the pace then. Within ten minutes they rode through the low scud of red dust stirred up by the hooves of the horses ridden by the fleeing men. Moments later, the sound of gunfire came from ahead, and the pursuers urged their mounts into a gallop. At that ground-eating pace, Smoke and Diego soon saw the backs of the two outlaws. One was on the ground, drawn up in a fetal position. The other, his horse shot out from under him, used the fallen animal as a breastwork.

Although wounded, he fired over the saddle at unseen adversaries as Smoke Jensen closed the gap between himself and the member of the Quinn gang. When Smoke and Diego came into clear view, whoever kept the outlaw pinned down ceased fire. In the silence that followed, the hardcase heard the hoofbeats behind him and turned to see Smoke and Diego less than twenty feet away. All resistance left him, and he laid down his revolver and raised his hands.

"I'm givin' up. Don't shoot me."

"Seems as how you tried like hell to do just that to us," Smoke growled.

His feeble protest would echo down the halls of the future. "I was jist followin' orders. Nothin' personal, you understand?"

Smoke snorted in contempt. "When someone throws lead at me, I take it right personal, y'hear?" Smoke dismounted as Alejandro Alvarado showed himself, along with three of the vaqueros.

Beaming, Alejandro extended a hand. "It is good to see you again. Poppa said you would come."

"He made it sound irresistible. Let's take a look at the fish you caught."

Roughly they searched the outlaw, supervised by Smoke Jensen. Two knives, a stubby-barreled Hopkins & Allen .38 Bulldog revolver, and a .41 rimfire derringer appeared from the voluminous clothing of the miscreant. For reasons known only to himself, Smoke found that amusing.

"Looks like whatever you lack in skill, you make up for in sneaky armament."

"Who are you, mister? You tore through our ambush like a bull through a corral of steers."

"Folks call me Smoke. Smoke Jensen."

"Awh . . . dog pucky. That ain't fair. It jist ain't fair. How was we to know you were around here anywhere?"

"Chalk it up to bad luck. Now, my good friend here, Don Diego, and I would like to know who you work for?"

Defiance flared in his eyes. "You'll never hear it from me."

Smiling, Smoke Jensen taunted the injured man. "I'll hear it when I want to. Although I don't think I really need to. Don Diego has told me all about your boss, Whitewater Paddy Quinn."

Ever so slightly, the gunman's eyes narrowed and tension

lines sprang up that did not come from the bullet wound in his thigh. He pressed his lips tightly together. Smoke shattered the man's newfound resolve with one terse, ominous sentence.

"If he won't confirm that, Alejandro, kill him."

That broke the last of his bravado. "Yes—yes, you're right, goddamn you, Jensen. And when Paddy Quinn finds out what you done to us, he'll be down on you like stink on a skunk."

Drily, Smoke answered him. "I can hardly wait."

"*Amigo,* we still have a league to ride to the *estancia,*" Diego reminded Smoke.

"Then, we'd best be going. I trust you can deal with this mess, Alejandro?"

"*Sí.* Any day, Smoke."

They left Alejandro to clean up after the ambushers and to send vaqueros to town to deliver the dead and living one to the sheriff.

Smoke Jensen was met by the entire Alvarado flock. The youngest, a totally naked toddler of two, crawled up on Smoke's knee and patted him on the cheek. Horrified by the overly familiar conduct of her infant son, Señora Alvarado, Lidia, rushed forward to pluck the squealing boy from his perch and apologized effusively to Smoke for the social gaffe. Smoke laughed about it and patted the youngster on the top of his head.

"But, you are a *caballero,*" Lidia protested. "You should not be bothered by the prattling of children."

Smoke smiled to show his sincerity. "He's no burden, Doña Lidia. I remember my own at that age."

Lidia Alvarado gave him a surprised look. "But they are all grown, yes?"

"All but one my Sally and I adopted not long ago. He has thirteen years."

"A burdensome age. I will leave you gentlemen to your tequila and old campaigns." With that, Lidia exited, her giggling youngster on her hip.

Diego took up the subject of most interest to both men. "Let me tell you what I believe is behind Clifton Satterlee's determination to secure all of the land for twenty miles around Taos. It is greed, plain and simple. Somehow he has found a way to make a profit out of land that sells for twenty-five cents an acre, due to its poor quality of soil. In its natural state, nothing much grows here, except for cactus and mesquite. Perhaps he has learned, as I have, of the value of irrigation. I do not believe that is the case. He means to plunder the land and leave it desolate.

"There is gold in the mountains. Not much, but enough to attract a greedy man. There is also the cattle that I and others raise. The price of beef is going up, now that it has been made more tender and palatable to the eastern taste. Satterlee's entire assets, at least those I have been able to discover, are not worth more than one hundred thousand dollars. The sale of our cattle would increase his holdings by tenfold. There is five times that value in the timber on the Tua reservation. Although the land is protected by your government in Washington, treaties have been broken in the past and will be again, given enough money changes hands."

Smoke smiled warmly. "You don't put much trust in the United States government, *amigo.*"

"No more than I did that in that of Ciudad de Mexico. Politicians are . . . politicians. It is the nature of government to become more intrusive, more controlling of people's lives and their property. Yours, ours now, perhaps less than many others. But who knows what the future may hold? Satterlee is a law unto himself. Therefore, I believe that he is not so much empire building as empire looting."

Smoke gave that some thought. "That's a strong accusation. Why would he want to acquire the town of Taos?"

"It is the seat of power in this part of New Mexico. We are far removed, by mountains as well as distance, from the government in Santa Fe. Our governor is a good man. I regret that I cannot say the same for some of those around him. Recently there was an affair that is being called the Lincoln County War. Governor Wallace offered amnesty to those of both sides. Secretly, some of those in power put out the word that certain among the combatants were to be killed upon their surrender. It seems that their continued existence would prove an embarrassment to some of our politicians.

"But, I digress, old friend. You are here to determine exactly what it is Satterlee intends, and if it is illegal or harmful to the best interests of the people, to put an end to it." Diego paused to refill his clay cup with tequila. He prefaced his next words with a low, self-deprecating chuckle. "That sounds remarkably like a politician, does it not? Forgive me, you came here of your own accord. If I have burdened you with too great a load, it is only because of my great concern."

Smoke shrugged. "If you'd put too much on my plate, I'd be riding out now."

"It's the people I am concerned about. Many of those who live around Taos work for me, or have sons and daughters who do. And Alejandro has business interests in the town. Then there are the Indians. Did you know that they rose up one time and slaughtered all the Spanish living around here? They are capable of doing so again. Now, let us go in to dinner. Fernando has roasted us a whole small pig. It will make excellent *carnitas de puerco.*" Diego added in explanation, "One of those traditional dishes that happened by accident the first time. Someone accidentally dropped chunks of pork into boiling oil. By the time they were fished out, the meat was crispy on the outside, juicy and tender inside. I'm sure you will enjoy it."

Smiling, Smoke emptied his cup of the maguey cactus liquor. "Anything Fernando cooks is an equal to my Sally's best efforts. I'm sure I'll like it."

Later, after the sumptuous meal, Smoke retired to a guest room for the night. As he lay on the comfortable bed, his thoughts strayed to the High Lonesome and to Sally. He fell asleep with visions of her in his mind.

Around noon the next day, Sheriff Monte Carson rode up to the main house on the Sugarloaf. He brought with him two dispirited, hang-dog youngsters atop a mule he led by a long rope. Seth and Sammy Gittings, although looking contrite, to Sally Jensen's expert eye managed to reveal their confidence that they would escape punishment. Monte reined in and greeted the two women who were picking spring flowers to brighten the interior of the house.

"Mornin', Miz Sally. Mornin', ma'am. These two belong to someone out here? Least they say they do."

Mary-Beth looked up with apprehension and surprise. "Why, they are my sons. Where did you find them?"

"In town, ma'am."

A fleeting frown spread on Mary-Beth's forehead. "Seth, Sammy, didn't I tell you not to leave this place? It is wild and dangerous out there."

"There's more to it than that, ma'am."

"Why, what do you mean—ah—Sheriff?"

"I caught them in the general store, stealin' horehound drops from a jar."

Predictably, Mary-Beth sprang to the defense of her sons. "That's not possible. My sons never steal."

Monte nodded to the boys. "Unlike these two, I never lie, ma'am."

"They don't lie, either."

"Oh? Then they are the sons of Johnny Ringo, and he and his gang will come get me if I don't let them go?" Monte maintained a straight face as he related the wild tale the boys had spun.

Shocked, her shoulders slumped with defeat, Mary-Beth Gittings resorted to a woman's best defense—tears. She dropped her bouquet and covered her eyes with both hands. Her body shook with sobs.

"Whatever am I to do? My hus-husband is nearly always away on business. And when he is home, he spoils the children abominably. I feel so helpless. Someone tell me how to deal with these things?"

Unconvinced by her performance, Monte snorted in disgust. Sally, equally dubious, smiled sweetly. "It's simple," she spelled out for her guest. "First, you talk to them and explain that what they did was wrong. That such behavior by children or adults is not tolerated by society."

"What do I do then?"

"Excuse me. I'll be right back and tell you."

Sally went into the house and directly to one corner of her kitchen. Then she returned, one hand held behind her. "Now comes the part that has the most positive effect. You yank down their britches and smack the hell out of them," she concluded, revealing the thin willow switch she had held behind her back.

Monte Carson whooped with laughter. "Now, that sounds like jist the thing. I'll haul them down and you do that, ma'am. You do that right now."

Dohatsa tugged at his forelock and looked down at his moccasin-clad feet in the manner his people had been taught since the Spanish first came. He was not conscious of his hand extended with palm up. The small bag of coins that dropped into it felt heavy indeed. It made Dohatsa glow inwardly.

"That's me good lad, Dohatsa. Now you go back to yer mud houses and stir up some mischief for me, won't ye now?" Paddy Quinn grinned at the young Tua warrior.

With another nod, Dohatsa tucked the money behind the wide, yellow sash that he wore over his shirttail and loincloth. Then he turned and trotted off toward the distant Tua pueblo located north and a bit west of Taos. Whitewater Paddy Quinn turned his horse and walked away in the opposite direction. He had other errands to perform.

There was that fat, stupid policeman in Taos who must be paid his monthly stipend, who reminded Paddy of another lawman he'd known, the reason Paddy had decided to come to America. Dead policemen, even a white pudding of a bobby in Dublin town, raised quite a row. In Boston he had quickly learned that the fine art of bribery got one far more benefit than did muscle. Not a copper, it had seemed, that wasn't on the take. Inevitably, Paddy had encountered the exception to the rule. A lad from the old sod at that. John Preston Sullivan. Which was what had brought Patrick Michael Quinn to the West. No doubt Sullivan still searched the alleyways of Boston for him. Ten years to the day and Quinn was now the boss of the largest gang of cutthroats, highwaymen, and robbers on the frontier. Which reminded him that Garth Thompson and some of the lads had something on for later that afternoon. Sure ought to stir things up a mite.

Smoke Jensen rode at ease alongside Diego Alvarado. The hacienda had put out flankers and two men on point for protection even here on his own huge ranch. Those visible rode with their rifles across their thighs, and were in sight of others farther out. It had been so, Don Diego had explained, since the first raid by the rustlers. More likely, Smoke reckoned, it had been so since the first Alvarados came here in the fifteen hundreds. He suggested the possibility.

"It was like this the last time I visited, if I recall correctly."

"Yes, *los Indios* were raiding."

Cougar whuffled softly, and Smoke popped his next question. "And in your father's time?"

Diego chuckled, a low, throaty sound. "There was a war. We had you gringos to combat, if you recall."

"And your grandfather?"

"The revolution against the Spanish. My family fought for Mexico."

Smoke waved at the vaquero bodyguards. "So this arrangement is nothing new?"

"I thought not to make you uncomfortable. This is a cruel, wild land. Most unforgiving. Not all of the danger comes from two-legged foes. Tell me, my friend, did you come to any conclusion as to how to deal with Satterlee?"

A smile crinkled Smoke's lips. "I slept too soundly. Too much tequila, I suppose. I'm not accustomed to much strong drink. Beer is more my style."

Diego appeared intrigued by this. "For a man who does not drink much, you show a lot of *machismo, amigo.*"

Smoke avoided a response by a study of the distance. Up ahead, he saw a flock of sheep, herded by half a dozen small boys ranging from ten to twelve. It made him think of Ian MacGreggor. "Diego, I have a friend who is looking for work. He speaks Spanish and rides well. But . . . he's a farmer's son. I promised him I'd ask you if you had need of anyone like that on the ranch."

Diego considered that a moment. "Enrique Toledo is growing old. His bones ache him. Perhaps he would welcome a younger assistant. When would this young man want to start?"

"After I've taken care of this business with Satterlee."

Diego cocked an eyebrow. "He is secretly involved in this?"

Smoke pulled a droll face. "In a manner of speaking. He is looking into some things for me. I haven't seen him in a couple of days."

Drawing a deep breath, Diego made his decision. "I will suggest something to Enrique. I am sure he will welcome the idea of help."

TEN

A large mesquite bush toppled down a rocky slope to block the road, located twenty miles outside of Taos. Its sudden appearance did not rattle the driver of the Butterfield stage that ground its way along the narrow, rutted trace. He hauled in on the reins and worked the brake with his booted foot, the long wooden lever operated by an angle iron that jutted from the underside. Too late, he realized the purpose of the fallen bush.

Swarming out of defiles and crevasses, a dozen men in the colorful, loose clothing and braided headbands of the Pueblo Indians closed around the coach. They wore high-top moccasins and long, black hair. All of them carried rifles or revolvers at the ready. With eyes keen and knowledgeable, the driver sized up these Indian highwaymen and reached a quick conclusion. He shared it in a whisper with the express guard.

"Injuns don't rob coaches."

At once, the shotgun rider brought up his short-barreled L.C. Smith 10-gauge and discharged a round. The shot splattered the shoulder of one pseudo-Indian, who howled involuntarily and cursed in English.

"I tol' you so," the driver hollered as he reached for his six-gun. "Ain't one of them's an Injun."

An arrow thudded into his chest and skewered his heart. He folded sideways as the six-up team came to a halt before the prickly branches. Two revolvers cracked, and the guard dropped his shotgun. Blood spurted from his shattered shoulder. "I don't believe a thing he said," he babbled.

They killed him anyway. While two of the Quinn gang held the headstalls of the lead team, another ambled his horse over to the coach and grunted in his best imitation of an Indian. "You get out. Put up hands. Give money. Much money."

"Make fast, squaw," another demanded of a hefty dowager who whimpered and jiggled as she climbed from the stage.

Quickly the outlaws gathered the valuables from the passengers while others released the draft team. After securing the strongbox, the members of the Quinn gang rode off, scattering the stage horses ahead of them. That left the frightened, demoralized passengers to fend for themselves. One of them, a portly man in a green checkered suit, expressed the astonishment of them all.

"Well, I never. Indians actually robbing a stagecoach. We have to get to the way station and find help."

Her cheeks ashen, the dowager suggested, "Someone should go on to Taos."

"Lady, we're on foot. It's too far to Taos. We'll find someone at the relay post with a horse. Then we'll report these Indians to the law."

On a low knoll, beyond his palatial hacienda outside Santa Fe, shaded by an ancient cottonwood, Clifton Satterlee watched the convolutions of an attractive young woman. Martha Estes was his houseguest, the daughter of one of his business associates. That did not serve as a deterrent for Satterlee, whose lust guided him. His wife had decided to return east and visit her family, so he knew himself to be free to pursue and conquer the lovely Martha. To do so, he had set forth on a subtle seduction.

From her position, where she exercised her horse, Martha Estes studied Clifton Satterlee from under the brim of a rakishly cocked, feminine version of a man's top hat. The bright green, crushed-velvet head adornment with its scarlet feather contrasted nicely with the red cape and riding skirt of the same material. She had become well aware that Satterlee was engaged in a skillful seduction, and it amused her. But why all the elaborate preamble, when all he need do was ask?

He needn't have given her pearls, or the promise of a luxurious house in Taos. She would have happily fallen into bed with him on the afternoon of her arrival. Her loins ached and throbbed with desire. Clifton represented power, raw, naked strength, and the willingness to employ it. Martha had hungered for him since her eleventh year, when he and her father had become associated in some slightly shady enterprises. Now, eight years later, her craving had not diminished. If anything, it had grown to unbearable dimensions. She abandoned her musings to give Clifton a cheery wave and rode up to join him.

"You are a magnificent horsewoman, Martha."

"Thank you, Clifton. It is one of my . . . lesser accomplishments." She lowered long, silver-blond lashes over cobalt eyes in a coy invitation.

"Let's proceed on, shall we? There is a charming little place I want to show you."

"We'll picnic there?"

"Yes, my dear Martha. And while away the hotter part of the afternoon. The natives call it *siesta,* and I heartily recommend it."

Half an hour's ride brought them to the reverse slope of a larger knob. There stately, ancient palo duro trees shaded a trio of deep tanks which had formed in depressions of solid rock. Martha clapped her hands in delight. Clifton Satterlee dismounted and helped her from the cumbersome side-saddle. He held the heavy picnic basket while Martha spread a blanket. He came to kneel beside her then, and put out their repast. Martha's eyes sparkled as she took in the elaborate fare.

"Is that really a *paté de fois en brochet*?"

"Yes, it is, Martha. Goose liver at that. And we have sliced ham, roast beef, pickled tongue. Oh, so many things."

Martha Estes affected an insincere pout. "You'll make me fat and unattractive."

Clifton patted one gloved hand. "Never, my dear. Many men are strongly enamored of full-figured women. I am, myself, I have to admit. Though I will say that you wear svelteness to perfection."

A trill of pleased laughter came from Martha. "You flatter me shamelessly. Um, I am hungry. A morning's ride always stimulates my appetite."

"I brought wine," Clifton offered.

"How thoughtful. I hope you brought a corkscrew."

Clifton produced the tool with a flourish. "I thought of everything."

Martha began filling her plate while Clifton opened the bottle. Then he availed himself of the splendid viands and poured wine for both of them. Sunlight sparkled off the clear water of the tanks. Overhead, cactus wrens twittered in domestic harmony while they sought grubs to feed their young. After some thoughtful chewing, Martha brought up the subject of the house in Taos.

"When do I get to see my house in Taos?"

"Soon. Within three days, I should think."

"Wasn't it once owned by a Mexican family?"

"Yes, it was. A family named Figueroa. They named a price I could hardly refuse."

* * *

Affecting a jaunty swagger he did not recognize as his own, Ian MacGreggor pushed through the glass-beaded curtain that formed the entryway of Cantina Jalisco, in Taos. Half a dozen hard-faced men had gathered at one end of the bar. They drank beer from glazed clay pots. Even to Mac's untutored eyes, they all appeared to pay deference to a burly, barrel-chested man at the center of the group. Mac walked up near them and ordered a beer. The bartender took in the six-gun at Mac's hip and served him without question. Mac lifted the foam-capped container in salute to the Irish-looking, beefy man and pulled off a long swallow.

It nearly choked him, but he did not let on since he felt all eyes turned to him. After another swallow, he walked closer to the hardcases and addressed the man in the bowler. "Might you be a gentleman known as Paddy Quinn?"

Eyes narrowed, Whitewater Paddy Quinn fired a question of his own. "Who might it be that is askin', is it now?"

"I'm known as Mac. Ian MacGreggor."

Quinn smiled. "A fellow Celt, as I live and breathe. It is said that the clan MacGreggor defended Queen Mary and the faith. Would ye be of those MacGreggors?"

Mac tilted his beer pot to Quinn. "Aye."

"And for what is it ye'd be wantin' Paddy Quinn?"

"I hear you are hiring gunhands for a man named Satterlee."

Paddy held up a cautionary hand. "Sure an' we don't be mentionin' certain names in so public a place. Say, rather, that I be hirin' for mesel', ye should."

"Well, then, for yourself?"

"What if I be? You don't look dry behind the ears."

Mac eyed Quinn levelly. "You have heard of Billy Bonney?"

That gave Quinn a good laugh. "Sure an' it's a lot of horse dung if yer tryin' to pass yerself off as Billy the Kid."

"No, I'm not. But, Billy was not yet dry behind his ears when he killed his sixth man. I'm not in his class, but I'm good with a gun."

"Are you now? Suppose we go out behind this place and you show me."

"I'm not calling you out, Mr. Quinn. All I say is that I am fast and I hit what I shoot at."

Quinn stepped forward, away from the bar, and patted Mac on one shoulder. "Nah—nah, don't fash yerself, lad. I was thinkin' of whiskey bottles, or better still beer bottles. They make smaller targets. One o' me boys could throw them up, say two at a time, and you draw and break them both before one hits the ground."

When there had been money enough for powder and lead to make reloads, Mac had practiced at that often enough to feel confident. "I think I can do that."

"Come along, then." Quinn turned to the bartender. *"Oye,* Paco. We're gonna take some of your empties out and make little pieces of glass out of them."

Paco shrugged. "Whatever you say, Señor Quinn."

Behind the saloon, the gunmen stood to one side, except for one, who reached to a stack of wooden cartons and extracted two beer bottles. He faced quarter front to Ian Mac-Greggor. Paddy Quinn gave his instructions at Mac's side. "When I nod, Huber there will throw the bottles in the air. You draw and fire at will."

With that, Quinn stepped behind Mac, so the youth could not see him give the signal. Not hesitating for a second, Paddy nodded to Huber. Two beer bottles sailed into the air. The moment they came into Mac's line of sight, he made his move. Before the two containers reached the apex of their arc, he had his six-gun halfway out of the holster. His first shot blasted a bottle to fragments a heartbeat later. The second

clear glass cylinder seemed to hover at the peak, then turned
to a bright shower of slivers as a second bullet struck. The
gun was back in Mac's holster before Quinn could recover
from his involuntary blink.

Quinn scowled, unconvinced. "Try that again."

Mac did, with the same results.

"One more time, lad."

Both bottles broke this time before either had reached the
apex. "B'God, it's fast ye are. Only one little thing, there is. I
wonder how you would perform if the target was shootin'
back at ye?"

Mac considered that a moment, then decided to answer
with a cleaned-up version of the truth. "A friend of mine and
I were jumped on the way here to Taos. Four men. I killed one
of them, and Joe took care of the others."

Quinn cocked an eyebrow. "Who'd you say that was?"

"You wouldn't know him. Joe Evans, from over Texas
way, where I come from."

"He your age?"

Mac kept his gaze cool and level. "No, sir. He's older.
Around twenty-five."

"Would he be lookin' for the same thing you came after?"

"No, sir, Mr. Quinn. He rode on to Santa Fe."

"Well, then," Quinn boomed with a hearty clap on Mac's
shoulder. "It looks like we got us only one more good gunhand. You'll do, young MacGreggor. At first, I'll be puttin' you
with someone more experienced. At least until ye get yer feet
wet, so's to speak. You'll be paid sixty dollars a month. Ammunition bought for you. Later, there'll be a share of any
spoils we bring in. Now, then, go settle up with wherever ye've
been stayin' an' meet us ten miles out on the road to Questa."

Their rumps sore from unaccustomed hours in the saddle,
two frightened and wounded survivors of the Butterfield

Stage Line robbery trotted their borrowed mounts into Taos in late afternoon. They asked for directions to the sheriff's office and for water to drink in that order. Next the two men stopped at a public horse trough and refreshed their flagging animals, industriously working the pump to bring up fresh water for themselves. The sheriff's office came next.

"Sheriff," one blurted as they stumbled through the door. "The stage from Albuquerque got robbed outside town about twenty miles. We were on it. Owens here took a nick in the shoulder. All I got's a scratch. But the guard and driver are both dead. It was Injuns done it, sure's you're born."

Sheriff Banner had strong doubts that the Tua, or any of the Pueblo Indians, had taken to robbing stages. "You got a good look at these highwaymen?"

"That's what we just told you, Sheriff. Long black hair, headbands, floppy clothing. Swarthy skin and mean as hell. Oh, they was Injuns right enough."

Banner remained unconvinced. "What way did they ride when they left?"

"To the west."

"Toward San Vincente?"

"What's that? We don't know the area."

"It's a pueblo and mission out that way. But the San Vincente Pueblos are even more peaceful than the Tuas."

"They talked funny English and rode bareback," Owens added helpfully.

"Anyone can talk funny and ride bareback. Did they speak any Spanish or Indian tongue?"

Owens cut his eyes to his companion. "Nope. Come to think, all they did speak was English."

Banner rubbed his hands together in satisfaction. "Well, gentlemen, I think you have been had. Sounds to me like white road agents done up to look like Indians. At last, that's the way I'm going to look into it." Banner turned to the door and called out. "Wally, come in here."

Wally Gower, who had been lurking outside the door to learn any gems of news he could sell to the editor of the Taos *Clarion*, popped around the doorframe and darted to the sheriff's desk. "Yes, sir?"

"Dang you for a rascal, Wally. But this time you can be of some good use. I want you to ride out to Rancho de la Gloria. Ask for Smoke Jensen and tell him to please come in. Say I have something interesting for him to look into."

"Yes, sir. I'll do it right now."

"Good. There'll two bits in it for you."

"Gosh. That much? I never get more than a nickel."

"You will this time. There's a lot of trouble brewin' out there. Now, get along."

Wally Gower led an ideal life for a kid. He was footloose and, for the most part, unsupervised. His father had been injured in a mining accident several years ago in Colorado. While his father remained unable to work and stayed at home to care for the seven children, his mother did custom alterations and general sewing for Señora Montez, the fashionable Spanish lady who owned a large women's clothing store in Taos. When school let out for the summer, Wally gleefully abandoned studies, shoes, and often shirt, to hang around town doing odd jobs for the money it brought in for the family. A lot of his time went to swimming with friends at the many *tanques* outside the town, or in pulling slippery rainbow trout from the icy creeks fed by snowmelt in the Sangre de Cristo range. He liked it most when the sheriff had something for him to do. The lawman paid better than anyone else. Wally was glad he had a pony he could use for this present assignment.

It was a small, shaggy mustang and only partly broken to saddle. But Wally loved Spuds with all his heart. He went to the small stable house behind their adobe home and saddled

Spuds. He led the snorting half-wild animal from its stall, plucked a parsnip from last winter's garden, and fed it to Spuds. Chomping pleasurably, the pony ground the pungent root vegetable into a mash which it swallowed. Wally put one bare foot in the stirrup and swung aboard. He angled Spuds toward the alleyway behind the Gower home. Had it been anyone else atop the little horse, it would have exploded into crowhops and sunfishing that would have unseated any but the most expert horsebreakers.

Wally trotted toward the western edge of town and the trail southwest to the Alvarado ranch. He reached the scattered fringe of small, poor Mexican adobe homes when he found out that life in Taos had drastically changed for the foreseeable future.

Three hardcases leaned against a low adobe wall, with two split rails atop. When Wally approached, the lean, tallest one eased upright and stepped into the road. He raised a hand and spoke in a low, menacing voice.

"Whoa-up, sonny. Where do you think yer goin'?"

A quick thinker, Wally invented something he hoped would be believed. "Out to where my paw works."

"Where's that?"

"Uh—the Bradfords' B-Bar-X."

Eyes narrowed in accusation, the clipped words challenged Wally. "He ain't come through here since we've been here."

"Oh, no. He goes out before dawn."

"Well, there ain't nobody goin' out of town from now on without our say-so."

Wally pulled another appeal from his ingenuity. "Bu—but my paw will beat my tail if I don't bring him his coat. He's got night guard tonight."

A nasty sneer answered him. "That's your problem, kid. If you're smart, you'll do what you are told. You go on back now, get lost, and tell that sheriff friend of yours nothing."

"Yes, sir. I suppose you're right, sir."

Being a plucky lad, Wally turned on the first side street, cut his way through several blocks, and went directly to Hank Banner's office. He made his report with wide-eyed excitement. Hank listened to him with a growing frown. Then he made a suggestion that appealed to the adventurous nature of the boy.

"Well, then, why don't you ride out the other side of town?"

"Sure enough, Sheriff. Right away."

Wally dusted out the door and swung into the saddle. He drubbed bare heels into the flanks of Spuds and started for the east end of town. He made it half a mile out of Taos this time. Four of the biggest, meanest-looking men Wally had ever seen in his eleven years blocked the entire road. A line of people on foot, in wagons, and on horseback had formed in front of them. The surly fellows allowed free entry to town, but denied departure to all except for the poorest *campesinos* and mission Indians. Patiently, though with mounting apprehension, Wally waited his turn. He tried his "taking a coat to Paw" story again and was again turned back.

On his own, Wally tried the south road out of town. This time he believed he had it all figured out. When he saw an angry-looking farmer and his family headed back for town in a wagon, Wally hailed them and asked if the road was closed.

"Why, yes, son, how did you know?" the wife asked.

Wally worked his shoulders up and down. "I got turned back two places already. What is goin' on?"

"Some bad folks up there, boy," the farmer told Wally. "Best thing for you to do is turn around and go back now."

Wally scrunched his freckle-speckled button nose. "How far to where they are?"

Scratching his head, the farmer figured on that. "Quarter mile, maybe a little more. Beyond that bend yonder."

"Thank you, sir," Wally replied politely.

He turned Spuds' nose to the west and cut across a field in

the direction of Pacheca Creek. Keeping constantly alert, Wally looked to the threat on his left as he progressed through a cornfield and into a pasture beyond. He did not see the men who he now knew to be nothing more than outlaws, so he felt confident they could not see him. A line of cottonwoods and aspen marked the course of the creek. He pulled up inside the screen and leaned down to pat Spuds on the neck.

"You're gonna get cold, Spuds. So am I. We gotta swim our way around those fellers. When we git outta the crick, I'll rub you down and dry off, then we'll cut to the southwest and head for the Alvarado spread." Wally reached in his hip pocket and produced another parsnip, which he fed to Spuds.

Dismounting, Wally led his pony to the creek bank and stepped gingerly out on the sandy and pebble-strewn streambed. They stayed in the shallows for a while, the water frigid and hip-high on Wally. When he gauged they had come close to being opposite the hardcases, he urged Spuds out into the current, and they both swam past, gooseflesh forming under Wally's shirt.

When he reached a spot he considered safe, Wally swam cross-current until he gained footing. Spuds reached solid underpinning first and surged forward past the boy's slim shoulders. Wally stumbled behind. On the bank at last, boy and beast stood shivering.

"That was colder than I thought, boy," Wally admitted through chattering teeth. "Gotta strip and warm up."

With that he pulled off his wet clothes and threw himself down on a sun-warmed rock. Before long, the chill subsided, Wally's eyelids drooped and he fell into a light sleep.

ELEVEN

Nearing the end of the first week's visit by the Gittings, tension hung over the Sugarloaf. Normally a direct, outspoken person, Sally Jensen repressed her instinctive reaction to Mary-Beth's feather-headedness and the constant misbehavior of her undisciplined brood. As a result, Sally's old friendship with Mary-Beth was in conflict with her good sense. Put simply, Sally knew she should firmly demand that they leave.

Especially when Seth and Sammy had escaped their deserved spanking for stealing the candy. Oh, Mary-Beth had switched them—two half-hearted whacks on buttocks that had not even been bared. Both boys shot sneers at Sally and laughed openly over the lightness of their punishment as they walked away. That had been two days ago, and the situation seemed to worsen by the hour. From the direction of the corral, a boy's voice, raised in anger, reminded her of that.

"Stop that! Stop it, damn you, Seth, Sammy. Those foals can be hurt real easy."

It was Bobby's voice. Sally wondered what devilment the Gittings boys had gotten up to this time. If it was serious enough, she would find out right soon. She had asked their foreman, Ike Mitchell, to keep an eye on the rebellious boys, and to take matters into his own hands if need be. Since he had been successful on earlier occasions, she also implied the same to Bobby.

The boy was more than capable of taking responsibility for himself. He could act in a responsible manner toward others as well, Sally reasoned. Bobby's voice once more cut through her self-examination. "Hey, what are you doin'? Quit that."

Then came a long silence. Sally's apprehension rose.

Bobby Jensen came upon Seth and Sammy Gittings at the small corral outside the foaling barn. There the mares and their newborn could exercise away from the rest of the herd. Both of the younger boys had taken it in mind that it would be funny to watch the reactions of the small horses when they pelted them with rocks. Bobby looked on in shock and anger as two missiles struck a stalky-legged foal and it ran off squealing in terror to find its mother. The building rage pushed out the disgust Bobby felt. He stepped in at once, voice raised to a strident shout.

"Stop that."

Seth and Sammy looked blankly over their shoulders at Bobby, and the younger boy stuck out his tongue. As one, they hefted fresh rocks and hurled them at another colt. Bobby's voice deepened with his outrage.

"Stop it, damn you, Seth, Sammy. Those foals can be hurt real easy."

"Oh, yeah?" Seth challenged in a quiet voice. "Says who?"

Sammy added his opinion. "Yeah. 'Sides, it's funny when they make that noise and run around."

Bobby's voice grew low and menacing. "You stop that or I'll make you hurt like you've never hurt before."

Seth sneered. "No you won't. Mother won't let you."

With that, both Gittings boys turned and chucked stones at Bobby Jensen. One struck his left shoulder with enough force to hurt, though it merely angered him more. He tried once again to end their assault. "Hey, what are you doin'? Quit that."

Laughing, the boys threw more rocks. For a moment, while he dodged the fresh onslaught, Bobby thought of pulling his six-gun and blasting the both of them to oblivion. A satisfying, warm rush washed through him. Then he remembered what Smoke had taught him. Only a coward settles something with a gun that he can handle with his fists. Accordingly, Bobby rushed the smaller boys and threw Sammy to the ground. Seth leaped at him and swung a fist that contained a healthy-sized stone. It struck Bobby on the forehead and split the skin.

Blood began to run down through one white-blond eyebrow and into Bobby's left eye. He ignored the discomfort and shot a fist to the nose of Seth Gittings, who dropped the rock, screeching his agony. Bobby grabbed the front of Seth's shirt with both hands and hurled him to the ground. He stood over the supine boys a long, silent minute while they whined and sniveled. Satisfied that the incident had ended, Bobby turned away and started off to clean up his cut and patch it. Another rock, hurled in defiance, decided Bobby that he would report the situation to Sally after all.

Sally Jensen looked with mounting fury at the rising lump on Bobby's forehead and the court plaster he had stuck on the cut. "That cuts it, damnit!" Although she rarely swore, Sally thought the situation called for it.

Bobby Jensen looked at her with clear, wide eyes. "What are we going to do?"

"You are going to stand back and make the accusation. I am going to take care of what has needed doing for a long time." She crossed to the stove corner and brought out her willow switch, then moved to the door to the hallway and called into the depths of the house. "Mary-Beth, come here right away."

When Mary-Beth arrived, she took one look at the limber willow wand, and her cheeks lost color. A hand flew to the corner of her mouth. "Oh, no. Not again. Not my boys."

"Oh, yes, Mary-Beth, dear. Take a look at Bobby's forehead. Seth attacked him with a rock. Smashed him in the head, then threw another that bruised him between his shoulder blades. You are coming with me right this minute and put an end to it."

Sally took a firm hold on Mary-Beth's left wrist and literally pulled her to the outside kitchen door. With Bobby at her other side, Sally strode to the foaling barn. They rounded the corner in time to see Seth connect with another of the frightened, tormented foals. Sally did not temper her words.

"You will stop that this instant, you little monster."

Impudent defiance shone in the eyes of Seth Gittings. "We don't have to, do we, Mother?"

Sammy let escape a revealing statement. "Yeah, you said we could do anything we wanted."

Shocked to the core at last, Mary-Beth stammered a partial denial. "I—I said no such thing. I said you could do anything you wanted, so long as it did no harm to others."

Seth whined in protest of his innocence. "We didn't hurt anyone. All we did was tease the little horsies some."

Bobby could contain his outrage no longer. "Then you turned on me and threw rocks at me. When I pushed Sammy down, you hit me in the head."

Sally advanced on the boys. At the last moment, she whirled to Mary-Beth. "Either you do what is necessary, Mary-Beth, or I will do it for you."

Faced with such determination, Mary-Beth came forward and took the willow switch from Sally. She started after Sammy first. His small face took on an expression of horror, and he tried to back away, arms extended, palms outward to ward off imagined blows.

"No, don't. You can't hit me with that. Poppa wouldn't like that. No, Mother. Please."

Without a word, her lips set in a grim line, Mary-Beth yanked down Sammy's trousers and bent him over one knee. Then she laid on with a dozen good, hard, swift blows. He howled, shrieked and wailed, tears flowed freely from his eyes. When she had finished, she put him on his feet again.

"You, young man, will not leave the house for the next three days. Now, Seth, it's your turn. You are old enough to know better."

"You can't do this! I won't let you," Seth screamed in utter panic. *"No, Momma, please! You can't, you can't."*

A wild light glowed behind golden lashes as Mary-Beth spoke wonderingly, more to Sally and herself than to the boy. "You know, I just discovered that I can indeed."

In a trice, Seth received the same treatment as Sammy. Only this time his mother delivered fifteen strokes before ending it. A very satisfied Sally Jensen looked on. When Seth again stood before her, still blubbering, she had further admonishment for him. "If you ever, ever again use a weapon on an animal or another person, whether it is a rock or a knife or, God forbid, a gun, I will beat you to within an inch of your life. Now apologize to Bobby this instant."

"Alejandro will round up those among my vaqueros who can shoot the best," Diego Alvarado told Smoke Jensen.

Ten minutes after Wally Gower arrived at Rancho de la Gloria, Smoke Jensen and fifteen vaqueros rode out for town. The boy kept station close beside Smoke, his chest puffed with pride. They soon came upon several disgruntled people who had been turned back from town, and from them learned more details of the roadblocks.

"Beats all hell," one long-faced rancher observed. "There was six of them when we made to enter town. Told me an' the boys to turn about and hightail it for home. Said that the town was closed 'til further notice. Who can do a thing like that?"

"From what I've heard," said Smoke Jensen, with a nod toward Wally Gower, "it's Whitewater Paddy Quinn."

A glower answered Smoke. "That no-account. Claims to be foreman for some outfit called C.S. Enterprises. Common outlaw, you ask me."

"I think you have the right of it, sir," Smoke agreed.

They rode on, allowing the horses to walk only when they began to retch and grunt from exertion. In that manner, they made it to a point where they could observe the roadblock from a distance. Smoke studied the activity, noting that people no longer queued up to attempt to leave town. Smoke sent Wally back beyond range and turned to the Mexican cowboys.

"First things first," he told them. "We're going to take out these *bandidos,* then move around to each road entering town and do the same."

"Do we kill them, Señor Smoke?" Bernal Sandoval asked.

Smoke eyed him levelly. "We're not here to kiss them, Bernal."

"Muy bien." He turned to his companions. *"Adelante, muchachos."*

Smoke led the way as they charged down on the outlaws ahead. With weapons at the ready, they closed in a cloud of red dust. Quinn's men turned at the sound of pounding hooves, and the one in the center of the road shouted a challenge.

"Rein in and turn around. Nobody gets into town today. This is your last chance. Do it now or you'll be hurtin'."

With a firm tug on Cougar's reins, Smoke halted first and took careful aim. He intentionally shot the hardcase in charge through the left shoulder. The man grunted and raised his own six-gun. It barked loudly, but without effect. Smoke had given him his chance, and he had not taken it. So the last mountain man put a bullet through the chest of the outlaw. At once the gunman's underlings opened fire.

Not lacking in courage, the vaqueros sent a storm of hot lead into the rank that partitioned the road. Slugs from both sides whipped and cracked through the air. More dust churned up, to mingle with powder smoke and obscure the view. From the midst of the haze, a man screamed. Another called for help. Alejandro silenced him. Two vaqueros cursed in Spanish. Another ragged volley rippled across the hilly ground. Then, on the far side of the melee, a horse sprinted free. Its rider cried out in near hysteria.

"Get out before they kill us all!"

Within five seconds, the roar of gunfire dwindled to silence. The dust blew away on a stiff breeze, and the vaqueros began to slap one another on the back and congratulate themselves for the easy victory. Smoke Jensen gave them a couple of seconds, then called them together.

"We'll go on to the next. Alejandro, you take half our men and come at them at an angle; we'll take them head-on. No time to waste until we clean out all of these skunks." He beckoned to Wally and the boy joined him expectantly.

Yank Hastings had been with the Quinn gang for three years. He had seen the scruffy rabble of low-grade highwaymen and rustlers turned into a finely tuned force, not unlike an army. At the constant goading of Paddy Quinn and Garth Thompson, they had cleaned up their collective ragtag, unwashed appearance. They had practiced with their weapons until they had reached a proficiency unheard of among most common bandits. Every man now took orders without questioning them, obeyed to the letter or died trying. They robbed banks like precision machines; they learned the skills of intimidation to add to their ability to use force; those most skilled at it stole cattle by the whole herd, rather than twenty or thirty head at a time. It made Yank Hastings proud to be among their number.

That was why it shocked him, then, when two of the gang ran down on their barricade on the Taos-Raton road on frothing horses. Their eyes wide with panic, they shouted that an attack was imminent.

"A bunch of Mezkin cowboys hit our roadblock jist a while ago," one blurted out "They shot hell outta Cort an' Davey and lit out after us toward here."

"Yeah. They'll be here any minute," his companion assured.

Yank had started to calm them and discredit their fears when a bullet cracked overhead. He looked beyond them with a stunned expression.

Alejandro Alvarado and seven vaqueros raced toward the roadblock at an oblique angle to the road. It had been Alejandro who had fired at Yank. Hastings holstered his six-gun and drew his rifle. He was not about to let this jumped-up "Mezkin" get the better of him. He worked the lever to chamber a round and felt a stunning pain in his hand as a bullet struck the small of the stock. Fingers numbed, he dropped the weapon as he stared in disbelief while seven more vaqueros, led by a white man, stormed toward them along the road. The air filled with deadly bees as the attackers blazed away at Yank and his men. He had to do something, and fast.

"Everybody dismount. Josh, take the horses back. The rest of you get in those rocks. Hold your fire until you have a sure target."

Quickly the men spread out to take positions of at least partial cover. Undeterred, the riders came on. Return fire spurted from the muzzles of guns in the outlaws' hands. From a peaceful, quiet afternoon, the world had swiftly changed into a place of noise, fury, and death. The fighting intensified.

Suddenly, a whole swarm of Quinn's hardcases appeared over a low rise and charged toward the attackers.

Smoke Jensen watched the approach of the reinforcements and made a quick decision. He turned aside and cantered back a hundred yards to where Wally Gower had hunkered down in a pile of boulders. He leaned forward and spoke urgently to the boy.

"Wally, I want you to ride like lightning back to where we cleaned out that first roadblock. Then skedaddle into town and go to the sheriff. Tell him what we are doing and to get some men here right now."

"Yes, sir, I can do that."

Wally sprinted off on his pony before Smoke could wish him good luck. Smoke turned back to the battle that had developed in his absence. The vaqueros appeared to hold their own. They kept moving, making difficult targets of themselves. Smoke located one outlaw, who had climbed high on the rocks and now took careful aim with a Winchester at Alejandro Alvarado. Smoke settled Cougar with a pat on the neck and sighted in on the exposed target. When he had what he wanted, he gave a sharp whistle and shouted to the hardcase.

"Over here!"

Obligingly the man turned, so that Smoke caught him in the upper left chest with his first round. Quickly Smoke cycled the action of his Express rifle and fired again. A shower of volcanic rock chips formed a plume behind the thug after the bullet exited along the midline of his body. He flopped back down and lay still. Smoke sought another target. He had no lack of them, he soon discovered.

Outlaws milled everywhere. The new arrivals had been slow in taking to the rocks. Diego's vaqueros made a good harvest among them. Bodies sprawled in the grotesque postures of the dead and dying. Smoke saw another man seeking a vantage point high in the rocks. Quickly he raised his Winchester. The discharge of a heavy .44 revolver close by caused Cougar to flinch and sidestep at the moment the weapon fired. A torrent of dark, red-brown, porous rock exploded in the face of the gunman.

His sharp cry of pain sounded over the tumult of battle. Smoke levered a fresh round into the chamber and felt the hot breath of a bullet kiss his cheek. Unflinching, he raised the sights into line and shot the author of that close call through the breastbone. Smoke made a quick count. They had taken a hefty toll on the gang. The advantage of numbers had shifted to their side. Only one vaquero showed signs of having taken a wound. And that, Smoke noted, seemed slight. Smoke was about to call to the Mexican cowboys to rally and storm the rocks when more of the outlaw gang closed in, led by Garth Thompson.

Santan Tossa kneeled at the edge of the sacred sand painting and examined the evidence. Someone had come again to the kiva and stolen several of the religious articles stored there. The footprint of the culprit was distinctive. Much wider than usual, longer also, it served as a signature. Santan Tossa knew to whom the splayed foot belonged. He and several others had been most vocal about raising up the entire male population of the Tua pueblo and striking at the outsiders who had invaded their land. And he thought he knew who it was that they worked for.

There was a white man, a round-eye, named Satterlee. This would be the one. He had come to the pueblo to talk the elders into giving him permission to cut trees, a whole lot of trees, on their land. It had been refused, of course. Many of the trees were very old, older than the memories of the Tua. So old as to have shaded the Anasazi, those mysterious dwellers of the time of legends. Santan Tossa had noted the glow of greed in Satterlee's eyes as he had looked upon the sacred amulets, bracelets, and necklaces in their niches. Now, fully half of them had disappeared. How much, he wondered, had Dohatsa taken to become a thief?

No matter the reason or the reward, this required help from outside the pueblo. Although he didn't like it, Tossa knew he must take his findings to the white lawman in Taos. He was powerless to investigate anyone not of the pueblo, but the sheriff would know how to go about it. Thus decided, Santan Tossa made a quick examination of the remainder of the kiva and exited through the hole in the roof. He went directly to the small corral on the southeast side of the compound and caught up one of his ponies.

Tossa rode the short three miles to the low adobe wall that surrounded the outsider town of Taos. There he went directly to the sheriff's office. To his surprise, he found it empty. He would wait. Now that he had committed himself to this course, he might as well see it through. While he bided his time, Tossa reflected on conditions at the pueblo.

Theft of the religious objects had been a shock to those who knew—and not all did—and also a source of much justified anger. As a tribal policeman, he kept his own counsel, but Santan Tossa did not question the rightness of his suspicions. Some of the hotheads among the young warriors had been most vocal in demanding retribution against the whites, whom they felt certain had stolen the object. Particularly Dohatsa, who had called a meeting of his warrior society in the kiva the previous night. After the meeting would have been an ideal time to steal the missing items. Santan Tossa had attended the gathering, although he had not been made to feel welcome. Now he recalled what had happened.

Firelight flickered off the bare, bronze shoulders of Dohatsa as he addressed the Puma Society members. "Brothers, we all know that precious articles of our religion have been stolen. It is clear to me who is responsible. It is white men. Not the Mexicans, not even the Spanish before them, would touch any of our holy relics. They considered them heathen and forbidden. Their lust was for gold not silver. So they discounted even the value of our most treasured works.

"I know that somewhere, our sacred squash blossoms and shells decorate the body of a white woman, maybe more than one. We must ask our mothers and sisters who work in the houses of the whites to look for them. Only they must do this carefully and quietly. And caution them not to say anything of this to anyone."

A young warrior raised a hand in protest. "Our women have never seen the sacred objects. How will they know what to look for?"

Dohatsa produced a wicked smile. "We will describe them, only not tell of their meaning and purpose. When they are found, we will move silently and swiftly. Our knives and lances will taste white blood. Not a one of the guilty shall live."

Santan Tossa could not keep silent. "If you do such a thing, outside the pueblo, you will bring much trouble to us."

Dohatsa turned a scornful sneer to Tossa. "What do you know? A policeman? You have already sold yourself to the whites. This is the best way."

Santan Tossa knew better. He believed it to be wrong that night.

And he believed it today as he awaited the return of Sheriff Hank Banner. More so for knowing now that the thief had been Dohatsa.

TWELVE

Another five minutes and they would be as dead as King Sol, Smoke Jensen thought to himself as the fresh wave of bandits rolled toward them. He took time to aim carefully and knocked another outlaw from the saddle. Still they came. Around him, the vaqueros from Rancho de la Gloria made the switch from a near victory to furious defense with smooth unconcern. Their expressions did not change as they pumped round after round into the advancing gang members.

Truth was, Smoke realized, they seemed to enjoy it. With a violent forward surge by the gang, little more than two dozen yards separated the contending forces. Any time now Smoke and the vaqueros would have to break and run or be annihilated. The outlaw leader sensed it also.

With a triumphant whoop, he urged his men on. They closed the gap by five yards. Suddenly a stutter of shots erupted behind them. It rapidly grew to a ragged volley. Confused, fully half of the bandits turned about. Smoke Jensen seized the moment to charge.

"At them! *¡Cuchillos y machettes!*" he yelled, calling for knives and the deadly long blades used for chopping jungle and high grass.

"Yiiiiiiii!" several vaqueros shouted in unison.

With bared blades in one hand, revolvers in the other, reins between their teeth or looped over the large, flat pommels of their saddles, the Mexican cowboys broke clear and thundered down on the astonished Anglo outlaws. The appearance of keen-edged steel unnerved many among the gang. They would gladly face down four or more blazing six-guns, but the thought of deep, gaping wounds, of severed limbs, or decapitation filled them with dread. Pressed from both sides, they abandoned all effort at resistance and fled in panicked disarray.

In no time, the posse led by Sheriff Banner and the vaqueros joined up. The field had been abandoned by Quinn's rogues so swiftly that the wounded had been left behind. Smoke and the sheriff rode among them. None of them appeared capable of further fight.

"It's over," the sheriff opined.

Smoke did not share Banner's confidence. "For now."

Back in the sheriff's office, Banner showed surprise to find Santan Tossa waiting. "It is good to see you, Santan. May I ask what brings you to Taos?"

"I wanted to check in. See what is going on in town."

Banner sensed the young Tua policeman's hesitation and decided to change the subject. "Oh, by the way, this is a very famous man among my people. His name is Smoke Jensen. Smoke, Santan Tossa, one of the Tua tribal police."

A smile bloomed on the dark copper face of Santan Tossa. To Smoke's surprise, he spoke excellent English. "Smoke Jensen. I have heard much about you. You have fought our brothers among the Kiowa, the Cheyenne, the Sioux, Blackfeet and Shoshone. But you were always fair. You've had a lot of run-ins with white men also. I had some of your exploits read to me by one of our people who understands English better than I do."

Smoke gave him a self-deprecating grin. "All lies, Santan. If I had shot at, let alone killed, as many men as the dime novels say, there would be an ammunition shortage in the country to this day."

They laughed together. When the sheriff joined them, the tension eased some. Banner decided to get to the point. "Now, what is it that brought you here?"

"We have had some thefts at the pueblo. Religious articles." He went on to explain about the stolen objects, and the desecration. He did not reveal the possibility of an uprising.

"Do you have any suspects?"

Tossa shook his head, looking unhappy. "Yes, I do. It had to be one of our own who entered the kiva. No Mexican or white man could get away with it. The one I think took the relics is Dohatsa. I think he stole them for a man named Clifton Satterlee."

"But why?"

"To cause trouble between our two people. I think he wants us to do something that will result in our being driven out. Satterlee wants the land. The trees most of all."

Smoke, who had listened with intense concentration to the conversation, looked up then and spoke what was on his mind. "I suggest that it might be time for me and this young man to pay a visit to Satterlee's hacienda in Santa Fe. Who knows what we might spook him into doing?"

Sheriff Banner snorted and shook his head. "That's it exactly. Who knows? I don't like it. There's too much can go wrong. But, I suppose there's no other choice. Be careful, Smoke."

Smoke gave him a curt nod. "Now that I will do."

Rapid, strident notes shivered brassily from the bell of a sliver-plated trumpet. The short, thin, dapper mariachi who played it had a pencil line of mustache that writhed above the mouthpiece as he articulated each tone. To his right, a big man with a huge bass guitar plucked the strings with gusto, rhythmic vibrations that directly strummed the heart. To the trumpeter's left, a standard guitar and two violins played out the melody. Under their wide-brimmed *charro* sombreros, three of the quartet sang lustily. The song was "Sonora Querrida." Clifton Satterlee looked with pride over the milling guests at his hacienda outside Santa Fe. Seated at the table on the palm-frond-shaded dais with him, his three partners and several of his eastern connections ate and drank to their hearts' content.

Across the patio, on which some of the guests danced to the music, two small, barefoot boys, dressed in loosely fitted white cotton shirts and knee-length pants, turned a spit over a large bed of oak and piñon coals. Their eyes shone with the excitement generated by the fiesta that swirled around them. Steam and smoke rose from the fat and juices that dripped off the split side of beef the youngsters tended. The aroma of the roasting flesh kept everyone in a constant state of hunger. Large, glazed clay bowls of beans were emptied and promptly refilled. Others of delicate saffron rice, mixed with onions, green peas, and tomatoes, suffered deep inroads. Mountains of freshly made tortillas, both flour and corn, disappeared with regularity. Beer, tequila, and bourbon flowed freely. The happy laughter of women tinkled from every quarter.

Obviously enjoying all of this, one huge-bellied, over-dressed man with pink pate showing through thinning hair leaned toward Satterlee and patted him on the forearm. "I have to hand it to you, Cliff, you know how to throw a party. All of this must cost a fortune."

"Not at all, Findley. Labor is cheap. Back when the Spanish, then the Mexicans, ruled this land, the law had it that when a man owned the ground, he owned everything on it. That included villages and the people in them. Of course, he was required to provide a livelihood for the peons, see that they had a roof over their heads, food to eat, even paid a small amount of money. The patron had responsibility for their well-being, but to all intents and purpose, they were his property. When I took over, they had nowhere else to go, so they stayed. I provide and maintain their houses in the village, employ them to run the stores and the cantina. I even support their church, although it is the Popish Roman rite."

"Rather like slavery," Findley Ashbrook said with a chuckle.

Satterlee affected shock and abhorrence. "Heaven forbid, Findley. They are nothing of the sort. After all, they get paid. Ten dollars a month is tops."

"You crafty devil," burbled Quinton Damerest, a burly man with a hang-dog face seated beside Findley Ashbrook. "You've gotten around that demagogue Lincoln and his emancipation, damned if you haven't. I admire you for it. Is that how you intend to log out lumber way out here, ship it all the way back East, and sell at a profit?"

Satterlee nodded, sipping from a clay mug of beer. "Precisely, Quinton. Once we have the workers living in company houses, buying only from the company store, getting their work clothes from the company commissary, just like my peons here at Santa Fe, then we wait until they are deeply in debt to the company and cut their wages by half, then half again. Before long, they'll also be making only ten dollars a month, like these Mexican peons."

Findley Ashbrook spoke up next. "What says they have to stay here?"

"The law, Ashbrook my friend, the law. We'll be their employer, and also the local law. If they try to get away from here, we'll take them in front of our tame justice of the peace, get an easy conviction for some trumped-up charge, then slap them and their whole family into jail. A little of that and they'll see the light, have no fear."

"What about the unions?" Findley asked darkly.

Satterlee smirked. "They'll never get a start here. If they try, or if they organize a strike, we have Paddy Quinn and his men to take care of such annoyances." He nodded to a slender, young, boyish-faced individual at one of the trestle tables, helping himself to another plate of *carnitas de puerco, carne de res barbacóa*, and all the fixings. "You see that one over there? He is a prime example of what I'm talking about. He looks like a baby, but Patrick Quinn assures me he is one of the fastest, most accurate gunhands he has ever witnessed."

Eyes wide, his cheeks gone pale, Quinton Damerest spoke in an awed tone. "Is that William Bonney?"

Satterlee chuckled indulgently. "Not at all, Quinton. He calls himself Mac. A Texas boy named MacGreggor. But he's hellfire with a six-gun. I've seen him in action."

Unaware that he had become the topic of conversation on the dais, Ian MacGreggor went about filling his plate. He had grown up on the spicy foods of the Southwest. The barbecued beef, with its hot, sweet, red sauce and the carnitas with the wide variety of condiments were among his favorites. He had consumed two plates so far. He could eat at least that much more.

"A growing boy," his mother had often said in mock irritation.

Well, it was true. For the last two years he had always felt hungry. At least being with the Quinn gang had that advantage. The food was good and plentiful. It had surprised Ian when he had been told he would be going along with a part of the gang to act as bodyguards at a fancy do put on by the Big Boss, Clifton Satterlee. The prospect excited him. He would get a chance for a close-up study of the man. He might also overhear something useful to Smoke Jensen. His plate loaded, Mac picked up a squatty clay pot of *jugo de tamarindo,* the savory extract of tamarind pods sweetened with honey and cut with water.

He could have had all the beer he wanted. No one would have questioned him. But he felt it wiser to remain alert and sober. His wisdom proved itself fifteen minutes later when Cole Granger rode in on a lathered, foaming-mouthed horse. Granger knocked the dust from his clothing and came directly to where Mac sat chewing industriously at his meal.

"Where's the boss?"

"Mr. Quinn? He's over there with the 'important' people on that platform," Ian responded between bites.

Granger was abrupt. "Thanks."

Mac sensed something important came with Granger. "Hey, what's up?"

Cole Granger made an all-encompassing gesture. "Big trouble. You'll find out soon enough."

With a sigh and a regretful backward glance at his abandoned plate, Ian MacGreggor drifted along behind Cole Granger. The latter stopped at the bottom of the three steps that led to the dais. There he waited to catch the eye of Paddy Quinn. Mac held back and turned away to avoid recognition. At last Paddy looked up and saw the agitated Granger standing on the edge of the tile patio.

"Sure an' what is it ye are lookin' so exercised over, Cole, me lad?"

"We've got some big trouble up in Taos, Paddy."

"Ouch, now, that's such fresh news, it is." Paddy had been hitting the tequila heavily. It showed clearly to an attentive Mac.

"No, really. We had the roadblocks busted up by a posse and some vaqueros who work for Diego Alvarado. About nine of the guys dead, some others near to death. Shot all to doll rags. An' I—well, I recognized someone fighting with the Mezkin cowboys."

"An' who might that be?"

"Maybe we ought to move away a bit before I tell you?" Cole Granger suggested, as he cut his eyes nervously to Clifton Satterlee and his partners.

Grumbling under his breath, Paddy Quinn grabbed a fresh shot of tequila and a lime wedge from the tray of a waiter and climbed from the platform. Ian MacGreggor had moved off, though not out of hearing. Granger led Paddy over by a palo verde. There he spoke in a low tone.

"It was none other than Smoke Jensen."

Shock and surprise registered on the face of Paddy Quinn. "Th' hell. I thought him to be dead and buried long ago."

"Not so. He's taken a hand in what's goin' on in Taos."

Quinn looked grim. "I'll have to tell Mr. Satterlee."

He went at once to where Satterlee sat and asked to speak alone with him. Off the dais, the head of C.S. Enterprises listened while Quinn explained. From the thunderous expression that shaped Satterlee's face, Mac could tell he liked the news even less. At last, Satterlee spoke in a low tone.

"The presence of Smoke Jensen could prove a major threat. Quinn, I want you to select some men and do something about Jensen. And do it fast."

Riding side by side, Smoke Jensen and Santan Tossa felt the warm sun on their right cheeks and shoulders. Santa Fe remained a full thirty-five miles away. They would not reach the bustling territorial capital until the next morning. As they neared a steep saddle, Smoke noted a large red-tailed hawk, its wings extended, tips down-curved, riding stationary on the strong breeze that blew through the opening.

Abruptly a shrill squeal came from a small, young rabbit crouched on the ground. Frightened beyond endurance by the hawk that hovered above it, it broke cover and sent spurts of red dust from under its hind feet. Instantly, the hawk folded its wings and dived like an arrow. Legs suddenly extended, claws flexed, the redtail snatched the tiny creature from the earth and soared away toward its lair. The pitiful cry of its victim faded as it gained distance. Smoke Jensen watched unperturbed. He never forgot that nature was indeed a harsh mistress.

Santan Tossa nodded toward the dwindling silhouette of the hawk. "The young of the redtail will eat well today."

"That is so," Smoke allowed. "Tell me, Santan, how long have you been a policeman?"

Tossa smiled, his chin lifted somewhat in pride. "Four years now. Although I will admit that this is the first real crime I have had to investigate. Most of the time I deal with a few drunks, or a dispute over ownership of a horse. What about yourself?"

Smoke had no need to search memory. "I've worn a badge, off and on, for well over fifteen years. I've fought outlaws and cleaned the riffraff out of towns, protected people in the government, even looked into the murder of friends and a few strangers."

Tossa looked expectant of Smoke's answer. "Do you like it?"

Smoke gave a snort of laughter. "A whole lot better than bein' on the other side of the law. I've not run into many Indian policemen. The Sioux and Cheyenne don't have them."

Tossa shrugged. "They are still controlled by the soldiers and the Indian agents. We are on our own. We're . . . pacified." The word sounded bitter to his mouth.

That decided Smoke to change the subject. "Do you have a woman? A family?"

"I am too young to raise children. At least that is the way we Tua believe. The padres of the *iglesia católica* want us to marry young and have many children."

"But that is not the Tua way."

A broad grin spread across Tossa's face. "No. And in that

way, we mystify them. A Tua man usually takes a wife when he has twenty-six summers—er—years. He is through with war and breaking wild horses by then. Ready to settle down, hunt and plant, and provide for a family. It is a good way."

"I agree," Smoke conceded.

They rode along making infrequent and idle conversation. They came down out of the Sangre de Cristo at Española and rode on a ways. The sun slanted far to the west and high-lighted red plumes to their backs. Smoke Jensen had kept notice of them for some five miles when he reined up.

"Someone is following us."

Tossa nodded. "I noticed it, too."

Smoke cut his level, gold-flecked gaze to Tossa. "What do you think we should do about it?"

The Tua shrugged. "Find out who they are."

Cole Granger and the four men Paddy Quinn sent with him rode hard and fast out of Santa Fe, in an effort to reach the halfway point between the Satterlee hacienda and Taos before nightfall. As it happened, they arrived in Española only minutes before Smoke Jensen and Santan Tossa passed through. Granger, who had been the one to recognize Smoke in the first place, spotted the tall, broad-shouldered, firmly erect figure as Smoke walked his mount down the main street. In spite of three hundred years of settlement, roads remained sparse in this part of New Mexico. It did not require great genius for Cole Granger to figure out where Smoke Jensen might be headed.

"Him an' that Injun are on the way to Satterlee's."

Pete Stringer eyed him dubiously. "How you know?"

"Where else would he be going? He's in a dust-up with us and right off, he heads south. He's goin' to call out the big boss."

Stringer eagerly went for the obvious solution. "Then, let's take him out right here an' now."

Granger shook his head. "Not likely. The marshal here's hell on killings in his town. Even if we let Jensen draw first—which would be a terrible mistake—we'd wind up in jail, most likely charged with murder. We're gonna follow along. Pick our spot, then jump the two of them."

"What does the Injun have to do with it?" another of the hardcases asked.

With a squint-eyed stare, Granger spat on the ground. "Who cares? He'll be only another dead Injun."

At Granger's suggestion, they gave Smoke and Tossa time enough to cover five miles, then rode out, retracing their hurried route to the small mountain town. The outlaws pulled into sight twenty minutes later. To their right, the sun floated over the western arm of the Sangre de Cristo range. Long shafts of orange and magenta light cast their features in unnatural colors. Dark, elongated shadows of horses and riders kept pace with them. Their quarry dipped below the horizon, where the road descended yet another three hundred feet to the more open desert land that stretched to Santa Fe.

When Granger and his henchmen reached the grade, the outlaw leader immediately discovered that the men they hunted had disappeared. The first cold, portentous inklings of extreme danger clutched the spine of Cole Granger.

THIRTEEN

Fat, dumb, and inattentive, four of the five hardcases who followed Smoke Jensen rode into a nasty surprise. Only Cole Granger hung back, acutely conscious that the missing men represented a threat that could not be ignored. Yet, had he warned the others, taken some sort of defensive position, Smoke Jensen and the Indian could have simply ridden off in some unexpected direction and disappeared for good. Jensen was slippery as a greased eel. Somehow, Granger knew, he had to allow them to spring any trap they had planned. That happened far sooner than he had expected.

His underlings had ridden on ahead, and only now became aware that their intended targets could no longer be seen. "Hey," Pete Stringer called out. "Where 'n hell did they go?"

"I'm right here." The voice of Smoke Jensen came from beyond a jumble of rocks that masked the right side of the trail from the view of Granger and the others.

"And I am here," Tossa answered from the opposite side.

Four astonished saddle trash cut their eyes from one side of the trail to the other. On their left they saw the squat figure of a Pueblo Indian, powerful shoulder muscles bunched as he drew the string of a thick, stubby bow back to his cheek, an arrow nocked and ready. In the other direction, a hard-faced white man held a six-gun on them in a competent, steady grip. All at once a terrible reality had caught up with them.

Given the alternatives, they decided to do what, to them, seemed the only thing to do. All four went for their guns. The arrow made a ripping cloth sound as it left its perch, propelled by a seventy-pound pull. It made an eerie moan through the air before it penetrated the chest wall of one thug and buried half its length in his lungs and other vital organs. He didn't even scream before he fell from the saddle.

From the other side, a .45 Colt Peacemaker barked with authority, and a hot slug smacked solidly into the gut of Pete Stringer. Pete's arm jerked, and his one shot went wild, to scream off the rocks. Another bullet brought an immense darkness to shroud him until a tiny, bright pinpoint of light began to swell and Pete Stringer rushed off to eternity. Pete didn't hear the next shot, which clipped Handy Manson in one shoulder and sent him in wild flight down the trail toward Santa Fe. The third, stiff-legged jounce threw Manson from the back of his horse. He hit the ground hard, folded into a ball to moan and writhe in misery.

On the opposite side of the trail, the close quarters left no time to string another arrow. Santan Tossa leaped from the back of his pony and dragged the remaining outlaw clear of his horse. They landed with a thud, the Tua Indian on top. Brigand ribs cracked like brittle sticks under the impact of Tossa's knees. Orange sunlight flashed on the keen edge of the knife Tossa whipped out and pressed to the throat of the winded thug.

So much for making a plan based on Jensen's expected attack, Cole Granger thought quickly. The only *plan* that made sense was to get the hell out of here. He reined his mount around and put spurs to its flanks. Smoke Jensen rode into sight then and threw a shot at the departing Granger with little hope of it hitting meat.

At the forefeet of Cougar, the youthful desperado had eyes

only for the knife that threatened him. After a cautious, though nervous, shudder, he raised his gaze to the white man who calmly sat his horse, looking down with apparent dispassionate interest. That sight caused him to lose it entirely. He began to shriek and utter great sobs. Only gradually did Smoke manage to interpret what the sniveling thug tried to say.

"Please . . . puh-leeeze! Save me from this savage. Drag him off me. You're a white man. You can't let him kill me."

Laughing nastily, Smoke Jensen bent down and spoke softly. "I'll let Tossa skin you alive if you don't cooperate. You and your friend down there." He gestured toward the fallen Handy Manson.

"What do you want to know? What? What?"

"Who do you ride for?"

"I can't—I can't tell you. He'll—kill me if I do."

Coldly, Smoke taunted him. "And you don't think Tossa there will kill you if you don't?"

Face ashen, he cut his eyes away from both of his captors. "Oh, Jesus."

Iron tipped Smoke's words. "He can't help you. I might. If you tell me what I want to know. Who do you ride for?"

"Whi—Whitewater Paddy Quinn."

Relentless, Smoke pressed on. "And who does he work for?"

Shaking with terror born of the impossibility of his situation, certain he would die no matter what he said, the craven rascal gulped himself into a fit of hiccoughs. His eyes squinted tightly shut, and great tears squeezed out. "C-C-Clif—Clifton Sa-Sa-Satterlee."

Smoke Jensen cut his eyes to Santan Tossa and asked rhetorically, "Why am I not surprised?" He made a curt gesture, and Tossa released the captive. "Get the other one. We'll patch them up and take them along with us while we go have a talk with Satterlee. Then, on the way back, we can drop them off in Española. The law can lock them up for us there."

* * *

Seth and Sammy Gittings intermittently wiped at the tears that streamed down their dirt-grimed faces with the backs of their hands as they saddled two small Morgan horses they had decided to take for their escape from the Sugarloaf. Horror and a terrible sensation of rejection burned in their minds. She had done it again. Their rumps still stung from the hard, swift swipes from the willow switch.

Seth sniffled loudly and smeared his upper lip with the mucous that ran from his nose. Then he spoke both their thoughts. "It ain't right. What did it matter if that dumb ol' pig got squashed. It was fun rollin' rocks downhill into the pigpen and watchin' the mud splash up."

"Yeah, Seth. It wasn't our fault that baby pig was stuck in the muck and couldn't get away in time. Mother had no right to spank us. She's never ever done it before."

Seth nodded energetically. "Poppa wouldn't let her. Now she's done it twice. It ain't fair," he whined. "We'll show her. She'll be sorry when we're gone."

Abruptly a rooster bugled his welcome to the pending dawn. Both boys jumped and looked at each other with the shock of fear reflected in their eyes. The cock crowed again, and a fit of giggles erupted from Seth and Sammy.

Through his sniggers, Sammy admitted, "That cock-a-doodle scared me. I about peed my pants."

"What's new about that?"

"Liar! I ain't done it in a year now."

"Shut up an' let's finish."

Seth completed the fold-over tie-off of his cinch strap, grateful that his older brother's friendship with Bobby Jensen had allowed him to learn how to master the tricks of saddling a horse, and he had in turn taught them. He went to check on his little brother. Sammy, as usual, had made a mess of it. He began to undo the bulky knot.

"Not like that, stupid. Here, watch."

Quickly Seth adjusted the cinch strap, slipped the leather end through the crosspiece, and jerked it down. Next he hung a canteen over the saddle horn and added a cloth bag that contained some biscuits, split and smeared with apple butter, two pieces of cold, fried chicken, and a hunk of cheese. An identical bundle already waited on his saddle. Through the barn window he saw a thin, gray line on the eastern horizon. It was time they left. Any more delay and they might get caught.

"Miz Jensen will be awake any time," he observed to his brother. "So'll the hands. We gotta go now and fast."

"Mother won't get up for hours," Sammy remarked.

"So what? We've gotta be way gone from here by then."

Both boys led their stolen horses from the barn and mounted up. Walking the animals to make the least amount of noise, they angled across the ranch yard and into the near pasture. Only then did Sammy notice the smooth, dark wood of a rifle stock in the scabbard on Seth's saddle.

"Gosh, what's that, Sethie?"

"Bobby's rifle."

"Why'd you take that; you don't like guns, do you?"

Seth had a wild gleam in his eyes. "Really, I think they're keen. Besides, we might need it. Mother says it is dangerous and wild out there." He put heels to the little Morgan and moved the beast into a trot.

Neither youngster had the slightest smidgen of horsemanship. Their thin legs bounced out from the sides of their mounts while their rumps banged up and down without even a hint about posting. By the time they had left the cleared fields of the Sugarloaf their thighs ached and their behinds knew more agony than any from the spanking. Tall fir, hemlock, and pine closed around them, and the sky disappeared above a thick mat of branches. Stunted aspens reduced visibility to twenty feet on either side. Sammy grew round-eyed with apprehension. It did not decrease when they picked up a game trail.

Seth pointed it out. "Look, there's a trail. I bet it leads to that dismal little town, you know the one?"

"Big Rock?"

"That's it, Sammy. We'll follow it, okay?"

"Sure."

Seth took the lead on the narrow trace, with Sammy close behind. They remained totally unaware that they were going in the exact opposite direction from Big Rock. Or that they grew more lost with each step their mounts took. They also continued into the vastness, ignorant of the cool, amber eyes that watched them.

Slowly the muscular, tawny body roused itself, lifted its blunt, white muzzle and sniffed the air. With a surge of new interest, the wily old cougar smelled a fresh meal.

Diamonds of moisture sparked on the leaves of Spanish bayonet and tufts of saw grass as Smoke Jensen and Santan Tossa reined in behind a low, sandy knoll outside the hacienda of Clifton Satterlee. Smoke nodded to their captives.

"We'll put them down and tie them to those mesquite bushes. Gag 'em, too."

Handy Manson had regained some of his former bravado. "You go in there after Clifton Satterlee an' you ain't comin' out alive."

Smoke gave him an amused expression. "You had better hope we do. Because no one is going to know where you are. Dying of thirst and hunger is a bad way to go, I'm told. So, hold a good thought for us, eh?"

"You—you ain't gonna leave us some water? Something to eat?"

Smoke appeared downright jovial. "Nope. You won't be

able to make use of it anyway, what with a gag in your mouth and hands tied behind a tree."

After securing the prisoners, Smoke and Santan rode on into the warmth of midmorning. Once out of hearing, Tossa asked of Smoke, "Do you think they will try to escape?"

"I imagine so."

"You do not seem concerned, Smoke."

"I'm not. The way I tied those knots, the harder they struggle, the tighter they'll become. Those two will still be there when we return."

"Don't they know a man can live five or six days without food and nearly as long without water, even in this desert?"

"I doubt it. Even if they do, it will take them some time to remember it. By then we should be back. In a case like theirs, fear can kill more likely than the doin' without."

Worry rode firm in the saddle on the back of Ian Mac-Greggor. A full day had passed since he had overheard the conversation between Cole Granger and Paddy Quinn. Four men had ridden out with Granger to "take care of Jensen," as Satterlee had put it. What had happened to Smoke? Pushing his concern to the back of his mind, he went about his assigned task of scanning the distant horizon. Motion caught his attention. He stared at the spot, and the dark silhouettes disappeared. He blinked and rubbed his eyes.

There they were. Two figures, clearly on horseback, headed toward the hacienda at a fast trot. Ian MacGreggor soon got the knack of looking slightly to the side of what he wanted to see, instead of dead-bang on. It let him decide that they were definitely both men. As they drew nearer, he determined that they did not resemble any of the gang he knew. What would strangers be coming here for? Mac turned aside and called down from the rampart that spanned the inner side of the high outer wall.

"Riders coming. I don't recognize them yet."

Another member of the gang repeated his announcement. Mac went back to a study of the approaching men. He could make out the color of their clothing now, and the style. Another dozen strides from the powerful shoulder muscles of their horses and Mac could make out their features. One of them appeared to be an Indian. And the other . . . the other rider Mac suddenly recognized as Smoke Jensen. It struck Mac like a fist in the stomach: *Smoke Jensen*. In a flash he recalled Smoke's admonition that if they saw each other, they would not give any sign of recognition. He shouted down to the cobblestone courtyard again.

"They're both strangers. One of them is an Injun. The other is a white man."

"Will ye come on down now, lad, will ye?" Whitewater Paddy Quinn called to him.

"Yes, sir, Mr. Quinn."

Hoofbeats rang loud in his ears as the horsemen grew nearer. Mac clattered down the rickety ladder that gave access to the parapet and joined a cluster of other outlaws who had formed up between the main gate and the house. Mac heard Smoke and his companion rein in. After a pause, the large iron ring that served as a knocker struck the portal with a hollow bang.

Old Jorge Banderes shuffled to the small, human-sized door in the thick wooden gates and opened the viewing port. *"¿Sí, señores?"*

"We're here to see Señor Satterlee."

"Lo siento, señores, Señor Satterlee is not receiving anyone at this hour," the grizzled Mexican retainer replied.

"Tell him that Smoke Jensen is here. He'll see us, I'm sure."

Jorge scuttled off to deliver the message. While they waited, Smoke exchanged an amused glance with Tossa.

Despite the age of the doorman, it took only three minutes. Jorge Banderes threw the bolt on the door and swung it wide.

"Come in, señores. Don Clifton will admit you to his salon now."

Smoke Jensen took a purposeful stride through the opening and cut his eyes to the gathering of hardcases. At once he saw Ian MacGreggor, then his gaze slid on without the slightest sign of recognition. Mac turned slightly as though to keep eyes on the Indian.

"We may regret this," Santan Tossa spoke in a whisper.

Mary-Beth Gittings entered the large living room of the Sugarloaf headquarters in a state of high agitation. Sally Jensen knelt on the hearth, removing ashes from the fireplace. Mary-Beth wrung her hands, and her face showed a puffiness unusual to herself. Sally noted her friend's perplexity at once.

"Mary-Beth, what is the matter?"

"I can't find them. No one has seen them this whole day."

"Who is it you cannot find, Mary-Beth?"

"Seth and Samuel. Your son says he knows nothing about them, only that his rifle is missing. Though I doubt his word on both counts."

Sally fought unsuccessfully to hold back a scowl. "That is entirely uncalled for. I resent the implication that Bobby would lie. It reflects on us as parents, and that is insulting."

Mary-Beth's face crumpled. "I'm sorry, Sally, dear. It's only . . . I am so worried. None of the hands have seen them. The boys are not at the corral, not in any of the barns, not in their room. I've been everywhere."

"Have you asked Billy about his brothers?"

"Yes, and he knows nothing either."

I could be mean, Sally considered, *and ask if Mary-Beth doubted her son's word also.* No, that would hardly do. "Ike

Mitchell has a good eye for reading sign. I'll have him take a good look around and see what he can come up with."

"Would you? I'd be so grateful. I worry so whenever they are out of my sight."

Sally found that unsettling. "Even when they go to school?"

"Of course not, Sally. I'm not an over-protective mother."

Oh, no, not by half, Sally opined silently.

Sally left her task for later and, with Mary-Beth trailing along, went in search of the foreman, Ike Mitchell. She found him in the smithy, pounding on a newly forged iron hinge. He looked up as they approached and wiped sweat from his brow with the back of one forearm.

"Ike, have you seen the younger two Gittings boys today?"

"No, ma'am. That I haven't. Told the missus that not two hours ago."

"Well, Ike, they've gone missing. Would you please take a good look around and see if you can come up with anything that might indicate where they got off to?"

"Sure, Miz Sally. Glad to be of help."

Ike completed leveling the hinge, doused it in a tub of water, and laid it aside to cool. Then he plunged both hands into another container of clean water and washed the charcoal smudges from his face. He rolled down his sleeves and started off to examine various parts of the headquarters ranch yard. Sally put a hand on Mary-Beth's arm.

"This is likely to take some time. Come back to the house and I'll make us some tea. We can let Ike work at his own pace."

Three-quarters of an hour later, a stern-faced Ike Mitchell presented himself at the kitchen door. Hat in hand, he knocked briskly. Although clearly uncomfortable, he presented his findings in a crisp flow.

"I reckon they done lit a shuck outta here, Miz Sally. I cut their sign west of the big corral. Tracks led northwest across the pastures. I followed them to the edge of tall timber. They kept goin'. Then I came back here and went over the stock. It appears they took two of the young Morgans, blankets and saddles, and hightailed it early this morning. Don't look like they reckon to come back. We'd best get some of the boys together an' go after them."

"I should say so," Mary-Beth blurted. Then the realization of the danger her children might face struck her. "My babies!" she wailed.

Blunt as usual, Ike had the last word. "They ain't babies anymore, ma'am. They're horse thieves."

FOURTEEN

Jorge Banderes escorted Smoke Jensen and Santan Tossa into the high, curved-ceiling passageway that separated the main entrance of the house from the gardenlike atrium at the center. Smoke found it to be cool and dark. Everyone blinked when they stepped out into the bright sunlight that washed the tiled central courtyard. A burly man stood beside the central fountain, his face a square mask that failed to conceal the boiling anger beneath the surface. Although Smoke had not seen him before, he surmised this to be Patrick Quinn. Leave it to a two-bit, gunslinging thug to choose as pretentious a moniker as *Whitewater,* Smoke thought.

Smoke Jensen had seen real whitewater on the Rogue River and sincerely doubted that Quinn had the stuffing to ride on it under any conditions. Paddy Quinn took a single step forward and extended both arms, palms up. "The guns. I'll take them now."

Smoke scowled, and his eyes went cold and flat, narrowed slightly. "That'll be the day," he growled.

Quinn proved himself no fool to Smoke's reckoning when he did not choose to press the matter. "Suit yerselves. An', sure ye'd not mind if me an' a couple of the boys stood close at hand while ye have yer little talk with Mr. Satterlee, would ye?"

Smoke could not resist the opportunity to tweak his enemy. "Not at all, a-tall."

For a flash, Quinn's expression grew even more furious. His eyes widened and revealed black centers that glittered malevolently. With obvious effort he reined in his emotion. "Come this way, then."

Framed by lush vegetation, an attractive young woman took her ease on a white-painted, wrought-iron settee near one side of the patio. Her silver-blond hair and fair, peaches-and-cream complexion glowed in the leaf-filtered sunbeams. She smiled warmly at the visitors and greeted them in a musical contralto. "Welcome to Hacienda Colina del Sol. I am Martha Estes, another guest of Clifton's. I trust we will be together for dinner tonight?"

Always appreciative of a good-looking woman, Smoke spoke his regrets with sincerity. "I doubt that such a pleasure will be possible. We must meet with Mr. Satterlee and then attend to other urgent matters.

Now *here* was a man who could make her knees weak. Martha breathed deeply, expanding her firm, medium-sized bosom, and gave him a melting smile. "What a pity. I—ah—don't believe I caught your name?"

"It's Jensen, Miss Martha. Smoke Jensen."

Martha raised an ivory Spanish fan to her lips and spread it in an agitated motion. "Oh, my. A regular celebrity where I come from. An honor, Mr. Jensen."

"Thank you. Now, if you will excuse us?"

No such warm welcome awaited Smoke Jensen and Santan Tossa when they entered the presence of Clifton Satterlee. The master of the house turned from his affected pose of gazing out the tall windows of his library and spoke with a petulant, condescending tone. "Don't you find it a bit presumptuous to be calling on me like this?"

Although not entirely certain of the meaning of the word, Smoke considered "presumptuous" to be insulting. So he accepted that the best defense would be a good offense. "Not at all. But I do consider it presumptuous of you to have sent men to follow us and attempt to kill us. Likewise to put up roadblocks to cut off all commerce and other traffic into or out of the town of Taos. And I am sure my friend here, a tribal policeman from the Taos Pueblo, sees it as presumptuous of you to inveigle someone among his people to steal certain religious articles from their kiva."

Clifton Satterlee affected a hurt expression, colored somewhat by indignation, and undertook to talk down to them like foolish boys who had been caught in some schoolyard prank. "Oh, come now. That's all quite preposterous. You can't possibly believe I would deign to stoop to such brigandish endeavors? I am a man of influence and substance in the territory. What flightiness could bring you to believe that anyone in my employ might be responsible for the difficulties in and around Taos? Dismiss the thought, gentlemen."

With that, Satterlee took Tossa by one elbow and began to steer the both of them toward the door to his library. Smoke Jensen set his boots and did not move. "One minute, if you please, Mr. Satterlee. You have not heard the full extent of our complaints, let alone our opinion of your condescending, self-serving response."

Satterlee stopped, rolled his eyes heavenward and sighed heavily. "Then, I suppose I must."

"You may have influence, and this layout proves your substance," Smoke told him levelly. "But in my book, you are just a grasping, greedy, lying son of a bitch. If you continue to send your third-rate gunfighters to enforce your will and to harm the people around Taos, I will have no choice but to keep on putting them in the *campo santo. ¿Comprende?*"

With that, Smoke allowed himself and Tossa to be escorted from the presence of the great man. In the garden,

Martha Estes gave them a lighthearted wave as they passed by on their way to the outside. At the tall, double doors of the main entrance, Paddy Quinn drew closer to Smoke Jensen and spoke heatedly, though softly, through a sneer.

"You're dead meat, Jensen."

Smoke gave Quinn a bleak, thousand-mile, gunfighter stare. "I'll remember that. I trust that you will?"

Riding away from Hacienda Colina del Sol, in the direction of Santa Fe, the two lawmen who had become friends on the ride south remained silent until well away from Satterlee's lair. Then Santan Tossa spoke what was on his heart.

"You really aren't afraid of Satterlee and his gunmen, are you, Smoke?"

Smoke held a moment before replying. "As a matter of fact, I am. Any man who faces death from so many enemies and says he is not afraid is a fool or a liar. But, knowing that, you can use that healthy fear to help you decide which enemy you are going to knock down first. Say you are facing three armed men. One is good, cool under fire, and fast with a gun. Another is a common thug with a gun. The third is edgy and unsure of himself. Which one do you go against first?"

Tossa rubbed his lantern jaw, absorbed in thought. "You take the easiest one first, right?"

"You might think that, but it is absolutely necessary to get rid of the greatest threat first. So you go for the best gun. Take him out while you are fresh and unharmed. Then go after the weakest one, because he's likely to do something cowardly. Save the average feller for last."

Santan Tossa stared at his companion. "I would never have thought of that."

Smoke Jensen gave Tossa a smile that reached all the way to the crinkle lines at the corners of his eyes. "No one does, first time out."

"All right, I'll accept that. Now, I have one for you. Did you see that squash-blossom necklace that Miss Estes was wearing?"

Smoke nodded. "Yes, I did. It's the most beautiful piece of its kind I've ever seen."

"It should be. It is one of the stolen sacred objects."

"You are sure?"

"Positive, Smoke. I have worn it in ceremonies a dozen times."

Smoke gave that only a second's reflection. "I think we ought to return later tonight and have a private talk with that young woman."

Santan Tossa stared in astonishment as they entered the outskirts of the territorial capital. Tiny Taos was the largest community he had ever seen. By the time they reached the business district of Santa Fe, which extended two blocks in all four directions from the Plaza de Armas, his head swam.

"So many outsiders," he gasped, then recovered himself. "Sorry. It is how we think of those who are not of the Pueblo people. And I have come to not think of you as an outsider, Smoke."

"I'm flattered," responded Smoke drily. "We'll find a saloon and start to ask around about Satterlee."

"I cannot enter any place that sells the white man's crazy water—uh—liquor."

"That's right, you can't. What do you reckon to do?"

"There are signs in Spanish on the walls that tell of a *charrida* ring. There I will find others of my Pueblo people. I will ask questions among them about Satterlee."

"Good idea. We'll meet—ah—there." Smoke pointed to a small restaurant on a corner at right angles to the cathedral. "Say, two hours before sundown?"

Tossa nodded and rode off. Smoke turned the other way

and reined in outside an arcade formed of plastered adobe arches. From the cool shade created by the sidewalk overhang, the door of a cantina invited him. Smoke dismounted and handed Cougar's reins to a small, brown-skinned boy with big, shiny, black eyes.

"The livery stable, señor?"

"No. Take him into the Plaza *jardín* and get him watered. Then bring him back and tie him off here." He handed the boy a coin.

Eying the silver U.S. quarter dollar, the lad's face glowed. *"Gracias, señor."*

Smoke touched him on a thin shoulder. "That is to ensure he is here when I come out. You understand?"

"Comprendo, señor. Muchas gracias."

Inside the cantina, Smoke stood at the bar, beside two white cowboys, and ordered a beer. He nodded to the men and their nearly empty *tubos.* "Buy you a refill?"

The older ranch hand smiled under a well-groomed walrus mustache. "Don't mind if you do. Thank you kindly. I'm Eric, this is Rob."

"Jensen," Smoke said shortly, then observed, "You two have the look of working stockmen."

Eric found that grimly amusing. "Working ain't the half of it. You must be new in these parts not to know that graze is so sparse we've gotta keep the cattle on the move all the time or they'll starve. Weren't half this bad in Texas. Used to be I could sit all night and play poker. Now I've got so many calluses on my butt I stand up to eat."

Smoke affected to consider that a moment, then put on a sorrowful expression. "Maybe I came out here on a snipe hunt?"

"How's that?" Eric asked.

"I got let out by the last outfit I worked for. There was this posting in our local paper about someone hiring out here. All sorts of jobs, including cattle work."

"What newspaper was that?"

"The Amarillo *Star*," Smoke replied, using the name of Mac's source.

Eric nodded. "Don't want to pry, but what's the name of this man who can spend so much money to get hands?"

"Didn't give a man's name. Some outfit called C.S. Enterprises."

"Cliff Satterlee." Eric spat the name as though it had a foul taste. Then he turned fully to Smoke and gave him a long, cool study from head to boot toe. "You look to be a straight shooter. I figger you're on the right side of the law. So, if you don't mind, I'll give you some good advice. Were I you, Jensen, I'd steer as far clear of Satterlee, an' any of those around him, as I could."

Pleased with what he had heard, Smoke pressed his luck. "He's crossed horns with the law, has he?"

Eric nodded. "More'n once. Nothin' ever proved, of course. Money talks. Though it's said by more than one that Satterlee's drovers throw wide loops."

Smoke knew what that meant. In cowmen's talk, throwing a wide loop implied that a man rustled most of his stock, or at the least, claimed more than his share of unbranded cattle. "There's more?"

"Some fellers have died of a sudden," Eric confided. "Satterlee has him a so-called foreman, name o' Paddy Quinn, who's prone to be quick to use his Colts. The rest of them that rides for the brand are jist as proddy."

"What brand is that?"

Rob added his bit. "C-Bar-S. There's some say it stands for his ranch, Colina del Sol. But it's for Clifton Satterlee and his C.S. Enterprises, you can be damn sure. Leastwise, it's an easy brand to use to blot another one with a runnin' iron."

"Thank you, Eric, Rob. I'll sure keep distance between me and Satterlee." Smoke downed the last of his beer and strode to the bead-curtained doorway.

Outside, Cougar waited for him, the reins in the patient hands of the small boy. Smoke looked left and right and located another saloon only three doors down. He spoke to the boy. "You keep him here. I'm going to walk down to the Cinco de Mayo."

Surprise raised black eyebrows. "Walk? You are not a vaquero, señor—*¿es verdad?*"

"That's right, son. I guess you could call me *un ranchero, un hacendado.*"

"*¡Por Dios!* It is an honor to serve you, señor."

Smoke ruffled the lad's thatch of black hair and started off to continue his information-gathering mission.

Santan Tossa sat on the top of the low, plastered adobe wall that separated the *callejón* from the performance ring at the *charrida* plaza. Elongated, like a hippodrome or the Circus Maximus, the Mexican rodeo ground lacked the circular symmetry of a Plaza de Toros. To one side and in front of Tossa, a young vaquero from the San Vincente Pueblo leaned his back against the wall, one leg elevated, knee cocked, boot resting against the inner surface of the barrier. The youth longed to be a recognized *charro,* but knew of the prejudice harbored by the Spanish-blooded Mexicans against anyone of pure Indian origins. Tossa understood this and used it to loosen the fellow's tongue.

"You will ride in the *charrida* this Sunday?"

A glum expression darkened the wide, Indian face. "I will clean stalls, saddle horses, and maybe, just maybe, ride as a header—to set up the bulls for the *charros* to rope. It is dangerous, but it lets people see what you can do. Another year . . two years, who knows?"

Tossa tried to be encouraging. "Chosteen, you will one day wear the *sombrero grande* of a *charro.* This is part of the land of the White Father in Washington now. He will not let the Mexicans keep our people out of the *Asociacion Nacional de Charros.*"

Chosteen turned to him. "And why not? Its headquarters is in Mexico . . . the old Mexico. The white eyes' laws do not apply there."

With a shrewd expression, Tossa offered his bait. "If you worked for C.S. Enterprises, perhaps the *charros* would accept you as an Americano."

Suddenly, Chosteen's features clouded. "I would rather work for Soul Eater. At last you expect Him to be evil." His eyes quickly narrowed as he thought of something. "Do you work for Satterlee? Are you here to try to get others to sell their Spirits to that outsider demon?"

"No—no," Tossa hastened to object. "I am interested in him, only. We believe that he, or someone he used, has stolen sacred objects from our kiva."

Chosteen spat on the sand. "Then he is as evil as I have been told."

"You know something of this Satterlee, Chosteen?"

"I do." For the next twenty minutes the two Pueblos spoke earnestly and intensely about Clifton Satterlee.

When they concluded their talk, Santan Tossa made his way to an outdoor barbecue pit where a small calf, which had been crippled in the day's practice, had been dressed out and put on a spit to roast. He watched the small carcass turn for a while, his stomach rumbling, prompted by the aroma. Mostly his people ate sheep, or wild meat. Over the years as a policeman, Tossa's frequent visits to the white man's town had given him a taste for beef. He pushed temptation aside to ask among the Pueblo men about Clifton Satterlee. One lean, young man, not yet in his twenties, gave him confirmation of a suspicion of his own.

"I have heard it said that he wants the land where your pueblo stands. He would cut the trees. All of them. He would lay our Earth Mother bare and let the rains wash gullies and ravines in her breast."

"Is nothing sacred to these pale skins?" another asked.

The first to speak went on. "They care nothing for the land. There is more, always more, to be taken, laid waste and then move on to yet more. Their god is formed of those circles of gold that they treasure so much."

Yet another advised, "Do not speak ill of the white outsider, Satterlee. He is a dangerous man."

Through the afternoon, Tossa heard much the same, and more, from those he questioned. He reached the conclusion that none of them admired or trusted Clifton Satterlee, and that most feared him. He ate some of the roasted veal, wrapped in flat, cornmeal cakes, and seasoned by a thick sauce of chile peppers and garlic. Then he made his farewells and left to join Smoke Jensen.

Smoke Jensen had finished his first swallow of beer in the Cinco de Mayo cantina and had settled down to weighing up the other occupants when Ian MacGreggor pushed aside the strings of glass beads and entered the saloon. Mac ambled to the bar and elbowed a place beside Smoke. He ordered a beer and drank deeply before speaking in a low tone, his lips not moving.

"I have something important. We need to talk soon. And it's getting too hot for me here. There's nothing much for us to do and too much time for the others to ask questions."

Smoke did not look at the young undercover deputy when he replied. "Find some excuse to get away for a while. Ride out from the estancia and join us on the road to Taos. We'll be there early tomorrow."

"I can do it. And, Smoke, you're not going to believe what I found out." Lapsing into silence, Mac finished his beer, then turned away from the bar. Smoke stopped him with a hand on one shoulder.

"There's one thing you can tell me now. Which room is Miss Estes using?"

Mac frowned slightly. "She's not. Not in the main house, anyway. She has a small cabin outside the place, near the north wall. It's the one on the south end of a row of three."

"Thanks." Smoke released Mac and the young man walked out the door.

In every saloon and eating place Smoke Jensen visited, he encountered someone who had heard of either Clifton Satterlee or Paddy Quinn or both. Not until the fourth cantina he looked into did he run into the first men to have anything good to say. In fact, they took immediate exception to Smoke even asking questions. Thrown from a blind spot, when he least expected it, a fist whistled past Smoke's head.

Smoke dodged it and spun on a boot heel. A hard-knuckled right fist drove up from waist level. Off balance from the missed blow, the pig-faced brawler caught Smoke's punch full in the gut. A loud grunt exploded from his lips. Eyes bulging, he bent double in time to take Smoke's swiftly upraised knee in the nose. Bright lights flashed in his eyes, to be swiftly followed by a blanket of blackness. He keeled over and struck his bloodied chin on the tile floor. At once, two others grabbed Smoke from behind and sought to yank him around.

Smoke Jensen set his powerful legs and twisted at the waist. One of the thugs went flying. The other hung on. *This shouldn't be happening,* Smoke thought. All he had asked was, "Anyone here know a feller named Satterlee? I hear he's hiring."

The others said nothing. Instead, they started swinging. They still remained silent as another one jumped into the brawl. Smoke rolled a punch off his shoulder and popped the hardcase who held him under the chin. His eyes rolled up, he blinked and tried to kick Smoke in the crotch. Smoke turned slightly and hit him again. He gave a shudder and let go of Smoke to sprawl with his face in the urinal trough that fronted the bar in most Mexican saloons.

Right then the fight took on a far more serious tone as two of the Quinn gang went for their six-guns.

FIFTEEN

Smoke Jensen saw their moves from the corner of one eye. He filled his own hand with a .45 Peacemaker in a blur of speed. One cut-rate gunfighter had time to gasp in astonishment before a 230-grain slug smashed into his left shoulder and he went flailing into a table, which collapsed under his weight. His six-gun, only partly out of the holster, fell to the floor at his side. Already, Smoke had swung his Colt to bear on the second gunman.

That unfortunate fellow had time enough to pull his barrel clear of leather and began to level the muzzle on the midsection of Smoke Jensen. His misfortune came from that fact, which caused Smoke to put a bullet through his heart rather than shoot to wound. The gunhawk slammed back against the bar and slid to a sitting position. It had all happened so fast that only now did the bartender react with a shout to his other customers as he ducked below the bar.

"Tengan cuidado! Los pistoleros."

A third gang member unlimbered his six-gun as Smoke swung his Colt that direction. He stopped the move instantly when Smoke raised his point of aim and the man could look down the black tunnel of the barrel. A thin curl of powder smoke rose from the muzzle. Smoke remained motionless while bar patrons dived for cover and the rest of the Satterlee partisans showed open, empty hands. A tense three minutes went by in which the only sound to be heard came from the wounded hardcase. Smoke lowered his revolver only when the law arrived.

Face a fierce mask, the town marshal entered the saloon with drawn six-gun. He cut his eyes from the downed men to the bartender, and then to Smoke. "All right, who started all of this?"

No one seemed eager to reply, so Smoke Jensen holstered his Colt and stepped into the breach. "They did." He indicated the wounded gunman and the dead one. "First off, three of those fellers over at the bar took offense to something I said and threw punches at me. When I knocked a couple of them flat, those two drew on me."

A skeptical raise of eyebrow projected the lawman's mood. "And you just happened to be faster."

"That's right. I was . . . or should I say am?"

"Do you have a name to go with all that speed?"

"I do. Could we talk about it at your office, Marshal?"

"You'll get there soon enough, I'd say. What's wrong with here?"

Smoke nodded at the gang members. "There are—other ears. What I have to say is for you alone."

With a shrug, and another dubious look, the marshal turned to one of his subordinates. "Nate, take care of things here. You, mister, come with me."

The marshal marched Smoke Jensen cattycorner across the Plaza de Armas to his office. Inside, the lawman took a seat behind a scarred, water-stained desk. "If it hadn't been some of Clifton Satterlee's hirelings, you'd be answering questions from inside a cell. So, speak your piece."

Smoke dug into his vest pocket and produced his badge. "I'm glad to hear that, Marshal. My name's Smoke Jensen.

I'm a deputy U.S. marshal. At the request of a friend, I am here to look into Satterlee and his dealings."

"Who is this friend?"

"Don Diego Alvarado, of Rancho de la Gloria, outside Taos."

"It's about time," the marshal snapped. "Governor Lew Wallace will be glad to hear that Satterlee is being investigated. By the way, I know your friend, Alvarado, and m'name's Ambrose . . . Dave Ambrose."

Smoke Jensen appeared more amused than relieved. "Well, Marshal Ambrose, I'm not here to investigate Satterlee. My job is to eliminate him."

Marshal Ambrose had a sudden change of mood. He snorted with contempt. "Another hired gun hidin' behind a badge."

Smoke immediately put him straight. "Nothing of the sort. What I should have said is that Satterlee has broken several federal laws, or at least arranged for others to break some for him. I'm here to bring down his business and put him away for a good long time."

Ambrose shot Smoke a disgusted look. "What if he chooses not to cooperate? Hell, man, he owns the judges."

Smoke gave the marshal a cold, hard smile. "Then I'll just have to eliminate him."

A bloated, red-orange ball hung over the snowcapped peaks to the west. Cold air rising off the white mantle distorted it into the wavy shape of an egg. Dark, purple shadows lay across the ground. Sammy Gittings sat on a fallen tree trunk, tears sliding silently down his chubby, round cheeks. They were lost. They had wandered off the Sugarloaf and no one would ever find them. He knew it, no matter what Seth said.

Seth looked up now from the pile of dry wood he had

gathered. "Don't just sit there. Help me. We need to get a fire started."

"What good will that do?" Sammy pouted. "We don't have anything to cook."

Seth stood, grubby hands on his hips. "You come down here and build a fire and I'll get us something to eat."

"How? You can't hit anything you shoot at."

"Shut up! Jist shut up. I'll get something this time."

A squirrel chattered alarmingly as it suddenly darted away through the tree limbs above. Seth looked up. "Maybe a squirrel."

Sammy made a face. "Ugh! They look like rats when they're skinned."

"Are you hungry or not?"

Sammy paused before replying to his brother. "Not that hungry."

"Then don't eat. I'll have it all."

Lower lip protruded in a pout, Sammy challenged Seth. "Won't either. I get my share. It's only right."

Seth started to laugh at his little brother, only to have it cut off by a harsh primordial cough. His face went chalk white. "What was that?"

Right then, the wily old cougar that had been stalking them uttered another hoarse hack, flexed its powerful hind legs, and with a strident snarl, launched itself. Sammy screamed at the sight of the tawny blur and fell backward off the tree trunk. Seth let go a yowl and scampered backward. He tripped over an exposed root and landed on his round bottom. His arm stretched out as he desperately searched the ground. His fingers found the cold steel of a rifle barrel, and he closed around it in desperation. The mountain lion missed Sammy by a foot when the boy toppled away from its spring and now whirled in the small clearing under large, overgrown branches. It lunged again at the terrified, smaller lad.

In that split second, Seth brought up Bobby Jensen's little

.32-20 rifle and fired at point-blank range. By sheer chance, the slug hit the cougar in the right ear and plowed a ragged furrow through its brain. It leaped into the air and fell back dead. One needle-clawed paw twitched three inches from the soft belly of Sammy Gittings.

"You got him! You got him, Seth," Sammy shouted.

Unfortunately for the boys, the ferocious charge and odor of the puma thoroughly frightened the horses. Neighing in terror, both animals slipped their insecure ties off and ran away. Only a haze of dust and pine needles marked their course as their rumps disappeared down the trail.

Seth stared after them in consternation. Sammy came to him then, wailing between great sobs. "What—are—we gonna—do? What are we—gonna do? We'll die out here all alone."

The moon would not rise until after midnight. It provided ideal conditions for Smoke Jensen and Santan Tossa to penetrate the security around the hacienda of Clifton Satterlee. Thanks to the information he had received from Ian Mac-Greggor, Smoke could pick the right place to scale the wall and be the least exposed to any of the watchers. The cabana occupied by Martha Estes was located close to the east wall of the compound, well away from the main house. Smoke had not come prepared to scale a high wall. Particularly he had not planned for the rows of jagged-edged, broken bottles that lined the top.

With gloves in place and moccasins on his feet, Smoke Jensen balanced himself on the shoulders of Santan Tossa. Cautiously, he reached up and felt his way between the blue ranks of dragon's teeth and found purchase. Smoke flexed his knees, then launched himself. He swung one leg upward to nudge against the outer row of bottle shoulders. He held on to the inside of the wall until his balance returned, then dropped the bite end of the rope around his neck to Tossa. Levering himself upward, Smoke went over the wall and dropped to the ground below.

Quickly he secured the loop of the rope to a post and gave the line a little tug. At once, it tightened and began to vibrate. On the far side, Tossa literally walked up the adobe palisade. In brief seconds he joined the last mountain man on the ground. Smoke pointed to a low, square adobe cabin to one side. A yellow square picked out a window, and indicated that someone occupied the premises. Silently, the two men moved in that direction.

Smoke eased to the corner of the building and peered around to take in the outer courtyard. Nothing moved, and he saw no sign of sentries. He beckoned to Tossa, and they went directly to the only door. Smoke put his ear to the panel and listened for ten long seconds, then grasped the latch, threw it, and swung the portal inward.

Startled, Martha Estes looked up from the book she had been reading, her expression showing her to be a bit frightened. "Wha—what are you doing here, Mr. Jensen?"

"I've come to see you, ask a few questions, Miss Estes."

Martha took a deep breath, reaching up with her hand. "This is—rather irregular."

Smoke made a pacifying gesture. "I apologize for that, but I have learned something of importance that I want you to explain for me."

Martha gathered herself. "I—I'll try to help if I can."

"Good. What it is . . ." Smoke hesitated, then went on. "That squash-blossom necklace you were wearing this morning. Where did you get it?"

"Why, Cliff—er—Clifton gave it to me. He has some other lovely pieces in the safe in the library."

Smoke eyed her levelly. "Are you aware that those are stolen property?"

Martha started an immediate protest. "That can't be. Clifton is a respected businessman, an enterprising investor."

Santan Tossa took over then. "Miss Estes, that necklace and the other items are religious objects, stolen from my people at the Taos pueblo. They are sacred to our kiva."

Martha's face twisted in a war between disbelief and outrage. "Why, that's—that's terrible. However could Clifton have gotten ahold of them? Perhaps he purchased them, not knowing their origin?"

Smoke Jensen shook his head. "I'm afraid not, Miss Estes. Santan Tossa here is a tribal policeman, investigating the theft. All of his leads have taken him to Clifton Satterlee. For all his mighty reputation around Santa Fe, Miss Estes, Satterlee is not what he appears to be."

"But . . . my father is a business associate. Surely he cannot be involved in such nefarious schemes."

Deciding to ease her mind, at last for the moment, Smoke offered a suggestion. "To get away with what he is planning, Satterlee needs the cover of honorable, legitimate businessmen. By reflection, you see, it makes him seem the same. Your father is most likely one of those."

Martha became more agitated. "No matter how he acquired the jewelry, it is simply unforgivable that your sacred items not be returned."

She rose and crossed to a large, walnut armoire against one wall. There she kneeled and slid open a drawer. From it, she took the necklace. A look of anger had replaced her earlier confusion and shock. "Here, take this back and put it where it rightfully belongs."

A thought occurred to Smoke Jensen. "What will you tell Satterlee if he notices it is gone?"

"I'll think of something. We women have our ways." Martha smiled for the first time since they had entered the room.

Tossa accepted the silver and turquoise work of art and folded it into a strip of purple velvet. "Thank you, Miss Estes.

I will keep it secret for a while that the necklace has been recovered."

"I thank you, too," Smoke added. "Now we'll say good night. It would be prudent if you did not let anyone know we have been here."

"Of course. Good night, Mr. Jensen."

Smoke built her a smile. "Call me Smoke."

Clifton Satterlee had stayed up late also. He paced the confines of his library, hands clasped behind his back. Thick, rich velvet drapes covered the leaded glass windows so that not a hint of light escaped. A small fire crackled in the bee-hive fireplace set into one wall. These early spring nights remained chill. Seated in a large, wing chair, his long legs sprawled carelessly across the Kermint oriental rug, Paddy Quinn sipped appreciatively at the Irish whiskey his employer had thoughtfully provided for him. At last, Satterlee stopped his measured tread, poured himself an inch of cognac in a snifter, and sighed heavily as he turned back to his guest.

"Obviously the men I sent to deal with Jensen failed in their task. He knew too much when he came here to warn me. *Warn me!* What impudence."

Quinn waggled a finger at his boss. "Every rooster likes to make his cock-a-doodle-doo before he gets his head lopped off for the stewpot, he does. Ye ask me, Mr. Satterlee, this Smoke Jensen is runnin' scared. He was flexin' muscles he don't have. He's tryin' to buy hisself some time."

Satterlee sipped the liquor and breathed out its aroma. "Somehow I don't quite believe that. There's more to the man than we saw in this room today. Are you familiar with his reputation?"

Quinn dismissed that with a curt gesture. "Reputations amongst the gunfighting brotherhood are gen'rally tall tales blown out of all proportions, they are."

"Even your own?"

For a long moment Quinn studied Satterlee until he decided the remark had been made in jest. He responded then with joviality. "Far be it from me to disabuse anyone of my ferocious nature."

Satterlee smiled tightly. "The same applies to Smoke Jensen. He is dangerous. I want you to send more men, enough this time to get the job done."

"An' what is it ye have in mind?"

"I want them to follow and finish off that inquisitive Smoke Jensen and the savage he had with him this morning. Then they are to continue on to Taos and join in the blockade Garth Thompson is conducting."

Quinn looked uncomfortable with the news he had to impart. "It might be more of a task than you think. Some of the boys had a brush with Smoke Jensen in town this afternoon. They came out the losers. Two dead."

"Damn that man. Neither you nor I can afford his arrogance. Too much of it will make us look bad. Perhaps I will have to take care of this personally."

Sheriff Hank Banner thoroughly enjoyed getting together with Doc Walters and several of the Taos businessmen once a week for a few hands of poker. This particular night had been especially satisfying, considering the step-up in pressure from the Quinn gang. To top it off, Banner had played only with other men's money after the third hand. Matter of fact, he had come away from the table about twenty dollars to the good. Not bad for a dime-ante, quarter-limit game. His boot heels echoed hollowly on the red tile sidewalk as he turned the corner and started to cross the Plaza de Armas to his office. Two men suddenly stepped out of the well-tended shrubs to block his path.

One of them worked his mouth in a nasty sneer under a poorly kept mustache. "Goin' somewhere, Lawman?"

"If it's any of your business, I'm headed back to my office."

"Unh-uh. Oh, no."

"Nope, you ain't," the second man added.

So far, neither man had done anything serious enough to justify drawing a weapon, but Sheriff Banner sensed the very real menace they exuded. His hand twitched to close on the butt of his Colt. Right then, two more hardcases stepped onto the crushed rock path behind the sheriff.

"No, you're not goin' to your office," the first one said again. "We're gonna go have us a nice little talk."

He recognized them then. The one doing the talking was named Islip; the one with him they called Funk. Drawing a deep breath, Banner mustered his nerve. "Were I you, I'd go have a nice talk with a bed, Islip. You're drunk. If you don't want to face a charge of disorderly conduct, clear out of my way and let me pass."

Grinning like an imbecile, Funk, the second gunhand, shook his head and tapped a forefinger on the center of the badge worn by Hank Banner. "Can't do that. We got our orders. You an' us is gonna have that talk, an' we're gonna reach an understanding."

At once, the two thugs at his back grabbed the sheriff and pinned his arms to his sides. With a smooth move, they lifted him off his feet and carried him toward the mouth of a dark alley that led off of the plaza on the north side. Once within its shadowy confines, they put Banner's boots on the ground and kept hold while the first pair caught up. Without preamble, Islip and Funk began to take turns, driving hard fists into the chest and stomach of Sheriff Banner.

After a little preliminary softening up, Abner Islip started speaking in a low, insistent tone. "You're gonna forget all about what's happenin' in Taos. No more backin' those who get crosswise of Mr. Satterlee. In fact, you're gonna take a nice little vacation. Go off and visit relatives somewhere, why not? Or go fishin'. I hear they've got some bodacious critters down in the Gulf of Mexico. A feller ought to try for 'em onest in his life, don't you think? Maybe you can take up lawin' in Georgia or Mississippi.

"Any way you want it, Sheriff, yer gonna shake the dust of Taos offen yer boots and clear the hell an' gone outta here by tomorrow morning."

Through the haze of pain, Sheriff Banner maintained his defiance. "You'll be in hell long before I do that, you and Funk, too."

Funk shoved his sweaty face in close to that of the lawman. "In that case, we've got other orders. We ain't to leave enough of you to do any fightin'."

With that, all four began to pound on the sheriff. Islip, his hands growing sore, switched to the use of his pistol barrel. He viciously pistol-whipped Banner until he drove the sheriff to the ground. Then all four formed a circle and began to kick him. Mercifully, blackness swarmed over Hank Banner, and he did not feel the last dozen gouges to his ribs, belly, and back.

Bare soles made hardly a sound as Wally Dower scampered along outside the closed and unlighted business fronts on the north side of the Plaza de Armas. In another five minutes he would have completed his final rounds. Only the cantinas remained open. He still had to go back and escort old Laro Hurtado to his house. He would be drunk of course. If he had any money at all, or could cadge drinks from some of the vaqueros, he would be falling down, piss-his-pants drunk. Oh, well, his wife always gave Wally a big, silver Mexican dollar for his mission of mercy. It was only worth about a dime American, but it felt nice in his pocket. When he neared the alley entrance, he heard the soft thuds and grunts that forewarned him that someone was in a fight. Wisely, Wally held back.

After what seemed forever to the boy, the noises ended, and Wally heard the thump of boot heels fading in the distance, toward the opposite end of the alley. He edged closer and risked a quick peek down the alley. Nothing. No, that wasn't right. He saw a darker lump in the blackness of the passageway. Wally watched for a long while, then hazarded to step into the opening. Five paces down the path, he came upon the huddled form of a body. Wally bent and rolled the man by his shoulder.

At once his eyes went wide. It was Sheriff Banner. A low groan escaped from bloodied lips. Wally did not need prompting to know what to do. He came upright and sprinted from the alley, then settled into a dead run toward the office of Doctor Walters.

SIXTEEN

Their wounded captives in tow, neither the better for wear and tear, Smoke Jensen and Santan Tossa cantered along the wide, well-defined road between Santa Fe and Taos. The sun, slightly over the meridian, warmed their backs and chewed away at the last of a low ground fog that had given dawn a hazy, closed-in quality. They would reach Española by mid-afternoon. With the prisoners off their hands, they could make even better time. Smoke wanted to meet soon with Sheriff Banner and Diego Alvarado. The encounter with Clifton Satterlee had awakened several questions. He felt certain the lawman and the rancher could provide answers. Always conscious of his back trail, Smoke cast another glance in that direction as they crested a low swell.

Immediately, he saw dust where none had been before. His eyes narrowed in concentration. It could be two, three, or even more riders. No doubt men sent by Satterlee or Quinn to carry out the threats of yesterday. Smoke turned back and made a gesture to Tossa.

"Behind us. We have company."

Santan Tossa's thoughts traveled the same trail. "You think they are men sent by Satterlee?"

"It wouldn't surprise me." Smoke thought a moment, eyes

searching the surrounding terrain. "See that bend up there? I think we should wait for our friends around there, out of sight."

Tossa flashed a wide, white smile. "Who surprises who— er—whom?"

Smoke nodded and laughed. *A very bright young man, this Santan Tossa,* he thought. *He's improving his English by simple exposure.* "It's the best way to be in an ambush . . . be the ambushers."

The dust plumes had grown noticeably closer by the time Smoke and Santan rounded the curve in the road. Shielded by the swell of a sandy mound, they reined in and walked their mounts off the road to either side. In moments, the faint thud of hooves could be heard. Smoke slid his .45 Peacemaker from the right-hand holster. Santan readied his stout bow, a triangular, obsidian point bright in the midday sun. Closer now, the hoofbeats became a regular drumroll.

When the heads of the horses came into sight, the gunfighter and the Indian policeman made ready to fire. Immediately, Smoke Jensen checked himself. "Hold it!" he barked to Santan Tossa.

Much to his surprise, Smoke had recognized the pretty face of Martha Estes over his gunsights. His command had the effect of halting her as well. She blinked in astonishment at sight of the drawn weapons. Beside her rode her maid, a young Zuni woman, whose carriage indicated that she would be capable of taking care of the both of them. On her other side rode Ian MacGreggor.

Hand to her mouth, Martha reacted explosively. "Oh, I . . . you startled me, Mr. Jensen. This nice young man thought it might be you. We were trying to catch up."

"You caught us, all right. Well, Mac, what do you have to say for yourself?"

"I was riding out to meet you like we arranged. She came

to the barn while I was saddling. Said she wanted to go with me. That's what delayed me."

Smoke gave Mac a sidelong squint "All night?"

"I couldn't get away last night. Ten of the gang rode out on Quinn's orders. From what I overheard, they were to find you and kill you. The watch was doubled all around the hacienda. As it was, she—the lady helped me leave this morning."

"Yes," Martha verified. "I told the men at the gate that he was accompanying me on my morning ride."

Smoke nodded to the maid. "What about her?"

"Lupe always comes with me, unless I'm riding with Clifton."

"Humm. You're here now, you might as well ride along."

Martha put a bite in her words. "You're too, too kind."

Smoke removed his hat in a sweeping gesture and bowed low. "My pleasure entirely, madam." Then to Mac, "Let's you and me ride up ahead and you can tell me this news you have."

Martha leaned forward in the saddle to press her case. "Let me make something clear, Mr. Jensen. I gave a lot of thought to what the two of you told me, and I've decided to leave Clifton Satterlee. There isn't any way he could have obtained that jewelry lawfully, is there?"

"Not that I can see."

"I only wish I could have taken the rest."

Smoke smiled fleetingly. "We know where it is. We can come for it later. And . . . you are a welcome sight."

"Thank you. And I mean it, this time."

Smoke and Mac trotted on ahead while Tossa escorted the women. Mac's jaunty expression changed as the distance between the parties widened. "Smoke, Quinn is bringing all of the gang north to Taos. Mr. Satterlee has ordered him to blockade the town until the people give in and turn over everything to him. Quinn will leave later today, and Satterlee will come along after. Wants to be there to gloat, I suppose."

A frown creased Jensen's high forehead. "That don't

sound good. Any talk of burning down buildings, killing people?"

"No. From what some of the gang said, I believe that Satterlee wants it to look all legal and proper. At least on paper. There were a lot of really important people at a party I was sent there to bodyguard for. Everyone but the governor, and he did send a representative. When things started calming down, they all went inside for a meeting. They seemed mighty pleased to be in Satterlee's company. I got the feeling, when I heard about the siege at Taos, that if Satterlee had the papers all signed and in order, his friends in government would not ask any questions about how he went about getting folks to turn over their land and businesses."

Smoke nodded, well pleased. "You've got a good head on you, Mac. You'll not be able to go back now, of course. Just sort of stay out of sight when we reach Taos."

"Hey, I'm not worried. I can outshoot near all of them. And, you'll need all the guns you can get on your side."

With a curt nod, Smoke sought to delay the inevitable. "We'll talk about it later."

Leaned back against rocks that reflected the heat of a hat-sized fire, Smoke Jensen listened while Martha Estes talked about her father. He was partners with Clifton Satterlee in a large firm that built houses back in the crowded East. Satterlee became involved because he had, or was going to get, large sources of timber. The lumber that came from the trees would be used to build houses. Some of them would be tenements, three or four stories, half a block deep, with limestone fronts.

Smoke didn't think there would be much of a demand for such expensive structures and said so. Martha informed him to the contrary. "Boats loaded with immigrants arrive at least three days of every week. Wealthy men will buy the tenements and rent apartments in them to the newcomers. With three or four to a floor, the profit will be enormous. The buyers won't mind paying twenty or thirty thousand for the buildings. Clifton—Mr. Satterlee and my father will keep ownership of the land and receive a percentage for the use of it."

Considering that, Smoke scratched at an earlobe. When he spoke, his voice reflected the mystery. "Something seems out of kilter about that, but I can't put my finger on it. It's sort of like having one's cake and eatin' it, too."

Martha's eyes shined. "Exactly. Any time Cliff—er—C.S. Enterprises wants to raise the percentage, they can. After all, the owners can't move their buildings off the ground." The image gave her a new thought. "That does sound a little crooked—no—unethical, doesn't it?"

"I liked your first choice of words. That's what bothered me before. Those rabbit hutches could be held up for ransom. And, from what I've gathered about Clifton Satterlee, he'd be likely to do it."

Martha gave him a puzzled look. "Is he really as awful as you make him sound?"

"Worse, no doubt, Miss Martha. I've just learned that he plans to force everyone out of Taos and take over the whole town for himself. That don't sound like someone who would refuse to squeeze the suckers who bought those houses."

"But, my father . . ." Martha started to protest when a muzzle flash bloomed brightly and a shot crashed out of the darkness.

Orin Lassiter smirked, unseen in the darkness. They'd had some difficulty finding the camp. The small fire, shielded all around by large boulders, gave off little light. He and the others had ridden through Española without finding the men they sought. Lassiter did learn that Jensen and the Indian had come through town about three in the afternoon. They now had three people with them. Two women and another man. One woman appeared to be that sweet thing the big boss was sporting with. How could that be? he asked himself.

Then he put that behind him when he remembered that two of the gang now languished in the jail at Española. He had immediately tried to see them. The sheriff had refused. Angry, he had stomped from the office to be given the only good news for the day. One of his men had informed him that they were only two hours behind their quarry. They had set out at once. Even so, it had taken them until two hours after full darkness to locate this place. The time of month favored them, Orin noted as he moved closer to the camp. The moon would not rise for at least four more hours. Conscious of the men to either side of him, he motioned them to greater silence when reflected firelight made their faces visible.

Then they were in position. Orin Lassiter raised his six-gun and fired at the figure of a man seated beside a woman at the base of a large, volcanic boulder. Dark, red-brown rock turned to powder six inches above the head of the man when the slug struck stone. Orin Lassiter watched as Smoke Jensen dived forward and took the woman with him. What he did not see, because it went too fast, was the big .45 Colt clear leather on the man's hip and snap in his direction.

He saw the muzzle bloom a split second before intense pain exploded in his left biceps as the bullet shattered his humerus. Dimly he was aware of the other boys opening up. The shock of his injury slowly numbed, and he remembered to move before another slug could find him. To his right, Baxter Young screamed horribly and clutched at a feathered shaft that protruded from his belly. Distantly, Orin heard the shouts as five of his men rushed the far side of the camp.

"Stay down," the man Orin Lassiter now believed to be Smoke Jensen shouted to the woman. A fraction of a second later, Jensen sprinted away from his exposed position by the fire.

Biting back his agony, Orin fired again.

"Stay down," Smoke Jensen commanded as he gave Martha Estes a shove on one shoulder. Before she could reply, he came to his boots and sprinted into the shadows away from the fire.

A revolver blasted from a few feet away, and suddenly another man loomed over her. Martha Estes looked up and stiffened when she recognized Orin Lassiter. He reached down to her. "Come on, you're going with me," he growled.

"No! Leave me alone."

Shock and pain ran through Martha as Lassiter slapped her with a solid, open palm. Her skin burned and tingled, and she could not prevent the sudden flow of tears that washed down her cheeks. Lassiter growled at her again. "Dry that up and do as I say."

Defeated, Martha raised a hand to be assisted upright. Automatically, Lassiter extended his left arm and immediately groaned at the new rush of agony. He spoke through gritted teeth as he holstered his six-gun. "Take my right arm."

She complied and hoisted herself to her high, black, narrow boots. At once, she heard the rustle of a full skirt that came from the darkness to her right. Lupe rushed at Lassiter with a knobby chunk of mesquite root held above her head with both hands. Hampered by Martha clinging to him, Lassiter could not completely dodge the blow. The hunk of wood slammed into his left shoulder, and he could not prevent the howl of agony that burst from his lips. Still aching, he pulled his good arm free of Martha's grasp and dropped the Indian woman with a hard right to the jaw.

Martha noticed the bloodstained shirtsleeve then, which

evened the score somewhat for the slap. "He shot you—good."

Mustering his waning resources, Lassiter snarled at her. "Shut up, bitch."

Her courage nearly fully recovered, Martha risked a further taunt. "Or you'll what? Kill me? Clifton wouldn't like that."

Her barb found its mark, and Lassiter only grumbled under his breath as he dragged Martha off into the night. He found another of his henchmen and jerked his head in the direction of the camp. "Go get that Injun woman and bring her along."

A flurry of gunshots alerted him to the fierce resistance his other men had met, and Lassiter let go a shrill whistle. The signal was picked up by someone nearer the conflict and repeated. A third man echoed the call. Heeding the signal, the outlaws broke off their fight and faded into the darkness. Lassiter led the way to the horses and saw to securing Martha and Lupe on dead men's mounts. Then they rode off into the darkness.

Ian MacGreggor counted the muzzle flashes and made note of their positions. Then he raised his .44 Marlin and pumped a round toward the black smear to the right of one red-orange blossom. The burning gasses ceased. To his left he heard the twang of a bow string, followed by the hideous shriek of the target. An outlaw staggered into the firelight, his hands clawing at the wooden shaft of an arrow that had sunk deep into his upper right chest. The Tua bow sang again, and he went down with a shaft through his heart.

Three men tried to rush at that point, overconfident that no bowman could launch arrows quickly enough to hit them all. How quickly they forgot about him, Mac thought as he took aim and began to fire as rapidly as he could cycle the Marlin and take aim. Smoke Jensen's .45 Colt opened up from Mac's right, and another hardcase left the earth. Then Mac heard a piercing whistle, repeated twice more close at hand, and the enemy fire ceased. Mac fired once more and then listened to the fading sound of boots thudding in retreat. It was all over. At least for now.

Yellow fingers of light reached through the second-floor window of the infirmary maintained by Dr. Adam Walters. They brushed invisibly on the eyelids of Sheriff Hank Banner. The lawman blinked and then abruptly opened his eyes. For the first moments everything registered as a blurred mass. Gradually individual objects came into focus. His head ached abominably. After three minutes of silent effort, he discovered that he could not see clearly out of his left eye. Only impressions of light and dark, all of it fuzzy. At last, he tried to move his arms.

A loud groan, brought on by that effort, summoned Dr. Walters from his office and treatment room. "What do we have here?" he asked with forced joviality.

His old friend and poker adversary looked like hell. His left eye was swollen nearly closed by a huge purple-yellow-green mouse. His left arm was immobile in a splint, in hopes the fracture would mend properly. Another device, created out of necessity by the good doctor, tried to give some semblance of the original shape to a broken—no, mashed would be more apt—nose. It consisted of rolls of cotton batting shoved into the nostrils, with court plaster holding in place two pieces of broken-off tongue depressor. A white sea of bandage held broken ribs immobile. Both lips were split, made three times normal size by puffiness. Without consciously thinking about it, Dr. Walters spoke his thoughts bluntly.

"You look like hell, Hank. How many of them were there?"

"Four I'm certain of. Maybe five."

"And I oughta get a look at them, eh?"

Banner tried a grimace and flinched at the result. "Horse manure. Adam, they done tom turkey tromped the crap out of me."

Dr. Walters winced and spoke ruefully. "No kidding. I had to get you out of your trousers to treat your injuries, so I know for a fact." A loud groan came from his patient. "Did I embarrass you? If so, I'm sorry."

"No, Doc, it's just your winning bedside manner. What brought that sorrowful noise on was that I just added up the score. It left me with one tail-biting question. What in hell's gonna happen to Taos with me bunged up like this? And, worse, with Smoke Jensen off sniffing around Clifton Satterlee? Those hardcases are going to be back, you can count on it, and who's to stop them from shuttin' down this town right permanent?"

From the bed opposite him came the voice of Pedro Alvarado. Pedro had come in to have the stitches and drain tube removed from his belly wound and stay for overnight observation. "My father will send as many vaqueros as you need."

"That's mighty kind of you, son. But the way I see it, they got us all outnumbered at least three to one."

"You just lie back and rest, Hank. I'll have my girl"—he referred to Dorothy Frye, his sometimes nurse and record keeper, as *my girl*—"bring you some broth. Though with the shape your mouth is in, I reckon you'll have to take it through a pipette."

"You're so full of encouragement and good news, Adam."

"Thank you," Dr. Walters said with more humor than he felt. Pedro might be encouraging, but for the life of him, the doctor did not have an answer.

Kyle Curtis, one of the Sugarloaf hands, reined in and raised up on his stirrups. He waved a gloved hand to draw attention from the searchers close at hand. "They're over this way. I can see 'em down in a draw about two hundred yards below me."

At once, the rider closest to Kyle drew his six-gun and fired three fast rounds into the air to summon the remainder of the search party. Faintly he heard cries of alarm when the last shot echoed away among the mountain peaks. Fully a dozen ranch hands, drawn by the sound, closed in on the shooter. Kyle Curtis then pointed the way to the missing Gittings boys.

When the youngsters saw them coming, they were overjoyed. Then a terrible thought struck Seth. They had taken horses without permission, and then lost them when the cougar attacked. No doubt they would be in for it now. And a worse paddling it would be than one that came from their mother. The idea of having their britches yanked down in front of all those men humiliated and shamed Seth beyond anything so far in his young life. Then a black lance of pure, boyish hatred thrust through him.

He was there with them. Bobby Jensen. How he'd sneer and make life miserable for them from now on. He swallowed back his outrage and looked up at Ike Mitchell, who led the search party.

"How—how did you find us?"

"Easy," Ike informed him as he bent forward and down from the height of his sixteen-hand Palouse horse. "We just backtracked those horses that got away from you."

Seth's eyes widened when he recalled how they had lost their mounts. "It was a mountain lion. He come at us and scared off the horses."

Ike narrowed his eyes and rubbed at his chin. "Somehow I doubt that. If he had much interest in comin' at you, you would be in his belly 'fore now."

"Nope." Pride swelled Seth's shallow chest. "I shot him dead. One bullet, right in his ear."

Bobby Jensen chose that moment to erupt. "You're a liar as well as a thief, Seth."

Seth shot out his lower lip in a pout. "I didn' lie, an' I'm not a thief."

"You took my rifle and those Morgans without permission. That's stealin'. Horse thievin' is still a hanging offense out here in the high lonesome. An' I brought along a good rope."

Real terror gripped both boys. His legs trembling, Seth dropped to his knees. Sammy flopped on his belly and bawled like a colicky baby. Seth turned to Ike Mitchell and beseeched him. "You can't do that. We're jist little kids. They don't hang children."

Bobby Jensen stung him with harsh words. "Like hell they don't. They tie a big sack of sand around your ankles so's to get the job done proper-like."

Ike had the last word. "Before we go back I want you two to show me this cougar. If it's like you say, I might put in a good word for you."

Face alabaster, the grime overlaying it became more pronounced as fat, salty tears began to stream down the face of Seth Gittings. Both brats had been thoroughly cowed by this revelation. All sign of rebellion was instantly banished. Heads hanging, they submitted without protest to riding behind two ranch hands, it being deemed that they did not deserve mounts of their own. Sammy cried and sniveled all the way back to the Sugarloaf. His butt made even more painful by the lack of support from stirrups, Seth regained some of his spitefulness.

He lost that quickly enough when the small party reined in outside the main house. Instead of rushing to them, wretched with worry over their disappearance, their mother remained in place on the porch, her face rigid with anger and affront. Slowly she raised an arm and commanded them.

"Come up here this instant."

Ike Mitchell dismounted and handed down the boys, one

at a time. With dragging feet, they approached the steps to the porch. Mary-Beth Gittings gazed beyond them and met the eyes of Ike Mitchell. "We know that they took horses without permission, and that Seth, for some insane reason, took a rifle belonging to Sally's son. What else have they done?"

"They left the ranch, ma'am. By a good twelve miles. What I reckon is that they was fixin' to run away for good an' all. Now, about that rifle, ma'am. If they didn't have it along, they would have been cougar meat long before now. Before we started back here, I had them take me to where the cougar jumped them. He was there, all right. Dead with one shot to the brain. Seth, here, saved his brother's life and his own."

Sally's face remained fixed in stern disapproval. "But that does not excuse the terrible things they have done."

By then, Seth had preceded his little brother up to the second step. He gulped involuntarily when he looked up at her rigid features. His mother darted out one hand and closed her fingers tightly around his upper arm, so tightly he squealed from the pain it caused. Then she yanked him off his feet and stood him on the porch. She reached with the other hand for the willow switch Sally Jensen held, pulled down his pants, and bent him over.

Seth got twenty-five lashes this time, and every one of them hurt more than he could stand. He was bawling by the fourth one, hoping to wring his mother's heart. He did not, and his humiliation grew greater when he heard some of the hands snigger.

SEVENTEEN

Wally Gower took the reins of the horse ridden by Smoke Jensen. The moment the tall, rangy man stepped down from the saddle on Cougar, the boy piped up with the news he had been bursting to convey. "Did you hear that the sheriff got beaten up the other night?"

Smoke gazed down at the boy. "No, Wally—Wally is it?" The lad nodded and Smoke went on. "Tell me about it, Wally."

Wally went on to describe what he had seen of the attack, mainly the results. He concluded with an unhappy expression. "I didn't see any of them, so I can't say who it was. But Doc Walters and the sheriff say it was some of the Quinn gang."

"Where is the sheriff now?"

"Over at Doc's, Mr. Jensen."

"Then I suppose the thing to do is pay him a visit."

Wally trailed along, hopeful of being allowed inside. At the foot of the stairs, Smoke turned to him. "You'd best wait here, Wally. If the sheriff has any message for you, I'll bring it to you."

Disappointment clouded Wally's face. "Awh, I wanted to talk to him."

"Maybe later."

Up in the office, Dr. Walters took Smoke in to Sheriff Banner. The man looked terrible, Smoke noted at once. "You look like you've been run down by a buffalo stampede," Smoke advised the lawman.

Banner made a sour face as best he could. "I feel like it, too."

"Tell me what happened?"

"First off, that stray, Wally Gower, saved my life right enough. I sure want to see him and thank him in person."

Smoke grinned. "He's downstairs, waitin' on word on your condition."

Hank Banner actually managed a smile. "Bring him up, bring him up. That boy's got him a double eagle waitin' for what he did. He come here right away and brought Doc to me. Hell, we'd jist finished playin' poker half an hour before. Next thing I know, I'm wakin' up in this bed, hurtin' like damn all. But I know who did it. Recognized two of em." Then he went on to identify the men and describe the beating he took before he lost consciousness.

Smoke Jensen listened with growing anger while the sheriff outlined the boot stomp he had received. When the lawman finished, Smoke spoke softly. "I'll go get Wally now. I don't think he needed to hear what you just told me."

Wally nearly wept when he saw the condition of the sheriff. But he was manly in fighting back the huge tears that welled in his gray-green eyes. "I'm sorry this happened to you, Sheriff. You're—you're the best man I know. *Please* get well."

"C'm'ere, Wally."

Obediently, Wally scuffed bare, callused soles across the wooden floor as he approached the bed. Hank Banner reached with his good hand and took a hinge-clasp leather purse from the table. He snapped it open and dug inside with thumb and forefinger. He withdrew a twenty-dollar gold piece.

"Here. This is yours. It's for saving my life."

Eyes huge with awe, the eleven-year-old gulped as he stammered out, "Twen—twenty dollars? I can't—can't take that much."

"You've got to, Wally. It's a reward. That's right, ain't it, Smoke? No one can refuse a reward."

Smoke reached out and tousled the lad's sandy brown hair. "That's right, Wally. Buy your mother a new dress with some of it, if you want."

"Really? I can do that? Oh, boy!"

Doc Walters cleared his throat. "Time's up, Wally. You'd best scoot on and do something like that. You're gettin' Sheriff Banner all exercised."

"Thank you, Sheriff. Thank you, thank you." With that, Wally scampered from the room and thundered down the outside staircase.

"Now, I have some news for you, Sheriff," Smoke Jensen announced.

"Give it."

"Don't tax him too much," warned the doctor.

Quickly Smoke related what he had learned from Mac and told the peace officer that he had proof Satterlee had the stolen Tua religious paraphernalia. Finally he added the abduction of Martha Estes. The sheriff digested it a moment, then spoke brusquely. "That does it, then. Smoke; considerin' the shape I'm in, I want you to become undersheriff. Take over for me. And, you can have a free hand dealing with Satterlee."

Smoke hesitated only a second. "I'll agree to it, Sheriff. Provided I can make Santan Tossa a deputy."

Distress displaced the pain etched on the lawman's face. "But, he's an Injun. Oh, I know, they've been peaceable for more'n a hundred years, and the Pueblos are civilized and organized. But . . . he'd have to carry a gun."

"Have any of your deputies been effective against Quinn

so far? Tossa has killed at least five of them, and with a bow and arrow."

Banner frowned. "You've got a point. If the governor gets wind of this, he'll have a fit. Armin' an Injun is serious business. There's some places it's still against the law to provide a firearm to any Injun."

"But not here, I gather?"

Banner nodded. "That's right. Okay, go ahead and fit him out from the rack in my office. Then I'll swear the both of you in."

"Not today you won't," Doc Walters interjected.

Banner scowled. "C'mon, Doc. I'm feelin' fitter every hour. If this town is gonna get besieged, we've gotta move fast."

Smoke agreed with that. "Just so. First thing, I'm going to send to Diego Alvarado for all the gunhands he can spare. Then, can you give me names of men in town who are loyal to the local government and willing to fight?" At the sheriff's nod, Smoke went on. "I think it would be a good idea for Tossa to try to recruit some help from among his tribal police."

Banner's good eye widened. "You really like to flirt with wrath from above, don't you, Smoke? All right, Smoke. You're undersheriff, so it's your ball game, as that feller Abner Doubleday would say. Now, you can start by askin' Ezekial Crowder, Marshal Gates, Warren Engals . . ." He went on to name two dozen more.

Sighing heavily, Sheriff Banner lay back on the bed as Smoke Jensen left the room. Within seconds he lapsed into a deep, though troubled, sleep. Even with help from the Tuas and Diego Alvarado, he knew Smoke faced a terrible dilemma.

A small drum tapped a staccato rhythm, and smoke rose from the square opening in the roof of the Tua kiva. Santan

Tossa handed the reins of his pony to his younger brother, who looked up at the tribal policeman with an expression of hero worship. He climbed the single-rail ladder and washed his hands and face before taking the descending steps to the floor of the religious center. He saw immediately that a dozen young men had gathered, seated on the circular, shelflike ledges that ringed the domed, circular structure. At the altar, sweet grass, pine needles and sage gave off their pleasant aroma as they smoldered on a small bed of coals.

Using an eagle-wing fan, the gray-haired shaman wafted the thin, gray tendrils of pungent smoke over the empty altar. Silently, Santan Tossa approached and kneeled before the medicine man. From his sash he produced the folds of velvet cloth and opened them.

"Grandfather, I have recovered one part of our stolen sacred heritage." Quickly he revealed the necklace.

For the first time since the theft, Whispering Leaves smiled. "You have done well, my son. Have you any idea where the . . ." Hope flared a moment in the old man's eyes. "The others might be?"

Torn nodded. "Yes. It is known to me."

"If he knows that, it is he who stole them," came the grating voice of Dohatsa from behind and to one side of Tossa.

Tossa whirled as he bounded to his moccasins. The muscles of his neck and arms corded. "You should guard your tongue, traitor."

Aware from childhood, as with all of them, that this was no place for anger or violence, Dohatsa did not respond to the challenge, merely shrugged and turned away. Inwardly, a striking sensation gripped his heart. Exactly how much did Santan know? He relaxed some as the soft words of the shaman came to his ears.

"This is not the place for hot hearts, Santan," he gently chided the younger man.

Santan Tossa lowered his eyes and nodded. "That is a true thing. I have come for another reason also." He turned to take in his fellow Tuas. "You all know of the gang of white outsiders who have tried to take our land. They work for a man named Satterlee. While I recovered the necklace from the house of Satterlee, I learned that the white gang is going to ring Taos, like the Spanish did our Pueblo in the first days of their coming. The gringos call it a siege. The purpose is to prevent anyone from entering or leaving, and to starve the people inside into surrender. The star man, the sheriff, has asked us for help. I am made a dep—u—ty of the star man. I want any who will join me to gather outside the kiva with their ponies. We must ride swiftly back to Taos."

His precarious situation forgotten in a flush of anger over this outrageous suggestion, Dohatsa snarled his challenge and contempt. "You are a fool, Santan Tossa. The white outsiders are using you. You will get no thanks from those people. And it is shameful that you ask we give any help to them."

"In other circumstances I would agree with you, Dohatsa. But this is different. These outlaw whites will only come here next. They want all the land, and they can take it if we do not fight."

Goaded by this, Dohatsa lost his composure and his reason. "You lie! Satterlee and his first warrior, Quinn, are our friends. I have spoken with them. To stop you, I will fight you."

Automatically, Santan Tossa's hand went to the unfamiliar butt of the six-gun at his hip. "Will you now? That is interesting. But, as Whispering Leaves says, this is no place for anger, or fighting. If I must fight you, I will. Wait for me outside this sacred place." He turned to the others. "Now, who will join me?"

Several among the young men of the pueblo made as though to come over, among them three of his tribal policemen. They hesitated, though, at a scowl from Dohatsa, who had begun to climb the ladder to the outside. Santan Tossa turned back to the shaman.

"Be patient, and hopeful, Grandfather. I will soon bring the rest of the sacred objects. With enough men, the white outsiders can be defeated, and I can go with my friends to get the holy dolls and the masks."

"Yes, Santan Tossa, but which outsiders are the real enemy?"

Tossa paused at the foot of the ladder. "Why, the gang led by the one called Quinn, of course."

With a mocking smile almost identical to the one worn by Dohatsa, Whispering Leaves nodded once. Santan Tossa continued out of the kiva. In a steady line behind him, the other young men followed. Tossa found Dohatsa waiting for him on the ground below.

"I will kill you if I have to," Dohatsa stated flatly.

"It is forbidden, you know that."

Dohatsa shrugged. "It does not matter. Take off that white man's weapon."

"Naturally."

While the other occupants of the kiva formed a loose circle around them, more men and a number of small boys of the pueblo gathered to watch. Santan Tossa untied the pegging string of his holster and slipped the buckle. He let the six-gun drop as he instantly launched himself at Dohatsa. The renegade had expected that and easily sidestepped Tossa. Dohatsa drove an elbow into the small of Tossa's back, smashing him to the ground, his strength robbed by the burst of pain in his kidneys. Some among the onlookers cheered. At once, Dohatsa whirled and kicked Tossa in the stomach. Renewed agony exploded in the tender parts of Tossa's body. He gasped for air and fought to get purchase.

Failing that, he scooped up a handful of dirt and hurled it in the face of Dohatsa.

"There is no honor in that," shouted two of Dohatsa's partisans.

Fire erupted behind the eyelids of the traitor, and he clawed at his face. Tossa fought back the debilitating effects of the blows he had absorbed and came unsteadily upright. He took two shaky steps forward and engulfed Dohatsa in a bear hug. Flexing his knees, Tossa tried to throw his opponent.

Heavier by far, Dohatsa did not move at first. Then, slowly, his moccasins rose into the air. Tossa swiveled his hips and threw his enemy to the ground. Dohatsa did not land flat. He hit his head first and his shoulders next as Tossa landed on top of him. Now Tossa dimly heard men cheering him. A spectacular nighttime shower of stars filled Dohatsa's head. He fought to suck air into his restricted lungs. When his chest moved, he dimly heard the brittle snap of three ribs. Fiery torment seared his chest cavity. Tossa had greater strength than he had expected. If he did not break this soon, he would not fight on this day, let alone win. As though from a distance, he commanded his legs to rise.

When the soles of his moccasins rested flat on the ground, he flexed powerful thighs and heaved upward. Although the burden of weight upon him shot up into the air, Dohatsa failed to dislodge Tossa. When the wiry young tribal police-man came down, he buried one knee in the slightly paunchy gut of Dohatsa.

Sour bile and the remains of his morning meal erupted from Dohatsa's mouth, preceded by a heavy gust of air. His head swam and his limbs went slack. In desperation, Dohatsa rallied his flagging resources and went for the knife in his bright orange sash. When it came free, he made a swift slash at Tossa.

Nimbly, the young Tua avoided the blade and sprang to his feet. A quick kick sent the knife spinning brightly in the sun-light. Then Tossa had the arm pinned. He rolled the offending hand of Dohatsa over, palm down, and stamped on it with a moccasined foot until he heard bones crack. Howling, Dohatsa doubled up, nursing his injured extremity. Tossa stepped behind him and knelt. He took a large hank of black hair and yanked back the head of his enemy.

"I could, I should, cut your throat. Instead, what I want from you is the truth. Tell me all about our stolen sacred articles."

Dohatsa surrendered all of his arrogance, along with his resistance. He had been in the pay of Satterlee for nearly a month. He knew that his confession would mean certain exile, if not death, under tribal law. Shamefacedly, he turned his head to look at the man who had bested him. "What you accused me of before is true. I have taken money from the white outsiders, Satterlee and Quinn, for a moon now. It is I who stole the religious objects and gave them to Quinn. What he did with them I do not know."

Disgust at such betrayal twisted the face of Santan Tossa. He came upright and turned to address the gathering of Tua men. "You heard what this disgraced one said. Confine him somewhere until the council can attend to his crimes. Now, who will join me? Come, it is a thing of honor. Without the help of the white lawman I would never have found the necklace."

Two young Tua men stepped forward. Three more joined them. Then half a dozen. One spoke for the others. "If you will have us, Santan Tossa, we will fight with you for the white men."

Before he left for Taos, Santan Tossa had acquired a force of twenty-eight.

Shortly before nightfall, Deputy Sheriff Sammy Jennings cantered up to the *casa grande* at Rancho de la Gloria. The majordomo greeted him politely and hailed a boy to lead the lathered horse to the stableyard, to be cooled out, watered, and rubbed down. He showed the lawman into the central courtyard.

Don Diego Alvarado sat there, on a white-painted wrought-iron bench, smoking a cigar. He roused himself to welcome his visitor. Jennings made it short and to the point.

"I've come from Smoke Jensen, Don Diego. He is under-sheriff in Taos now."

Jennings, an uncomplicated man, missed the sardonic note of irony in the grandee's chuckle and words. "My friend Smoke is coming up in the world. I gather that there is something of importance that I should know?"

"Yes, sir. Smoke sent me to tell you that the Quinn gang intends to lay siege to Taos. Shut off the town and starve out the occupants. He asks that if it is possible you send as many vaqueros as you can."

"I can fill forty saddles within the hour. Will that do?"

Jennings swallowed hard. "Oh, Lordy, sure. Fine as frog's hair, señor."

"Excellent." He raised his voice and called to his eldest son. "Alejandro! Come out here and round up the vaqueros. I want forty of the best."

Alejandro appeared in a doorway of a room on the second floor. "What is it, Father? Have the rustlers returned?"

"No. We ride to Taos. Smoke Jensen has need of our fire-power." He turned back to his visitor. "As I say, this will take an hour. You must be in need of refreshment. Come, I'll have Maria prepare food and get you something to drink." Steering the young deputy toward the doorway to the detached kitchen, Don Diego shouted ahead to his cook to fix some meat and cheese and tortillas. Also to have Pepe bring up three beers from the springhouse.

* * *

After sending off his last messenger, Smoke Jensen settled down in the sheriff's office to a plate of beef stew from the corner eatery. This being Taos, the stew had potatoes right enough, but with tomatoes, onions, garlic and chile peppers instead of turnips, carrots and garden peas. The gravy was rich and thick, which he scooped up with folded flour tortillas. A soupy bowl of beans came with it, and a side dish of some mashed, yellow-green substance. Guacamole, he had been told. Avocado, Wally Gower had informed him. Again with the ever-present tomato, garlic, onion, and chiles. It had been flavored with some pungent, green herb and it tasted delightful. Smoke had just finished wrapping his lips around another bite of it when a loud crash and the sound of breaking glass summoned him from the office. From the knot of excited onlookers in the street, he learned the disturbance came from La Merced, one of the more unsavory saloons in town.

Smoke headed that way at once. He had to shove his way through a cluster of brown-faced spectators who crowded the boardwalk and entranceway. Three steps led to a grime-coated tile floor. Again, Smoke had to grab shoulders and heave men out of the way. This time, he noted that the faces wore expressions of anxiety and concern. He soon learned the reason.

A quartet of white thugs worked systematically at breaking up the place. Their apparent leader snarled at the bartender, who cringed in the far corner of the back bar. "You damn greasers like to have poisoned two of my men last night. We're takin' over this town, so you might as well get an idea of what happens to folks who put funny powders in drinks for the Quinn gang. You understand? *¿Comprende?"*

Bobbing his head frantically, the barkeep, who knew not the least word of English, and could not understand a thing being growled at him, covered his eyes as a wrought-iron legged chair went hurtling toward the mirror behind the bar.

The big plate of glass shattered into a million shards on impact. The complaining hardcase yanked a jug-eared, slightly built fellow from his chair and flung him after. Two of his henchmen turned to check out the disturbance between them and the doorway. In the next instant, Smoke came face-to-face with them. Neither ruffian suffered from being slow. As one, they balled fists, and the nearer one drove a hard-knuckled hand toward the face of Smoke Jensen.

EIGHTEEN

Smoke Jensen jerked his head to one side and let the fist whistle past. Then he brought one up from the cellar that connected with the brute's jaw. Teeth clopped shut, and the yellowish whites of his eyes showed as his pupils rolled upward. Smoke closed in and gave him two hard shots to the heart for good measure. Then he felt a sharp jolt as the second thug caught him in the gut. Smoke took a step back and braced himself.

At once, the brawler came on. Smoke let him get in close. Then he flexed his knees, fired his best right cross, and put shoulder and hips into it. The outlaw's boots left the floor. Squalling like a cinch-galled horse, he pitched face-first across a nearby table. The legs broke and went four directions, as did the stacks of coins and bills. By that time, the first one to assault Smoke had recovered himself enough to launch another attack.

He came in low, intent on taking Smoke off his feet. Smoke stood his ground and, at the last instant, smartly raised his right knee. Face met knee and the face lost. Blood flew in a shower from a mashed nose. Three teeth snapped loudly, and more crimson ribbons streamed from the damaged mouth. The legs stopped churning and the eyes gradually crossed. The

would-be tough dropped two feet in front of Smoke Jensen.
Which left the other assailant to tend to.

Smoke turned to face him as the member of the Quinn
gang put himself back on his boots. He had lost his cocksure
smirk. His eyes glazed, he took an unsteady step toward
Smoke Jensen. Blindly, he tripped over the broken table and
sprawled again on the green baize. One of the men, who'd
had his game disrupted and his winnings scattered, boxed the
outlaw's ears. Which got him up right smartly. He spat a curse
at Smoke Jensen and came on.

Smoke snapped a right-left combination to the head, then
lowered his point of aim to work on the chest and gut. His
elbows churned back and forth while he delivered short, pun-
ishing blows. When the ruffian's guard disappeared entirely,
Smoke took a quick back step and launched a solid left jab
that rocked his opponent to the toes. He spun half left and
shuddered while still erect. Then he wilted like a stalk of
grass before a prairie fire and thudded on the floor. Seeing
the pair so hastily dispatched, the leader and his remaining
henchman went for their guns.

Smoke did not even change stance. His right arm already
across his body for counterbalance, he simply grabbed at the
butt of his second Colt and hauled it from the horizontal
leather. He snapped back the hammer and tripped the trigger.
By that time, and much to his later regret, the subordinate
section leader of the gang had cleared leather. He had not,
however, leveled his weapon when a hot poker jabbed him in
the belly and his six-gun discharged into the floor. Beside
him he heard his underling utter a boast he knew could not be
fulfilled.

"I got him! I got him—got him!"

What he got was the center of the forehead of a big black
bull that hung on the wall behind Smoke Jensen, as the bullet
of the last mountain man smacked into his chest and burst his
heart. Smoke crossed the short space between him and the

dying man and kicked the Colt from his grasp. Then he turned on the gut-shot leader.

Plucking the Merwin Hulbert from his numb fingers, Smoke observed, "You won't survive that. So, I'll let you go. I have a message for Paddy Quinn. Tell him to keep the hell away from town or I'll bring down a firestorm of hurt on him."

Gasping, the hardcase observed, "You've got a mouth on you. Who are you?"

"Smoke Jensen."

"Awh . . . shit, shit, shit." With that, he passed out.

Smoke turned to the customers. "Will four of you bring those two to the jail. *La carcel, ¿comprende?*"

Volunteers nodded their heads eagerly. They roughly grabbed up the unconscious hardcases and dragged them from the saloon. Smoke faced the bartender. "Whatever money you find on those two, I'll add what I get from the others to help offset damages."

One vaquero at the bar translated. It brought a beaming smile from the worried brow. Smoke had earned his gratitude.

On a small mesa to the west of town, Whitewater Paddy Quinn listened to the sound of gunfire in Taos. All of his section leaders sat horses around him. All except Slim Vickers and three of his henchmen. From what he had learned from one of the seven who did report on time, Slim had remained behind to teach a lesson to some greasers who had poisoned some of them the previous night. Now, hearing the gunfire, Paddy Quinn beckoned to one of the hardcases who waited farther away with many of the gang. The man walked his horse up.

"What do you want, boss?"

"Baker, tell me about this poisoning, will ye?"

Baker looked embarrassed. "Awh, well, boss, it wasn't

poison for real. Jist some green beer. It was right skunky. Bunch of us wound up squirting through the eye of a needle at ten paces. Two of the boys got sick. Threw up over everything."

"Where did this happen?"

Baker frowned. "Some place called La Merced. Don't know what it means."

Paddy gave him a patronizing smile. "It means, 'the mercy.' Though I don't reckon ye got much mercy from them, eh, bucko?"

"That's right, boss."

"Sure an' what did Slim have in mind to do about it?"

Surprised that Quinn would take it further, Baker blinked. "Uh—well, ah, he and three of the boys was gonna go back and bust up the place. Kick some greaser butt."

"He say anything about shootin' them?"

That set Baker back. "Uh—no. Jist wanted to cause some damage."

Quinn's face went hard, his eyes narrowed and he gazed at the distant town. "Then it's that damned Smoke Jensen doin' the shootin'. An' I've no doubt that the boys will not be comin' back. I don't."

"Rider comin'," called out one of the outlaws.

Slim Vickers came on slowly, slumped in his saddle, one arm supporting him on the neck of his horse. When he drew nearer, Quinn saw that the man's face had turned a ghostly white. A green tinge surrounded his mouth. Then he saw the red stain on Slim's belly.

"Awh, saints above. What's happened to ye, darlin' boy? Where's the rest of the boys?"

"Two's in jail. One's dead. An' Smoke Jensen has done killed me." With that he fell off his horse and into eternity.

"Awh, damn Jensen's black heart." Quinn threw up his hands. "Nothin' for it, then. We'll be leavin' now, we will. Spread out, boys. An' hold back until the rest of the lads arrive. When they do, we'll be takin' our positions. This time it will be a regular siege," he told them. "Ye have your assignments. Ye are to pursue them and show no quarter."

Merchants and townsmen alike turned out to not be so hot for the prospects of standing off a siege. Feeding all of the volunteers became a problem long before Don Diego Alvarado and his vaqueros reached town. Several other ranchers had brought cowboys in to supplement the defenses. The opposition became even more vociferous when the new undersheriff strode through town with a bundle of posters, which he attached to the door of every cantina and saloon.

"What's the meaning of this?" one unhappy saloon owner demanded. "You can't take the opportunity away from us to make a nice profit."

Smoke Jensen stared at him with disdain. "The last thing we need is a lot of boozed-up men with guns on their hips. We won't have time to round up drunks when Quinn and his gang get here. The flyers mean exactly what they say. You will restrict yourselves to the sale of beer only. Any violators will have their establishments locked and spend the duration in jail. It would be a good idea to limit your customers' intake, also. I've known men to get fallin'-down drunk on good, strong beer."

Bristling, the owner offered defiance. "You ain't no dictator. What if we refuse?"

Smoke snorted. "Are you volunteering to be the first to get locked up?"

Short and stout, with the flabby muscles of a man unaccustomed to hard work, the bar owner gauged the look in the eyes of Smoke Jensen and rightly read his expression. "Well—ah—well, no. I reckon I'll do what you say, but I don't have to like it."

"No, you don't." Smoke moved on.

When that task had been completed, Smoke had to hurry to the town hall for a meeting he had scheduled with the women of the community and the restaurant owners. In the public meeting room, Smoke stepped to the lectern and addressed the gathering.

"Ladies, we have a good fifty outsiders in town. None of them have the facilities to feed themselves. And there will be more coming. I have been assured that the eating places in town cannot handle the increase except on a continuous operation basis. What we need to do is set up a cookhouse here at city hall. I'm asking for volunteers to cook and serve."

Abigail Crowder, wife of the Taos fire chief, raised her hand. When Smoke recognized her, she stood to ask her question. "Where will we get the food?"

"I have spoken with Mr. Hubbard at the general store. The city will purchase all supplies from him. There will be no charge for the meals. If you give of your time, it won't empty the city treasury, what there is of it."

Another woman stood. "How long will this go on?"

Smoke frowned, scratched at his jaw. "Hard to say. At least two or three days. The mayor and I have sent a message to Santa Fe. We're asking the governor to call out the militia. But, politicians move slowly. Troops under arms move even slower. We'll be on our own for a goodly while."

She had another question. "Will there be enough to eat?"

Smoke nodded reassurance. "I reckon so. For the volunteer fighting men, I suggest you concentrate on fixin' what there's the most of. Such as corn bread, biscuits, potatoes, rice and beans. Hubbard has dozens of barrels of those. Plenty of pickles, too. If you can come up with some chickens from home, it would help. Now, if you'll step over here, Mr. Dougherty, the town clerk, will sign you up, put down the times of day you want to work."

* * *

Small columns of outlaws streamed down off the mesa. They spread out, and those tasked to the detail made ready to close off the roads. Others waited two miles from Taos to set up roving patrols to prevent anyone from sneaking out of town from houses on the outskirts. What Paddy Quinn did not know would soon prove to have fateful consequences for his plans.

Less than ten minutes earlier, twenty-five young Tua warriors, with Santan Tossa in the lead, had ridden into Taos and assembled outside the sheriff's office. Their faces were set, emotionless, the stereotypical Indian visage. At the direction of their tribal police chief, they filed into the office and came out with far more animated expressions. Each of them clutched a rifle or a shotgun. Faces of horror flashed through the Mexican and white residents of Taos when they saw this. Enough so that Santan Tossa went inside and spoke briefly with Smoke Jensen.

Smoke came outside and went among the troubled citizens of Taos. He spoke briefly and earnestly to small groups. "They are here to fight Quinn's gang. They can't do that with bows and arrows. If more of you had volunteered, it would not be necessary."

One indignant, pudgy man in a banker's suit protested hotly. "It's not our fault. You can't blame us. We're not lawmen. It's your job to protect us."

Such whining complaints quickly wore thin Smoke's sparse layer of patience. After the third such outpouring of whining self-justification, he snapped hotly. "And if you had the brains of a gnat, you'd realize that is exactly what I am doing."

"The governor will hear of this," a voice warned darkly. The banker had slunk back to launch another feeble barb.

Smoke laughed in the man's face. "Not until you can get out of town, he won't."

* * *

Diego Alvarado, along with two of his sons, Alejandro and Miguel, at the head of thirty-eight vaqueros, thundered up the long slope from the high desert flats where Rancho de la Gloria was located. All of the cowboys had heavily armed themselves. Twin bandoliers of rifle cartridges crisscrossed their chests. Obrigon .45s rode high in holsters on their belts.

Eight of their number cast frequent, nervous glances at their saddlebags, which had been packed full of crudely made grenades. The hand-thrown bombs were made of wine and tequila bottles, tightly packed with black powder and horseshoe nails, then fused and stoppered. The prospect of using them excited some of the more reckless among the vengeance-hungry vaqueros. Ahead waited the men who had murdered their *compañeros* and stolen their pride when they had stolen the cattle they tended. This would be a day for *El Degüello*. No quarter would be given. In the heads of some of the older ones echoed the brassy refrain of the "Cutthroat Song," which their grandfathers had played outside the defiant walls of the Alamo. That these *ladrónes* they rode to fight were gringos only sweetened the revenge. Five miles from Taos, Diego Alvarado signaled a halt.

"Alejandro, Miguel, here is where we will divide into three groups. Miguel, you will take ten men and ride directly down the road to town. Alejandro, take fourteen and circle a short way to the north. Not more than half a mile, mind. I will take the rest and go to the south. When Miguel and his men open fire, we will sweep down on the *bandido* scum and kill them all."

Alejandro and Miguel made their selections and drew the men apart. After signaling to their father, Diego stood in his stirrups and waved a gloved hand over his head. *"¡Adelante, muchachos!"*

With an enthusiastic, shouted cheer of encouragement, the indomitable company of vaqueros thundered off to bring the force of destiny to the unsuspecting outlaws.

Three members of the city council came bustling into the sheriff's office while Smoke Jensen was spooning a plateful of beans into his mouth. From the fiery flavor, Smoke judged that the women cooks had found a ready and willing source of chile peppers among the Mexican households. A florid-faced man in a brown suit and matching derby hat spoke for the politicians.

"What is this we hear that you have actually armed the Indians?"

Smoke chewed and swallowed his most recent mouthful and gestured with the spoon. "Yes, I have."

"Why, that's outrageous. And, it is totally unacceptable."

Smoke shook his head. "No, it's not. Think about it, gentlemen."

Agitation darkening the rosy color of his face, the spokesman yapped at Smoke. "We have thought about it. We do not intend to be massacred in our beds or our own homes. We demand—"

Smoke raised a hand to silence him. "Let me acquaint you with some very real, although unpleasant facts of life. When the gang and its hangers-on get here, Paddy Quinn will have between forty-five and seventy highly capable gunfighters at his command. The Tua warriors have come here and are willing to defend your town for you. They can hardly do so against such odds with weapons out of the Stone Age. The mayor agreed with me that we should properly arm them, and that has been done."

"Why were we not consulted about this?"

Smoke Jensen smiled coldly. "To save time. Politicians, from the White House on down, believe that they can talk troubles to death. We could be arguing over arming the Tuas until winter came."

The councilman cut his eyes to his associates and fired his last barb. "Banker Elwell tells us that you refused to notify the governor."

Smoke lowered his gaze a moment. "I—ah—stretched the truth a little when I spoke with the banker. In the letter requesting the militia, I informed the governor of our decision. The mayor assured me it was all right to arm the Indians for—how does the territorial constitution put it?—'the purpose of hunting game and for the defense of the common good.'"

Defeated, and hating it, the spokesman snapped at Smoke. "For a man with so low an opinion of politicians, you can sure quote law like one."

Grinning, Smoke affected to preen himself. "A man of many talents, wouldn't you say?"

Shocked at this effrontery, the senior councilman's eyes bulged. "Well, I never!"

"Nope. Reckon you haven't."

Smoke's mockery sent them to the door. Heads held high in indignation, the delegation had only reached the porch when they collided with Wally Gower and three other town moppets of about his age, who surged past them, into the office. "They're comin', Sheriff Jensen. The Quinn gang's closin' in on town. It looks like there's enough of them, they're gonna ring the whole place."

NINETEEN

When the news the boys carried got out, it quickly changed a lot of minds. First to scurry into the sheriff's office was the banker, Elwell. "You're the undersheriff. Do something," he bleated. "We need all of the protection we can get."

Smoke Jensen could not resist a final tweak of this whining hypocrite. "You've changed your mind about arming the Tuas with modern weapons?"

"Yes—yes, anything. Just save us from those vandals out there."

"Well, then, I'd suggest you go home, get your rifle, and help us."

Elwell eyed him with suspicion. "Sheriff Jensen, I've not fired a rifle in years."

Smoke gave him a grin. "It's like ridin' a horse, Elwell. You never forget." To Santan Tossa he suggested, "Let's go out and take a look at the new arrivals."

What they found, as they made their rounds, stunned even the usually unflappable Smoke Jensen. Instead of the expected forty-five to seventy outlaws, Smoke counted fully two hundred border trash, drifters, and genuine hardcases spread out around the town. All of them seemed to be cold, grim-faced, hardened killers. Smoke turned to a deputy who stood nearby nervously fingering his Winchester.

"Hardly what we counted on, is it? I want you to go back into town and get those volunteers to speed up filling sandbags. Tell them I want stacks built to line the outer walls of all wooden buildings to the height of a kneeling man. Then come back here and take charge."

The lawman gulped and broke his fixed stare at the outlaws. "Right away, Sheriff." Grateful to be away from there, if only for a few minutes, he hurried off.

Then Smoke advised Tossa and all the men within hearing, "Now all we have to do is wait and find out what the enemy has in mind."

Back at the Sugarloaf, Mary-Beth Gittings worked industriously to load the valises they had brought into the fancy carriage. Her sons, red-eyed from yet another switching, dragged their own packed luggage from the house. Her face drawn and tight-lipped, she remained ominously silent as she walked past Sally Jensen, who stood on the porch and watched. Sally's face revealed a poorly restrained expression of pleasure.

When the last piece had been loaded, Mary-Beth advanced on Sally, fists on hips, her face a study in self-righteous indignation. Her cheeks burned, not only with her umbrage, but from humiliation. She had allowed this woman to dictate to her how she should deal with the minor infractions her darling children committed. She was the first to admit they were not perfect. All children did naughty things from time to time. But to *spank* them? To viciously punish and degrade them—and one's self—in such a barbaric fashion? It would have never occurred to her that when on another person's property, and under their roof, one should abide by their rules. She should have never listened to Sally, her angry thoughts continued. Especially after she learned what she knew now.

It had come out only an hour ago, while she once again reluctantly put the switch to the boys up in the room they shared. Wailing in hurt and fright, their bottoms a cherry red, they had sobbed out how that monstrous creature had threatened their lives. Horrified, Mary-Beth had decided on the spot to leave. Now she let all her outrage boil out.

With a visible effort, she restrained most of her dudgeon as she addressed her hostess for the final time. "I never believed that such a dear old friend would be so shamelessly protective of such an ill-bred child."

Her patience exhausted, Sally glowered back. "What is it this time, Mary-Beth?"

Mary-Beth let it spill out. "Why, it is about murder. My precious sons revealed to me not an hour ago that Bobby threatened to hang Seth and Sammy when they ran away."

That banished the last of Sally's sense of obligation. "Mary-Beth, don't you recall that after all they had stolen horses? Horse thieves are hanged out here."

Sally might as well have smacked Mary-Beth in the middle of her forehead. Shock silenced her to a small squeak. Then she hoisted her skirts and turned away. Briskly she walked to the carriage and boarded the driver's seat. She picked up the reins and snapped them. Without a farewell or a backward look, she and her troublesome children rolled down the long lane. At the last moment, only Billy Gittings turned back and gave a friendly, forlorn wave to Bobby Jensen.

Soberly, Bobby returned the gesture. The next instant, Sally and Bobby fell into one another's arms in relief and joy. "They're gone. They're finally gone," Sally shouted happily.

For the defenders of Taos, the wait to see what Quinn had in mind proved a long one. Both sides restlessly eyed one another from across the separating distance. Tension increased among the besiegers when the faint drumming of many horses came from the southwest. Paddy Quinn and a dozen of his immediate subordinates lingered on the far side of a bridge that spanned a narrow creek in a deep, red rock gorge. They conversed quietly there with the men assigned to operate the roadblock. It was toward them that a party of eleven men, dressed as vaqueros, cantered in midafternoon.

Quinn trotted forward a few lengths and raised a hand in a gesture to halt. "Turn back. No one enters town without our leave."

Several seconds went by before their identity became clear to Quinn. Then he shouted over his shoulder. "B'God, it's that Diego Alvarado's outfit. Turn about, boys, an' give 'em hell."

Miguel and the vaqueros had anticipated that. At once their weapons blasted in a volley. They fired again, and three of the outlaws left their saddles. Paddy Quinn barely escaped with his life. Bullets cracked past his head, and one grazed the shoulder of his mount. He turned first left, then right, only to see a swarm of more cowboys appear on both sides of the road. Determined to salvage what he could of his subordinate leaders and the men, he put spurs to his horse as he shouted to his underlings.

"Follow me! It ain't worth it; let 'em in." Then he cut off at an oblique angle between the hostile forces.

At once, the vaqueros converged on the road and cantered into town in a column three wide. Diego and Alejandro waited at the side until the last of the cowboys got through. He halted six of them.

"Stay here and keep the road open," Diego commanded.

One of the younger vaqueros looked nervously over his shoulder. "Sí, patrón. But you saw what they did when we rode in. There are so many of them."

Diego nodded. "They cannot all come against you. They

are here to close the town. When some of them come back, use your rifles. Keep them at a distance."

With that Diego rode on into town. He stopped at the sheriff's office and was greeted by Smoke Jensen. "It's good you're here, Diego. How many men did you bring?"

"Thirty-eight, and two of my sons."

Smoke laughed and wrung Diego's hand. "Make that three. Pedro insists he is healed enough to take part. He wants a rifle."

Diego nodded his understanding. Then he asked the question foremost on his mind, "How many of them are there?"

"By my count, close to two hundred."

Diego frowned. "That is a formidable force."

A smile bloomed on Smoke's face. "We have nearly as many, thanks to you and our Tua friends. Come, I'll show you how we're set up."

Smoke Jensen set off on a tour of town, explaining the defenses to Diego Alvarado. They had covered two sides of town when a flurry of gunshots broke out.

Being run off from the barricade rankled some of the gang. A dozen of the outlaws on the east side received a blistering lecture from their section leader on holding their place at all costs. Being of the criminal class, they saw any orders, especially those couched as criticism, as an affront. It made them restless, and eventually their patience wore out.

One hothead gave his opinion. "I say we can take that town full of sissies just by ourselves."

Another slightly more intelligent one disagreed. "Those Mezkin cowboys are in there now."

"Don't matter. Mezkins is dumb like Injuns. They think it's the noise that knocks a man down, so they don't aim."

A third piece of trash had news that slowed them for a while. "These must; they done knocked two of the boys outten their saddles."

"Lucky shots," the first insisted. He kept on for another ten minutes, until he had them all convinced.

They trotted their horses to the east road and passed through the blockaders without restraint. Then the reckless hardcases spurred their mounts to a gallop and, with six-guns out and ready, rode like a whirlwind into Taos. They met immediate opposition. A hail of lead came from the second-floor windows in buildings near the center of town. Rifle fire, they soon learned to their regret. Two of the frontier trash left their perches and sprawled in the dirt of the street. A third gritted teeth and clapped a hand to a hole in his shoulder.

From closer at hand, more guns sought out the survivors. Bullets clipped through the air around them. For all that the defenders had been instructed to take good aim, the fact remained that there was more air out there than meat. Nine of the outlaws managed to reach the Plaza de Armas, which they proceeded to ride around, firing into the building fronts. They had made half the circuit when Smoke Jensen and Diego Alvarado arrived on the scene. The situation changed abruptly.

"That shooting is coming from the Plaza." Diego Alvarado announced something that Smoke Jensen already knew.

"We'd best get there the fastest way," the last mountain man opined.

Diego pointed to an alley that cut through several blocks at a sharp angle "Take this *callejón*."

They set out at a fast trot, both men with six-guns in hand. At the far end, Smoke could now see the fountain in the center of the square. A horseman obscured his view a moment as he rode by in the Plaza de Armas, firing into buildings as he went. Another followed, then another. One block to go. Smoke held his fire as another of the Quinn gang—he figured it could be none other—rode by the alley mouth. In another three seconds they came out into the open.

498 William W. Johnstone

"Here's a couple of 'em," a strange voice brayed from behind Smoke Jensen.

He crouched and whirled in the same move. The Colt in his right hand bucked, and the outlaw who had called to his friends took a bullet in the right side of his chest. To Smoke's other side, the Obrigon in the hand of Diego Alvarado belched flame, and a .45 slug struck another bandit in the gut. His eyes bulged, but he kept coming. The odd, foreign-looking revolver—the barrel, cylinder and frame had not been blued—in his hand raised to line up on the chest of Diego Alvarado.

Diego fired again and put his bullet in the brain of the man with the 11mm Mle. '74 Saint Etienne, French-made six-gun. He died before the shock of his first wound faded. The heavy, soft-gray steel weapon fell from his hand. Immediately more of the outlaws came at them. By then, a scattering of defenders had reacted to the sudden appearance of the enemy. The volume of fire raining on the intruders grew rapidly. It soon had an effect.

Three more went down, and Smoke Jensen found himself nearly run over by a riderless horse. He jumped to one side, tripped over the body of a hardcase, and fell to the red tile walkway around the base of the fountain.

"I've got you now," a triumphant voice shouted from above Smoke.

Instantly, Smoke Jensen rolled to his left and brought up his Peacemaker. He fired the moment he saw a human form. By the sheer perversity of chance, the slug struck the front of the outlaw's revolver cylinder. The thug screamed and dropped his now useless weapon while Smoke rolled again. This time, Smoke took better aim.

"Dutch!" the dying man screamed, in spite of the hole in his throat. "He got me, Dutch. Did me good." Then he groaned softly and fell across the neck of his mount. The frightened horse carried the corpse away from the plaza.

Smoke rounded the base of the fountain, forced to dodge bullets from both sides. Inexorably the numbers mounted. Suddenly Dutch Volker found himself and only two others cursing and firing defiantly at the defenders. He opened his mouth and bellowed loudly enough to carry above the tumult of gunfire.

"Get out of here! We're all that's left."

Swiftly, they clattered away through a low screen of powder smoke. Diego Alvarado, his face grimed with black smudges, walked over to where Smoke Jensen stood with the loading gate of his .45 Colt open for reloading. "If they are all as stupid as those were, we should have an easy time— *¿no, amigo?*"

Smoke gazed at the litter of the dead. "I wouldn't count on it."

Soft shafts of yellow lanced through the wrought-iron barred windows set high in the outer wall of the second-floor master bedroom. This side of the Satterlee hacienda outside Santa Fe faced the south. It provided a slight, though noticeable, temperature advantage during the winter months. Clifton Satterlee selected articles of clothing from a large armoire, which he handed to an Indian woman servant, who diligently folded and packed them into a large carpetbag.

Satterlee spoke aloud to himself as he decided on his wardrobe. "I think something elegant, perhaps a morning coat. For the formal capitulation of Taos nothing less would do." A soft rap sounded on the open door, and he looked up.

His majordomo stood there, a sparkle of expectation in his ebony eyes. "A rider just in from Taos, *señor.*"

The expression on the face of Satterlee reflected that of his servant. "Show him up."

In two minutes the official greeter of the house returned

with a smiling Yank Hastings. The young outlaw did not dwell on formalities. "Ever'thing's goin' fine, Mr. Satterlee. Paddy Quinn says there's no need for you to hurry up there. We'll have 'em flushed out by tomorrow morning. That's his guarantee."

Satterlee stretched his thin lips to even narrower proportions. "Mr. Quinn may well want his hour in the sun, but I have no intention of being denied my triumph. I will be ready within the hour. You will accompany me and my personal retinue to Taos at that time."

Sundown lingered only a quarter hour away. Rich orange light bathed the bowl in which Taos lay. It painted the red, yellow, and brown buttes, mesas, and volcanic mountains in muted shadow. Following the ill-thought-out charge of the hotheads, the gang had settled down to strengthen their stranglehold on the town and its occupants. On the three sides not influenced by the creek and its deep gorge, the bandits edged in close enough to be well within range of their weapons. They opened up in a fury.

Windows became the first targets. Every visible pane ceased to exist in a wildfire storm that lasted twelve minutes. By then, the town custodian, whom no one had thought to inform to the contrary, had begun to light the streetlamps. They quickly became the objects of punishment for the outlaws.

Glass flew into the street first, followed by thin streams of kerosene. It did not take long for one burning wick to be dislodged from the body of a lamp and fall into a pool of the flammable liquid that formed at the base of the post. Flickering blue at first, to be reduced to yellow-white, the flames swept the length of one block, then a second. At once the alarm sounded at the fire station, and volunteers had to abandon their fighting positions to answer the call. Always a curse, fire could reduce the city as surely as the outlaws who had caused its release.

Chief Ezekial Crowder directed his firemen from the shelter of a doorway. Bullets from the gang continued to be a hazard. One young firefighter suddenly dropped his length of hose and yowled as he grabbed at his ear. Blood trickled between his fingers.

"At least it ain't like fightin' a structural fire," Crowder observed to Smoke Jensen, who had come at the first alarm. "So far, that is," Barnes amended.

His volunteers quickly spread out to beat down the flames. To Smoke it appeared the very earth burned. Black smoke vaulted the sky above town, and the outlaws cheered and shouted in derision. Gradually, the blazes subsided. After ten hard minutes the last one went out.

Encouraged by the diversion the fires had created, half a dozen scum charged the vaqueros who had been holding the west road. One of the Mexican cowboys reached to the saddlebag at his feet, grabbed up a bottle, and used his hand-rolled cigarette to ignite the fuse that protruded from the cork in its mouth. When it began to sputter, he counted to three, stood and threw it out the open window.

It turned end-for-end four full times before it exploded violently at shoulder level in the midst of the gang members. All six screamed piteously and went down in a heap. That quickly changed the minds of those who thought of joining them. The effect on those who had witnessed the grenade became obvious as the fire it had caused began to dwindle. The last shots came from the outlaws only minutes after nightfall.

Half an hour later, Smoke Jensen finished off a piece of pie, sent over by one of the restaurants, and licked his lips. "I think that ends it for today. Diego, I'd keep a few people on the lookout for any effort to test our strength. The rest can get a little sleep, at least until an hour before daylight."

"And you, *amigo,* what will you be doing?"

Smoke gave him a wicked grin. "I'm going to go out and raise a little hob."

TWENTY

Smoke Jensen chose to leave town by way of the road controlled by the vaqueros from Rancho de la Gloria. The ranch hand on watch gave him a silent salute as he crossed the bridge on foot. Thick coatings of burlap muffled the hooves of his stallion, Cougar. They would remain on until Smoke slipped past the pickets of the outlaw army. So skilled was the last mountain man that when the vaquero lookout who watched him depart blinked, Smoke had completely disappeared.

It did not take long after that for Smoke to find targets for his night's mischief. Silently he wormed his way in among the outlaws at one campfire. One look at his gunfighter rig and they accepted him as one of their own. He was offered coffee, which Smoke accepted.

"Thanks, I needed that. Maybe it'll settle my nerves."

"What are you gittin' at—er . . . ?"

Smoke dropped into the loose grammar and dialect of his mentor, the old mountain man called Preacher. "They call me Jagger. An' what I'm gettin' at is that there's Injuns in among the folks in town."

"Naw," another hardcase disputed. "They're Mezkins, Jagger. You've jist caught a case of the spooks."

Smoke played the trump in his rumor hand. "Mezkins wearin' moccasins, loincloths, and floppy shirts? Hair down to their shoulders? Believe it. I've seen 'em myself. They're all sharpenin' scalpin' knives."

A shiver passed over his audience. Smoke added more to their unease. "There must be as many fightin' men in thar as out here."

The doubtful one again challenged his statement. "Not accordin' to Whitewater Paddy."

Smoke cracked a grin. "Mr. Quinn don't know ever'thing. I've seed 'em. There's Injuns, an' Mezkin cowboys, and a whole lot of townies."

Smoke answered a string of troubled questions with inventions calculated to fan the blaze of fear he had introduced. After ten minutes of yarn spinning, Smoke drank off his coffee, came to his boots, and drifted on.

"I'm makin' the rounds, checkin' if anyone needs anything," Smoke explained at the next fire. Using the names he had acquired at the first gathering, he deepened his cover. "Are you Zeke? Well, Rupe told me to tell you howdy for him. He's holdin' his own. 'Cept for what he found out about the Injuns in Taos."

Zeke eyed Smoke. "What's this about Injuns?"

Smoke launched into his tall tale about scalping. Then he added another log to the overloaded wagon. "That's not all. A feller who's been in close to town tells me that this Smoke Jensen has put up a hundred-dollar bounty on every one of us who gets killed."

Zeke denied that at once. "I don't believe it. Nobody, especially a rovin' gunfighter, has that kind of money."

Smoke ignored him. "Somethin' more about those Injuns. Jensen's armed them with rifles and shotguns."

"No!" Agitated, Zeke came to his boots. "Ain't no way

them townies would stand for that. It's fools' work givin' guns to Injuns."

"Makes no never-mind. That's what I saw with my own eyes. Injuns runnin' around with Winchesters. An' that's not all of it. Not by half." Smoke went on to add yet another burden to the worried outlaws. Then he quietly left the uneasy souls to these imaginings.

After three more such visits, Smoke decided that his rumors would take sprout and grow with satisfactory speed. Crouched low, he worked his way in among the horses of those who ringed the town between roads. With a cautious hand, he reached for the cinch ring of one animal. He kept the other on the nose of the animal to calm it.

Ever so slowly, Smoke eased the leather end free of the ring and loosened the cinch. Next time the owner tried to straddle his mount, he would wind up with a lap full of saddle. Smiling to himself, Smoke completed the task and moved on to another critter to do the same. He repeated the loosening of cinch straps a dozen times, then switched tactics.

Along the west side, he fitted front hooves into black leather hobbles on ten other horses. He started to come upright from the last one when a voice challenged him from the darkness. "What are you doin' here?"

Smoke had a ready explanation. "Cleanin' the frog on the right forehoof of my horse. On the way out here he come up lame. Figgered it wouldn't do for us to jump up a fight and me unable to ride."

"Good thinking." The speaker moved closer. "Say, I don't think I—"

Prepared for that, Smoke had already slid his left-hand Colt from its pocket and gripped it tightly around the cylinder with his left hand. He swung the weapon now and connected the butt with the outlaw's temple. The alert section leader went down without a sound. Smoke bent and checked him, then tied the man's wrists and ankles and dragged him off toward the rear. His night vision in perfect condition, Smoke sought a place to stash his burden.

He found it in the form of a small ravine. He lined up the bandit parallel to the gully and rolled him down, out of sight. During his brief search, Smoke had come upon a secondary ring of campfires. These had not as yet been ignited. He carefully marked their location for later attention. For now, he moved on to find more who had straggled away from the picket line.

Nate Carver had his mind on a glass of whiskey, a hand of winning cards, and a pretty bit of fluff to sit on his lap. He eased his cartridge belt upward and unbuttoned his fly in order to relieve himself. While he fumbled with one stubborn button, visions of the sort of celebration he would have once this was over danced behind his eyes.

That whiskey would sure taste good. His mouth watered at the thought of it. And a nice big steak, well done, the way he had learned to eat it in Texas. And four of the stupidest fellers to ever hold pasteboards in a poker game to play against. Yeah. And then that tingling feeling that came every time a feller walked up them stairs with a floozy on his arm. The small room, the soft bed, the tender flesh. His self-distraction prevented him from sighting the ghostly movement against the lighter darkness of a star-lit horizon. All too late, he sensed another presence an instant before Smoke Jensen smacked him on the side of the head.

Nate would have rather died than be found by his friends in the condition that resulted from sudden unconsciousness and a full bladder. Smoke Jensen trussed him up and set him in the center of a collection of large, fat, barrel cactus. There were bound to be more, Smoke told himself.

* * *

Ten minutes later, Smoke found the reason for the second ring of firepits. An outlaw wearing a cook's apron gathered dry mesquite branches and stacked them beside a chuck wagon. Well beyond rifle range, this would provide a safe place for breakfast. Smoke quickly thought out a way to spoil the meal for them. Ghosting in on moccasined feet, he closed with the belly robber. Smoke's lips thinned to a grim line of disapproval when he saw the curly gray hair on the head he intended to thump. A feller his age should know better than to run with outlaws.

Smoke's regret was not tempered by mercy. He eased up behind the unsuspecting rascal and put him to sleep with a solid blow from his Colt. Quickly he grabbed the man and eased him to the ground. He pulled another prepared strip of latigo leather from a pocket and bound the bean burner's wrists. Then he pulled off the man's boots and removed a sock. After binding the ankles, he stuffed the dirty, smelly wool stocking into an open mouth, careful to remove a poorly fitted set of dentures first, and used another pigging string to secure it in place.

"Time to get to work," Smoke muttered to himself.

He went directly to the rear of the chuck wagon, where the oversized tailgate/worktable had been lowered into place. He opened the drawer that contained about five pounds of salt. This he poured into a bowl for the time being and refilled the receptacle from the sugar bin. The salt then went in to replace the sugar. A quick search under a rising moon located an anthill. Using a tin plate, Smoke scooped up a generous number of the busybody insects and delivered them to the flour barrel.

Half a dozen road apples, from the team of mules that pulled the wagon, completed his sabotage when he dropped them into the liquid that covered the corned pork. Then he hoisted the supine cook over one shoulder and carried him off a goodly distance to where he would not be found for some time. Someone else would be fixing breakfast for the Quinn gang. Someone Smoke felt confident would not have the skill to recognize the change in the ingredients. That attended to, he began a round of the prelaid fires.

Into each of ten, he inserted a capped and fused stick of dynamite. Being careful to cover them well with dirt, he replaced the kindling and larger wood, then faded off into the night. He reflected on what he had done and counted it a good night's work.

Clifton Satterlee fumed over the delay. A wheel had broken on his surrey not thirty miles north of Santa Fe. Fortunately there had been a posada close by. One that did not have vermin swarming in the mattresses and climbing the walls of the kitchen, he noted grudgingly. The food had been good, for a change. Not the excellent meals his cook prepared, yet flavorful and generous in quantity. Much against his best instincts, Brice Noble had come with him. They sat now at a small table in the alcovelike cantina off the lobby of the inn. Noble poured for both of them from a green glass bottle of Domeq Don Pedro brandy. Not so good as his preferred cognac, but it would do, Satterlee considered.

Taking a sip, he spoke to Brice Noble. "This delay is inexcusable. A spare wheel should be brought along at all times."

"It's your carriage, Cliff." Noble did not mention that the damage had been done as a result of Satterlee's insistence that they travel at the fastest possible speed.

Satterlee cued on his partner's tone. "Meaning?"

"You are the one who has to order a spare being lashed on the surrey."

With a snort, Satterlee took a long pull on the amber liquid. "I hate people who ooze practicality." Abruptly he changed the subject. "We may have some difficulty with some of the people in Taos. They are a stubborn lot. But our time is running out. Quinn has assured me he has rounded up enough gunfighters and rough types to overcome any objections. We'll have about two hundred men."

Noble winced. "That's going to cost a lot of money."

"Yes, but it is necessary. We may have to take the town by force." He paused, sighed heavily. "Although I would prefer not to resort to that. It might affect our credibility when it comes to filing for new deeds. No matter what, we will have Taos, and we will log that Indian land. That is all vital to our project. I think I've had enough of this." He nodded to a quartet of mariachis playing to a Mexican couple at a corner table. "I'm going to retire. Hastings has assured me that they will have the wheel fitted by morning. Good night, Brice."

Smoke Jensen returned to Taos, linking up with the route he had used to depart only at the last moment. His keen night vision, augmented now by a hazy full moon, allowed him to pick out the significant differences from when he had left town. Seven darker lumps stood out against a background of twinkling pinpoints of light in a black velvet sky. Slowly they resolved into human figures. All faced inward toward the community they invested. Smoke had already dismounted. Now he clapped a hand over Cougar's muzzle and eased the big Palouse off the roadway. He ground reined his horse and slid off into the night once again.

One of those who attempted to reestablish the roadblock under cover of night had taken a position some fifty feet from the verge of the road. He had hunkered down, the stock of his rifle used as a prop. He constantly cut his eyes from side to side and up and down to enable him to better see what lay across the deep gully and its creek that divided him from the outermost houses. He had no way of knowing that Alvarado's vaqueros knew to do the same and had picked out his position to within an inch. Had he known so, it would not have done him any good. He lost consciousness before they could do anything about his presence.

Smoke Jensen eased up behind the gunman and slammed the butt of a Colt Peacemaker into the side of his head. With a soft grunt, the outlaw fell over onto the sandy red soil. Smoke quickly tied him and moved on.

Another of Quinn's ragtag army sat cross-legged with his back against a low palo verde. Smoke Jensen found him and decided upon a little trickery. "Hey," he whispered harshly. "Over here. We've got a problem."

Almost dozed off, the response sounded quarrelsome. "What's the matter. Ground too hard?"

"Come here. An' be quiet."

Roused from his near snooze, the outlaw came to his boots and duckwalked over. "Now, what's this problem?"

"I am," Smoke told him before he clouted him on the temple with the barrel of one .45. The thug went rigid and then dropped face-first to the ground.

Smoke moved on in an instant. He suddenly realized that he had allowed himself to grow overconfident when a voice growled at him from the side. "Hold it right there."

Moving slowly, so as not to startle the speaker into shooting, Smoke faced his challenger. "What do you mean? I was only goin' down to bum a smoke offa Hank."

Suspicion thickened in the outlaw's voice. "There ain't no Hank with this outfit, an' I ain't seen you before." He beckoned with the muzzle of his rifle. "Come over here an' let me get a look at you."

Smoke complied, easing his left hand around out of sight. When he got within a long arm's reach, he stopped. The distrustful hardcase peered closely at Smoke's face. "Nope. Never saw you with the gang before. Who are you?"

Smoke came out with his Greenriver sheath knife in his

left hand and, with a short lunge, drove it horizontally through the costal region between the fifth and sixth ribs on the left side. The pointed tip penetrated the heart and sank the blade deep into the pulsing organ. Then Smoke jerked the haft to rip sideways. The man died without a sound. Smoke maneuvered to hold the dead man between him and any outlaw bullets and called out loudly to the defenders across the way.

"¡Oigan, vaqueros de la Gloria! Ayudenme!"

He got his help right away as the Mexican cowboys opened fire on the hardcases they had previously located. Smoke gave a shrill whistle, and Cougar trotted toward him. Quickly he flung the body away from him and swung into the saddle. With heels drumming into his sides, Cougar jumped to a fast canter and sprinted across the bridge and into the shelter of the buildings on the outskirts of Taos.

Smoke had thoughts only for sleep. But he found a delegation waiting for him at the sheriff's office. The mayor, Fidel Arianas, and Dr. Walters occupied chairs, along with Santan Tossa and Ed Hubbard. All except Tossa wore worried expressions.

Arianas opened the session. "How long do we have to hold them off?"

Smoke studied on that. "Three or four days, however long it takes for the militia to get here."

Arianas turned pale. *"¡Chingada!* There's not maybe fifty hombres in the militia. And that's on a good day. This *ladrón* has four times that many."

"Not anymore. I took care of a few. And tomorrow's sure to do in more."

Dr. Walters addressed a more serious problem. "We cannot hold out for more than four days. There is not enough food. There are too many mouths to feed."

Smoke frowned. "Make sure the vittles at the town hall get served only to the fighting men. The townspeople will have to fend for themselves."

Horrified at that prospect, the mayor thought first of votes. "The people will not stand for that. They'll blame me."

Smoke Jensen cut hot, angry eyes to the politician. "They'll have to live with it, if they don't want Paddy Quinn campin' on their doorstep." He had not the slightest concern over the mayor's reelection possibilities.

Dr. Walters had another idea. "What about the water supply? If they poison the creek we have only a few cisterns, fewer wells."

Smoke looked to Tossa for a solution. "Can you have some of your warriors slip out of town and make sure Quinn's men do not put anything in the water?"

Santan Tossa smiled. "That will be easy. They will never be seen."

"Then that's settled. Reduce rations all around and guard the water that is in town. No matter how this goes, we'll all have to tighten our belts to survive. And . . . you can expect another attack in the morning. I reckon those scum will be spoilin' for a fight."

TWENTY-ONE

Four o'clock in the morning was entirely too dang early to get up and get around, the swamper for the missing cook complained as he trudged through the darkness toward the chuck wagon. All around him, the tiny flames twinkled as men struck lucifers to ignite their fires. They would boil their own coffee. It was up to him and old Snuffy to turn out the grub. Where was Snuffy? he wondered as he reached the wagon and did not find the belly robber anywhere. By now he usually had a lantern going and the first rollout of biscuit dough ready to cut.

"Snuffy! Where are you? Come on, we're fallin' behind."

Right then, at a firepit not far away, flame hit the split and frazzled end of a length of fuse. It sputtered and hissed gustily, consumed the powder train that ran down its middle, and reached the detonator cap. A bright flash drew the swamper's eyes as a stick of dynamite let go with a tremendous roar. An instant later a shower of dirt and burning kindling mushroomed over the fire ring nearest the chuck wagon. Concussion knocked men rolling. One, who had leaned over, blowing gently to encourage the flames, died instantly.

Five seconds later another buried stick let go. Then a third.

The sound of the eruptions echoed off the walls of buildings in Taos. Reverberations had not died out when a fourth fire ring erupted in a gout of dirt. A fifth followed on its heels. By then, the swamper had dived to the ground and hugged red-brown clods of earth in a forlorn hope that a similar fate would not overtake him. Light the cook fire? Not very damn likely.

Two more blasts shattered the predawn quiet. An eerie silence followed. Then the swamper heard the cries and moans of the injured. Gradually his heartbeat began to slow. Then an anguished shout chilled him anew.

"Don't light that! Nooooo!"

BLAM!

No, there was no way he would light that fire. Two more explosions quickly dotted the i's and crossed the t's of that decision. No matter what Snuffy might say, he would absolutely, positively never even strike a match.

Smoke Jensen stood in a second-floor window, an old pair of brass army field glasses to his eyes. Ignited by the exploding dynamite, tufts of prairie grass had burst into flame, along with mesquite bushes and greasewood. The conflagration illuminated the disordered ranks of the enemy enough to let him clearly see the results of his night's work. It turned out to be better than he had expected.

Those outlaws already awake and not injured took to their horses. Shouts and curses blistered the air when some of them put a boot in a stirrup and wound up flat on their backsides. Several forked their mounts only to pitch face forward to the ground when their hobbled beasts jerked to sudden stops. Some rode off in the direction of Raton without a backward glance. Yet other hardcases ran around in confusion, their horses scattered in fright by the explosions.

More men helplessly stood in place to shout curses and shake their fists. Dust thrown into the air by the dynamite explosions began to settle and obscure the entire scene. Acrid smoke from the explosives hung in undulating waves over the former fire sites. The others who had crowded into the room with him were laughing and slapping one another on the back. Smoke Jensen felt no such elation. Men had died, and others had been maimed by his actions. If it served to break the resolve of the outlaws, well and good.

"What happened to them?" Diego Alvarado asked Smoke.

Smoke lowered the field glasses. "That's what I'm here for anyway, isn't it? I prepared a little wake-up call for them."

Don Diego studied Smoke's handiwork in awe. "It looks . . . devastating."

"Who was it said something about omelets and eggs?" Smoke asked aloud.

He shifted the glasses again as a pearlescent ribbon silhouetted the jagged mountain peaks to the east. There. He had found him. Paddy Quinn stood on a knoll, the reins of his horse in one hand. His expression was one of disbelief. What next? he seemed to be asking himself. If need be, Smoke Jensen decided, he would show Quinn what.

"Begorrah, there's a blackhearted bastard at work here," an enraged Paddy Quinn exclaimed as Garth Thompson approached to report on their condition.

"You'll think it is Old Nick himself when I tell you where we stand right now."

Quinn cut his eyes to Thompson. His black orbs, which usually twinkled in harmony with his perpetual smile, had become flat mirrors. The beaming expression had melted away. "What is it yer sayin', boy-o, what is it?"

Garth had never seen his boss like this. He noted the black

smudge of unshaven jaws, the little mouth set in an angry slash, high forehead furrowed, the muscles of his head so rigid that his small ears literally twitched. To Garth, Quinn looked ready to explode like one of their firepits.

"We've had fifteen men killed. There's another twenty injured. Twenty-five men just plain rode off. I don't reckon they'll be coming back. Old Snuffy, our cook, and his swamper have plain disappeared."

A foul stream of curses gushed from Paddy's mouth. At last he curbed his fury. "By damn, this is the doing of Smoke Jensen. I've got to talk to whoever is in charge in Taos. He's got to curb his mad dog. And, he's got to see reason, he does. Even with our losses, we've enough men to wipe out the entire town. There's other places to live, an' men start over all the time, they do." Paddy went on for a good five minutes, as though rehearsing his presentation to the leader of the defenders. When he wound down, he issued his orders to Garth Thompson.

"Rig a white flag. Then ride down there and tell them I want to meet and talk with whoever is in charge. We'll meet after break—awh, hell, we don't have a cook, ye say. How am I gonna get some breakfast?"

Smoke Jensen and Diego Alvarado rode out to the meeting with Paddy Quinn later that morning. As they swung into their saddles, Smoke offered a word of caution. "I think it would be wise to have some of your vaqueros keep a close eye on every hardcase in rifle range of our meeting."

Diego cut a knowing eye to Smoke. "You suspect that Señor Quinn will not honor his own flag of truce?"

"That's putting it mildly. I'll keep watch on Quinn. You do the talking."

Smoke's arrangement worked out excellently. Paddy Quinn knew Diego Alvarado from previous encounters and naturally addressed him as the leader. He chose to ignore Smoke Jensen, whom he also recognized. The snub was wasted on Smoke.

"Don Diego, it's good to see you again, it is."

Diego's black hair and mustache and chiseled features gave him a sardonic appearance. "Somehow I doubt that. What is it you want, Quinn?"

"Ah, no time for pleasantries, is it? A busy man ye are, no doubt. Well, then, we might as well get to it." Quinn paused and drew a deep breath, which he sighed out before he continued. "There's no denyin' that ye hurt me some. An' Mr. Satterlee will be sore distressed over that, an' that's a fact. But, it's also a fact, it is, that we've the strength to wipe out any resistance ye might choose to put up. So, me fine grandee, I've come to discuss the terms of your surrender. Not just the town, but that grand ranch of yers."

Diego Alvarado swallowed the rising anger to request in a cold, grave tone, "In return for what?"

Paddy Quinn leaned back in the saddle, as though considering that question, then produced his usual cherubic smile. "Now, Mr. Satterlee was perfectly willing to pay fair market price for all the property he desires. But . . ." His expression changed to the mask of deadly fury witnessed earlier by Garth Thompson. He nodded toward Smoke Jensen. "Then the devilment wrought overnight by this hired cur of yours changed all that, it did. So, Señor Alvarado, here's what we'll be havin'. All hostilities will end immediately. We will be allowed into town at once, without hindrance, to select which properties Mr. Satterlee desires."

To Paddy Quinn's surprise, it was Smoke Jensen who answered. "You'll be dancing with the devil before that happens."

Quinn masked his reaction and raised an arm to make a curt gesture. Two of his henchmen appeared over a low rise. Between them they held Martha Estes. They brought her forward until Smoke could plainly see the fear in her eyes. Quinn openly gloated over his prize, his voice a velvet purr.

"So, then, unless we are allowed into Taos, and the people are lined up eager and ready to sign over their property to C.S. Development Company, a division of C.S. Enterprises, Miss Martha here will be slowly killed right out here before your eyes."

Smoke Jensen's face took on a rock-hard stillness, his amber eyes and expression thunderous. "I sincerely doubt that's true. Clifton Satterlee would not be at all pleased."

Quinn appeared not at all affected by that judgment. To further prove he did not bluff, he made another signal. Four houses on the edge of town, which belonged to some of the poorer Mexican farmers, suddenly burst into flames. The dry thatch of their roofs burned rapidly. Women and small children ran screaming from their fiery homes. In the distance, the fire bell began to clang. Smoke and Diego looked on, unable to do anything.

Paddy Quinn watched with them for a while, then turned his horse and spoke over his shoulder. "You have one hour." Then he posed a question for Smoke Jensen. "Tell me, Smoke Jensen? How does it feel to at last meet your better?"

Smoke Jensen's flat, level gaze pierced Paddy Quinn and fixed him in place. "I don't think I have."

For a long, tense moment Paddy Quinn did nothing. Then he turned about and rode swiftly away without another word.

Smoke Jensen looked up from the lists of preparations that had so far been completed. A delegation of some eight local merchants stood in the sheriff's office. He clearly read the fear on their faces. Smoke erased the frown that had creased his brow and forced a smile.

"Something bothering you gentlemen?"

He noted that they were among those he had rated as the

most timid among the businessmen of Taos. They fidgeted now, like schoolboys caught in some naughty act. One ran an index finger around the interior of his celluloid collar. Two shifted their feet in an uneasy manner. All eight clearly wished to be elsewhere.

"Come on, no need to hold back."

Charlie Lang, the haberdasher, cleared his throat and bobbed his Adam's apple. "Well, ah . . . we—that is, it's gotten around that we have an hour before those brigands just come in and take what they want. Is that true?"

Smoke shook his head. "No. We have an hour before they supposedly murder a young woman before our eyes and then come in and take what they want."

"Oh. That—ah—that makes a difference."

Smoke's face registered his discontent. "Mr. Lang, I was trying to be sarcastic. I chose the wrong words. The facts are that they cannot take this town no matter how hard they try. A lot of them are along out of curiosity. They have no real loyalty to Paddy Quinn or Clifton Satterlee. When they get a taste of our firepower, a lot of them will drift away. More than twenty of them ran out this morning before sunup."

"What about the young woman?"

Again, Smoke made a negative gesture. "Quinn will never kill her, not even hurt her in a serious way. He believes she is still the lady friend of his boss. With all the gunfighters he commands, Quinn would never buck Satterlee."

Lang persisted. "Why is that?"

"Mr. Lang, do you pay your employees at the start of the week or at the end?"

Charlie Lang frowned. The question puzzled him. "Why, at the end of the week, for all that it matters."

"My point. You don't pay them until they have performed the work for which they are being compensated. I firmly doubt that Satterlee has paid Quinn, and won't until the job is done. If Quinn and Satterlee got at odds, and Quinn didn't get paid, he'd have a whole lot of angry, broke gunhawks to contend with."

Lang thought on that awhile. "That makes sense. Even so, we've been talking about the danger we're in, what those outlaws can do to us. We have families, investments, roots in the community. We don't want to risk harm to our wives and children and lose everything we have. This Clifton Satterlee has offered to compensate us fairly for our property. It seems wise for us to accept what he is proposing."

"Not anymore. Quinn says our resistance has changed all that. Satterlee is going to take what he wants, and that's all of Taos. As to protecting what you have at stake, I suggest that all of you grow a pair of stones and fight for what's yours."

Lang and three others began jabbering as one. "But some of us will get injured." "We'll be killed." "We have a right to be protected."

Smoke Jensen's disgust spilled over. "Listen to me, you yellow-bellied rabbits," he thundered. "You are going to have to fight for your rights; we'll be too busy protecting the town as a whole. Here's my final word. Not a one of you will give in to such cheap intimidation. If I need to, I'll put a Tua warrior in every store, eatery, and saloon to prevent your surrender. Now, get out of here."

Paddy Quinn rode to the abandoned adobe farmhouse where Martha Estes had been imprisoned. Following his instructions, his underlings had lashed her arms to a chair and left her sitting at a table, with only a crumbling wall to stare at. Quinn entered and stood between her and that unpromising vista. At once, Martha's gorge rose, and she began to unload onto him all her disgust and loathing.

"You are the most disgusting, foul, misbegotten piece of

human refuse I have ever laid eyes upon. Your every act shames your mother and father."

She stopped for a breath, and Paddy seized the opportunity to get in a word of his own. "My mother, God rest her soul, is dead these twenty long years. An' me father is a drunk, who would not feel insult if someone crapped in his hat."

Eyes narrowed in her rage, Martha spat, "When Clifton discovers how you have treated me, he'll have you horse-whipped."

"Ye've got the right of it, lass. He's not got the balls to do it hisself." Realization that Jensen's taunt had struck home made her reminder even more unwelcome. "It's well an' good, it is, that ye know I'll not be for carryin' out me threats against you. That was for those dogs from town. Let them be worrin' over it. But, between you an' me—ah, an' Lord, there's somethin' I'd love to have between you an' me, there is—before this is over, I intend to get to know you better. *Intimately* better, if ye catch me meanin'?"

Martha twisted her face into an expression of disgust. "I'll see you in hell before that happens."

His smile bright as ever, so disarming it did not lend credibility to his words, Paddy Quinn spoke lightly as he started for her. "Will ye now? An' what's to stop me? All I need do is hoist them skirts and have at you with a will."

A sudden clatter from a carriage outside halted Quinn. He stopped, then took two hasty steps back. The next moment, Clifton Satterlee stormed through the askew doorway. His face flushed, Satterlee pointed a glove-covered forefinger at Quinn.

"That lout of yours out there tells me that you have Martha Estes in here as a prisoner, trussed up like a Christmas goose."

Paddy gestured to his prisoner. As though jerked by a string, Satterlee took two steps toward the young woman, then turned on Quinn. "Release her. *At once!*" Then to

Martha, "My dear, this is inexcusable. I'll have you freed in a moment. And I promise you nothing like this will ever happen again. Where is Lupe?"

Martha turned her cobalt gaze on Clifton. "She's . . . being held someplace else."

Ice formed around the words of Clifton Satterlee. "Quinn, you will finish untying this young lady; then you will go and fetch her maid. And be certain that she has with her everything needed to restore Miss Martha to her usual loveliness."

Paddy Quinn had recovered himself enough to bark back. "She ran away from you, did you know that? I didn't send men to take her, I didn't. She went off with none other than Smoke Jensen."

Satterlee cut his eyes from Quinn to Martha. "Is that true?"

"Yes and no. I left on my own. I encountered Mr. Jensen on the road, and he was to escort me here to Taos." Hurrying to get it out before her nerve failed, Martha added, "I felt so terrible when I learned that the jewelry you gave me had been stolen. And that they were sacred objects to the Indians here. I wanted to do what I could to make amends."

Satterlee's anger found a new source. "Lies. Jensen must have told you that. It is not true. Trust me in that."

Martha clenched her jaw a moment, then braved it out. "I talked with a young Indian policeman who identified the necklace I wore . . . when they visited in Santa Fe."

"A copy perhaps," Satterlee suggested.

Martha held her own. "They do not make copies."

Satterlee took another tack. "Come, my dear. Let's put all that behind us. I am so relieved to find you safe and sound."

"Not so safe, nor so sound, if that one had his way," Martha challenged.

Clifton Satterlee rounded on Quinn again. "I thought I gave you an order. Now do it."

"You may regret this, Mr. Satterlee," Quinn muttered softly while he undid Martha's bonds.

Satterlee winced as though the threat had hit home. In that instant, after her release, Martha bounded upright and made a break for the door. Before Satterlee could react, Quinn passed him in a flash and snagged Martha by one arm.

"Not so fast, me fine colleen."

Martha did not resign herself so easily. She clawed at Paddy Quinn, scratched his cheek and neck, kicked him in the shins, and pounded one small fist on his chest. While she struggled, Clifton Satterlee took it in with an astonished, bemused expression. Martha tried to knee Paddy in the crotch, and he hurled her against a wall.

All fight left her as she slammed painfully into the adobe blocks. Shoulders slumped, she faced the two men like an animal at bay. Her chest heaved from her exertion, and her face had turned a pale white. Clifton Satterlee studied her with new eyes.

At last he spoke. "Perhaps I have been hasty. I may have misjudged you, Mr. Quinn. Yes, I think I far underrated Martha's spirit. It seems that for the time being, you will have to detain her forcibly if she persists in such unbecoming activity."

Paddy Quinn touched fingers to his cheek. They came away bloody. Then he saluted his employer with a tap to the brim of his hat. "I'll see to it right away, that I will." Before departing, he added, "When that is done, there are some changes I want to discuss with you as to the taking of the town of Taos."

TWENTY-TWO

Shortly before the hour deadline, Smoke Jensen came to Santan Tossa with a suggestion. "I want you to gather your warriors. Have them start to drum and sing, do a war dance out in plain view of Quinn's gang."

A huge grin spread on the mahogany face of the Tua. "We haven't done a war dance in fifty years. This will be a true pleasure. We'll make it look very bloodthirsty indeed. Lots of howls, leaping in the air, swinging war clubs and knives." He went off, gleefully listing loudly the terrorizing features they would use.

Twenty minutes later, a drum began to throb in the outskirts of Taos. Tua warriors started to prance and stomp in a circle around a large fire. High, thin voices chanted the challenge to fight and die to all who could hear. Knife blades flashed in the sunlight. The drum beat louder. Some among the outlaws became visibly uncomfortable. Several exchanged knowing glances. They had heard the rumors about scalping.

Some few did not want to test it further. Two drifters, who had joined up for the fun the siege promised, went for their horses. They rode off five minutes later. Five minutes later, three more, who were not part of the gang, held a whispered conference, nodded agreement, and left for other parts.

A grinning Santan Tossa waved a lighthearted farewell to Smoke Jensen as Smoke eased himself into the gorge that contained the streambed and set off to locate Martha Estes and her maid.

Smoke followed the creek upstream to the southwest until well past the ring of outlaws. Then he led Cougar up out of the ravine and mounted. Carefully he worked his way back toward the siege lines. He left Cougar behind a screen of young palo verdes and proceeded afoot. Bent double, he presented a far diminished profile to any eyes that might look outward, instead of toward town. There would be few places where Martha might be kept, he reasoned. With silent determination, he set about eliminating those.

Ten minutes went by. Smoke found himself on a small produce farm. No doubt the Mexican owner sold to the general store in Taos, and to others who happened by. Yes, there, beyond the work sheds, barn, and house, a palapa had been erected over a stairstepped set of shelves. Baskets of peppers and fresh vegetables lined them. Two small boys, under the age of thirteen or so, kept watch and called out to passersby.

Making little sound in his moccasins, Smoke eased his way up to the side of one shed. The sound of splashing water came from within. Women's voices came from inside, chattering in Spanish over the latest gossip. Smoke's command of the language, slight at best, had not improved over years of disuse. Even so, he made out a number of juicy items.

"Raquel is going to have a baby," one woman revealed as she energetically sloshed a bowl of red and green jalapeño peppers in a tub of water to remove the red-brown dust.

"How can that be?" asked a much younger, more innocent voice. "She is not even married."

"*Sí, esto es verdad.* She has no husband, but she has a baby."

"Padre Domingo says that is a sin." Smoke could almost see the blush her words produced.

"That is true, little one. And you will promise your mother that you will never, ever do what it takes to make a baby . . . until you are safely married."

Another woman brought a change of subject. "I hear that Juanita Sanchez is going to marry that Guerrero boy."

"Which one?" several asked.

"Mateo, I think. Or is it Raul? No, it is Enrique."

"Carlos Guerrero has nine sons. How can you tell which one?"

A titter came from the youngest. "It's not Ricardo. He's only ten."

A superior-sounding voice discounted that. "What difference does that make? My sister, Esperanza, was married at twelve."

A snippy voice followed a nasty laugh. "Everyone knows she had to. It was that Dominguez boy, although she married Sancho Valdez."

A wounded squeal came from the defender of early weddings. "Cow."

"Pig."

"*¡Bruja!*" her target spat, then repeated, "Witch!"

"Ladies, please," a matronly woman commanded. "We are here to work, is that not true? Someone hand me some of those squash."

Grinning, Smoke moved on. Small wonder that men who owned businesses preferred not to hire women. The metallic screech of metal against stone directed Smoke to another shack. The farmer sat under a thatch palapa, working a pedal-powered whetstone to sharpen a machete. Smoke coughed softly to attract the man's attention.

"*¿Sí, señor?*"

"Have any of the *ladrónes* around Taos come around here?" Smoke asked. When the man shook his head in the negative, Smoke tried another. "Have you seen any of them taking a young woman somewhere?"

Another shake of his head, then, *"¡Ay, sí!* Early this morning, I was turning water into my corn. Two men rode over toward the old Olivera place. They had a woman with them. She did not look happy."

Smoke nodded in satisfaction. "That's the one. Thank you, señor."

Then Smoke asked for and was given directions to the Olivera farm. He headed that way on foot. He had covered half a mile when he came upon the first of several layers of lookouts. Smoke skirted the man easily and continued on. The second one proved not so simple to evade.

He sat his mount, alertly searching the surrounding terrain. From time to time, he stood in his stirrups and peered beyond low obstructions. Smoke, clad in buckskin, hugged the ground. The man's diligence and regularity became his undoing. After carefully timing the outlaw's routine, Smoke was ready when a missed gaze beyond the low brow behind which Smoke waited signaled a change. He came up and moved out in a split second.

Habit had outweighed diligence. The man had his head down, intent on rolling a cigarette. Smoke leaped and landed on him like a stone statue. Tobacco flakes flew everywhere. Dragged from the saddle, the outlaw landed heavily with Smoke on top. Rancid breath shot out of his twisted mouth. His lungs empty, it took only a hard right to the jaw by Smoke Jensen to put him asleep. Smoke quickly tied him and hurried on.

Another watcher lounged in the doorway of a partially fallen-in adobe house. Smoke froze and sank to the ground. For five long minutes he studied the man who leaned against the doorframe. He looked bored. He also looked sleepy. Another minute passed, and the thug abruptly jerked awake, stepped out of the shade, and paced to each corner of the building, Winchester held at the ready. He looked around the wall and returned to his position. Once more he slouched.

Such kind were dangerous, Smoke reasoned. If the hunch hit him at the wrong time, he might see someone sneaking up on him. Smoke inched his way behind a rock ridge and circled widely around the crumbling structure. He came at the adobe building from the rear.

Through a small, high window he had a clear view of the interior. Across the single room, he saw a large loft, obviously where the family slept when they lived here. In the middle of the room he noted a small table. Seated at two sides of it were Martha and her maid. They had been tied tightly to their chairs. To one side, Smoke observed Paddy Quinn and two of his men in the room conferring quietly. The bad news became immediately obvious.

There wouldn't be time enough to take out Quinn and his fast guns and free both women. This small farm lay too close to the ring of outlaws. Any exchange of gunfire would draw two dozen gunmen in seconds. He could not free them, yet he had a firm belief that Satterlee would not want her harmed. What happened next reinforced that attitude. Quinn's voice raised suddenly, and Smoke listened carefully to each word.

"You're right, Huber. These two are poison. I think we can get away with it if we do it that way, I do. We just take 'em out in the desert and lose them somewhere."

At once, Martha snapped hotly at him. "Clifton will have you gelded if you actually go through with killing me. You heard what he said when he had you bring my maid here."

That was news to Smoke. The criminal overlord was here now. That gave him some fresh ideas. Quietly he slipped away, headed back for Cougar and a ride to town.

Never one to take strict notice of exact time, Smoke Jensen found himself eying the big, octagonal face of the

Regulator wall clock that hung on the wall of the sheriff's office. When the hour deadline arrived, he strode out to where Quinn had confronted them earlier. It did not surprise Smoke when he found none of the outlaws present. Particularly, Smoke noted, no torturers and no Martha Estes. In the next instant, he learned why.

Rifle fire broke out on two sides of town. With shouts and curses, the outlaw gang opened an attack on Taos in earnest. Smoke could not understand why the entire force that ringed the defenders did not press the engagement. He needn't have speculated. Smoke had no sooner reached the line of houses that defined the city limits than riders thundered down the slope where he and Diego had met with Quinn. They opened fire as the range closed.

Immediately, Smoke ducked behind a low adobe wall and drew a .45 Colt. Two .44 slugs slammed into the outer face of the brown mud bricks, which sent a plume of dust upward to obscure Smoke's vision. He triggered a round, and a hardcase cried out in pain, his right arm limp and useless. That concentrated more fire on Smoke's position. He could not stay in such an exposed place for long, Smoke reasoned.

Sheriff Hank Banner sat propped up in bed by rolled blankets and plump pillows. At his insistence, Dr. Walters had rolled the bed over close to a window. Now he stood in exasperation at his patient's request.

"I'll do no such a thing, Hank Banner," the physician snapped, his well-scrubbed hands clasped in front of him.

"Awh, come on, Adam. We've got the fight of our lives goin' on out there, and I ain't in it. Hell, man, even you've got a six-gun strapped on."

"That's to protect my patients and my medical equipment," Dr. Walters responded testily.

"You gave Pedro Alvarado a rifle. All I'm askin' is you get me one, too."

Unmoved by the argument, Adam Walters answered primly. "Pedro is thirty years younger than you, Hank, and he's ambulatory. Besides, how are you going to operate a Winchester from that bed?"

Bushy eyebrows knit over his nose, Banner grumped at the doctor. "Easy if you'll give me a rifle and open the damned window. I mean it now, Adam. I can see out of both eyes now, and things ain't so fuzzy I'd shoot one of the town folks. I'm the sheriff, and by damn, it's my duty to help defend the people out there."

Dr. Walters knew that Hank was right. But he was his friend, and Adam Walters did not want to see Hank Banner taking unnecessary risks in his weakened condition. While his thoughts roamed over that little dilemma, Dr. Walters heard a light smack and the musical tinkle of falling glass. The bullet cracked loudly when it struck the wall opposite the window.

"Goldag it, Adam. That does it. If they're shootin' at me, I've got the right to shoot back."

Sighing, Dr. Walters turned from the infirmary and entered his treatment room. From there he proceeded to the office, where he picked up a Winchester and a box of cartridges. He returned to the room where the sheriff continued to fume at the attackers. Adam's face wore a sheepish expression.

"Here. And try not to shoot yourself in the leg." The doctor busied himself with opening the sash. From the end window, which faced the alley behind the building, a rifle barked in the hands of Pedro Alvarado.

For all the fury of their resistance, small groups of Quinn's outlaw band penetrated the defenders' barricades. Six of them from the west side of town headed directly for the center.

They made their approach by way of one of the radiating alleys that formed an X based on the Plaza de Armas. To reach their goal, they had to go past the window where young Pedro Alvarado waited with a ready Winchester. The moment one of them came into view, he immediately regretted his hastiness.

Fiery agony spread in his leg as Pedro put a round into his hip. The outlaw fell at once and painfully crawled, crablike, toward the shelter of a doorway. Pedro fired again, ending the thug's movement forever. As his life ebbed from him, the hard-case faintly heard the voices of his comrades.

"Up there."

"Yeah, I see him. In that window."

Funny, the dying rogue thought, *I didn't hear any shots.* He did not hear the return fire as his fellow outlaws opened up and darkness engulfed him.

Up in the infirmary, Pedro Alvarado flattened himself on the floor as a rat-a-tat of slugs punched through the thin wall. Glass shattered in the window above him. The moment a lull came, Pedro popped up and sighted on one of the five. The .44 Winchester recoiled smoothly, and the target clutched his chest and slammed back against a wall. Pedro got off another round before he had to dive for the floor again.

Ian MacGreggor held his own from his second-floor room in the hotel. He had been on town patrol duty during the night and had returned to grab a few hours' sleep only to have the attack break out after only forty minutes' rest. Over his sights, he saw one hardcase who appeared to be directing the ac-tions of a dozen others in a push to breach the defenses to the south of town. A long shot for a rifle, but Mac retained the confidence of youth.

He elevated his aim to the maximum and fired. After what seemed a terribly long time, the section leader jerked in his saddle, then slowly folded forward at the waist. He clung to his horse for a moment, then dropped away to land in a puff of dust on the hard ground. Mac levered another round into his Winchester and sought another target. He found one much closer than he would have liked.

Two hardcases ran out of the mouth of an alley and randomly discharged their weapons upward toward second-floor windows. Mac pulled a quick bead and let fly another .44 slug. One of the outlaws continued to run forward while the other did a crazy little jig and crashed blindly into a rain barrel. He died before he hit the tile walk.

Mac charged his rifle again and sighted on the remaining gunman. The Winchester bucked, and Mac remembered this time to shove three fresh cartridges through the loading gate. He ejected the empty and chambered a loaded one. If this kept up, they could easily reduce the enemy by half, he speculated.

Someone else had figured out the same thing. Shouts to pull back went from one outlaw to the next. Slowly they began to withdraw from town, yet they continued to pour a withering fire on the defenders from a distance outside Taos. Whitewater Paddy Quinn sought out his second in command.

"We'll give it a little time, then go back again. I want to get that bastid Smoke Jensen in me sights, an' that's a fact."

Garth Thompson did not sound so eager. "I've heard he is hard to kill. So far, I have no reason to doubt that. How many did we lose?"

Quinn raised a hand and swept the hillside. "That's what I want you to find out, boy-o. Didn't seem to me that half the lads what went in there came back. With losses like that, we can't keep this up for long. Whether Mr. Satterlee likes it or not, we may have to use fire to drive those stubborn folk out."

"He'll have a fit if we do. But, I agree with you. We can't

let them whittle us down like that much longer. When do we go back?"

Quinn rubbed a powder-grimed hand across his brow. "Find out where we stand an' we'll give it an hour."

Ezekial Crowder and Ed Hubbard had taken positions on the south side of town, close to Smoke Jensen. They looked first to the sky when they heard a distant rumble. When they found it to be clear and bright, they lowered their gaze to observe the ominous approach of a large body of outlaws. They exchanged a worried glance and tightened the grip on their weapons. Over the growing thunder of hooves, they could hear the voice of Smoke Jensen, low and calm.

"Steady . . . hold it . . . let 'em come in real close. Make every shot count."

Smoke knew it would not happen that way. Excitement or fear would make the inexperienced men fire carelessly. They would rush their aim and no doubt jerk the trigger. It would only get worse when the outlaws opened fire. Some, though, he knew would make good account of themselves. Like young Mac, who had shouted to him during the brief respite.

"Hey, Smoke, I got three of them. Those two down there and another on his horse outside town."

"Good shootin'," Smoke praised. He continued on his way to check the other defenses. His inspection gave him the impression that some twenty outlaws had gotten inside the town. Perimeter defenses had to be shored up. He had arranged for that, though only just in time.

They were going to have to keep the gang from entering town this time, Smoke thought as he watched the outlaws close once again. A few seconds later, Ed Hubbard proved a better gunhand than expected when he cleared two saddles in rapid succession.

"Did ya see that?" Hubbard called out, surprised by his own success. He took aim again.

With a loud crash, the hardcases opened up. It drowned out Ed's third shot, which hit Dutch Volker in the side. It was a severe enough wound to put him out of the action. With a blistering backward look and a hot curse, Dutch steered his mount away from the conflict. He would get patched up and come back, Dutch thought.

Smoke Jensen had other ideas for him. Careful aim with his .45-70-500 Winchester Express paid a dividend to Smoke. For enough time to make it count, the head of Dutch Volker sat like a hairy ball on the top of the front blade sight. The upright post rested in the notch of the rear, buckhorn sight. Smoke squeezed the trigger. Volker's head snapped forward and back as the bullet bore through his brain and exited the front, taking with it his entire forehead. A fountain of gore splashed on his horse. Without a controlling hand, it went berserk.

Crowhopping and squealing in fright over the smell of blood and brain tissue, the animal cut crossways to the advance, scattered several other riders, and at last dislodged its odious burden in a thicket of mesquite. Already, Smoke Jensen tracked another outlaw. The volume of defending fire increased from other points as Smoke concentrated on his aim. He discharged a round that missed one hardcase by a finger's width and drove into the shoulder of the man behind him. Smoke risked a quick glance toward Hubbard and Crowder while he cycled his lever action.

Both men so far remained calm. They took time to aim, worked the action of their rifles in a controlled manner, and shoved fresh cartridges into the magazine between shots. Hubbard spoke up loudly enough for Smoke to hear him above the rattle of gunfire.

"You're doin' all right for a fireman."

Crowder grinned. "So are you . . . shopkeeper. I'd sell my soul for a shot of whiskey and a cool beer."

"If I was the devil, I'd take you up on that." Hubbard broke off to fire his Winchester again. "Got another one," he commented.

"The way they're comin', this could last until sundown," opined Zeke Crowder.

Hubbard blinked and swallowed hard. "It had better not."

Sheriff Banner thought much the same as Chief Crowder. From his vantage point he watched the huge gang swirl around Taos. Here and there, one would slump in the saddle or fall to the ground. Not nearly enough, though, the lawman concluded. He watched as three of them charged a barricade made of two overturned wagons.

Their mounts easily cleared the obstacle, and he had one of the men in his sights before the hooves touched ground. An easy squeeze and the sheriff's rifle fired. His bullet drilled the outlaw through the chest. Quickly Banner worked the action and sighted in on another. Before he could fire, one of Diego Alvarado's vaqueros dashed into the street. He carried a large yellow and magenta cape. Swiftly he unfurled it and billowed it out into a fat curve; the skirt flapped in the breeze his motion created.

At once the horses sat back on their haunches and reared. One rider fell off; the second barely hung on. And then not for long. Another rippling pass put the animal in a walleyed frenzy. The rider had all he could do to regain control. While thus occupied, Sheriff Banner shot the hardcase through the heart.

Fierce fighting continued through the afternoon. Smoke Jensen made periodic visits to the defenders positioned on the outer edges of Taos. He always had a word of encouragement and usually replacement ammunition. Braving the chance of a bullet, the older boys of the town, organized by Wally Gower, brought food and water to the fighting men. The fury promised to go on forever.

When night fell, the gang withdrew, much to the relief of everyone. To their immediate discomfort, the defenders of Taos soon discovered that the enemy had not gone far enough so that anyone could escape.

Smoke Jensen's words were not greeted with enthusiasm when he made his dark prediction. "They'll be back tomorrow."

TWENTY-THREE

"They're comin' back!"

Early the next morning the shouts of the lookouts roused the wearied protectors of Taos from uneasy sleep. Too many of the townspeople moved with a lethargy that they would soon regret. Caught between their homes and fighting stations, most looked on in numbed horror as the outlaws easily penetrated the thin defenses and streamed into town.

"We ain't got a chance this time," one less courageous townie wailed.

"We're goners for sure," the fainthearted barber took up the cry.

Smoke Jensen would hear none of it. He seemed to be everywhere at once as he worked to rally the resistance of the battle-tired people. "Quit your whining," he growled at the timid souls. "Take your weapons and form up in the streets. We can stop them easier when they don't have room to maneuver."

"Say, that's right," one of the more imaginative townies declared. "We can trap them between the buildings. It'll be like shootin' fish in a water trough."

Smoke moved on, praising the idea over his shoulder.

"That's the idea. Get to it." Smoke's confidence rose more when he came upon the more reliant among the defenders.

Those Tua warriors not on water watch were the first to respond. Santan Tossa stood on one side of the Plaza de Armas and directed his fighting men to vantage points on the roofs of buildings. Unaccustomed to the Spanish tile roofing material, one of the Tua men put a moccasin on a loose one and all but fell.

"Be careful," Tossa cautioned. Then he produced a fleeting smile at that choice of words in the face of an all-out assault by men determined to kill them all.

On two sides of town, Don Diego's vaqueros labored valiantly to keep more of the trash from entering Taos. The dapper senior Alvarado shouted encouragement to his cowboys. *"Buena suerte, compañeros.* Shoot their eyes out."

Gradually, men caught by surprise on the west side of town began to calm and take better stock of their situation. Smoke Jensen quickly exhorted them. "This isn't the end of it. Not unless you want to go belly-up. Get some backbone, dammit. All of you there, quit milling around and form up to drive and trap those who got past the barricades in the center of town."

Slowly they began to respond. As the first remotivated men spread out, more joined them. Before long they had enough to ring the business district and began to close in. From the moment of the first encounter, the fighting grew more fierce with each passing minute.

Smoke Jensen soon saw that the outer defenses had been completely breached. The vaqueros fought valiantly as they retreated street by street from the pressure put on them by the Quinn gang. Here and there they managed to rally as those facing them turned out to be drifting bits of frontier trash with no deep-set loyalties. That sort crumbled rapidly, especially when confronted with a revival cry from the Mexican cowboys.

"Con nuestra Señora, Santa Maria de Guadalupe! Maten- los maten!"

Even Smoke Jensen developed chills down his spine the first time he heard it and translated the words. *With our lady, Holy Mother of Guadalupe! Kill them, kill!* He had to admit it had a galvanizing effect. The vaqueros swarmed back down the street, a wall of death with six-gun, rifle, and knife. At one point, a saddle tramp who had become overwhelmed by their ferocity dropped to his knees and began to howl like a dog. It did him little good. He got his throat slit anyway.

On the next street over, the vaqueros put a full dozen to flight. Horses surged into one another and spilled two riders to face the advancing fury of the Mexican cowboys. They screamed a long time as they died.

Paddy Quinn shoved his way into a cantina to catch his breath and reload. He found Garth Thompson there ahead of him. Whitewater Paddy flashed a big grin. "We're doin' fine. Another half hour and the town will be ours."

Thompson looked at him in consternation. "Are you kidding? We have men dying out there by the handful. It doesn't make sense. These townies are fighting back like madmen."

"Awh, Garth me bucko, yer not seein' clear, yer not. Most of those who are being killed are not part of the gang. What that trash is here for is to soak up bullets for us, it is. Let's go upstairs where we can better see what's really happenin'. Ye'll be surprised how good it's goin', ye will."

Two blocks down, in a narrow alley, three of Quinn's men found the situation more like Garth Thompson saw it than their boss. Seven Tua warriors rounded the corner and started toward them. Clearly they had heard the rumors started by Smoke Jensen. The trio cut their eyes to the Indians and began to run in the opposite direction. Not a one made an effort to fire a weapon.

"Lou, Lou, we gotta get out of here. They're gonna scalp us."

Lou looked ahead and paled. The rear of a building closed off their escape route from the narrow alley. "We're trapped," he wailed.

The others saw it, too. Unnerved by his belief in the scalping story, one of the outlaws turned his gun on himself. His body had hardly hit the ground when Santan Tossa and his brother Tuas opened fire. One of Quinn's men jerked spastically, staggered two paces to his left, and keeled over. The other got off a shot before Tossa put a bullet through his screaming mouth.

"They were cowards," the Tua policeman pronounced over the cooling corpses.

Gradually the tide turned. The shock of their earlier failure began to wear off, and the men of Taos ceased in their headlong flight from the threat of the gunmen. They turned back in twos and threes in one place, half a dozen in two others. Instead of two men fighting a desperate rear guard, while the others fled, the mass of harried men turned about and lashed out at their enemy.

At first it did not look like much. Then an angry growl raced through the defenders, until it became one voice. Five of the gang rounded a corner, laughing and firing blindly. Halfway down the block a solid mass of growling, snarling men began to run toward them. A high, clear cry raised above the roar of their discontent.

"Fire! Open fire!"

A ragged volley crackled from the weapons in the hands

of shopkeepers and clerks, bank tellers, and wheelwrights. A stream of lead scythed into the startled outlaws and they began to die. Two of the gunhawks wisely opted to flee. One made it to the corner they had rounded half a minute before. The other one took two faltering steps along his escape route before he fell over dead.

Throughout town the spirit of defeat disappeared as he died. Shouting, the defenders charged in a massive counterattack. Determined men soon swept the byways of Taos of the dregs of humanity who had attacked them. The only resistance that remained centered around the saloon named Cantina del Sol. Smoke Jensen reached that strong point in the vanguard of the revived defenders.

Curly Lasher and eight relatively capable gunfighters had been stationed outside the cantina to protect their leaders. He and his underlings listened to the shift in mood among the defenders with growing apprehension. When four of them rounded the corner with a determined stride, the outlaws realized that the seeming ease of their capture of the town was an illusion. Weapons already in hand, the townsfolk had the advantage when the hardcases reached for their six-guns.

Curly had time to shout only brief advice. "Spread out!"

Gunfire roared in the confines between two-story buildings. Two of the outlaws went down. Curly Lasher took cover behind a watering trough and traded shots with the aroused residents of Taos. That lasted until Smoke Jensen and six vaqueros rounded the other corner and closed in on them.

"Make for the saloon," Curly yelled to his surviving men.

Curly backed up the steps to the portico over the entrance to the cantina. A quick check showed that the others had preceded him. He had almost disappeared through the beaded curtain that screened the doorway when Smoke Jensen stepped out into the center of the street and pointed his left index finger at the outlaw leader.

"Curly Lasher, you yellow-bellied pissant, come out and face me like a man."

Smoke Jensen had recognized Curly Lasher the moment the man came to his boots and started for the cantina. Although quite young, Lasher had a respectable reputation as a gunfighter. He was reputed to have killed ten men in face-downs in Texas and New Mexico. Rumor had it his total number of kills included three for-hire assassinations and a dozen ambush shootings. At the age of twenty-three, he was about as good as they came these days. But not in Smoke Jensen's book.

The way Smoke saw it, it was time to cancel Curly's pay book. After issuing his challenge, Smoke waited now, ignoring the random bullets, fired by Lasher's henchmen, that cracked into the ground near him. A second stretched interminably long, then another. Smoke counted to five before Curly waved a grubby, rumpled bit of cloth out the opening to La Cantina del Sol.

"You make those others stop shootin' at me an' I'll face you, Jensen. Hell, you're an old man. You can't be much good anymore."

There it was again, *old man*. Smoke's expression grew grim. "We'll see, won't we? And have those back-shooting gun trash with you holster their irons."

Another second went by. "You heard him, boys. Put 'em up." A nervous giggle escaped Curly. "This is between Smoke Jensen an' me."

With that, Curly Lasher stepped out into the street. He looked formidable enough, except for the muscle tic that twitched his left eye. Smoke Jensen sidestepped to line up with Curly Lasher. Curly's hand hovered over the butt-grip of his Smith & Wesson .44 American. He nodded evenly to Smoke.

"Your play, Jensen."

"No, you go first. I want this to be fair."

Another giggle burst from Curly's throat. "Fair? Hell, Jensen, you better be pickin' out your coffin right now."

"You reckon to jaw me to death? If so, it'll be like ol' Samson, eh? Killed with the jawbone of an ass."

That tripped Curly's hair-trigger temper. "Goddamn you, Smoke Jensen, kiss your tail goodbye."

Curly Lasher drew then, confident that he had beaten Smoke Jensen by a good half second. Not until a stunning force slammed into his chest did he realize how terribly mistaken he had been. His lips formed a perfect *O,* and his legs went rubbery. Enormous pain spread through his body, followed instantly by a frightening numbness. Try as his brain might to send signals to his heart, they never arrived. A fat, 230-grain .45 slug had destroyed that vital organ.

His eyes rolled up in their sockets, Curly discharged a round into the street and fell in a crumpled heap. In the moment after he fired, Smoke Jensen moved. He waved at the astonished townies to follow him.

"Come on, let's get in that saloon."

"B'God, that was fast," Warren Engals muttered. "I never seen his hand move."

"Neither did that cocky gunhawk," Buell Spencer snorted in satisfaction.

Midmorning came and went. Still the fighting lingered, as Smoke Jensen and five of the men from town entered La Cantina del Sol. Theirs could hardly be called a conventional means of entry. Smoke sent four vaqueros around to the rear to make a show of breaking in through the service door. He gave them enough time to be convincing, then dived low through the front doorway. Smoke hit the floor and did a roll, to come up with his Colt blazing. He got immediate results.

One hardcase slammed into the bar, his back arched to the point of breaking his spine. Smoke fired again and the bones cracked. The outlaw dropped to flop on the floor like a headless chicken. A townsman and one of Diego's vaqueros entered behind the last mountain man. Flame gushed from the muzzles of their six-guns.

Another hardcase died in their hail of lead. A third had dived for cover behind the bar when Smoke first entered. He popped up now and shot Ransom Clover between the eyes. The feedstore proprietor died on his feet. But not before Smoke Jensen sent the killer off to eternity with a similar wound. Terrible discordance came from the upright piano in one corner as another thug hastily fired a bullet at Smoke's back.

Smoke ducked and spun on one boot heel. The muzzle of his Peacemaker tracked with him, and he squeezed off a round the moment the back shooter came into view. Hot lead punched through thick leather and then did awful damage to the hip bone of the man. By then, Smoke had cocked his .45 and put a second slug into the chest of his assailant. Restricted by the muslin safeguards suspended below the ceiling, viscous layers of powder smoke undulated in the room, obscuring the whereabouts of other enemies.

Ears ringing from the enclosed gunfire, Smoke made for the stairway. There had to be some reason why a fairly reliable gunfighter like Curly Lasher and eight men had been guarding this place. He had reached the first riser with a boot toe when another of the gunmen appeared at the top of the stairs. Smoke acted at once.

So close to the wall, the force of his gun blast nearly ruptured Jensen's eardrum. Yet he did not even flinch as he re-cocked his six-gun and sent another .45 round winging upward to seal the fate of the hardcase who menaced him. Hit twice in less than half a minute, the outlaw staggered back and rammed slack shoulders into the wall of the upper hallway. Smoke paused at the landing and called back to the ground floor to one of the vaqueros.

"Joaquin, come up here with me." When the slender, boyish-faced cowboy reached the top of the stairs, Smoke gave terse instructions. "Stay here. Watch my back."

Smoke set off to search the rooms in the rear portion of the second floor. Someone of importance had to be up here, his gut feeling told him. He readied himself at the first door, cocked his leg, and planted a boot beside the doorknob. A loud crack followed and the panel flew inward. Following his six-gun, Smoke entered the room in a crouch.

Empty. He turned on one heel and started for the next. His explosive entry caught two outlaws with their backs to him, taking shots at Taos residents in the street below. The slam of the door against the inner wall brought one around in a blur of movement. His eyes went wide as he gazed at Death with a outstretched hand. The six-gun in that hand fired a second later, and reflex drove the bandit backward to crash through the window, taking both sashes with him as he fell to the ground. The second hardcase wisely released his revolver and threw up his hands. Smoke Jensen stepped up close and rapped him on the skull with the barrel of a Colt. That left three more rooms to check.

The next proved even more empty than the first. It did not even have furniture. Smoke moved on to the next in line.

His vicious kick surprised Garth Thompson and Paddy Quinn in the act of reloading. Thompson swung his six-gun up first and fired at Smoke. The man from the Sugarloaf had already fired a round which ripped into the body of Garth Thompson a fraction of an instant before the outlaw's bullet punched a neat hole in the left side of Smoke Jensen's waist. It burned like hellfire, but it did not even stagger him. Thompson tried to fire again, not realizing he looked at his target with a dead man's eyes.

His bullet cut air beside Smoke Jensen's left ear as the legs of Garth Thompson gave way. Smoke gave him a safety round and turned his attention to Paddy Quinn.

Stunned by the swiftness of action by Smoke Jensen, Paddy Quinn only belatedly closed the loading gate of his Colt Peacemaker. Instinctively, he knew he did not have time for a shot. Not if he wanted to continue living. Instead, he diverted his energy to his legs and sprinted past the wounded Jensen out into the hall. Smoke bit back the pain that burned in his side and turned in pursuit.

Out in the hall, Paddy Quinn raced toward the far end of the building. A window in the center of the corridor there bore a sign above it that read *Escalera de Incendios.* "Fire Escape" for those who could read Spanish. Smoke Jensen pounded down the bare board floor behind Quinn. The outlaw leader made better time.

Without a break in his stride, Paddy Quinn threw his arms up to cover his face and hurtled through the glass partition. Fragments of the sashes clung to him as he hit the small, square projection that served as a platform for a ladder. Legs still churning, Paddy cleared the railing in a single bound and dropped out of sight before Smoke reached the shattered window casement.

Quinn landed flat-footed and hard on the packed earth below. Pain shot up his leg from a broken heel bone. His horse, and those of Thompson and another hardcase, had been tied off at the rear door earlier in the day. So unexpected and precipitous had been his arrival from above that the vaqueros sent to break in the rear stood in immobile surprise while Paddy limped to his mount, retrieved the reins and swung into the saddle.

Smoke Jensen sent a bullet after Paddy Quinn as the latter called out to his men. "Pull back. Get clear of town. We've lost it for now."

TWENTY-FOUR

His face twisted in anger and contempt, Clifton Satterlee rounded on Paddy Quinn. "What do you mean you had the town taken, and then got pushed out? How can that happen?"

Whitewater Paddy's answer came low and meek. "Smoke Jensen. That's how it happened. He killed Garth, he did, an' he near to finished me in the bargain. He found out somehow where we were and came after us with some of those Mezkins."

Satterlee paced the confined space in the ruined adobe farmhouse. "Better that you and a dozen like you die than that I lose Taos."

Stung by the insult, Paddy's eyes narrowed. "Pardon me, Mr. Satterlee, sir. There's no denyin' yer smart an' all that. But, truth to tell, your chances of takin' Taos without me are somewhere between slim an' none, they are."

Face florid with his fury, Clifton Satterlee raised a fist as though to strike the gang leader and bellowed up close in Quinn's face. "Then get out there, gather up what men you have left, and go back. And keep on going back until their resistance crumbles. Brice, you're going with them."

Brice Noble gaped at his partner. He knew himself to be good with his guns, better than most of the petty criminals in Quinn's gang. Yet, he realized he was not any sort of gunfighter like Smoke Jensen. The man was entirely too good. "You're not serious. What could I possibly do?"

Sarcasm dripped from Satterlee's words. "You could be like a famous general. An inspiration to the men."

"That's uncalled for. There's simply no reason for me to go there."

Satterlee turned even nastier. "But there is . . . because I insist. Now, get going, Quinn, and bring me back a town on its knees."

Shortly after noon, the gang came back to Taos. Those in the lead met with a shower of wine-bottle grenades. The black-powder bombs exploded with sharp cracks and bright flashes. The shards of their containers, and the scraps of metal within, whizzed through the air. Many pieces bit into vulnerable flesh, both equine and human. One went off so close to two hardcases that both of them and their horses were disemboweled. Their shrieks of agony engendered pity even among those they attacked.

Soon their distressed wailing faded under the tumult as the fighting rose toward a crescendo. Paddy Quinn had centered nearly all of his men on one side of town. Only a few snipers and riders kept the defenders on the other three sides occupied. As the volume of fire increased at the center of the offensive, a voice rose from the assailants.

"They broke! They broke! They're running."

It was quickly picked up. The shouts merged into a roar as the allies could no longer withstand the onslaught. Outlaws poured into the gap in the line and spread out through the streets of Taos. Pushed to the forefront of the vanguard, Brice Noble found himself the first to enter the small town. When the resistance melted away his confidence soared. This might be easier than he had expected. His horse trotted down the narrow avenue toward the center of town.

At the Plaza de Armas, Noble found a tall, broad-shouldered man directing the fight. He forcefully snatched demoralized residents off their feet and shoved them into a position from which they could engage the invaders. His calm demeanor told Brice Noble that if they were to succeed, this man must be eliminated. He edged closer and formed the words of a challenge as he raised his revolver to accomplish that. Off to the side, someone yelled the gun-fighter's name.

"Smoke! Smoke Jensen. I've got ten men here ready to fight." Then, sighting Noble, he pointed out the menace, "Look out, Smoke!"

Smoke Jensen turned his cold gaze on the man who sought to kill him. He backed it up with the muzzle of a .45 Colt. Instantly, fear eroded his guts, and Brice Noble swallowed his provocation. He lowered his right arm and released the six-gun. It dropped to the grass with a thud while Noble raised his hands over his head.

"I surrender. I've not fired my weapon. Don't shoot me, Mr. Jensen."

"Get down." Smoke's command moved Noble with alacrity. He swung a leg over and dismounted while Smoke walked up to him "Who are you?"

"I—I'm Brice Noble, a business associate of Clifton Satterlee."

"Umm." Smoke swung from the belt line. His hard fist connected with the lantern jaw of Brice Noble. When the arch criminal crumpled, Smoke reached out and caught a towns-man by one arm. "Drag this piece of dog dung to the jail."

Diego Alvarado sought a single man among the outlaws. His wide experience in fighting a variety of enemies told him that the majority of these vermin would flee if they lost their leader. Smoke Jensen had killed Garth Thompson that morning. That left only Paddy Quinn. He left Alejandro and Miguel in charge of the vaqueros and started off to locate the gang boss. Mayor Arianas, an old friend, approached him as Diego crossed the Plaza de Armas.

"Diego, I am astonished at the valor of the Tua warriors. They fight for us as though this was their town."

Alvarado gave him a wry smile. "They know that if Taos falls, their pueblo will be right behind. Satterlee wants everything around here. I, for one, am grateful for their aid."

"As am I, *amigo*." Arianas paused a moment, uncertain of the propriety of his question. "May I ask, where are you going? Most of your men are on the east side."

"Don't worry, my friend. I am looking for Paddy Quinn. When I find him, I am going to kill him and end this madness."

Arianas clapped Diego on one shoulder. *"Buena suerte,* then."

"Gracias. I can use all the good luck I can manage."

Diego Alvarado strode off, headed north. As he went by the flight of granite steps that fronted the church on the plaza, he automatically crossed himself and cast a reverent glance at the impressive structure. Suddenly the bells began to toll. Padre Luis threw wide the tall, oak doors and stepped out onto the wide flagstones at the top of the stairs.

"Men of Taos, rally your strength. Fight for your freedom," he exhorted the confused and demoralized defenders who huddled in the plaza. "Remember your women and children. Drive out the invaders."

A gunshot cracked across the plaza, seemingly louder than all of the others. Father Luis jerked at the impact and swayed, a large red stain spreading on the shoulder of his cassock. Diego Alvarado looked in the direction from which the shot had come. Seated on his horse was the man he sought. Paddy

Quinn had a smoking six-gun in his hand and a nasty sneer on his face.

"Easy for you to say, priest. You who hides behind his own skirt," the apostate outlaw snarled. Oblivious to Diego Alvarado, Paddy Quinn started to raise his revolver for another shot.

Diego Alvarado filled his hand with his Obrigon .45 with all the smoothness and almost the speed of Smoke Jensen. He cocked and fired in one even motion. The bullet took Quinn in the belly. He winced, but seemed otherwise unaffected. His icy black eyes turned on Diego.

"So, cowherder, you defy me one last time, is it now? The priest can wait. This is between you an' me, bucko."

Before the last word left his mouth, Quinn fired the Colt in his hand. The slug cut a deep, painful gouge across the top of Diego's left shoulder. Then Alvarado fired the Obrigon again. His aim off because of his wound, he nailed Quinn in the right thigh. That proved enough to unhorse the gang leader. He fell and sprawled on the cobbles that paved the street in front of the church. Immediately Paddy Quinn learned how mistaken he had been in shooting the priest.

Rather than demoralizing the residents of Taos, his blasphemous act served to electrify the defenders. A great roar of outrage filled the plaza from Protestant, Catholic, and pagan alike. Suddenly the peons, who did not possess firearms, swarmed over the fallen outlaw. Sunlight glinted off the well-honed edges of their machetes. Their arms rose and fell in a steady rhythm while Paddy Quinn shrieked and screamed his way into oblivion.

Blood streaming from his own wound, Diego Alvarado hurried to the injured priest. "Padre, you are hurt. I will get the doctor."

Gentle brown eyes settled on Alvarado. "Care for your own wound, Diego. God will tend to my needs."

Diego would not back down so easily. "Dr. Walters can give Him a lot of help. Let me take you inside. Then I will go for the doctor." Diego Alvarado cut his eyes to the mutilated corpse of Paddy Quinn. "He has answered for his crimes here, now I hope he burns in the hottest corner of hell."

Word quickly spread about the demise of Paddy Quinn. It restored the fighting spirit of those who protected Taos, especially when they learned how and why he had died. It proved to have the opposite affect on the outlaws. Leaderless, and with no assurance of being paid, the hangers-on deserted in droves. Harried by the emboldened townsmen, they streamed out of the city and made tracks toward Raton. The first two dozen to desert opened the flood gates.

Fighting continued for another twenty minutes while the headlong flight reduced the number of outlaws by more than half. Three of Quinn's subordinate leaders held a hasty meeting in the shelter of an adobe house on the west edge of town.

Yank Hastings came right to the point. "We have to get out of here. Those gutless cowards have left us in a fine fix."

Vic Tyson nodded, his face a grim mask. "Tell us something we don't know."

Hastings faced the sarcasm without a reaction. "The boss was right about puttin' all our force on one place. We got in, didn't we? I say we can do the same to get back out."

"Then what?"

"We run like hell for someplace else, Vic."

"What about our share of the loot?"

"There ain't gonna be anything to share. We can rob a couple of banks if we need money. Only I ain't stayin' around here any longer. You with me?"

"We'll do it," the other two agreed.

* * *

It did not take long. Hungry for revenge, the guardians of Taos roamed from building to building, street to street. Those outlaws who offered resistance they gunned down. The wiser ones they drove ahead of them. Smoke Jensen and Diego Alvarado led two thirds of them, Santan Tossa the remainder. Within half an hour the streets had been cleared.

"Now what?" a tired, powder-grimed Diego Alvarado asked over the top of a tubo of beer. A thick bandage bulged under his coat.

"Do you think they will be back?" Alejandro Alvarado queried.

Smoke Jensen had been thinking along those lines. "There's always the chance that they will. Though I hope not. We've lost fifteen men killed, and twice that wounded. If there's none of them left except the original gang, they can overwhelm us, given the right leader. To keep that from happening, I reckon to go out late tonight and cut off the head of the snake. That'll end it once and for all."

Alejandro looked eagerly at the big man. "I want to go along."

A smile spread on Smoke's face. "Welcome you'll be, Alejandro. Now, let's drink up and get something to eat. We need to rest before going out there."

Vic Tyson's concern over losing their pay proved baseless. While the remains of the gang fought its way out of Taos, Clifton Satterlee and his bodyguard, Cole Granger, rounded them up and persuaded them to listen. Reluctantly, others joined the gathering.

"Listen to me, men. We have to control Taos in order for our development scheme to succeed. You will all be rewarded. And most generously, I might add. In fact, I will offer you a bonus of one half your original share if you will agree to do what must be done. You will remain here, deny the people in town any contact with the outside. Cut off their food supply. Shoot any armed man you see on the streets. In short, maintain the siege until more men can be recruited and sent here to make the final push." Satterlee paused and let his gaze sweep over the assembled outlaws. "Do you understand what I'm saying? The whole project now depends upon you. You have good leaders in Yank Hastings, Vic Tyson, and Coop Ellis."

Coopersmith Ellis flushed slightly at that praise. Satterlee continued his harangue. "What I want is for you to do this. Return to positions well out of rifle range, and encircle the town again. Concentrate on the roads. Roving patrols can take care of anyone who tries to slip away across the fields. That's simple, isn't it? When enough men reach here for another attack, go at it with a will. Don't let anything stop you."

His stirring words brought a ragged cheer. But not enough to change Satterlee's mind on a matter of some considerable importance. When the remotivated gunmen started out to take their new positions, Clifton Satterlee huddled with Cole Granger and explained what he had in mind.

Darkness had covered Taos three hours earlier when Smoke Jensen and Alejandro Alvarado left town to spy out the enemy. It had taken that long for the gang to settle down. Some of them still had strong reservations about staying there. Several voiced their opinions loudly while Smoke and Alejandro slipped quietly through their line, headed for the adobe ruin where Smoke had earlier seen Martha.

"I think this is damn foolishness," one tough spared no effort in informing those near the fire where they prepared a meal and a pot of coffee.

"Biggs is right," another put in. "Without Whitewater Paddy, we've got no one to stand up to this Satterlee. Who says he'll for real pay us when it's over?"

"I'm glad you agree," Biggs included the man. "I say we walk our horses out of here right now, hit the high road to Santa Fe and don't look back."

"Hell, yes. Those Injuns could be out there, sneakin' around with their scalpin' knifes right this minute."

"Don't even mention that," a third hardcase replied. "It gives me cold chills."

Smoke and Alejandro crept on in the moonless night. When they reached the spot where Smoke thought the building should be, they found nothing. Smoke motioned for Alejandro to separate from him and look for the adobe. Quietly, both men went about finding the place.

Smoke located it first and saw that the farmhouse was unlighted. Had everyone gone to sleep? Somehow he doubted that. Moments later, Alejandro joined him, having made a wide, half circle. Smoke leaned close and whispered in the young ranchero's ear.

"I want to get a look inside. But if you were to ask me, I'd say the place is deserted. No light, no guards."

Smoke's speculation proved correct. He cautiously entered the structure through a crumbled rear wall. There he quickly discovered that Martha and Lupe no longer occupied the chairs. The table where they had sat had been overturned. He saw no sign of Clifton Satterlee either. Back outside, Smoke suggested they check along the line of fires where the watchers remained at the roadblocks.

A careful search among them revealed no sign of Martha Estes, her maid, or Clifton Satterlee. When they approached the last of the barricades, Smoke suddenly realized that Alejandro's appearance would give them away. Smoke made an abrupt signal that told the youthful *caballero* to wait outside the firelight and cover him while he went in to talk with the outlaws. Alejandro disappeared into the night, and Smoke continued to the fireside.

"Quiet as a graveyard," Smoke observed as he walked up.

"You coulda picked something better to say about it," grumbled one of the saddle trash. "What you doin' here?"

"You've got coffee goin', I smelled it. So, here I am."

His earlier jitters forgotten in light of no forays from town, the outlaw chuckled. "Pour yourself a cup."

Smoke took a blue granite tin cup and filled it. "Where's the big boss? He was so hot for us stayin' here," Smoke probed casually.

A low curse answered him. "Didn't have the grit to stay here himself. A little while after that pep talk, he took the women an' Granger and they hightailed it outta here. Off to Santa Fe, I reckon."

One of his companions spoke up in support of Satterlee. "He's goin' to get more men. Remember what he said about sending us some fresh blood?"

"Yeah. And blood is what it'll be, you ask me."

Smoke let them talk for a while, then drained his coffee and handed back the cup. "Thanks for the brew. I'd best get back to rovin' from place to place or someone will have a hissy."

"Yeah, that's right. So, you're with Vic Tyson's crew, eh?"

"Yep. For better or for worse. See you fellers."

Reunited with Alejandro Alvarado, Smoke Jensen and the ranchero made a rapid return to town. On the way, Smoke weighed the alternatives facing him. Not unusual, he did not like any of them. Back in the sheriff's office, he sent loungers to summon a war council. This would be a long night, Smoke knew.

"There's nothing for it but that I go after them," Smoke announced after relaying what he had learned beyond the town.

Mayor Fidel Arianas nodded thoughtfully. "I can understand that. But how are you going to go about it?"

Smoke Jensen had his answers ready. "First we have to

break this siege. They are mighty spooked over two defeats in one day. And we've not attacked them at night before. What we are going to do is organize an assault force from the local volunteers and Diego's vaqueros and wipe out their roadblocks, scatter the patrols around the town and plain raise a lot of hell."

Diego Alvarado's eyes glowed. *"Muy bien, amigo.* Naturally, all of my men will volunteer."

Smoke shook his head. "We only need half of them. Someone has to hold the fort. Gather five groups of ten each, and meet me in the Plaza de Armas in half an hour. One bunch will take each road out of town. The fifth will make a sweep of the roving patrols. Tonight we're going to kick hell out of these scum."

Thirty minutes later, grim-faced men gathered in the plaza. All were heavily armed. Every man had a horse. Smoke quietly gave them their assignments and moved out himself with those going after the mobile pickets. When everyone had gotten into position, they watched the hands on one of the clocks located on the four sides of the church steeple. The minute hand closed on 10:45, and the deadly bands moved out.

Three hundred yards from the roadblocks they urged their mounts to a gallop. Weapons out and ready, they opened fire at seventy-five yards.

With Quinn and Thompson dead and Satterlee gone, the attack quickly became a rout. Already demoralized by the turn of the day's events, the outlaw trash had little heart for a fight. Muzzle flashes in the night, followed by the crack of bullets and roar of weapons, undid even the most courageous among them. Men seemed to be shooting at them from all directions. Riderless horses ran past, and those securely picketed whinnied in the mad desire to join their fellows.

"To hell with this, I'm gettin' outta here," the hardcase known as Rucker spat as he ankled over the ground to his horse.

He slipped on a bridle and swung up bareback. No time for the niceties. Too many guns out there. He drummed his heels into the flanks of his horse and broke clear of the melee behind him. His mount nearly ran into the chest of a big, gray, spotted-rump 'Palouse. Veering at the last instant, he caught a glimpse of the rider.

"Oh, God, Smoke Jensen," he wailed aloud.

Then Smoke shot him.

In twenty minutes the last of the vermin had been exterminated or surrendered. Diego's vaqueros herded them back toward town. At the jail, Smoke confronted the leaders of the resistance. "Thank you all for what you've done. You've saved your town. The end of this is up to me. I'm going after Clifton Satterlee. Mac, Alejandro, I'd like you to come with me. We'll take about twenty-five men to handle any opposition Satterlee can muster. Even with them, it's gonna be mighty hard to end this."

TWENTY-FIVE

Smoke, Alejandro, and Mac rode out of Taos at the head of a twenty-three-man force. Even pushing to the limit, they would not reach Santa Fe until early morning of the next day. Smoke used the time to review how they should go about cornering Satterlee. His options were limited; that he accepted. He had no way of knowing how many gunhands Satterlee might have at the large *estancia* outside the territorial capital. Whatever the count, he wanted to keep the number of injuries and deaths small among his volunteers. Most of all he wanted to give Mac a chance at building a satisfying life for himself. All such considerations aside, he wanted to end it quickly. Could he count on the sheriff in Santa Fe?

That question remained with him as they rode through Española. False dawn caught them still two miles from Satterlee's lair. To Smoke that answered his preoccupation with the sheriff. They simply did not have time to ride past the road that led to the ranch and into Santa Fe. They would have to do it on their own.

Half a mile from the estancia, Smoke halted his small force and informed them of what they would do. "Mac, I want you to take charge of everyone but Alejandro and myself. Take on any gunhands Satterlee has at the ranch and keep them busy. Alejandro and I will go in to find Martha. Also to get Satterlee." Then he added with a crooked smile, "If something happens to let us open the gates for you, we will."

"I want to go with you, Smoke," Mac protested.

"Not this time. Keep in mind, youngster, that you are only fifteen years old. I'm not going to coddle you, but I want you in a responsible position, doing something that has to be done. Something that keeps you out of the center of most danger."

Mac blurted his objection. "But I want to be there, to help."

"Hell, boy, you're gonna get shot at anyway. Why make it worse?"

Grudgingly, Mac saw his point. "I'll do my best, Smoke. Count on it."

Alejandro nodded silent approval. He couldn't help but like this boy/man. "I think my father will find it impossible to continue his food production without you, young Mac. We want you around to make our gardens more productive."

Mac flushed and put on a foolish grin to hide his elation at this praise. "Yes, sir—uh—Alejandro. Do they—ah—ever call you Alex?"

Alejandro flashed white teeth in his olive face. "Only my gringo friends. So, I suppose you can, too."

Smoke concluded his strategy session. "Let's get to it, then. Mac, circle wide around and hit the place from the rear. Once you have their attention, we'll come at 'em from the front."

A short while later, Mac and his mixed force invested the walls around three sides of the hacienda. Under cover of darkness, Smoke and Alejandro approached the front gate in the twelve-foot wall that surrounded the compound. Smoke had a little surprise that he had not mentioned to the others. With the battle raging around them, he quickly went to work sheltered by the inset of the massive portals.

"Alejandro, gather up all the big rocks you can find. Bring them here."

Diego's eldest son went to work with a twinkle in his eyes from sight of the cylindrical sticks in Smoke's hands. By the time Alejandro returned for the sixth time, Smoke had attached a bundle of five sticks of dynamite to the center of the gate, where the crossbar would be.

"Mix some mud," Smoke commanded as he bent to place more dynamite against one of the hinges.

Alejandro found water in a horse trough and plenty of desert soil right where they needed it. He carried the liquid in his hat to make a quagmire under the sheltering lip above them. When he thought he had it right, he stopped to watch Smoke packing rocks against the charge on the hinge.

"Smoke, it is ready."

Studying the consistency of the mud, Smoke passed judgment. "Thicker. Make it sticky."

When it reached the desired texture, Smoke began to pack it around the explosives in the middle of the gate, then poured more over the rocks. That completed, he cut his eyes to Alejandro. "We'll let that dry awhile."

The volume of gunfire rose and fell as the outlaws traded shots with the men from Taos. It served well to keep attention off Smoke and Alejandro. After ten minutes, the surface had returned to its natural color, and cracks began to appear in the mud. Smoke nodded approvingly and bent with a lucifer in his hand.

"You light that one and I'll get this. Then we get out of here . . . fast."

With the fuses sputtering, Smoke and Alejandro ran from the gateway and flattened their backs against the wall to either side. Three minutes went by, and then a tremendous roar shattered the sporadic gunfire from within the hacienda. Dirt and acrid smoke billowed out of the arched opening. Splinters of flaming wood mingled with them. The ground shook, and Alejandro smelled the nauseous fumes of the burned dynamite. In the numbing silence that followed, Smoke and Alejandro heard a shrill shriek, followed by an enormous crash.

"Let's go," said Smoke tautly.

Quickly they rounded the corners that had sheltered them. Alejandro's jaw sagged at sight of the damage the explosives had wrought. One side of the thick gate hung askew. The other lay flat on the ground, blown out from the bottom. Smoke jumped on top of it and ran into the courtyard. They met with no resistance until they reached the main entrance to the hacienda. Two dumbfounded thugs with bestubbled jaws stood inside. They gaped at the damage until the figures of Smoke Jensen and Alejandro Alvarado filled the range of their vision.

"Lutie, it's him. It's Smoke Jensen," babbled one.

"Then git him, Frank, git him."

Each man made the fateful mistake of reaching for his six-gun. Smoke beat them both, with Alejandro not far behind. The Colt in Smoke's hand bellowed, and Lutie doubled over, shot through the liver. Frank fired a round before Alejandro ended his life with a bullet in the head. Sidestepping the dying men, Smoke and Alejandro pushed on into the house. Cole Granger and three men waited for them in the inner courtyard.

"There they are," shouted one piece of human debris as Smoke became visible at the inner opening of the corridor.

Smoke, the .45 still in his hand, shot him through the heart. Two others dived for cover behind the cheerily splashing fountain. Granger dropped behind a huge clay olla that held a stunted banana tree. From there he triggered a round that ripped along the left ribs of Alejandro Alvarado.

Face grimaced in agony, the young grandee spun to one side and leaned back against the wall of the arched corridor that connected the front door to the patio. "Go on, Smoke. I'll be all right."

Alejandro extended his right arm along the wall and took aim at a pale face that appeared above the lip of the fountain. Biting his lip, he squeezed his trigger. The slug slammed into the edge of the marble basin. Water and stone chips showered into the air. The face disappeared, an irregular hole in the center of its forehead. At once, Smoke was on the move.

He bounded to his left and dropped behind a long, earth-filled planter. Three slugs pounded into the opposite surface. Smoke inched along to the end and hazarded a quick look. Granger had come to his boots, peering across the open garden in a attempt to get a sight on Smoke. It would be all too easy.

Smoke raised his arm and fired at the center line of Granger's body. The bullet smashed into Granger's belly, and he staggered backward. Smoke came to his boots and jinked off another direction. He learned that he had miscalculated Granger's strength a moment later when Alejandro shouted from behind him.

"Smoke, look out!"

Cole Granger fired his six-gun with less than acceptable accuracy. A hot tunnel opened in Jensen's left arm an instant before he discharged his Colt and put another bullet in Cole Granger's chest. To his surprise Granager absorbed the punishment and turned his gun on Alejandro.

This time he wavered unsteadily so that the slug struck the stucco-plastered, adobe wall before it plowed into the chest of Alejandro Alvarado. Cursing his bad luck, Smoke raised his point of aim. He fired at Granger's face and blasted the life out of his assailant. Quickly he bound his arm and chaged his empty Colt for the fresh one. Then Smoke began to search for the final hardcase.

Sagged to his knees, Alejandro called out to Smoke "He's gone. Ran out to the others."

"What about you?" Concern rang in Smoke's voice.

"It's . . . not bad. Go on. Find Satterlee and get the girl to safety."

Smoke Jenson started for the stairway that led to the second floor. Behind him a door flew open. Smoke spun on one heel and snapped off a shot. Another of Satterlee's henchmen died. Halfway up the stairs, he paused to look back. Alejandro sat spread-legged against the wall, his face pale, but his breathing regular. The bullet must not have reached his lung, Smoke speculated.

He took time then to reload, then ascended to the open-sided hallway that ran around the upper story. Now the search turned serious. Smoke stepped to the first door and kicked it in. A startled hardcase turned from the window where he had been exchanging rounds with Mac and the attackers, who had swarmed into the compound through the damaged gate. Smoke shot him in the shoulder, took his weapons, and locked the door behind as he left. The next two rooms were empty. Smoke worked his way out into the open.

From below, Alejandro spoke to Smoke, his words light and breathy. "I can cover you from here."

Smoke nodded and went on. The next door he found locked from the inside. His .45 Peacemaker at the ready, Smoke lined up and kicked the center panel beside the lock case. It hurt like hell. Made of stout manzanita, the door did not yield. Smoke kicked again, with the other foot. Wood splintered in the frame. Dimly, from behind and below, Smoke noted the arrival of Mac and some of the vaqueros. They swarmed through the courtyard as Smoke lashed out with his boot a third time. The door flew open to reveal a frightened and startled Lupe and a bulldog-faced hardcase.

"Down," Smoke shouted to the maid.

She dropped without hesitation. Smoke popped a cap on

the outlaw at close range. The slug pierced a forearm and entered a vulnerable chest. Smoke shot him again, and the thug's six-gun flew upward out of his hand. It discharged when it struck the ceiling. The bullet went through the thin plaster and exited the building by way of the tin roof. A stunned expression washed over the dying gunman's features, and he fell face-first to the floor.

Smoke pointed to Lupe. "Stay here."

Footsteps pounded in the stairwell as Smoke faced the next door. It was also locked. Smoke reared back for a good blow with his boot as Mac and three of Diego's cowboys ran toward him.

"We got 'em all, Smoke. Most just gave up."

"Stay back," Smoke cautioned. Then he slammed his boot sole against the door.

It happeded in a blur. Smoke saw a thick-shouldered gunman facing the door and fired instinctively. The lout dropped his revolver and clasped his belly with both hands. Smoke shot him again. At once her looked to his left.

With a long-legged stride, Clifton Satterlee moved across the carpet toward a wide-eyed, visibly shaken Martha Estes. He had a .44 Colt Lightning in his left hand. Too, late, and knowing it, Smoke swung his Peacemaker toward Satterlee and fought to gain time with his voice.

"Don't move!"

"Stop where you are." Mac's voice broke as he stormed into the room, eyes fixed on Satterlee.

Satterlee swung his Lightning away from Martha and fired double-action. His bullet hit Mac in the notch at the bottom of his throat. Quickly, Satterlee shot again. This .44 slug punched through Mac's right lung and ripped out his back. Instantly, Clifton Satterlee grabbed Martha Estes and pulled her in front of him. Driven backward by the agony of his wounds, Ian MacGreggor stumbled into the corridor. He teetered on the banister for a precarious moment. Then his legs went out from under him, and he caught himself with his elbows.

Smoke did not have time to check the youngster and knew it. He faced Satterlee, who now held the muzzle of his Colt to Martha's temple. "I'll kill her. So help me, I will. Holster your iron and get out of my way. Let me go and she won't be harmed."

Reluctantly, Smoke complied. Then he heard a miserable groan from Mac, and his eyes narrowed to furious slits. "You're a dead man, Satterlee. There's no way you are getting out of here."

Satterlee cut his eyes to a large carpetbag on the floor. It bulged with his portable wealth. Two finely wrought pieces of Tua jewelry spilled from the open top. "I'm taking that and her and leaving.

Smoke eyed the loot and returned his attention to Satterlee. "You killed that boy for nothing, Satterlee. More than for any other reason, I'm going to kill you for that."

Clifton Satterlee forced a nasty chuckle. "Not likely, Jensen. I've worked too hard for that." Again his eyes shifted to his ill-gotten gains. "You make a try and the girl dies."

Suddenly, Martha Estes moaned and uttered a huge sigh. She went limp in the arms of Clifton Satterlee. The instant her head fell away from the gun barrel, Smoke Jensen drew with blinding speed and triggered a round. The slug hit Satterlee at the top of his nose and pulped the empire builder's brain. He did not have time to send a signal to his trigger finger. He flew away from Martha Estes and sprawled across the bed.

At once, Martha straightened and opened her eyes. A big smile adorned her face. "I thought you might do that," she told Smoke a moment before she rushed to him and gave him a big hug.

Gently Smoke disengaged her. "You're safe now, Miss Martha. I'll arrange for passage to your home. Now, if you'll excuse me."

Smoke stepped out into the hall and gazed down at the bloody, sweating, pale-faced Mac. Ian MacGreggor worked his throat, and his lips moved. He spoke in a low, wheezy voice. "I—I guess I'll not be needing that gardening job."

Something stung Smoke's eyes, and he blinked rapidly. "That was fool thing to do, Mac. But you did save a girl's life. I'm proud of you." No reason to hide the obvious from the boy. "I'll see that your family gets your pay."

"Th—thank you, Smoke. It was—was an honor to fight at . . . your side." That said, Mac heaved a mighty sigh and died.

Eyes wet and burning, Smoke Jensen turned away to discover that Don Diego Alvarado and his remaining vaqueros had arrived. Smoke went to his friend. "Alejandro took a couple of bad ones."

"Yes, I saw. What about you?"

"I'll live. But . . . Mac didn't make it. I'll have to see that the Marshal's Office sends his pay to his parents."

"It's a beautiful day," Martha Estes opined as she joined the two men.

Still deeply moved by the death of Ian MacGreggor, Smoke looked across the early morning vista. The rising sun cast a pink hue on the white caps of the Sangre de Cristo range. No matter the cost, peace could return to Taos and the Tua pueblo. He nodded to Martha.

"Yes, it is a right nice day." *She's right, it's beautiful,* Smoke mused. *Almost as beautiful as the Sugarloaf.*

Sally and Bobby Jensen greeted Smoke's triumphant return to the Sugarloaf with unbounded joy. After a long, energetic embrace, Smoke looked around and then kissed Sally on one cheek.

"It doesn't look like anything has changed. What did you do while I was gone?"

Sally pursed her lips, fought to banish her sour memories, then answered. "I had a visit fron an old school friend."

"That's nice. Did you have a good time?"

"Like heck," Bobby put in. "Her kids sure are a bunch of brats." In spite of Sally's sharp look, Bobby went on. "It's the truth. And you're always after me to tell the truth, Smoke. An' to be man enough to stand up for it."

Smoke put and arm around each of his family and started for the porch, hugging them tightly. "So, tell me about this friend of yours, Sally. And don't forget the brats."

Connect with Us

Visit us online at
KensingtonBooks.com
to read more from your favorite authors, see books
by series, view reading group guides, and more.

 Join us on social media

for sneak peeks, chances to win books and prize packs,
and to share your thoughts with other readers.

facebook.com/kensingtonpublishing
twitter.com/kensingtonbooks

Tell us what you think!

To share your thoughts, submit a review,
or sign up for our eNewsletters, please visit:
KensingtonBooks.com/TellUs.